The Girl King

Meg Clothier studied Classics at Cambridge, spent a year sailing a yacht from England to Alaska, then – after a few false starts – became a journalist. Her last job was working for Reuters in their Moscow bureau before coming back to London to study for a Masters degree in post-Soviet politics. She first read about Tamar while writing a paper on Georgia and decided not to get another proper job but to write a novel instead. She has visited Georgia several times, most recently on honeymoon. She likes mountains, boats, learning languages and adventure stories.

The Girl King

MEG CLOTHIER

C

CENTURY · LONDON

Published by Century 2011

2 4 6 8 10 9 7 5 3 1

Copyright © Meg Clothier, 2011

Meg Clothier has asserted her right under the Copyright, Designs
and Patents Act 1988 to be identified as the author of this work.

This book is a work of fiction. Names and characters are the product of the
author's imagination and any resemblance to actual persons, living or dead, is
entirely coincidental.

First published in Great Britain in 2011 by
Century

Century
Random House, 20 Vauxhall Bridge Road,
London SW1V 2SA

www.rbooks.co.uk

Addresses for companies within The Random House Group Limited can be found at:
www.randomhouse.co.uk/offices.htm

The Random House Group Limited Reg. No. 954009

A CIP catalogue record for this book
is available from the British Library

ISBN 978-1-846-05820-2

The Random House Group Limited supports The Forest Stewardship
Council (FSC), the leading international forest certification organisation. All our
titles that are printed on Greenpeace approved FSC certified paper carry the FSC logo. Our
paper procurement policy can be found at www.rbooks.co.uk/environment

Mixed Sources
Product group from well-managed
forests and other controlled sources
www.fsc.org Cert no. TT-COC-2139
© 1996 Forest Stewardship Council
FSC

Typeset in Bell MT by
Palimpsest Book Production Limited, Falkirk, Stirlingshire

Printed and bound in Great Britain by Clays Ltd, St Ives plc

For Rupert

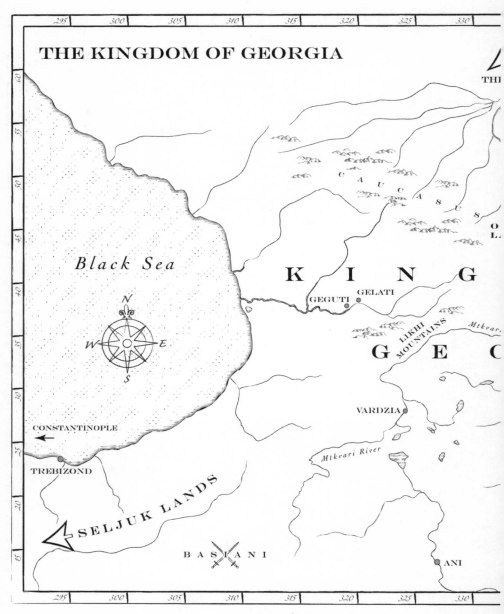

THE KINGDOM OF GEORGIA

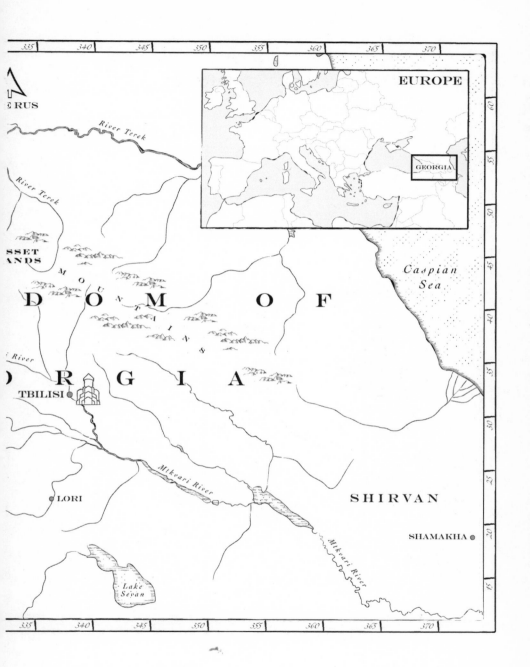

Prologue

It is 1177 in Georgia, the land of the Karts.

Hemmed in by mountains to the north, two great seas to the east and west and unfriendly neighbours to the south, the small kingdom in the Caucasus has always struggled to survive. It isn't many years since the Seljuks all but obliterated the country and its people – only the great King Davit saved them from ruin. The kingdom's natural ally, the Christian emperor, or basileus, in Constantinople, could not help. His power is waning as the might of the Seljuks and the audacity of the Frankish crusaders increases.

And so the Karts stand alone.

Davit's grandson, Giorgi, has defended his throne against all the odds for twenty years and now stands on the threshold of old age, proud of the victories of his reign – but he faces a grave new threat. He has no son to rule Kartvelia when he is gone.

Part One

Chapter One

The palace nursery was so hot it was hard to stay awake, hot and powerfully sweet-smelling as every morning Nino threw pine branches in the grate to ward off fevers and chills. Bearskins covered the walls, heads dangling down, eye sockets empty, the claws scraping the floor, while rich red rugs, brought up by mule train from the south, lay two or three deep to protect the girls' bare feet. Books half read, games half played, food half eaten littered the room.

Winter had lain unusually hard on Tbilisi that year. The Mtkvari, which in the summer tumbled mindlessly towards the eastern sea, rolled thick and cold between banks crisp with ice. Storm winds scythed down from the mountains, packing the narrow streets with snow and driving everyone indoors. Prayers to the city's many gods floated up to the skies, mingling with the woodsmoke and freezing mists.

Tamar burrowed her nose through the layers of felt draped over the windows, wanting a sharp lungful of daylight. An upside-down forest of icicles hung from the roof like the jagged teeth of a big beast, droplets skimming down their sides. She smiled to herself. Spring, at last, was near.

Ladders clattered and boots thumped overhead, followed by a couple of warning shouts. Tamar snatched her head away from the window as a party of palace servants set about shovelling the slush off the roof, hacking at the icicles with long poles. Two years ago a boy from the kitchens looked up at the pale sun and was dead a second later, a blade of ice in his eye. Her sister, Susa, had cried for hours.

Tamar grimaced across the room at where Susa was lost in lazy contemplation of her pink-white hands, folded neatly in

1

her lap. She was three years younger, soft and delicate, her hair heavy about her face. Just like her mother. Everyone said that. Just like Burdukhan, the mountain flower, the Osset rose. More like a caterpillar, thought Tamar. *A caterpillar coiled up on a leaf.*

Susa looked up and saw Tamar. 'I'll tell Nino.'

'Tell her what? What will you tell her?'

'Tell her you're letting the cold in. Again. You know Nino says it's bad for me.'

'But it's good for me.'

Tamar tucked her legs underneath her, cupped her chin in her hands and turned back to her inspection of the day. The sliver of frost that snaked over the trees in the courtyard was melting. On summer nights lanterns would wink in their branches and the soft whisper of their leaves would mask wonderful secrets in the shadows.

'Nino says your legs will grow bent and crooked and knobbly as a beggar's if you sit like that,' Susa said, giving Tamar the pitying look she normally saved for dead animals.

Tamar clenched her back teeth together, clamped her throat shut and tried to keep calm. She longed to leap across the room, wrench Susa to the floor and shake her until all serenity vanished from her perfect little face.

It had been the worst winter of Tamar's life. When she was younger, the slow, dark months meant playing hide-me-find-me or endless bouts of the Persian battle game or hours with the beautiful books that Shota bought from Armenian merchants. Or else – best of all – her father's men-at-arms would spin her gory stories about her great-grandfather Davit's wars with the Seljuks. She would sit on the floor at the feet of a rheumy old Kipchak soldier, arms gripped tight about her knees, as each deliciously bloody episode made her flinch and cower.

Death came like a wind from the east. It blew men's heads from their shoulders. Their skulls were like balls in a playground. Their bodies like tree trunks stacked in a forest.

But this year courtesy had crept into men's words, restraint into their eyes, the same uncomfortable feeling as when the cold wormed through the cracks in the palace walls and fingered the nape of her neck. She was never alone. She could not cross a room without being followed by a pair of half-lowered eyes. But nobody did anything with her. Her old friends avoided her, mumbling something about sword practice and no she couldn't come this time, sorry. The women handed her embroidery and told their own stories, which also made her shudder, but not in a way she liked. So Tamar retreated inside the nursery, inside herself, while her sister laid siege with digs and hints.

A shout flew up from the gatehouse.

Tamar, most of her head already outside, saw a shapeless figure on a muddy bay horse canter into the courtyard and skid to a standstill. The day was cold enough for both to be sheathed in a snorting cloud of sweat. The man leant forward, swung his left leg stiffly round the horse's rump and dropped heavily to the ground. His hood fell back.

Dato.

At last, he was home. After weeks of careful eavesdropping, all she knew was that he had been sent deep into the south on the king's best horse with the king's kinzhal strapped to his side, the dagger that was as good as the king's word. And now he was back.

'Who is it? Who's come?' Susa tried to squeeze up next to her on the seat. 'Make room, Tamar, let me see, I want to see.'

Tamar shoved her shoulder in the way. 'Remember what Nino said. Cold air is bad for you. Get back to your fire.' She shoved a bit harder, knocking Susa off balance and on to the floor. A huff, a stamp and her sister was out the door, shouting, 'Nino! Nino!'

She paid no attention, but listened to the scrape of the triple-planked, iron-backed doors of the great hall as they arced slowly outwards. King Giorgi filled the entrance. Tamar held her breath. It was days since she'd seen her father.

'Dato, at last! Get inside, man.'

His voice was always a little less terrifying than she remembered, but it still made her stomach jerk.

3

'You – bring food, wine – you – take his horse. Come on, faster, the man's exhausted. Here, lean on my shoulder.'

He strode into the courtyard, orders flying left and right as he clamped an arm round Dato's back and walked him slowly inside. Tamar leapt to her feet – she would try to bump into them before they holed up in the king's rooms – but a hand landed on her shoulder. She looked up into Nino's face, the thin eyebrows raised, the thin mouth turned down.

'Fighting again, my girl?'

Susa was behind her, tears standing in her eyes.

'I . . . she . . .'

As always, Tamar struggled to remember why she wasn't in the wrong.

'I just wish she wouldn't hurt me so,' her sister stammered.

A tear broke away from one of her eyes and curved gracefully down her cheek.

'There, there, kitten. Your sister doesn't think. She's not like you.'

Why can't you be more like Susa?

The unspoken words sent angry red blood to her head. Standing tall – she already towered over them both, which helped – Tamar marched out of the room, making her most gruesome face as she passed. She heard Susa protesting and Nino ordering her to come back, but she ignored them, hoping the old nurse wouldn't actually give chase.

But she had not gone far before she heard the determined flap of Nino's feet behind her, with Susa's slippers dancing alongside. Ahead of her, around the next corner, two Kipchak guardsmen would bar the way to her father's chamber. There was only one thing for it. She ducked into the cramped, windowless antechamber where the palace women stored clothes and bedding out of season, and scrabbled between two mounds of quilts, squashing herself against the far wall. The thick scent of lavender and juniper, scattered everywhere to ward off moths, made her eyes tickle.

'She's in here somewhere, Nino, I know she is.'

She froze as the door opened.

'For shame, Susa, your sister would not behave so childishly. But one of the maids does seem to have left this door unlocked. We'd best set that to rights.' Tamar heard the jangle of Nino's keys. 'Now, let me see, ah yes, here we go.'

Nino shut the door with an expressive humph and Tamar heard the key turn triumphantly in the lock. Their footsteps retreated back up the passageway. Tamar cursed – then laughed. Nino was unbeatable in her own domain. She wasn't going to scream and shout and beg to be let out, so she settled down to wait.

Now that her breathing had stilled, a distinct mumble and rumble sounded behind her. She swivelled round, making sure she didn't knock over the stacks of material, and pressed an ear to the wall. Men's voices, several of them, but all talking at once so it was hard to make out what each was saying.

As she dropped to her knees to make herself more comfortable, she came level with a thin line of light, a gap between two planks of wood. Gingerly, she pressed her eye against it and saw a row of backs crowding round something in the middle of the room. She was as good as inside her father's chamber.

Suddenly, to her right, close but out of sight, she heard a door open and the king, taller and broader than any man there, shouldered his way into the room.

'Give him some air.'

The men stepped back to the sides of the room. Not one leant against the walls. Not one sat down. Her father was so close it felt as if every pair of black eyes was trained on her. Some of them she knew well, others she knew only by name. They were the men the king fought with, the men he hunted with, the men who used to play with her. Many were Kipchaks, fighting men from beyond the mountains in the pay of the king. All had been born outside the tight circle of noblemen, the proud tavads who had long ruled Kartvelia.

Now she could see what they had all been so interested in. Dato, quietly massive, sat on a low chair. His right arm was bound across his chest and his face was bruised. His left knee

5

stuck out straight in front of him while his free hand rubbed the joint rhythmically. Tamar sought out his eyes, wondering what she would find there, but his gaze was down, his face still.

'Come,' said her father, 'tell us what has happened.'

Dato looked up and took in the room with his familiar slow stare. 'I travelled south to Lori,' he began. His voice still carried traces of an Osset accent although he had come down from the mountains years ago, as part of her mother's guard of honour when she married. 'I went to talk to Orbeli.'

Tamar frowned. Ivani Orbeli was her father's amir-spaslari, the commander-in-chief of his armies. Was he the reason why everyone had been so tense and strange all winter? She pressed her eye so tight to the wall that she was worried her lashes might protrude the other side.

'The king sent me to ask why his tribute did not arrive in Tbilisi before the snows. Sent me to ask if his wagons had been attacked, if his harvest had been poor, if our enemies troubled him. I was to offer understanding and aid. At first, Orbeli's people received me well, with much food and honour. But after five days I still had no answer. After five days I had spoken to Orbeli only once. I demanded an audience, in private. I waited another day. I asked again. And then I went to his chamber and encouraged his advisors to let me see him.'

Tamar caught the looks shared by a couple of men in the room. She too had some idea what it might be like to receive Dato's encouragement. Even her father's lips twitched.

'The news is bad. Ivani Orbeli renounces his . . .' – he stumbled, searching for the right word – '. . . his fealty.'

Some men blinked, shifted and rubbed their faces. Others rocked on their toes and pursed their lips. They might be trying not to show it, but Tamar could see they were all thinking that was worse than bad.

'There is more. Orbeli says Demna is now old enough to rule.'

'That hermit's boy,' Giorgi spat. 'The weakling son of a weakling. A newborn lamb is more fit to rule my kingdom.'

Demna was her cousin, the son of her father's elder brother

who had been king before him. Her uncle had not been long on the throne when he'd heard God's call and hidden himself away in a monastery, and so the crown had passed to her father. All this had happened before she was born, but she'd heard whispers that her father had somehow been responsible for his brother's passion for religion. Not that she believed them. It was simple: her father was meant to be king and her uncle wasn't. A real king would never have put on a monk's cowl and then collapsed and died of a stomach upset.

'Weakling, maybe, but he has Orbeli behind him now,' Dato replied, sterner than any other man would have dared speak to the king. 'They tried to keep me prisoner, but I left and returned here to bring word. I fear they are not more than three days' march behind me. They boast that Demna will be on the throne by midsummer.'

Tamar now understood why Dato was limping and pale. She also saw that her father's face had changed. His thick black brows, blacker than the hair on his head, had knitted tight together.

'They, Dato? What do you mean they?'

'An army is moving against you, my lord.'

'You'd call Orbeli's band of thugs and pretty boys an army?'

'No, I would not. But he has Qutlu Arslan and Gamrekeli with him. Jakeli and Dadiani, too. I saw them all gathered at Lori. I fear the lord Mkhargrdzeli also rides with them.'

He had named five of the most powerful men in the kingdom. Her father looked shaken.

'How is this?' he asked the air in front of him. 'Qutlu plays some game of his own – that I expect. Jakeli and Dadiani would only have needed a few days sucking grapes from the fingers of Ivani's slave girls to be persuaded. But Gamrekeli . . . Mkhargrdzeli . . .'

He turned away, his words unfinished. His back was to the others, but Tamar could see his face. It looked beaten. But, suddenly, a fierce, joyous light flared in his eyes, as when a watchman on a high wall removes the hood from a signal light. It burned brightly for a moment and then disappeared.

7

'So,' he said, slowly, the word fading to nothing. 'So,' he said again, facing the room once more. 'We have come to it at last.' He looked searchingly at each man in turn. 'Speak, men, speak.'

The king's black eyes, hooded until now, shot wide open and tracked slowly about the room. Tamar dug her nails into her palms as all eyes fell on Kubaza, the commander of the Kipchaks and the one man whose opinion truly mattered. Short and broad, his head hairless, he squared himself to speak. He did not need many words.

'I hate treachery. Orbeli will regret this day.'

As if on cue, the others echoed him, and as each man spoke, her father nodded to himself.

'Your loyalty warms me. I am relieved no man here is thinking that I have no son, nobody to rule after me. Or am I wrong? Is not Demna my nephew? The only son of my only brother? Speak up. What have you to fear?'

Silence. Every eye in the room was fixed on the floor.

'That is well. My brother was soft in mind and body. His son is worse. Demna does not have the stomach to ride north with an army at his back and call me out to fight – instead he cowers under Orbeli's cloak. I will not allow him to cheapen the throne of my grandfather, the throne of Davit Bagrationi.'

He circled round the cramped room, men shrinking deeper into the shadows as his voice tore into them.

'Burdukhan will produce an heir, one you will be proud to call your king. But until that day comes, I remain master of my fate and my kingdom.'

Every man nodded in furious agreement.

'Now, leave me, all of you.'

The men trooped out under the low door. Dato swung his left leg to the floor and stood up, wincing, but the king put a hand out. 'Not you, stay awhile.'

Dato sank back into his seat. The king crossed over to the window and tore aside the coverings. Cold air swarmed into the room and he breathed in deeply.

'So, Dato, war it is. The thought does me good, although I did not expect to find myself so outnumbered.'

'Yes, you look like a boy ready for the spring hunt. I admit I had thought my hunting days were done. Yours as well.'

'Never. Fear not. We will prevail. We must prevail.' The king grasped the back of Dato's neck with one massive hand and embraced him. 'One thing troubles me. My family. I must send them to safety before Orbeli attacks. My wife could go to the monastery at Gelati – she loves to be surrounded by the monks – and Susa could go with her. They do well together. But for Tamar, I would prefer somewhere more remote. You understand?'

Dato nodded. 'You fear what would happen if Orbeli had hold of her.'

'Yes. If a man wanted power over me he would have but to show me Tamar in the palm of his hand. Akilleus the Hellên hero had his heel. I have a daughter. And I fear that Orbeli knows it.'

Tamar's eyes widened.

'Dato, is there anyone in your lands you would trust? Someone deep in the mountains. A man of honour. A man who does not talk.'

'Yes,' he replied eventually, almost reluctantly. 'Yes, there is. But are you sure? The mountains are hard and lonely, with their own dangers.'

'Maybe you're right.'

Tamar couldn't bear it. She had never heard anything so appealing.

'No, no, I'll be fine. Let me go.'

The words had burst out before she even thought of stopping them. The two men gaped at each other.

'Where the hell are you?'

The king sounded furious. Dato looked amused. Maybe she should keep quiet. Maybe they'd think they'd heard a spirit voice. But her father had already flung open the door as if expecting to find her crouched outside.

'Come here now or I'll flay the skin off your back.'

He waited, obviously expecting her to trot round the corner and into the room.

'I can't.'

'Why can't you? You have legs, don't you?'

'I'm locked in.'

'Locked in where, for God's sake?'

'In the linen cupboard in the women's quarters.'

The king snorted, then nodded to Dato who stumped out of the room. Tamar wondered what he was going to do without a key, but the door gave way with one shove of his shoulder.

'Out you come.'

She emerged, blinking.

'Hello, Dato. Welcome back.'

One of his eyes flicked shut and open, a whisper of a wink.

'Hurry up – we don't want you to lose your skin.'

She stood before her father, not sure what to do with her hands. Men normally rested their right hand on their sword hilt or, if they weren't wearing one, looped their thumbs into their belt. She didn't have a sword, nor was she wearing a belt. She put her hands on her hips, but that felt stupid. She tucked them behind her back, but that felt pathetic. She was just about to fold them in front of her when at last he spoke.

'Tamar. We shall pretend I have just summoned you here from your quarters where you were busy doing something appropriate with your sister and Nino.'

She nodded. 'Yes, father.'

'Tamar. Your cousin Demna is trying to steal my throne. Do you know why he is not to be my heir?'

'Yes, father.'

'Why?'

'You don't will it.'

'Good answer. Are you pleased I don't will it?'

'Yes, father.'

Tall as she had grown, she barely came up to his chest, but the same gold light glittered in both their eyes.

'Even better. Now, listen close. It is too dangerous for you here on the plains. Fortune's favour switches faster than a falcon can dive and I will fight better knowing you are out of reach.

You understand that, don't you? They will try to find you, hold you hostage, use you against me. Do you understand me?'

She nodded. I *matter*. The thought was as invigorating as thunder.

'One question remains. Where are you to go? Orbeli's arm would have to be long indeed to find you under the Kavkaz peaks. You go north, to Osset country. There you can disappear from sight, from rumour until I send for you.'

Thank you Mary, thank you Jesus, thank you, thank you. Tamar felt as if she were already racing through a high meadow.

Her father's tone changed. 'Daughter, now listen close. Remember these words. Whoever comes to tell you that I have sent for you, whatever story they bring, they can tell you I am alive, dead, captured, plague-struck, devoured by vultures, I care not what they say, you must not believe them, you must not trust them, you must not follow them unless they show you this sign.'

He turned to Dato. 'You still have my kinzhal.'

Dato swiftly unbuckled the king's dagger from his side and held it out, the blade perfectly balanced in the palm of his hand.

'You know this?'

'Of course.'

'I do not know who will be dead and who living once I've whipped the whelp back into his kennel. But I do know that my messenger will be carrying this. Trust no man else. Do you understand?'

She nodded, entranced. 'But father, how will I know they haven't stolen it? How will I know the message truly comes from you?'

She expected him to bawl at her. But then, slowly, every line in his face softened. He reached out, put both hands on her shoulders and looked hard at her. She kept her eyes turned up, on his face, without quite daring to meet his gaze.

'So, I am right to believe there is something in there. Well, daughter, a second sign you want and a second sign you shall have. If you have the stomach for it.'

Dato broke in. 'But, sir, she's only—'

11

'Silence, man. Tamar, if your belly does not like the man who comes to fetch you, say *There is a second sign.* The man I send will put out his shield hand and say *I am ready.* Take up the dagger and make as if to cut. He will not flinch. That is how you shall know he is true. Now, enough talk. You leave at dawn. Both of you.'

Tamar grinned.

'Yes,' said the king. 'Dato will be your escort to the mountains. He will see you safe there. Now, go.'

Chapter Two

If I just see him and explain. The thought sustained Sos as he drove his yellow horse north. The quicker he made it home, the quicker his father would let him return. He refused to consider that Jadaron might be even less amenable close up than at a distance. *I'll explain . . . he'll understand . . . he must understand.* Like a chant, a prayer, the words thrummed in his head in time with the horse's hooves. Nobody overtook him, but he passed small trains of merchants, families walking to markets and a broad man and a slight girl on horseback.

Twelve hours earlier he'd been creeping, less than quietly, down a corridor in the palace towards the stone hall he shared with a dozen other boys of the court. The moon had set long before. The torches had burned out and would not be re-lit for another hour. In the darkness his heart was running wild, filling his eyes with blood, blocking out everything but love, his great discovery, the one thing in life better than fighting, better than hunting, better than blood congealing at the neck of a skewered boar, the sight, the smell that made him dance for sheer joy at being alive, that was nothing compared to her. *Chito . . .* He ricocheted off the door and swerved blindly inside.

Sos disentangled himself from his cloak and boots and slumped on to his narrow bed, as unsteady as a boy swinging in a hammock on his first sea voyage. He flung himself on to his front and buried his head in the pillow, wriggling ecstatically in rejection's sweet grip. Her face danced indistinctly on the back of his eyelids, he smelt her hair and felt a long white finger trace his jawline.

'I quiver like a sunbeam on water. I twist like a serpent

13

with a bruised head. My heart bubbles like a jar of sweet new wine.'

He mumbled the magical Persian words through lips swollen the colour of pomegranate flesh. Sleep hovered attentively at his side, ready to step in when the delicious anguish ebbed. His eyelids flickered and he passed out.

Sunlight tiptoed across his bed, lingering to dance amongst his curls. The other boys laughed at his slack-jawed snuffling and left him to sleep it off. Nothing disturbed him until an exasperated servant shook him roughly awake long after noon. He smiled up through gummed lashes at the shape looming over him.

'Soslani?'

'S'me. Wha' you want?'

'For you. A letter. The low road out of the mountains is open.'

The servant placed the roll of parchment on the boy's chest and exited, shaking his head. Sos was now unpleasantly awake.

A letter from his father. Correction, he thought. A letter from his father's steward. Jadaron didn't approve of writing and had refused to master the art. Sos had sent word before the snows asking leave to remain in the plains in the king's service for one more season. He had heard the rumours that war was coming and longed to fight. But the captain said he needed his father's permission before he promoted him out of the schoolroom.

He fumbled the message open and started to read. It didn't take long. There were only two words and his father's mark.

Home. Now.

His cheeks flared red. No explanation, no apology, nothing. He turned the paper over a couple of times, wanting to make it mean something else. He damned his father to hell.

Ever since Burdukhan had married the king, the noblest-born Osset boys travelled south in their fourteenth spring to live with the Karts in the plains. Sos's father had nearly forbidden it, but to go to Tbilisi was a great honour, the greatest there was, and

Jadaron's love of honour conquered his loathing of *ssifilissation*, as he always hissed the foreign word. So Sos set forth, unescorted, a wildly exciting journey, and plunged into the rough, bloody, brilliant world of the court. There were boys from all corners of Giorgi's kingdom, living on top of each other, no fathers to contend with, no mothers and sisters to undermine them. There was some attempt to corral them into book-learning, but for the most part they hunted, fought and experimented with love and wine. In short, they grew up.

Sos had been in Tbilisi for three years. He stood taller than most of his friends and could outrun anyone, but he was still beardless and his chest, shoulders and thighs lacked power. Lithe, wiry, fit, agile, he was all those things. But maybe not quite a man.

And now, just when everyone would be going to fight, his father ordered him home. Could he just not go? He tried out the idea, but fast realised it was impossible. Without his father's blessing, his father's gold, he was just another penniless camp boy, brushing horses, polishing shields, hurrying through the city carrying other men's letters to beautiful girls.

Girls. The night before flooded his memory. A large – and cheap – meal, a dare, a bet, some unsteady creeping around the snow-silent streets and a precarious ascent of Chito's house. *Chito.* Her shutters had opened and he'd caught a glimpse of her shocked face before she hissed at him to be gone. Maybe she'd have let him in if she'd known he'd be spending the rest of his life with his father's goats. *Damn him.* His belly smouldered with resentment, smoking and hissing like a damp wood fire.

Without quite realising what he was doing, he started to bundle his odd collection of things together – a book of Persian poetry he'd have to hide from his father, a boar tusk, the result of a lucky spear thrust, a couple of coins, clothes – and made for the steward's quarters to see about provisions for the journey home.

Shota was an unusually popular steward. He was dangerously

open-handed but because no man mistook him for a fool, he was never cheated. He knew when to give credit and when to refuse. He knew when a young man genuinely needed coins for a new horse and when the silver would be squandered on amber ear-bobs or mink slippers. Unlike most stewards he had a comfortable face, enjoyed good health and, stranger still, was poor. One look at his room and it was plain to see why.

The walls were crammed with dozens of books, a private collection unrivalled in Kart lands. Only the greatest monasteries and the king had more. Shota could bargain mercilessly over silks and spices, cheese and honey, but everyone knew that faced with a book he wanted – and there was no book he didn't want – he was defenceless. Merchants who tucked an Athos bible or a beautifully copied *Iliad* in their saddlebags always made a profit on that trade, even if they were bested over their main cargo.

The door was open, but Sos knocked anyway. Shota looked up and beamed.

'Come in, Sos, come in. What can I do for you?'

Sos started to speak, but his voice sounded odd in his ears so he stopped. Shota smiled encouragingly and waited. Sos tried again.

'My . . . my father calls me home. I need money for the journey. I have less than I thought. It seems I . . .' His voice trailed off again.

Shota was already nodding, businesslike. 'I understand. Winter's end is a bad time for us all, but you must bring gifts for your aunts, your sisters. I imagine you'll have no end of trouble otherwise.'

He took a key from the loop at his waist and opened a wrought-iron box at his feet. He took Sos's right hand and placed two coins in it, clapping him on the shoulder. 'No need to put it in the book. Just pay me when you return.'

'If I return,' said Sos glumly.

'Come Lord Misery, you've money in your pockets, a spring journey ahead of you and you'll leave behind more broken hearts and jealous husbands than a pup your age has any right to. You'll be back. Fathers just need to remember what their sons look like every once in a while, that's the truth of it.'

Sos refused to smile. 'But the war. Maybe it'll all be over by the time he lets me return.'

'War?' Shota asked, one eyebrow cocked.

'You know, the war everyone says is coming. The war with . . .' Sos stopped. 'Shota, you know everything, who is attacking? Is it the Seljuks?'

The steward snorted and made to cuff Sos about the back of the head, but he ducked just in time. 'The Seljuks? No, Sos, the king's enemies are closer to home. The Seljuks have been too busy with the basileus in Constantinople and his Frankish friends to pay heed to what's afoot in our kingdom – and we must all pray it stays that way.'

'But—' Sos began.

'No, no, I don't have the time to give you politics lessons, not today anyway. Off with you and ride safe.'

Sos was out the door before he heard Shota call him back.

'Word of advice.'

'What?' Sos followed the steward's gaze. 'My boots? What? What's wrong with them?'

'In my experience, fathers don't have much time for Constantinople fashions. I'd save those handsome fellows for the plains.' He winked, picked up his quill and started scratching away on a piece of parchment.

I'll explain . . . he'll understand . . . he must understand.

His father's messenger had come via the long, low road but Sos decided to take the direct route home through the high Kavkaz peaks, where spirits and demons crouched nameless under the Fire Mountain, the Ice Mountain and the Mountain of Chains. Only a bishop could fail to hear the voices of the old gods in the summer storms and autumn rains, feel their power in winter avalanches and spring floods.

The path all but disappeared once he was in the foothills, but by then every spur, every ridge, every peak was as familiar as morning. Day by day he wound higher and higher, leaving the forests behind, until he came to the great pass that marked the boundary of his homeland.

He was too early. He should let spring creep higher up the mountainside, but he was impatient. Death from a snowslide was less daunting than waiting. So he crossed, slow, silent and tense, leading the horse until it was safe to ride again.

Two days later, as dusk deepened into night, Sos glimpsed houses planted deep into the rocks, part-cave, part-hut. Little black smudges, fingerprints in the granite. Woodsmoke bobbed in the air, like a ghost at rest. A chill north-easterly wind carried the smell of evening cooking fires. Smoke and animals and mud caught in his throat. He was home.

He galloped up to his father's house, chickens flapping out of his way, and tied his horse to the gatepost, wincing a little at the squalor, the meanness. He did not see his father standing in the shadows at the door until he spoke.

'So, boy, you are home.'

'Yes, father, I am.'

Death was tracking him close, like a wolf lying unblinking in the long grass at the forest edge at dusk. Anybody, even Sos, could see that, but he could not accept it. He could more easily imagine looking up and finding the mountains had grown legs and jumped off the rim of the world than that his father might be near death.

Jadaron, standing deep inside his furs, cast a long, sneering look over his son.

'I hardly recognise this fine knight.'

He turned stiffly to enter his house. Sos ducked under the door beam, squinting in the gloom, and stood uneasily as his father placed himself on a high stone chair.

'Tell me news.'

Sos swallowed hard. Conversations with his father had always terrified him, but now he also had to contend with the embarrassed deference of vitality before age, the painful awareness of his own strength. Jadaron's face had collapsed, every bone was prominent, the flesh gouged. With everything else stripped away, his eyes had grown more intense until it seemed there was nothing but glowering black between him and his father's mind. Sos stumbled his reply, incapable of saying what he meant and hating himself for it.

'I . . . I know not what news you seek, sir. I thought to ride with the king when he went to fight. I thought to serve. I want to—'

'Want. Thought. I care not for those things. Tell me news. Who is loyal? Do the Kipchaks still have the king's ear? Who will follow Orbeli and the boy?'

Sos looked blank. 'I know not—' Again his father interrupted. 'You would know if you had spent your time at court wisely.'

Sos had the unpleasant feeling that his father knew everything he had done – and failed to do – in the last three years.

'If you had, then you would know that times have changed. The king of the plains is weak. Weak. He has no heir. And you speak of serving him. No, my boy. Orbeli sent to tell me he will rise. He asked for my blessing, my support, and I gave it. Giorgi's rule is over. It is time to say *No*. It is time to say *Enough*. We will rule ourselves. And then we will drive every last Kipchak back over the mountains.'

Sos gulped. For numberless generations, Kipchak nomads from beyond the mountains had sought pathways between the peaks and crept south, their fingertips freezing at night and rotting by day. They came in the spring, beardless men with broad faces, hunting goats and women and gold. They took what they wanted, then vanished. But it was different now. His father must understand that. He tried to explain.

'But father, the Kipchaks fight with the king against the Seljuks, against all men of the desert prophet. They are our allies, our friends—'

'Friends? Do friends take your land? Your cattle? Your horses? Defile your shrines? The woods and waters, the hills, the valleys: they have not forgotten, they have not forgiven and neither shall

19

we. Not until we have our revenge on those who let them in. Davit. That fame-fat fool.'

It had been a long time since Sos had heard the king's grandfather's name hissed with such malice, and it startled him. He knew what was coming. He had heard it many times before.

'Davit marched to the Darial pass. We thought he had come to our aid. But he betrayed us. He had come to let the Kipchaks in. They were waiting for him. Forty thousand of them. Their horses. Their women. Their swords. And he let them in.'

Anger made Jadaron's face even paler.

'Davit had his army at his back. What could we do? We watched, sick with shame, as they rode unopposed. We will never repay the dishonour done that day. We . . . but what do you know of honour? Do you even understand what I am saying?'

Sos had only one thing to say, but he didn't dare. *If you hate them all so much, why did you send me to Tbilisi?*

'Why did you send me to Tbilisi?'

Aloud. He had spoken aloud. He hadn't meant to. He tensed, waiting. His father did not reply immediately. He wet thin lips with an outsized tongue and looked at Sos, hard and unblinking.

'I thought it would make a man of you. I did not think you would forget your home, your family, your people, the earth that gave you flesh, the spirits that gave you breath.'

No young man, unless he's mad or a liar, can ignore his father's scorn. Maybe with time, when he is a father too, maybe then he can shrug off contempt and banish it. But for now that was impossible. Sos breathed slow, as if before a bowshot, wishing he was not so riled, wishing his father was not so still.

'Well, father, I am back. And, father, I am a man, whatever you think. What would you have me do now?'

He knew he sounded petulant, boylike. His father arched one brow, which pulled up the left side of his face into an expression so supercilious that Sos had to look at his feet.

'You, Soslani, you will remember you are an Osset. You will do your duty here. You are my heir. You will learn how to follow me when I am gone. Do you have anything else to say?'

20

The levelness of his gaze mocked Sos's furious efforts to keep himself under control.

'No. I see you do not. Maybe that is just as well. Now go.'

Sos dipped his head, the closest to the bow owed to an ageing father as he could bring himself to offer.

Chapter Three

Journeying to a remote mountain hideaway was not as much fun as Tamar had expected.

Giorgi's haste for them to be gone was so great that they arrived at the final pass into Osset country too soon. Tiny green leaves had been fluttering on the walnut trees when they rode up out of the plains, but by now spring was hundreds of feet below them. The last snowfall of the season lingered on the heights above, heavy, wet and lethal. If they didn't wait, Dato said, they could be buried under a snowslide, leaving their frozen bodies to be discovered by travellers who weren't so stupid as to try to beat the mountains. So they spent ten chill, grey days, in bullock-hide tents under a rocky outcrop in the lee of a cliff. It was not quite freezing but the air was clammy, the sun rarely seen. The last trees were two days' ride away, so they only had a fire when Dato made an evening meal.

At first, exhausted by the long ride, Tamar sank gratefully into a numb daze, rocking gently inside her fur wraps, stuffy and sleepy, her limbs too heavy to move, her mind too heavy to think. She wanted the journey to be over, but dreaded having to move. But soon she grew impatient. Every morning Dato trod a path to where they would start their final ascent. Every morning he returned and shook his head.

'Not today, my lady. Today it is not safe.'

'But whose are those tracks? Somebody has passed recently.'

'Whoever that was had no respect for his own life. Nor did he have to answer for the king's daughter. Please, my lady, let us talk of it no more.'

He paced back and forth outside his tent, his boots grinding the shale, while she lay and listened to the strange winds that raced around the peaks, gusts arguing ominously overhead, making sleep impossible.

She remembered Nino's quiet tears with embarrassment and a tinge of guilt. Susa had sobbed prettily about how much she'd miss her beloved sister, but Tamar was sure she was just jealous that she hadn't been singled out for a secret journey.

Her mother hovered in the nursery while Nino packed, her hands fluttering aimlessly as she kept asking if there was anything she could do to help. Eventually she had sat down on a low divan and called her beautiful girls to her. Susa nestled picturesquely in her lap while Tamar perched uncomfortably at her side. Burdukhan, her saucer eyes swimming with unshed tears, stroked her cheek.

Her father came to bid her farewell before dawn, folding her in an embrace that startled her so much that she almost failed to notice that he was whispering something urgently into her ear, repeating it over and over, squeezing the back of her head as if to grind his words into her brain. Those words now swam ceaselessly inside her, looming larger, fading smaller, but always there.

The sword hand, daughter. Only you and I shall know. The sword hand.

What about Dato?

I would trust him with my life, daughter, you know that. But I trust no man but myself with yours.

A thin daylight entered the tent and behind it came Dato. He bowed.

'My lady, there is food.'

'I'm not hungry.'

'Hungry or not, my lady, there is food.'

'I'm not hungry.' She rolled over, expecting to hear the tent flap fall shut. Nothing. He was still standing there, waiting. It was like trying to ignore a mountain. She rolled back over.

'All right, I'm coming. What is it? Buckwheat?'

He nodded. She grimaced.

'My favourite.'

'Mine too.'

'Are you being funny, Dato?'

'No my lady, when you've journeyed and fought for as many years as I have, you grow to love buckwheat, even without salt.'

She crawled out of the tent, pulled her cloak tight about her and sat on a rock, aggrieved without knowing why. She stuck her wooden spoon into the pot. It stood upright for a second or two, then slowly started to keel over away from her. Dato didn't react. She grabbed it before the handle was completely submerged and took a mouthful.

'Dato?'

'My lady?'

'Why do you my-lady me? You never used to.'

'You never used to be a lady, my lady.'

'Hardly a lady now, am I?' She gestured vaguely at the pot, at the slush.

'It makes no difference.'

'I thought we were friends.'

Dato smiled, but shook his head.

When she was little, still dressed in an unbleached Hellên tunic, she would stand sentry by the guardroom door, pacing back and forth until he came out, then jump up and down in front of him until he'd agree to a morning exploring the woods around the city. She'd skip by his side, playing the fool, trying to make him laugh, pelting him with questions, theories, demands. But it had been four, five years since the two of them had stood on the heights above the palace, looking down, her face pink, her skirts flapping in the wind, the setting sun on the back of her neck.

When she woke on the tenth morning the inside of her tent was dry and she heard Dato leading their ponies back to the camp.

'My lady, we await your pleasure.'

She bounded outside, breathing the morning air, violently pleased to be alive and moving on the top of the world. The sky was blue. The sun hot.

'No, captain. My legs feel stupid as tree stumps. Today I walk.'

'As you wish, my lady. I also like the feel of the ground under my feet.'

Tamar grinned inside. She wanted to grab his hand and bolt up the slope. Instead she sat, suddenly prim as a snowdrop, and laced up her boots.

They walked up the face of the mountain in long lazy loops, single file, Dato and the two ponies leading the way to tread down the snow. Tamar followed, staring at her pony's tail. The slender scoop between the two peaks, etched sharp against the sky, sank closer within reach until after three hours' trudging there was nowhere left to climb and they stood panting on the rim of the pass. Specks of ice danced in the sunshine.

'We must go carefully here. The snow is heavy with spring and the ground underneath is treacherous.' Dato reached through the snow, picked up a handful of small, dark grey flints and let them run through his fingers. 'Easy to slip. Easy to start a snowslide. Tread softly, my lady, and watch where your feet fall.'

She stood to one side as the squat ponies crunched after him, a tang of sweat rising from their bodies. The hair at their shoulders was matted and their eyes flailed left and right as they ground the iron bits in their mouths. She fell into line behind them, feeling lighter on her feet as they lost height, her legs swimming easily as she jolted left, right, left, right, down and down.

The sides of the valley met in a V so steep that the river running along the bottom was hidden, but a thick tangle of sound rose from it, like the summer afternoon hum when blue-bottles and fat bees race around a meadow, louder than thought.

She began to tire, scuffing not stepping. Dato halted and cupped his hands to swing her into her pony's saddle. She dozed as the sun dropped behind the peaks and cold shadows stretched over them. Deepening shades of blue and violet, the colour of three-day-old bruises, lingered in the east. A lacklustre finger of moon trailed sulkily after the sun.

It was most of the way to night when they followed a kink in the valley to a small plateau of land bisected by a stream jumping down to join the river below. She could make out a dull glimmer of orange where a hearth fire shone through the cracks in the walls of a house. A man's voice, indistinct, shouted down the hysterical barking of unseen dogs and then a larger patch of orange shone as a doorway was uncovered, silhouetting his legs.

'Where are we? Who—?' she began.

'No questions now. We must not linger here. We don't want anyone to know about our arrival, not if we can help it.'

The night was suddenly charged with a sensation she did not like, as if a thousand pairs of eyes were trained on the small of her back. She glanced fearfully over her shoulder as they splashed across the little ford in silence.

As they approached the house, the man called out a challenge, first in a language Tamar did not understand, then in something she recognised as her own, but strangely spoken, as if the man had sharp rocks in his mouth and was trying not to cut himself.

'Who comes this night? Speak!'

Dato pulled up his horse and replied urgently in the stranger's language. Although it was her mother's tongue, she could not understand what they were saying. Only the shape of the words felt familiar, as if she could catch their meaning by bending her mind. She remembered sitting at an open window, listening to her mother sing the songs of her own childhood, the words spilling over her head. Then the king's boarhound pack, red-jawed from the hunt, raced into the courtyard below and her mother covered her eyes with her fingers.

'What are you saying?' Tamar asked softly.

'He was not expecting us, Tamar. Strange things live in the mountains and the people here do not trust those who come after dark. But fear not, we are now his guests. Come, you must greet him.'

The man bowed slow and low, a bow for a palace feast not a mountain night. One of his eyes was stitched shut, a badly knit

26

scar running from brow to ear. She swung herself out of the saddle and dropped to the floor, her cold feet jarring uncomfortably as they hit the dirt. She wanted to fling her cloak at a servant, demand a bath and drink warm cinnamon milk under soft blankets. Before she could say anything he clasped her hands, rubbing them between his own.

'Your mother, my friend. Do not fear. We talk tomorrow. Now – food, sleep.' She nearly burst into tears.

Tamar woke deliciously slowly the next morning, letting sleep release her bit by bit, her mind wallowing. Kitchen sounds, animal sounds, all oddly close, filled her ears. She wanted to stay hidden as long as possible, but her throat was dry from the smoke in the house and she needed a drink, so she pushed a corner of curtain aside and peered underneath.

A sturdy woman kneading dough at a rough table glanced up.

'Water, please,' said Tamar, miming drinking. The woman pointed through the door and mimed scooping. Tamar grimaced. The woman shrugged and returned to her bread-making. So Tamar pulled on her dirty clothes and eased her way down the ladder and out of the house, screwing up her eyes against the mid-morning sunshine. Their ponies were grazing at one side of the house, their legs hobbled. A couple of tree trunks, their branches hacked off, lay in front as benches of sorts by a stone table for summer eating. Dato was sitting on one of these, sharpening his long knife. He looked up as she approached.

'How did you sleep?'

'It's better than tents, I suppose.' She walked over to where a large rock and a small hollow had formed a still pool, a foot deep, in the stream. She knelt down and drank mouthful after mouthful of meltwater.

'I don't suppose there is a bathing room?' she called to Dato.

'You're in it.' She held his gaze, looking for any hint of mockery but to her disappointment found none. Dato stood up and bowed. 'I will intrude no longer, my lady.' He thrust his knife in his boot, turned his back and strode away up the valley.

She stalked back into the kitchen where the saddlebags were propped in a corner. She had no idea what was in them. She undid the tie-ropes and rifled through the packs, clothes flashing gold and scarlet as she pulled them out and threw them on the floor. A snort came from behind her and she snapped round, glowering at the woman, who was not bothering to hide her amusement – as if Tamar couldn't order her chopped into tiny pieces. Finally, at the bottom of the second pack, she found an unadorned wool dress and a spare travelling cloak which she bundled under her arm.

She kicked off her shoes and stood on the bank, the cold mud squeezing up between her toes. She struggled out of her dress under the cloak and crouched over the stream, splashing her face, the back of her neck, under her arms, between her legs until her fingers were numb and her body smarted from the cold. She took a deep breath and plunged her head under water, counting to ten while it whipped around her. She wrestled into the clean dress, perched on one of the stones to splash the mud off her feet, roughly dried them and shoved her shoes back on.

The woman dropped what was probably a curtsey when she walked back inside, pointed to a stool and sloshed milk into a lopsided clay mug. Tamar sipped, eyes narrowed slightly as she looked about her, the milk frothing warm on her tongue. The woman dumped a plate in front of her, flat bread balanced on top of a mound of unidentifiable meat. Tamar leant forward to sniff the brown mess. It did not smell unpleasant but there was no spoon. She tugged at the woman's sleeve and mimed again. The woman looked blank for a moment, then rolled her eyes and pointed to the bread. Tamar rolled her eyes right back, hunched her shoulders and shovelled her breakfast down.

When nobody took away her empty plate, she picked it up and carried it out the door. And that was how Dato found her when he returned, crouched on her haunches, her skirts riding up over her knees, rinsing her dish and mug in the stream.

'Where've you been? Aren't you meant to be guarding me?' she asked him over her shoulder.

'Retracing our steps, scouting. Until the snow melts nobody can follow us over the pass undetected.'

'And? What did you see? Why do you look strange?'

'I look strange?'

'Yes, you do.'

'I wish the snow would melt. Until it does our tracks glow like fire on a moonless night. Any fool could follow us. What have you told the woman?'

'Nothing! You forget I cannot speak their language. Your language.'

'But, surely, your mother . . . ?'

'My father did not like to hear it. He said the look in her eyes when she spoke it made him want to throttle her. I think she believed him. She always was scared of him.'

He said nothing, but his expression had suddenly darkened.

'Well, she is,' she countered. 'I don't know why.' Her voice tailed away and she took a new tone. 'So, captain, here we are and here we stay. If there is no escape from the sour old sow in there, so be it. I'm going to look about.'

As she turned away, he put his hand on her shoulder and pulled her back to face him. He spoke low.

'You understand nothing. That sour old sow – as you so handsomely call the woman who has sworn to hide you – is brave, kind and terrified. Soldiers will soon be scouring every scrap of land between the two seas. Hunting you. And they will kill whatever stands in their way. This is no time to pout at the company you are forced to keep.'

Her eyes turned dark like the sea when the first clouds of a storm overtake the sun, chasing away light and shade. She too spoke low to start with, but a hiss of anger escaping between her teeth distorted her voice.

'I will do as I please. No man, not even you, speaks to me like that. I don't care how far away the court is, you will not forget yourself like that again.'

Dato hadn't been afraid of anything since he was four and first had to walk by himself across the pine trunk that bridged the river by his parents' house, terrified by the water demons snatching at his ankles. But Tamar's eyes made him uneasy. He dropped his gaze.

'Forgive me.'

'It is forgotten.'

A pause.

'But, my lady, believe me, nobody must know who you are. Aton and Albina, them we can trust. At least they have nobody to tell. Few people come this way. But we don't want a shepherd to talk of a strange girl at the ford. Not one dressed so fine.'

She looked at her plain grey dress, then realised he was serious.

'Well, what do we do?'

'You must either stay inside, out of sight, until your father sends word.'

'Or?'

'I was thinking of a simple disguise. To speak plain, you are not quite a woman.' She flushed. 'Cut your hair. Borrow some clothes. Even as a boy you will still have to keep close to the house, avoid people, but from a distance there should be no danger. Aton can mention a great-nephew, a feud in the plains. That should serve.'

Tamar turned this over in her mind. 'Agreed.' She smiled, her eyes dancing once more. 'At least boys must not be seen scrubbing pots.'

Dato returned her look soberly. 'Quite.'

He stood up and ran his hands through his hair, combing out invisible tangles.

'And now, my lady, I must ride south once more. With your leave, of course.'

'But Dato, why? You haven't even been here a day. I don't know these people. Dato, I can't understand a word they're saying. Stay, stay at least a seven-night.'

He shook his head. 'No, I cannot. We were long on the road, longer than I or your father expected. I must tell him you are here, tell him you are safe, then fight at his side.'

'But what am I to do?'

'What are you to do? Is that all that's worrying you? What

about your father? The situation is grave. Very likely Tbilisi is already under siege.'

She shook her head. Fear for her father? The idea had not occurred to her. 'He is the king. No man will defeat him.'

Dato laughed, quietly. 'Such faith. That is why wise men hope to father daughters. Well, to answer your question, haven't you always complained about being, what do you call it . . . *cooped up*? Well, there's no coop here, only the mountains, the valleys. I envy you. You are in hiding, but I'd say you are more free now than you have ever been. And Aton's a kind man. You could learn a great deal from him – if you are minded to listen.'

'Will he show me how to shoot a bow from the back of my pony?'

'I was thinking more about plant lore, fishing and the like,' he said ruefully. 'But ask him, by all means. Now, my lady, I must ride.'

Sadness settled in her stomach as she watched Dato swing himself into his saddle and pull his travelling cloak tight around his neck. He reached out to rest his hand briefly on her head, then he kicked his horse into a rolling canter, one arm raised in farewell.

'Dato!' she cried out after him, but he did not hear. He had already crossed the ford and was pounding up the valley, riding hard for the plains.

'I'm sorry,' she muttered. 'You're right. She's not a sow.'

Chapter Four

Sos looked down at the horse's sides heaving between his thighs and tasted again the deep satisfaction of being high in the mountains, close to the sky. His cousins were somewhere behind him, but only he had followed the stag and taken the leap at the gorge, a glorious bound that nearly stopped his breath. The next pony refused, falling back on its haunches, its front hooves scrabbling at the edge.

'They always know when a rider's scared,' he called over his shoulder as he gave chase. The others now had to weave back half a mile through the forest to where the cliffs narrowed enough for even a child to hazard a jump.

He plucked an arrow, poplar wood, tipped with eagle feathers, and notched it into the gut of his bow, letting his breathing grow still as he scanned the way ahead. Nothing in his head but the hunt, the need to be first with the kill.

He heard a rustle in the bushes and half a heartbeat later swung his bow round. A boy, not a stag, stood uncertainly before him. It was too late to stop the arrow, but as he released it, he jerked up and sideways so the shaft did not burrow into the boy's throat, but instead flew four fingers wide and ripped into the flesh above the collarbone.

Sos tumbled off his horse and dropped to the boy's side. His eyes were still open but blank and black with pain. His mouth hung open, the lips waxy. But he made no sound. He had not even cried out.

Sos tore open the boy's shirt and shifted the arrow back and forth. Blood flowed faster from the wound, but it was not deep, not fatal, at least he didn't think so. He twisted the point free with his right hand and clamped the wound shut with his left.

'Here, come on, where are your hands, either side, no, no –
harder, pinch, pinch.'

He guided the boy's fingers to the wound, jumped up and ran
to his horse, which was worrying at a gorse bush, to find a rag
to soak up the blood. When he looked round, the boy had fainted
backwards. Blood was pouring from his shoulder, pooling in the
hollow at the base of his neck. Sos swore, ran back. What a
child. But now that the boy's eyes were closed, he saw how soft
the face was, how young. A child. His anger left him and he felt
sorry.

The others cantered into the clearing and started hallooing
when they saw the yellow horse without its rider.

'Too fast again, were you?'

'Come out, come out, don't whimper in the bushes!'

He called back, rude and cheerful, and they followed his voice
to where he knelt by the boy.

'Oh noble huntsman—'

'Lion and boar tremble at your footfall—'

'God's hand guides your arrows—'

A year ago he would have let fly with insults, maybe fists, but
now he could shrug off jokes, just about.

'So that's what you and your Kart friends hunted, was it?
Boys?'

That question came from Vakhtang who never missed a chance
to needle Sos about soft city habits.

'Only when wives weren't in season Vakho,' Sos answered to
much laughter.

'There'll be a blood price to pay, you know, whoever he is,'
said his cousin, sulky now. His father could not afford to keep
him at the king's court and he had never left the mountains.

Sos lifted the blood-soaked cloth and looked underneath. The
blood was no longer flowing and the pulse was strong.

'I know that, Vakhtang. But God doesn't want this little shepherd, not yet anyway.'

'Well then, for the love of God, wake your little shepherd up
and send him on his way.' Some sniggering.

Sos scooped the boy up and hung him over his shoulder. 'You go ahead. I'll leave him at Aton's house. He can reunite him with his mother, or with his sheep, whichever has a greater claim on him. Give me a hand, one of you.' He hefted the boy over the back of his horse and climbed up after him. 'See you before sundown.'

As he jogged towards the mountain house, he prayed Vakhtang didn't track down the stag before he caught up with them and wished Aton's first sight of him in almost four years was with something more impressive than a wounded boy slung over his horse. He'd meant to ride up and visit the old man ever since he'd come back from the plains, but the right moment had never come.

Aton was a brilliant huntsman, although Sos hadn't always appreciated it. When his father first sent them out together, the eight-year-old boy thought the old man's style was plodding. For a start, he hunted on foot. *You can't see a thing perched up there.* And when after hours of hot and prickly creeping and crawling they came up on the stag or the boar, Sos bursting with the effort of keeping quiet, Aton never let him make the kill. *That's the easy part, lad.* Instead, he'd point out a knot in the trunk of a tree, a few handspans shy of their prey. *Show me you can hit that.* Then they'd traipse back to his father's house empty-handed.

But when Sos joined the court hunt, even in the strange terrain of the plains, he knew instinctively which way an animal had gone. Time and again he'd make the right turn and come up first on the beast, just as the dogs had brought it to bay. The others found it so uncanny they mocked him for being part animal or possessed by spirits, but he knew it was jealousy and his heart danced at his skill.

As he approached, Sos saw Aton laboriously splitting logs at the side of the house. He called out, shading his voice with respect for his age and his scars.

'Honour to your sword!'

Aton's head snapped up, his stance wary, but almost immediately the tension vanished and he unwound a broad smile.

'And strength to yours. It's been a long time, Sos. How many winters since you rode away? By the mountains, you're tall as a pine tree.'

Sos grinned back. 'Size isn't all.'

'Indeed it's not. I'm glad some of what I taught you took root under your curls.'

Aton worked his axe out of the stump, hefted it over his shoulder and strode towards him. 'Well, don't sit up there when there's shade and wine.'

He frowned suddenly and his voice changed.

'What is that? What's on your horse?'

Sos swallowed and patted the boy's back. 'Oh, this boy? I came across him in the forest. Do you know where he belongs?'

As he reached down to show Aton, the boy came back to life, slithered down the horse's flanks and bolted behind the old man like a kicked cat. Aton put one arm round him and kept tight hold of the axe with the other.

'I see, he's yours,' said Sos, flushing under Aton's stiff gaze. 'Well, tell him he shouldn't skulk in the bushes when men are hunting. It's dangerous. Foolish.'

He trailed off. Aton took in the deep red stain, the boy's grey face and spoke low.

'Off your horse. Now.'

Sos would have scowled if his father had spoken to him like that, but Aton only made him feel guilty and his words tumbled out.

'I'm sorry I hurt him, truly, I swear it. How was I to know he was there? You're right I should have looked. I rushed. Forgive me. Will he be all right? Who is he? Forgive me.'

He might have floundered for ever, but Aton's face softened and he laughed.

'Sos, my lad, the seasons passed quietly when you were safe down in the plains. Quiet. But slow. The boy will live. You were right to bring him here. Now, let's see if Albina can mend my nephew. Albina! I need you!'

Sos flashed the old man a grateful grin, which faded fast when he saw Albina bearing down on him in a cloud of flour, rolling pin in hand.

'Sweet heavens, what has happened?'

'Young Sos mistook our boy for a stag. But luckily he still can't shoot straight.'

Sos opened his mouth to protest, but thought better of it.

'Don't you joke, husband,' Albina puffed. 'And as for you, you misbegotten monster, who taught you to gallop about shooting children? Is that what you learned from the Karts? Is it?'

She flourished her pin so menacingly that Sos took a step back and put his hands up.

'Yes, yes, that's right. I can do as much damage with this as your tavads can do with their swords. Shooting children! The shame . . .'

Still scolding, she swept the boy inside, patting and stroking his head.

'Let's leave them,' said Aton. 'Come, my lord Soslani, we'll go down to the river and you can tell me your news.' He clapped Sos on the shoulder and they walked off together.

'It's good to see you, Aton.'

'You too, Sos, you too.'

Tamar sank into her mattress, weak-limbed, her eyelids dragged shut, listening as the beats of the young man's horse sounded fainter and fainter, first in her ears, then in her memory, mingling with the blood pounding inside her head. She did not have the strength to sit or stand, but something invisible was careering wildly back and forth inside her ribcage, like a puppy hurling itself headlong at the walls of its pen. Her head raged at the way he'd looked at her, but did not see her.

Albina mopped and dabbed and scrubbed the wound, keeping up a stream of imprecation, incantation as her warm dry brown hands padded it with green stuff and bound it tight. Her words flowed insistently, heavy as mud. Tamar was foolish, reckless, heedless, thoughtless, thankless, the Lord was blessed, merciful, beneficent, bounteous, bountiful – but the fingers were kind, the tone a caress. She tucked a pillow under Tamar's head and pulled a blanket about her, stroking her forehead, smoothing her hair, and murmuring, quieter and quieter until Tamar fell deep, deep asleep.

Chapter Five

Spring became summer. Nothing disturbed the shimmering peace of the valley. The endless, windless days dawdled past, indistinct in the heat. The grass turned a pale green-brown, notched with little dust tracks as if a giant had idly scratched his fingernails on the ground as he passed on his way north. Goats, who had long lost their winter scrawniness, fanned out behind their herders, criss-crossing in their wake as they headed up to the high pastures. If the children carrying food parcels up to their fathers in the meadows noticed a slight figure cantering his pony along the river they never thought twice about it. Everyone had heard from someone that a boy was summering with the old man. Everyone assumed, without the need for discussion, that he was hiding until a matter of blood could be settled. Some guessed it was to do with Sos's time with the Karts – he often stopped by the high house.

Another day dawned, bright. Tamar had risen early, risen before the sun had crested the valley's sides. She pulled on her loose-fitting breeches and tunic, threw a fond look at Albina, gargling the night's final snores on her back, took a piece of yesterday's bread from under an upturned bowl, unhooked her basket and rod from the wall by the door and ducked outside. Inside it had been deliciously cool. Outside it was deliciously warm. She hurtled down the steep bank to the river, her momentum nearly accelerating her out of control as the pebbles slid away under her bare feet.

Aton was wading upstream to the forest side where the close-growing pines shaded the far bank, seeking the bigger fish that wallowed in the back eddies, the green-dark pools. He waved Tamar a good morning before he disappeared from view. She paddled softly out to a rock in the middle of the river, propped the basket next to her and sat down, the water splaying left and right around her. She looked down at her feet, wriggling and splashing them, the water just too cold for comfort, then reached into her basket, selected a worm and baited her hook the way Sos had shown her.

When they'd first gone fishing, she'd almost dropped the worm he'd chucked at her. She'd had to cup one hand under the other to stop it wriggling through her fingers and plopping into the water.

Don't you know how to do it?

Of course I do.

No, you don't, or otherwise you'd have done it by now. Don't you have rivers where you're from? Do you live in a desert?

She'd flung the worm back at him but his hand shot out just before it slapped into his cheek.

Stop playing and fish – or we get no supper. That was Aton, who'd been watching.

Go on, it's easy. He'd tossed it back and she'd wrinkled her nose and jammed the hook through the worm's head. When she'd glanced back at him, he'd been grinning at her. *Fish are easy. We'll go and hunt something bigger when I next come, I promise.*

She'd nodded eagerly – although she knew there was no way Aton would ever agree to it. He never let them out of earshot, let alone out of sight. She was secretly relieved. She had no idea what boys talked about when they were alone. What if he guessed she was a girl? That would be a disaster. But what if he didn't? She frowned. That might be worse.

She wasn't paying much attention to the rod in her hands, but automatically whisking it upstream and letting the line drift back down with the current. The tiny ripples danced in the sunlight. Fish broke the surface with sudden sharp splashes. Time slid.

She felt them before she heard them, heard them before she saw them. The thump, thump of hooves drumming like war, the crick-crack of breaking branches, then one, two, a dozen horses cantered out of the forest. The lead rider yanked his horse to a halt. It plunged and reared, snorting, startled by the sudden stop, its hooves kicking up water, grinding the stones at the river's edge. Tamar tasted shock like nausea in her mouth. From the moment they sprang out of the forest it was already too late to run and hide. For three breaths they looked around them, their eyes adjusting to the glare after the gloom between the pines. The men were alert, purposeful, their horses unusually large for mountain riding. The leader wheeled his horse in her direction, one hand lightly on the reins, the other shading his eyes as he bore down on her.

He had an ugly cast to his soft, pale brown eyes and a small cleft in his chin. As his eye caught hers she quickly lowered her gaze and stared down hard at the rock between her legs.

'You, boy, go, run, tell your lady we are here. Tell her Bakhar has come at the king's command.'

'My lord, I do not understand,' she mumbled in Osset, hoping the stranger could not speak it.

He spurred his horse at her until she could feel its hot, wet breath on her forehead. There was a sharp hiss as something cut through the air. She looked up in time to see his whip arching down towards her. Instinctively, she flung herself backwards, tumbling off the rock into the river, struggling back on to her feet, wet, wild-eyed, a red welter on her right cheek. She backed away from him as he drew closer, then as he was about to strike again, she dropped her rod and bolted for the bank.

Bakhar gave the other men a quick, grim nod and kicked his horse into a trot. As he followed, the last rider aimed a kick at the basket, upending it and sending a cascade of small silver fish into the river. Their bodies were already stiff as knives, gills parched, eyes clouded. They slid between his horse's legs down to the rapids below.

Tamar dived under the low doorway into the main room, her stomach leaping over itself as her throat ached and her head prickled with fear. The horses would struggle to scale the bank and would have to come the long way round but she could already hear them pounding up the dry dirt track. They'd be there in seconds.

Her mind raced. Could they be friends? Her hand went involuntarily to her cheek. How did soldiers normally behave? Where was Aton? Where was Albina? Already she could hear the men hitting the ground outside as they leapt from their horses. *Trust nobody*. Time was short. She wouldn't flap like a chicken in a coop.

'Where is she?'

Bakhar's voice sounded surprisingly quiet and normal. She gripped the table behind her, willing herself to make the right decision. She opened her mouth to speak but the words stopped in her throat when she heard Aton's voice close outside.

'My lord. How do I serve you? Wine for men? Grass for horses?' She could imagine his good eye levelled coolly on the strange soldier.

'No, old man, nothing. We seek the king's daughter. We seek Tamar. The king wants her back at court and we are to take her there. Where is she?'

Tamar swallowed hard, waiting for Aton's answer. 'This not palace, lord. No princess here.'

'You lie.'

Tamar heard the untidy scrape of a sword leaving its sheath.

'Stop,' she cried, her voice strangely high but still powerful. 'I am here. Don't touch my servants if you value your lives. I am coming.'

She ripped off her clothes, hunted for her bags and pulled one of her untouched dresses over her head. She pushed her tufts of hair under an embroidered cap and tucked her feet into silk slippers. Something was missing. She rummaged for her cross, as big as her hand and the finest thing she possessed – emeralds, rubies and pearls set in gold – and hung it about her neck. Her eyes landed on a barrel of apples, waiting to be boiled down into sticky sweet preserve. She snatched one up.

Any doubts she had about declaring herself vanished. Aton was sprawled face down in the dirt, his shoulders heaving as he struggled for breath. He fought to his knees, coughing uncontrollably.

41

Only one of the other riders was visible. The others must be on guard further off. Bakhar, sword still drawn, dropped an ornate bow. His eyes darted to the red rip down her cheek, and he looked away fast.

'Your name, sir,' said Tamar, horribly aware of his height, his weight, the smell of his sweat fogging the bright air. She took a bite of her apple and forced herself to chew slowly.

'Bakhar, my lady.'

'I have been away from court for a while. Tell me, Bakhar, is it now the custom to stand with head covered and blade bare in front of the king's daughter?' Another bite.

'You must excuse us, my lady. My men and I have ridden long and hard. My joy, my relief, at finding you alive makes me forget my manners.'

The word *alive* sent a chill through her. She noticed that although he pulled off his hat, his sword stayed where it was, its edge catching the sun, his knuckles white on the hilt.

'You come from my father?'

'My lady, yes. You've had no news here?'

She shook her head slowly, her eyes never leaving his face. He continued.

'Your father sends word that you are not safe. It is no longer a secret that he hid you in these mountains. Men, twenty, thirty, maybe more, follow fast behind us. We must ride now.'

She ignored the command in his voice and flung the apple core down the bank. 'How did Orbeli learn where I was? Who betrayed me? Why did my father send you? I do not know you from court.'

He shrugged. 'The king ordered me. I asked no questions and obeyed. And I have a token, one he said you would recognise.'

The word *token* kindled a tiny spark of hope inside her. Maybe she could trust him. It was a brutal time. Her father probably needed men like Bakhar to survive.

'Show me.'

He unslung a black bundle and let it unravel. The king's kinzhal landed in the palm of his hand.

'How came you by that?' she demanded.

He smiled and spoke softly. 'Princess, it is the truth-token, is it not? He gave it to me with his own hands. He said you would recognise it and know to follow me. How soon can we depart?'

She did not answer, but held out her hand for the knife. How could he have her father's blade unless the king had given it willingly? He slept with it in his hand. When he ate he buried the point in the table or drove it into the earth. There was one way to find out.

Only you and I shall know.

She smiled at Bakhar and spoke soft. 'You must know, my lord, that the dagger alone is not enough.'

The summer flush evaporated from his neck and face, leaving only stung-spots of red in the hollows of his cheeks. He placed his hand on the stone table, the fingers extended. He bent his head so she could see the afternoon breeze lifting the fine hairs at the back of his neck.

'I am ready.'

She turned the blade over in her hand, examining the familiar handle, testing the edge with her thumb. Her chin was high, her eyes steady, but her body was rocked by almost imperceptible spasms that she had to fight to keep under control. She took three steps over to where Bakhar was standing, his face turned aside. She gripped his wrist with her left hand and lifted the dagger. Bakhar did not flinch. She made up her mind.

The blade dropped, swimming easily through skin, sinew, bone.

Bakhar's head snapped back towards her, his eyes squinting with pain and shock. Tamar stared at the fingers lying next to each other in the dust.

'Wrong hand,' she said.

And ran.

Bakhar's horse was ten desperate strides away, a wall of flesh. She flung herself at it, clawing her fingers deep in its mane, kicking like a mule to propel herself messily on to its back. Its spine ground into her chest. She thumped its sides, yelling, 'Go, go, go.'

'Stop her!' Bakhar's voice rasped, furious behind her. She had bare seconds.

43

A hand seized the hem of her dress, trying to get a grip on her leg under the layers of silk. But the startled horse crabbed sideways and shook it off. She drove her thighs together, crouched low over its neck, willing it forwards.

Voices roared behind her. 'Don't shoot! Ride her down! Drop your bows! After her!' But she heard nothing except the blood in her ears, saw nothing except the forest across the ford. *Go, go, go.*

Horse and girl streaked down the slope and thundered towards the river, but instead of crashing across, the animal swerved downstream, breaking left as one of Bakhar's men, swearing hard, galloped up behind, trying to head her off. Tamar pounded its haunches, wrenched its mane, willing it to hold its line. *No good.* The soldier was overhauling her, herding her back to the house.

She shifted her weight to the right, pulling up on the reins. The horse lurched, stumbled, almost collapsed to its knees. As she'd hoped, the other horse shot past. *On, on, on.*

But instead of plunging across the ford, her horse kicked its hind legs high in the air, trying to shake the lunatic off its back. She wrapped her arms tighter round its neck as it bucked then reared up almost vertical, paddling the air with its front hooves. She lost her grip, slid backwards and at the next kick cannoned to the ground, winded, her head filled with black spots and bright lights.

She couldn't breathe, her eyes were shut, her arms over her head. There was a lot of shouting, yelling, the thwack of the flat of a sword, then hooves as the horse bolted.

She struggled to her feet, bundled up her skirts and was about to try for the ford when suddenly she was face down on the ground, a man grinding her nose into the pebbles. His knee was between her shoulder blades and he grabbed at her hands, twisting them behind her back. She wriggled and squirmed, convinced she could rip free, but soon he had her pinioned. He took a fist of her hair and wrenched her head back. She stared at the dust, panting as sweat rolled down her face.

'Still, girl, be still.'

She could no longer move even if she'd wanted to. Steps sounded behind her and a pair of boots appeared under her nose.

'Up.'

It was Bakhar, his left hand swaddled, his right gripping Aton. He pushed the old man aside, drew his sword and rounded on Tamar, his face contorted.

'You mustn't!' gasped the soldier holding her.

'Fool. I know that.'

He turned on Aton, eyes blazing. Aton snatched a dagger out of his boot and backed away, holding it in front of him, like a shepherd brandishing his crook at a winter-hungry wolf. Bakhar advanced and with one blow knocked it out of his hand, sending it spinning to the dirt. He raised his sword and Aton closed his eyes, almost leaning into the blow he knew was about to land. Bakhar struck a merciless slice to the neck. Aton collapsed to his knees, hands clasped about the ragged wound in his throat, blood bubbling as he tried to breathe.

Tamar's mouth filled with something bitter. She spat, sobbed and started towards Aton's side, but came up against the point of Bakhar's sword.

'Leave him. Give thanks to the Virgin that we need you whole or you'd be joining him.'

Tamar fought the panic that threatened to choke her like sun-warmed seawater. She had to survive.

Chapter Six

They rode up the valley. A small girl, eight or nine winters, her hair falling out of day-old braids, hopped, skipped, hopped behind a trio of white goats, flicking them with a pine switch as she marched them downhill. She threw a glance at the party of men and dismissed them instantly, her attention caught by a shower of yellow butterflies flirting with a bush. She danced past, trying to net the butterflies in her hat, singing the goats' names, hearing the river join in the chorus.

Tamar watched her go.

The sun was too high for riding in the open. It burrowed blindly into the back of her skull, making her brains throb. The ugly trot made her sick. Thirst made her tongue swell. The skin beneath the cords around her wrists reddened and wore away.

She was wedged, ungainly, in front of Bakhar on his horse, her fingers entwined in its mane as she tried to hold herself upright. It would have been easier to lean back and rest her head and shoulders against his chest, but the thought was repulsive. She wanted as much distance between them as possible.

Her eyes latched on to their cramped shadow bumping up the path ahead of them. It stretched, found form, turned into a horse as the day advanced.

By nightfall they were walking in single file along a track littered with twisted, fractured rocks, unsmoothed by time. The mountains climbed high on all sides, trapping her at the bottom of a well as deep as the world. The mud and stones at their feet were starved of sunlight. There was a dark, old smell, like poverty or plague.

The moon must have risen an hour ago but it was still sweating up the black rock wall to the east so it was almost perfectly black at the foot of the cliffs. Some light had found the snow near the underbelly of the night sky, turning it dirty white. Tamar thought of her mother's cheeks, all colour, all texture long beaten out of them. Not the defiance of marble but the helplessness of fat under a deer's skin.

When the path next brought them close to the river, Bakhar called a halt for the night. He jumped off the horse and reached up to lift her down. She ignored him and clambered awkwardly down the other side, too exhausted to think.

Bakhar was sheltering a small pile of tinder between his knees, sending sparks cascading from his flint. He stopped what he was doing and looked at her.

'It's a lot harder without fingers,' he said with a sudden lack of malice, holding up his roughly bandaged hand before returning to his fire.

'It's your fault. You should have just grabbed me. Why didn't you?'

'I never thought a precious royal princess would hack off my hand.'

'Fingers.'

'What?'

'I didn't hack your hand off. Just your fingers.'

The soldiers started to eat with great focus in complete silence. She forced a couple of mouthfuls down, the dry bread catching in her throat, and some of the tension in her body vanished, leaving her more tired than before. She shut her eyes and slept where she sat.

The day dawned, the dull yellow of sickness. All night clouds had been pouring into the valley, spilling over the ridges to the north into the bowl where they camped, leaching the heat out of the stones. The air was wet, heavy, lying like rot on the peaks. Her skin felt uneasy, her brain foggy.

'My lady, the first meal is ready.'

She bridled. 'Call me Tamar. Or better, call me nothing. I'm not your lady.' She thrust her wrists out, the chafe wounds turning yellow as they struggled to heal. 'And take these off. If I run, you can just catch me again.'

Bakhar ignored her and put a bowl of something colourless on one of the firestones.

'How am I supposed to eat?' Again she stuck out her wrists. Again he ignored her, spooning whatever food it was supposed to be between his full lips. She took up the bowl in the palm of her left hand and tried to feed herself. She felt stupid. She would rather not eat than eat like a pig at a trough, like a baby. One of the men's daggers was thrust into the ground by the fire. Fine. She took two steps. Before she could take a third she felt Bakhar's hand round the back of her neck, his voice wet in her ear.

'That is not yours to touch. Nothing is yours unless I say so. Nothing. You ride when I say, sleep when I say, eat when I say. And now I say eat.'

He pushed her to the ground, hard, knocking the breath out of her body. On all fours, her face a handspan above the clumps of ashes, she nearly collapsed, buried her face and hid, but something more powerful raced up inside her, a clear bright rage, the thunderclap that breaks the gathering dread of a summer storm.

She flung herself at Bakhar with a wordless howl. Her shoulder slammed into his testicles, her head ploughed into his stomach, her hands flailing high scratched for his eyes. For a whisper of time she was winning. He was on his back, trying to protect his eyes, trying not to whimper at the impossible pain between his legs, twisting frantically to the side as her right knee ground into his groin.

A whisper of time. Soon he caught her wrists, his hand easily circling them, and hefted her off him, standing up and dragging her with him. The others laughing loudly, enjoying it.

'That's enough, Bakhar.'

Dato. *Dato!* Bakhar's grip slackened enough for her to wrench free. She threw herself towards his voice, babbling.

'Dato . . . I knew . . . see I fought . . . where, where . . . thank God, thank God.'

She wrapped her arms around his chest, buried her face and gripped him close, about to allow the sobs of relief to bear her away. For a moment she felt his hands brush lightly, tenderly, over the hair above her ears, then he unclasped her and pushed her gently away.

When he spoke, it was if he was speaking to himself or to his God. Not to her. He wasn't even looking at her. He was looking into the mist.

'Understand Tamar, this is nothing to do with you and me. You . . . I will see no harm comes to you. You have my word.' He stopped. Swallowed. Started again, this time looking hard and straight at her. 'There are things you cannot understand, not yet.'

She heard the words, but they made no sense. They were just sounds, little barks and hisses, as meaningless as the wind. He was right. She didn't understand. Already he had turned away and was talking furiously to Bakhar. Her eyes watched Dato's lips as he spoke. A fake Dato or Dato possessed by a demon. Not her Dato. Slowly, the light in her eyes turned cold, like the last log on a watchman's fire, and then went out altogether.

'Orbeli promised she would come to no harm.'

'*Promised.*' Bakhar spat the word back at him. 'You promised she would come quietly. You promised I wouldn't lose these.' He waved his left hand in front of Dato's face.

'Your shield hand. Why did she—?'

'Looks like Giorgi didn't trust you after all.'

'Of course he did. What reason had he to doubt me?'

Bakhar curled his lip. 'What reason indeed?'

The horses trudged up through the clouds, dark shapes swimming in the mist, their hooves grating loud as a forge on the stones in the silence that surrounded them.

Dato had looked at her dress and wordlessly found her a tunic and leg coverings, but he'd tucked her cross and her father's kinzhal inside his own pack. He'd suggested she ride in front of him, but she gave him such an appalled look, empty of anger, empty of everything, that he mounted alone and she shared with

Bakhar, her head lolling like an ox at a poor man's plough. Only his arms kept her from crashing to the earth.

Suddenly, they came out from the clouds. The blue light burst upon her, as it did when Nino drew back her thick curtains on a summer morning. The sun, the height, the cold danced in front of her and every line and shape was unnaturally sharp. Bakhar ordered a halt.

Would the clouds below hold her weight? They looked so solid and she felt so insubstantial. She could dive in, swim away south, kicking through the billows and wisps while the soldiers watched helplessly. Or she could just shut her eyes and sink, letting the whiteness close over her head.

'Where are we going?' she demanded. Her voice sounded loud in her head, as if she had just unblocked her ears.

Dato and Bakhar looked at her, surprised.

'Where are we going?' she repeated.

Bakhar got to his feet. 'Hallelujah. She speaks.'

She stiffened, but kept going. 'Tell me. Who am I to tell? You're not going to kill me. So, what's going to happen to me?'

'What harm after all?' It was Dato who spoke. 'She'll find out when we reach the plains. It's better for her to accept it now.'

Bakhar shrugged. 'As you wish. Do you want to explain? No? I thought not.' He turned to Tamar. 'My lady, we have reached a stalemate outside Tbilisi. Demna will not raze the city. Giorgi will not surrender. You, girl, are needed to tip the balance. Think of yourself as a new kind of siege engine. Happy?'

He turned to mount his horse.

'No,' she said, louder this time. 'Not happy. There's one more thing I want to know.' She took a deep breath and tried to ignore the tears prickling at the corners of her eyes. 'Tell me why.'

Bakhar opened his mouth to speak, but she cut him off. 'Not you. I care nothing for you. Dato. Tell me why, Dato.' Her voice was so hoarse she could make no more words come.

Dato's silence roared back at her.

'Tell me!' she shouted and the sobs followed.

Dato started towards her, but Bakhar stepped between them, pushing him out of the way.

'Enough, Tamar. This is life. We have a long road and no time for tears.'

'I'll cry as much as I want. You can't stop me. Go on. Hit me, hit me. Warrior! I don't care. You can't kill me. You can't touch me. You can't, can you? You can't!'

With each *can't* she poked at his chest, her eyes and nose streaming, her lips swollen, her face red and very ugly. Then, quick as a hare, she ran to where the mountain dropped sheer away. Dato saw what she was going to do, but he was too late. She had already scrambled over the rim and found a precarious foothold on the cliff face.

'Back, back, back, back, back or I jump.'

They hesitated. She seemed to be standing on nothingness. All they could see was a small face in anguish, two white hands burrowing in the shale trying to find something solid to hold on to – and an invisible drop behind. They stepped back.

'Would she?' Bakhar asked Dato.

He nodded. 'She would.'

A couple of the soldiers had worked their way down the path and were now looking up at her. 'Boss,' one of them shouted up, 'she can't get down. She can't get nowhere. We can't get her, neither.'

A pause. Bakhar's brow was furrowed. 'What do you want, princess? If you want to die, do it. We won't let you go.'

'I want to talk to Dato. I want him to tell me why he's doing this.'

Bakhar took a step forward. 'What the hell difference does it make?'

Tamar, her eyes big with watching, snatched her hands out of reach balancing on her toes as she tried to ignore the emptiness pulsing behind her. One step and Bakhar could have her collar in his hand. Or nothing. Nothing in his hand, and she would be wheeling down to the valley floor, a brief flight, a crunch, a thump. She tensed her muscles, ready to spring.

'Tamar! Don't!'

Dato grabbed Bakhar's belt, lifted him like a grain sack and flung him back. 'Tamar, I beg you, this is better than death.'

'Not true. Death is better than betraying my father. Better than letting myself fall into the hands of his enemies. You were there. You heard him.'

'He wouldn't care that you were in their hands, so long as you were alive.'

'You think so? You really think so?'

'I know it. Tamar, not for all the world would he see you dead.'

'That only shows how little you understand him. He would sacrifice anything to keep his throne. Even me.'

'Even peace.'

'Is that why you've sold me to Orbeli?'

He hesitated. 'Yes, for peace. Your father is wrong. Blind. Orbeli is right. Tamar, believe me, this is the only way. Come, what do you say, will you come?'

'I say you're weak. A coward.'

She scrambled back up over the lip of the cliff.

'But I'll go with you. If I die, then how can I make you pay?'

Her jaw was set, her eyes did not flinch, but the joints at her knees felt as soft as an hour-old calf.

Chapter Seven

Sos had left home under an overcast sky, but by the time he emerged from the forest a blue-gold breeze had burned through the cloud and only a few idle wisps straggled above him. He splashed through the ford, looking forward to a day's fishing followed by Albina's robust cooking, as well as the chance to make the old man happy by showing favour to his agreeably awestruck nephew.

A sweet sticky smell made his nostrils twitch. And then he saw the flies. He sprang from his horse and dropped to Aton's side. Most of the flies retreated, but a few, braver or greedier than the rest, lingered around the eye sockets. Hundreds of waxy yellow things squirmed and writhed in the gaping neck, like grains of corn come alive. Something hungry had got hold of the dead man's innards and unravelled them. A retch and a sob warred in Sos's throat.

A bloody end in battle needed no man's pity. It was glorious to fall when trumpets howled like devils, when men shrieked and horses roared. But Aton had lived long enough to deserve a gentler end. Sos cursed whoever had cut down a half-blind old man.

He staggered to his feet and ran up to the house. Albina lay across the threshold, her eyes shut and her face soft. There was no blood. But the angle of her neck told him enough.

Where was the boy? It wasn't the first time a young son of a feuding family had been stashed high in the Kavkaz mountains. Aton's killers must have been after him. They might have hacked off his head or hands as proof, a trophy to flaunt, but they would have left the body as a treat for the vultures. They had captured him, then, for ransom or to bargain for one of their own. That must be the answer.

Sos ducked outside and started scouting for the killers' tracks, jogging low over the ground like a hound as Aton had taught him. It was easy. They had made no effort to hide the route they had taken from the ford. It would have been a lot harder if they had waded downstream before setting out. Twelve horses. Moving at a steady trot. He could follow them as easy as kill a chicken. Sos whistled his horse to him, swung on to its back and cantered after them.

The mountains became hills. The way underfoot was hard and dry. The air was hot and full of dust. But the landscape was softer, the slopes and leaves rounder. On the last rise Tamar had looked south and seen the plain unfold before her, long evening shadows stretching across the brown-gold grass where the trunks of tall trees blocked the rays of the sun. The sky was pink and orange, colouring the undersides of the clouds that hung like ripening fruit on invisible branches. It was beautiful. She breathed in and out, filling her blood with joy, forgetting her bound hands, her hobbled feet.

The men made camp, ate a meagre supper and settled to sleep round their fire, with one man watching Tamar by hers. She lay on her back, following the sparks buffeting in the night breeze. The moon would not rise for several hours. It would be a dark night. The man on guard was wrapped deep in his cloak, busy being bored. Poking the fire with a stick. Peeling the bark off a branch. Shifting his weight. Picking at his nails. Tamar rolled over, her face turned away from the fire. Her cheeks grew cold, but slowly her eyes lost their night blindness.

The horses were grazing under the shadows of the forest. A gentle snicker, the frisk-swish of a tail, the clink of a hoof on a pebble. Those were the only sounds. Then she saw a deeper dark between the tree trunks. She shut her eyes. Opened them. She had not been mistaken. Somebody was there. Somebody was watching, and watching her. It's hard to sense a careless glance. But this was not careless. It made her tingle.

There, between the horses, there he was. A man crouched on

all fours, hooded. Moving so slowly she had to blink furiously to force her eyes to focus. She froze as the watchman stirred. But he only reached for another log, threw it on the fire, making it crackle, pop and burn brighter. Good. The shape was now flat on the grass. Writhing forward on its stomach. A patch of black creeping closer and closer. A flash of teeth where his lips curled round a dagger. So close now she could see the fire in his eyes.

She held her breath, shut her eyes, cursed herself for a coward and opened them to see the dagger open the watchman's throat. His legs kicked out, scrabbling in the ashes, louder than a trumpet blast. Then he lay still. Blood pumped between the man's knuckles where he held his hands over the soldier's face.

Slowly, gently, a mother laying a sleeping child in its cot, the man let the corpse's head drop onto his knees. He wiped his hands on his cloak and edged backwards. He looked everywhere but at her face. She too was shy. She held out her wrists, pulling her hands far apart to expose as much taut rope as possible. He sliced through the cords, then leant over her and sawed at the ropes around her ankles, his body almost on top of hers.

Without looking back, he started to crawl away towards the bushes at the edge of the clearing. She followed, everything blotted out by the silent terror that one of the men sprawled around the larger fire would open his eyes. Her heart was trying to beat free from her ribcage, her blood nearly erupting from her veins. But hand, knee, hand, knee, she followed him. The sounds of the sleeping men faded.

The trees loomed over them. He stood up, reaching down to help her to her feet. She put a hand on his arm and felt it shuddering furiously and realised she too was shaking uncontrollably. He took her hand, his hot and dry like a man with fever, and led her deeper into the forest.

His voice came to her, speaking soft-mouthed, soft as blossom on the wind.

'S'me. Sos. Horse. Not far.'

Five paces, ten, twenty. Every second a miracle. Every step

worth an armful of gold. She counted – *thirty-three, fifty-six, ninety-seven* – anything to make herself walk calmly, not burst into a mad, panicked sprint. The fire was lost, a glow behind the trees, like a full moon about to rise behind the hills. Suddenly, ahead and slightly to the right, she heard a snicker, a snort and the shuffle of hooves. Sos dropped her hand to reach out patting, stroking, scratching. The horse stilled. A bird flapped up into the sky, hooting crossly, its hunt disrupted. And still there was no sound behind them.

He leant in close to her left ear, his nose just brushing the cropped curls at her neck.

'Do you ride without saddle?'

She nodded, remembered it was dark, and whispered, 'Yes. Of course.'

She felt for its mane and with a little leap swung herself on to its back, rubbing its neck, settling her weight. He moved quietly in the darkness, untethered the horse and jumped up behind her.

They rode away from the fire, away from the mountains, losing height with each footfall. Her eyes returned again and again to the pool of orange, still visible through the trees. It swelled and beckoned, diabolical. The heat would be drying the watchman's blood on his shirt front, the toes of his boots would be starting to smoulder.

She had been expecting it with every heartbeat, but when the roar of discovery erupted above them, she gasped and urged the horse faster. Sos stopped it.

'No, no, now we must be still,' he mouthed. Then his tone shifted, a glimmer of light in his voice. 'Don't even breathe.' And she heard him take in a giant lungful of air, like a child about to plunge to the bottom of a pond. She was about to do the same, when she heard him breathe out and realised he was joking. *Joking.*

He was right, though. The shouting stopped. Tamar and Sos listened to them listening. She willed herself inside the horse's head, begging it to be still. It pulled at some roots, a cacophony of lips smacking like a hundred drunk soldiers at a feast. She heard Bakhar's voice. The words did not carry, but his anxiety did and her spirits leapt.

'Now we go.' And Sos kicked the horse on, choosing a path by some instinct, some knowledge that thrilled her.

They dropped down into a shallow gunnel, dislodging stones. A river bed, dry since the spring. It was steep, tough going, but she gripped tight with her legs and made sure she didn't fall. Above and behind she heard shouts, hooves, but they were out of sight. He had planned it well.

The horse wound down through the storm bed, until the ground levelled out and the way widened. The sun was not yet ready to show itself, but night was vanishing fast, the darkness evaporating, nothingness disappearing into nothing, leaving the strange colourless non-light that shrouds the world before dawn.

The Kart plain opened up before them, the grass bowing low before the light easterly wind that sprang up with the day. They climbed down and let the horse rest while they watched the sun race free, turning the land brown and green, colouring their faces pink and gold.

Tamar's hair wandered over her eyes. Her lower lip was sun-blistered. Her hand went to her shoulder, she reddened and her eyebrows bunched together, a little furrow in her forehead.

'Why?'

Sos grinned. 'Because I could. Because I wanted to.' His smile faded a little. 'And because of Aton.'

'I'll make them pay for that. For Albina too.'

His lips twitched. 'You. A girl?'

So he'd worked that out.

'Yes, me,' she nodded firmly. 'With help from my father.'

'Is he a rich man? Powerful? Would I know him from court?'

It was Tamar's turn to smile.

'I am sure of it. I am Tamar. You have saved the king's daughter.'

Chapter Eight

Sos trudged unseeing through the forest, kicking the rotting pine needles underfoot, smacking the trunks with the flat of his sword. Every dozen paces he stopped short, spun round, growled something under his breath and set off back the way he had come, then changed his mind and carried on north, his indignation spilling out in passionate snorts.

'Bet she gets pitched off. Bet she breaks her neck. No, not her neck, both her legs. And her arms. Then dies of thirst.' He stamped into a clearing, slumped to the ground, pulled off his boots and glowered at the burst blisters under his big toes. 'Pecked to pieces. Eaten by worms.'

He felt a bit better and started hauling branches to the same blackened cook-stones where he'd watched the kidnappers build their fire. Grey-white flakes of ash flew into the air, into his eyes and nose, making him sneeze and blink.

He'd been tucked high in a tree, an owl's-eye view. The clearing below him had been full of bearded men with dirty faces, some leaning against the trees, scratching and spitting, others sprawled on their backs. And in the middle, alone, a small, stiff figure perched on a log.

That was when he'd realised. He'd breathed in looking at a boy. Breathed out staring at a girl. She'd shape-shifted, like old earth magic. What had stopped him seeing it before? Her eyes were lost in blue-black circles. Her face pale, grimy and sun-warmed all at once. Her head swaddled in a dirty white shawl although the midday heat was long past. She needed help. She needed him.

After nightfall, masked by the crackle of the fire and the murmur of the leaves, he'd felt his way out of the tree and crawled, then walked, then run back to his horse.

Later, waiting until they were asleep, watching the branches brush the face of the night sky, his imagination softened her, added curves, made her a woman, made her like all women. He dressed her in silks, put emeralds about her neck, made her eyes wet with grateful tears. He shook hands with her father, her brothers and uncles, and laughingly declined gold and horses. Drank her helpless adoration, gently unclasped her hands from his neck, kissed her forehead and promised always to think of her. Then rode away without looking back.

He started to rip the skin off a pair of rabbits, cursing himself for a sentimental fool.

Even the rescue had been perfect. The shock of the man's blood, hot on his hands, his body twitching. The rough cords between his fingers. Her body perched between his arms, her thighs against his. The shouts of the men fading behind them. The sun rising to admire what he'd done. The warm smile of morning had bathed her in a glorious light, like an almond-eyed icon gazing down at him from the walls of a cathedral.

He hacked the rabbit's thighs into cubes and threaded them on to his dagger, balancing it above his fire.

The king's daughter. Even more perfect. He'd smiled, grinned. He was happy for the love of God. He'd risked his life. Done the right thing. He'd waited for her to say something else. *Thank you. That was very brave. What would I have done without you?* Something. But instead, she'd rolled her eyes.

'All right, there's no need to smirk.'

He'd blinked. That was unexpected. He couldn't think what to say – but that didn't matter because she was still speaking.

'You should see your face.'

His face? What was wrong with his face? He liked his face. Everyone liked his face. It was a likeable face.

'What—'

'I've never seen anyone look so pleased.'

'But—'

'Smug, even.'

'How—'

'Never mind. We're even now.'

'Even?'

'Yes. You practically kill me – me, the king's daughter. Then you rescue me. So we're even. Think about it.'

The golden light had vanished.

'But,' he spluttered, squirming and flapping like a pigeon, 'but that was an accident and I've already said I was sorry and you said you'd forgiven me.'

'Well I lied, I hadn't, I haven't. You can't shoot me, dangle me from your saddle like a dead goat, patronise me all summer as if you were a prince of the purple not some stupid mountain farmer and think I wouldn't mind.'

'What d'you mean patronise? And what the hell d'you mean mountain farmer?'

'What d'you mean? What d'you mean?' she mimicked him. 'I mean puffing your chest the whole time. I mean explaining any words longer than two syllables to me. I mean telling me who Akilleus was. Even a real shepherd boy would know that—'

'—' Sos tried to cut her off, but he didn't know how to stop her without shouting *shut up, shut up* or punching her to the floor. It was worse than an argument with one of his sisters.

'—and that ridiculous way you spring off your horse when people are watching. You don't do it when you think nobody's there. And anyway, how could you think I was a boy all that time. Are you blind or just really, really stupid?'

Sos turned his back but she ran round him and planted herself in front of him. He made to push her out of the way but she jumped back, talking non-stop.

'And now you rescue me, for what? For fun? To show off? So you've got something to boast about to every single person you ever meet?'

That, finally, sliced through his confusion. He grabbed her shoulders and shook her as hard as he knew how.

'Do you want me to take you back to them? Is that what you want?'

She thrust her chin higher, ignoring his hands.

'You killed one of them. They'd kill you.'

'It was dark. They've no idea who did it. And if you really are who you say you are, I could ransom you for a fortune. I bet they'd be so pleased to have you back, they wouldn't waste time asking awkward questions.'

'You wouldn't dare.'

'I would. And I will too if you don't start showing me some gratitude.'

'All right, I'm sorry. I am grateful. Now, will you let go of me, please? You're hurting me.'

He dropped his hands and turned away, suddenly embarrassed by the red marks his fingers had left at the base of her neck.

That was when he heard his horse snort in surprise.

He whipped round and saw her on its back. He lunged, but she danced it out of reach, all eyes and smile. He stood, dumb, helpless, while she pranced in a circle round him.

'Goodbye, Sos.'

Their eyes locked. He thought she was about to say something, but then she let out a great cry and galloped south. There was nothing he could do. He couldn't even shout and curse. He gaped while girl and horse melded into a dark spot where the sky met the plain.

Sos shivered. His rabbits were burnt black and the fire was nearly out. He must stop thinking about it. He'd go home and never have anything to do with Karts – or women – ever, ever again.

But as he settled to sleep a different voice whispered inside his head. She'd moved as sure and stealthy as any man, hadn't she? Nor had she squealed at the sight of blood. And she'd looked remarkably fine – not beautiful, maybe, but not bad, not bad at all – when his horse had reared underneath her and borne her away.

Chapter Nine

Tamar rolled herself up in her cloak in a tangle of trees set back from the road and stared at the starlight, trying to ignore the grinding hunger in her belly and the scuffle, rustle and swoop of invisible creatures. She clamped her eyelids shut and ordered herself not to think, not to be scared, but night fears circled like moths. Every time a twig snapped she saw Bakhar's face and imagined his men creeping towards her, daggers drawn, their footsteps muffled by the wind in the leaves. The glow of the old moon loomed soft above her and her thoughts spun out of control, unearthing old nursery terrors, feeding her greedy new ghosts. She clenched her body into a tight ball and begged the day to hurry, then when she could bear it no longer, she woke to pale blue morning and felt the dew on her face.

She catapulted to her feet, looked down at her sunburnt hands, her filthy feet. She waggled her arms and legs to crunch the cricks out of her joints and peered out from under the cool shadow of the trees, one hand stroking her horse's neck. The road to Tbilisi unrolled ahead, the mountains blurred purple behind. She took a run up, bounced herself on to the horse's back and settled into a fast canter, thanking the saints that at least he had a decent animal.

As the sun raced up the sky, the road started to fill with travellers, all bound in the opposite direction, making the going difficult. Bakhar would have waved his sword above his head and shouted them out of the way, but Tamar didn't have so much as a knife and even from on top of her handsome horse, her voice would carry no threat. She swerved to the side of the road, where the grass grew tall, and watched for a while as they trailed past. The men's faces were grim, the women's fearful. Babies squalled pathetically in the heat.

'God be with you! What news from the city?' she called.

Only one old woman looked up and answered.

'Turn around, boy. They say Tbilisi will fall on the morrow.'

Soon after dawn the next day Tamar stood on the heights above the city, her face glazed with sweat. The colourless morning was still young, but the sky already slouched low, a grey gauze patterned with slow-moving birds. She'd ridden all night and was stupid with exhaustion, swaying like an overloaded mule. She took in the empty courtyards, the shuttered houses and the two massive armies that squatted on the brown grassland beyond the walls.

The siege was over; the battle was about to begin.

As she watched, a signal arrow flew up from her father's camp, a long tail rippling behind it, dazzling white against the black rainclouds that were mustering in the east. An answering arrow shot up, then two smudged figures strode into the middle of the plain to parley.

Tamar hauled herself back on to her horse and galloped down through the deserted streets. She skidded and swerved past the wagon men as they trundled food and water back inside the city and then bucketed into the army's rearguard. Six burly mounted men barred her way.

'Hey, lad, what's the idea?'

'Horse too strong for you?'

They weren't unkind, but they weren't going to let her past.

'The king. I need to see the king.'

They grinned.

'He's kind of busy, son.'

'I must see him, I must.'

'Calm down. What's so important? Does he owe you money? Or has he pinched your girlfriend?' He enjoyed the chuckle from the others.

'It's . . . it's about his daughter.'

63

His eyes suddenly focused.

'The princess Tamar? I heard those bastards have her.'

'No! No, they don't. She's escaped. She's safe. She sent me to tell the king.'

'You know where she is?'

'Yes, yes, I do, please, it's urgent.'

'But he's already—'

'I can see that. Take me to Kubaza. Any captain with a brain in his head. Now.'

'The general Kubaza? I cannot interrupt him—'

'Now, I said.'

The ragged child perched in front of him evaporated and the soldier heard only a voice of command. He nodded.

'Leave your horse. Follow me.'

They plunged through the camp to where the Kipchak stood on the front line, his shoulders set, his eyes never leaving the king, flanked by two bodyguards as stern and motionless as himself.

'My lord—'

'Not now, damn it,' he barked. The man retreated, abashed — he couldn't argue. But Tamar stood her ground and tugged desperately at Kubaza's sleeve. He whipped round and grabbed her by the ear, twisting it hard.

'Not now, I said.'

'Kubaza, it's me.' Her voice was painfully small.

'What the—' Tension bulged in the veins about his neck.

'Me, Kubaza. Tamar. It's me. Look.'

A rare start of surprise ran across his face and slowly he let go of her ear.

'So they lied.'

He said nothing more, but ripped an arrow from the turf at his feet and thrust it into the outstretched hand of the archer by his side.

'Fire!'

All around her, soldiers scrambled for their weapons when they saw the black tail sweep into the darkening sky. *It's me.*

They shot the black arrow because I'm here. Me, father, it's me. Tamar wanted to sprint across the hundred paces that separated them.

But at a word from Kubaza, two soldiers had her by the collar and were dragging her away from the front line. They bundled her into a tent that was dim, stuffy, its roof sagging. A half-eaten leg of something and a torn-off chunk of flatbread called out to her from a low table. She dropped to her knees, and was about to cram it all into her mouth when her father's voice boomed above her.

'What rascal is this? Stealing my leftovers?'

She stumbled to her feet, suddenly scared he would be angry she had let herself be captured. She should have guessed about Dato. Or not let Bakhar take her so easily. Now she was here, sodden, half starved, in rags, in the middle of his army, the last place she was meant to be.

But before she could explain everything, she was hoisted clean off the ground, her face crushed against his breastplate, her feet dangling in empty air. Giorgi held her for long moments then placed her on her feet and stood gazing at her, shaking his head slowly from side to side, a triumphant smile curling under his beard, his eyes shimmering.

'Well met, daughter.'

She looked at her feet, not at him.

'Father, I'm sorry, they came, I couldn't help—'

He snorted, seized her chin and made her look straight at him.

'Tamar! Why in thunder are you cowering like a kitchen boy? Damn it, that whoresucked, bullfucked Orbeli sent last night to tell me they'd plucked you from the mountains and had your cross and my dagger to prove it – look.'

He tugged them out. They shone against the dull metal of his body armour.

'Said they'd cut your throat at noon if I didn't give the throne to Demna – they had Dato there to swear every word was true. The one man I thought I could trust. I was in agony, daughter, in torment. I should have guessed they were lying.'

65

'But they weren't lying. They did have me. I . . . I escaped.'

'Escaped! You outwitted that brute Bakhar and now you're standing there like a guilty scarecrow and apologising? *Father, I'm sorry!* God's love, I ache to hear the tale, but we have no time now. My heart cries war. My belly hungers after blood. I must buckle on my shield, cut a path back to Orbeli and disembowel him and the fools who follow him.'

'Spare this one poor fool at least, King Giorgi,' a voice called from outside the tent.

Tamar looked at her father. She did not know who had spoken, but the king evidently did, for his expression locked into a cold, triumphant smile that vanished as fast as it had come.

'In you come, Qutlu, in you come.'

'First bid your man stand aside.'

'Kubaza, come, let him in.'

The tent flap opened and two men entered. Kubaza first, plainly furious, followed by a tall, spare figure Tamar recognised as Qutlu Arslan. He looked odd in full battledress, not uncomfortable or comic as a lesser man might, but disdainful, as if he wore it on sufferance like a costume – an uncle dressing up to entertain children on a feast day. He removed his helmet and bowed deep.

'My lord. Forgive my jest. We have indeed been guilty of much that was foolish.'

Never had a man spoken of a jest with less humour, nor of guilt with less remorse.

'Do not apologise, Qutlu, the sight of you is as welcome as lambs in springtime. Say on – why are you here?'

Tamar tried and failed to picture Qutlu gambolling across a meadow in a fluffy white coat. Her father was being facetious. He only did that when he was inordinately pleased about something.

'Demna has proved a disappointment. A great disappointment, my lord.'

'Ah . . .' A long sigh escaped her father. Even Kubaza shifted from one foot to the other.

'He had his chance. A bolder commander – a bolder man – would have seized Tbilisi months since. But he had reservations, *scruples* he liked to call them, about the damage an assault on the city would do. He trusted that your *sense of realism*, another ill-judged phrase of his, would prevail and we would see the white flag fluttering above the walls before midsummer.'

'The boy should have known his uncle better.'

'Yes,' said Qutlu. 'I told him as much.'

'He was impervious to your famous powers of persuasion? I can't help liking him a little – a very little – better. Go on.'

'There followed, as you now know, Orbeli's reckless scheme concerning your daughter.' He did not look at her, but Tamar did not doubt he knew precisely who she was. 'Kidnapping is for mountain savages, not civilised people.'

'Mountain savages might have made a better job of it,' the king snorted. 'You seize my daughter, then, astonishingly, you lose her. So one of you – I can't help but wonder who, Qutlu – comes up with a little piece of deception. *Pretend we have her. Show him her cross. Make Dato swear. Play upon a father's love. He'll believe us.* And it might have worked, too, had I not had word Tamar was safe. A dirty game – one you lost. So I ask again – why are you here?'

'To beg forgiveness from my sovereign and to offer what little aid I may.'

'You would offer your sword, Qutlu?' asked the king as if that were no great prize.

'Yes, my lord, but much more besides. The tavads are wavering. If you attack now, you will find that the army that withstands you is smaller – much smaller – than the one you imagine is ranged against you. You will be able to obliterate Orbeli and the boy with ease.'

'Who do you speak for?'

'Not Orbeli, of course, nor those tied closest to him. His feelings for you will not allow him to see reason: not today, not ever. But of the rest, the majority are eager to – how shall I put it? – bask once more in the light of your goodwill.'

'Mkhargrdzeli?'

'He is a man of action. Demna's hesitation sickened him.'

'Jakeli and Dadiani?'

'Oh, you may be sure of them. I found them receptive to sound advice.'

'Gamrekeli?'

'The man's sense of honour troubles him, as always. It is too delicate to allow him to drive his own dagger between your nephew's shoulder blades, but he is happy enough for me to do it. You can count on him and those who follow him.'

'I see you have been busy, Qutlu. Very well, wait outside. You shall have my answer shortly.'

Qutlu bowed – not quite as deep as he should – and left them alone. Tamar wondered why Kubaza was so grim when Qutlu brought such good news. He looked as if a lump of maggoty fish had settled on the floor of his stomach.

'Kubaza,' the king turned to him, 'what do you make of this?'

'I say this. Dog returns to vomit. Fool returns to folly'. Normally, only the oddly musical inflection of his voice betrayed Kubaza as not Kart born, but now he was angry, his words sounded closer to the broken soldier-speak of the other Kipchaks. He drew breath. 'He offers his help now, but who knows when he will next change his mind.'

Giorgi reached out and gave Kubaza's shoulder a friendly shake.

'I bear Qutlu little enough love, as you know, but he has proved himself useful.'

'Hmmmph.' Kubaza evidently disagreed, but was not going to contradict the king outright. 'I would rather teach those traitors – starting with Qutlu Arslan – a lesson they will never forget. We should have attacked sooner, before this slippery diplomat sniffed out which way the wind was blowing. The fight would have been harder, but I would have enjoyed it more with his head as my prize.'

'At least you do not suspect a trick?'

Kubaza considered. 'No. What he said rings true. But one thing troubles me.'

'What is that?'

'Why did he ask for nothing in return? I expected him to bargain. It is his way to set up his stall like a merchant in the marketplace.'

'He did not need to. I am in his debt and he will not let me forget it. You should give him more credit, friend. He has a strange power over men and I have yet to see him back the wrong horse.'

'Are we nags that race for his pleasure? I think—'

'No more thinking. Thinking is over, for today anyway. Forget him. Give thanks that my daughter lives. And help me break this siege and secure my throne.'

He beamed at them both, an infectious smile, carefree. Tamar couldn't help but grin back. He clapped her on the shoulder and strode to the entrance of the tent. There he stopped and spoke gruff and low.

'And those fools wanted that boy on my throne.'

Then they were gone.

Tamar started after them, tiredness forgotten, awash with excitement that at last she would see a battle. She tore aside the flap and walked straight into two crossed spears. She tried to duck past them but one of the soldiers blocked her way.

'With respect, princess, you're to stay inside.'

'Why? I want to—'

'Inside, the king said.'

She weighed him up and decided he was too big to bargain with. She retreated meekly into the tent, dropped to her knees at the far side and rooted around until she found a wobbly peg. She ripped it out of the ground, squirmed under the side of the tent and crawled outside. A curtain of rain swept across the plain, driving the birds before it as she heard the roar of the first charge.

All she needed now was a good vantage point to watch the battle unfold.

Dusk was beautifully cool and clear. The storm had eaten itself up and there was nothing in the sky. The clouds had fled or collapsed or climbed beyond sight. The sun had sunk to the west, leaving only a few forgotten streaks of colour.

From her perch on top of a stack of water barrels, she had watched with pride and delight as her father and his horsemen tore a hole in the rebels' line. The army, which had looked invincible when it was marching on Tbilisi in the spring, had shrunk, melting away at Demna's feet. She could not tell how many had fled, how many had fallen and how many had joined the king's side, but she knew the day was theirs and a profound, smouldering glow warmed her heart.

Black figures, silhouetted against enormous bonfires, were walking to and fro across what an hour before had been a battlefield. At first she thought they were carrying logs, swinging them back and forth and then tossing them up high until they crashed out of sight, sparks shooting into the air. Then a shift in the light breeze sent the smoke writhing towards her. It smelt like the riotous summer feasts in the hills above Tbilisi when men crouched in circles, turning sheep on rough spits, upending great skins of wine, their faces sticky with animal fat. She dug her fingers into her sides. They were corpse pyres.

'That, daughter, is victory.'

Her father was standing below her. She looked down at his face, bloodied and smoke-blackened. His eyes gleamed like bleached bones, his pupils a swamp of mud, his hair caked with battle. He was wonderful and repellent.

'Come and see for yourself.'

He held up his arms and she jumped down into them — as she had not done since she was a little girl. Flanked by a guard of twelve men, they waded through a morass of song and boasts and delirium, through clumps of soldiers unconscious from wine or exhaustion. Soldiers wrung the king's hand, touched him, they were all the same, all one. He slapped backs, gripped arms, pinched cheeks, while Tamar trailed three steps behind, dazed and superfluous. She was the only person under the night sky who did not have another man's life smeared on her clothes.

For the first time in days, maybe weeks, she thought about

her mother. She saw her sitting by the window in a cool stone cell high in the monastery. There was a soft breeze about her face, her hair was covered and a prayer hovered about her lips. She was gazing at the stars. Tamar shook her head and jogged to keep step with her father.

The fingers of a stockade sprouted from the plain, ringed by mounds of wet, fresh-dug earth. Brushwood torches burned bright around the perimeter. She trod slower. When she was little, she'd played a game called prison pit, piling into a small dark pantry with the palace children, giggling and nudging, while a guard made ghoulish threats outside until somebody came and saved them.

Orbeli's men, flung on top of each other, did not yell or scream or curse. It was worse than that. A black groaning throb hung in the air. The guards kept well back from the edge. The ground was slippery, the sides sheer and no man would live long if he fell. It already stank.

'What are we doing here?' Tamar whispered.

'There's somebody you should see,' her father replied, a smile licking up one side of his face.

'Orbeli? Is he here?'

'No.' He paused to savour his reply. 'He died on the field, by my sword. He could hardly see by the time I reached him. I'm not sure he knew who he was, who I was. But he fought, I'll give him that, he fought well and did not fear death.'

'But you said he was a coward, a snake, a Persian dog.'

'So he was. All those things and more. But why hate a dead man? Dead is dead, I can't touch him now. And anyway, I might have done the same had his grandfather, not mine, made the Kart lands his own.'

Tamar struggled to understand.

'What will happen to all these men?'

'See who's who. Then ransom or death. But forget them.'

'Then who . . .' The question was forming on her mouth when she saw.

A young man, barely older than herself, hung upside down

71

from a scaffold. The ropes coiled round his legs squeaked against the top bar as he twitched, jerked and swung slowly from side to side. His face was turned towards her. His eyes were open, the pupils rolled into the back of his head. His tongue sat thick in his open mouth and little animal noises sounded in his throat.

'The boy who thought he could defeat me. Your cousin Demna.'

Chapter Ten

Sos fidgeted on the edge of his father's chair. The sun would be near its peak, but that meant nothing inside. No warmth came through the thick stone walls and only pathetic tendrils of sunlight could squeeze through the arrow slits. People thrummed outside. They all wanted something and it was his job to work out what. The steward probably knew, but Sos couldn't face appealing for help.

Money, marriages, matters of blood. What was the point?

He missed being *young Sos*. Everywhere he went, men dropped low bows that he didn't trust for a second, the kind of bows he used to give. His young cousin Niko intoned *my lord Soslani* with a straight face and laughing eyes. His sisters chanted it and ran off giggling, and when he chased them his mother gasped *my lord Soslani* as if overnight it had become blasphemy for him to wallop Maka or yank Keti's plaits. The steward lisped it delicately as if he had a mouthful of unripe berries and punctuated his duties-and-responsibilities monologues with wistful references to *my lord Jadaron* and his wisdom, his mercy, his foresight.

A barrage of excited voices sounded outside. Vakhtang and the others whooped past the hall – as they did every morning – to remind him he had to spend all day being *my lord Soslani* while they could do whatever the hell they wanted. Vakhtang's father had been a wall-eyed, drunken fool, a nobody who couldn't shoot straight, but at that moment Sos would gladly have swapped places. He sighed aloud and Niko scurried over.

'My lord Soslani? What do you wish? Sir? Sos?'

'Nothing! Nothing!' Sos bellowed. Then he remembered the

boy was bound to be miserable too, penned up with a grumpy, overbearing master on a perfect autumn morning.

'Nothing, thank you,' he added, more gently. The boy sank back into the shadows by the door and Sos returned to his brooding.

There was worse to come, he was sure of it. His mother and his aunts had been throwing long glances whenever he visited their quarters, talking out of the sides of their mouths.

'Such a good family . . .'

'So respectful . . .'

'The stars are perfect . . .'

When he tried to pin them down they changed the subject.

'Nothing, dear.'

'Pay no attention, dear.'

'Just women's talk, dear.'

How stupid did they think he was? They were trying to marry him off to Alde. Simpering, cow-eyed, placid, flaccid Alde. He'd never agree to it, never, but trying to tell them that worked as well as setting a half-grown puppy on a flock of pigeons. They jabbered and scattered.

Forgetting the boy in the corner, he groaned out loud and hung his head in his hands. His father would have said he was too young to marry. *Don't have children until you can teach them something.* Sos sighed again. He'd longed for his father's death so fervently, resented him so completely, that he had no idea why a hole opened up in his stomach whenever he thought of him.

It had been a long walk home after the princess stole his horse, and Jadaron was bed-bound by the time he returned. Air hissed in his throat, the hairs above his mouth quivered, tiny signs that he yet lived. Very rarely his eyelids flickered or he worked his lips and then Sos, on a stool by his side, would lean close and whisper, 'What, father, what?' But his eyes never opened and no words came. The gap between breaths grew longer. And then one night, at the cold hour before daybreak, Sos started awake and knew he had gone.

'My lord Soslani! My lord Soslani?'

This time it wasn't the mocking chorus inside his head.

'What? I'm busy.'

'A messenger, my lord. From court.'

Finally. She was going to apologise.

'Enter.'

A young, rotund soldier appeared in the doorway, stared blankly into the gloom, then bowed low, hat swept off, boots clamped tight together.

'The king sends you greeting—'

Sos catapulted out of his father's chair. It was Zakari, his greatest friend, the son of Sargis Mkhargrdzeli.

'Zak, you donkey, it's me!'

Zak sprang back upright, looked left and right and said in a higher-pitched voice, 'Sos?'

The young lord's exuberant hug nearly winded him.

'Geroff me!' Zak shook himself free, grinning just as cheerfully. 'I'm the king's messenger so you better give me a bit of respect.'

Sos solemnly raised his eyebrows. 'And I, master messenger, am lord of the Osset lands east of the great pass, south of the ice-river. Who respects who now?'

Zak goggled. 'Your father . . .'

'He died soon after midsummer.' He shrugged, shaking off commiseration. 'I've no brothers. My cousins are making no trouble, or not at the moment anyway.'

'What luck—' Zak stopped himself, looking a little sheepish.

Sos punched his shoulder. 'Oh, it's all right. I know what you mean. The trouble is, I hadn't realised how tedious it would be. Did you see all those people out there? They never leave me alone. Never for a minute. And the women. They have horrible, horrible plans about some girl, I can't tell you how ugly she is, Zak. I swear it's hell dreamt up by every devil who ever walked.'

His friend laughed. 'Enough, enough. I can see it all. A great future settling quarrels over whose dog savaged whose goats while your lady spins your tunics.'

His father's ghost brushed past his neck, but he ignored it and joined Zak's laughter.

'Well, what are you doing? Scampering around the kingdom running the king's errands? By God, Zak, it still is the same king, isn't it? Does Giorgi still rule?'

'Sos, do you hear nothing in these mountains?'

'What? You mean the . . . the . . . the man from the south won?'

'No! It was close, though – have you honestly not heard?'

Sos shook his head and Zak's face lit up.

'Really? You must be the last man in the kingdom not to know all about it. Well, it goes like this. The king's daughter, not the beautiful one, but the other one, the older one, Tamar, the king sent her into the mountains to hide when it all started. Don't ask me why he didn't hide the other one, I'd be much more interested in finding her.'

He breathed in deep, shivered dramatically and licked his lips.

Sos laughed. 'Have you actually ever seen her?'

'Yes. Well, no. Not really. But if I had seen her—'

Sos laughed even more.

'Oh, shut up. It's not like you know anything about princesses.' Zak turned to Niko. 'Go on scamp, get me some wine seeing as your lord and master seems to have forgotten.'

The boy looked at Sos, who nodded. 'Yes, yes, wine, food, the best we have, and tell the cooks they have the son of the great lord Mkhargrdzeli to impress tonight.' The boy ran off. 'Poor lad. You could see how much he wanted to hear the rest. Go on.'

'So, Dato, your giant countryman – turns out everyone was wrong about him. He led Orbeli's men to the princess. He stole the king's kinzhal so she'd trust them and took them right to her. Now comes the good bit. She escapes. A girl. Captured by hundreds of men. She kills half a dozen of them at least and escapes.'

'She does, does she . . .' He bit his tongue before he could say more. He'd be glad to tell Zak all about Sos, the bold saviour

76

of princesses, but he'd rather keep quiet about the other Sos, the one who'd had his horse swiped from under him by a girl. It'd be better to pretend he knew nothing. 'How did she manage it?'

'God, I don't know. But that's not the point. The point is that Orbeli tells the king that they have her anyway. Him and the king are standing out on the plain in front of everyone and Orbeli says the king must swear to give the throne over to him – well to his nephew, but it's all the same, really – or otherwise they'd . . . they'd . . .' Zak frowned. 'You know, I'm not sure what he was going to do to her, but something really, really horrible.'

'Really, really horrible? You're a real bard, Zak.'

'Shuddup. Do you want to hear the good bit?'

'Go on, go on.'

'The king is about to swear he'll do what they say when the princess appears from nowhere on a golden horse.'

'Golden? Not yellow?'

'No, no, no, it was definitely gold. She appeared from under the sky on a cloud with lightning all around her. She looked amazing.'

'Were you there?'

'Well, no, not exactly, but that's what everyone's saying. After that Demna and Orbeli didn't have a hope. There was a huge battle, which the king won, and now the fastest riders have been sent all over the kingdom.'

'And that's where you come in?'

'Yes, Sos, that's where I come in.'

'So what's the message?'

'The king wants every lord in the kingdom who can speak for a hundred men or more to be at the palace by the next new moon. There's to be a feast at the season turn. If you're not there, the king will judge you an enemy and come looking for you after the snows. There you have it. The perfect excuse to get away.'

Sos clicked his jaw from side to side. 'I suppose,' he said.

'Suppose? You're not planning to go against the king's command, are you? You do some crazy things, Sos, but please not that.'

'No, no, of course I'm not going to.'

'Then what?'

'Is your father content to follow the king?'

Zak grimaced. 'You mean, would he rather answer to no one? Of course he would – but he says we need a strong king, a leader who isn't scared of a fight. My family's lands are open, hard to defend. My grandmother can't even remember her own name, but she'll still tell you all about the Seljuks. It used to scare me half witless when I was young, really young I mean, the things she said they'd do. Even to babies.'

He paused as Niko came back in with glasses of wine, decided they weren't going to ask him to stay and scuttled out again.

'That's why my father joined up with Orbeli at first,' Zak continued. 'He didn't want to go against the king. They campaigned together during the wars in Ani when they were young – he still talks about it all the time. But Giorgi can't live for ever and it angered my father that he wouldn't make Demna his heir when it was the only sensible thing to do.'

He stopped and took a step or two closer to Sos and spoke almost in a whisper.

'I understand what you're thinking. Taxes, tributes, having to kneel and bow and wait to speak. It's not the Kart way. Even less the mountain way. But when Giorgi's gone, maybe we can make it fairer. Demna is the last Bagrationi – and I doubt he'll be alive much longer. The tavads will be able to choose who follows the king – and whoever that is will have to listen to us. That's what my father says.'

Sos nodded. That made sense. He imagined his father sitting here talking to Zak. He'd have refused to talk Kart at first, leaving Zak to stumble along trying simpler and simpler phrases, sounding like an idiot, until he decided to speak. His father would never have gone to court. His father had never bowed to anybody, man or, Sos guessed, God.

'Sos? Sos?' Zak nudged him. 'You all right?'

'Mmmm. What? Yes. I'm fine. Listen, we should stop grumbling in here like a pair of greybeards. Let's take my dogs and go and enjoy ourselves. What do you say?'

'I say lead on.'

Chapter Eleven

'They should be home today.'

'Who?' Tamar asked, her voice wary.

'Your mother and sister.'

Giorgi glanced up from the sheaves of messages on the table in front of him, took in her expression and laughed.

'Come, daughter, at least be civil enough to pretend to look pleased.'

'It won't be the same when they're back.'

'You've been slouched in that chair for a month. You'll enjoy a change.'

'I won't. It's been fun,' she replied.

He shook his head and went back to his work.

It had been fun, whatever he said. With the women of the court still miles to the west – and only capable of returning over the Likhi mountains to Tbilisi in the easiest of stages – nobody had tried to make her do anything that was not to her taste.

She'd told her father that the safest place for her was by his side, and he hadn't argued. So she'd dragged a comfortable chair into a dark corner of his chambers and settled herself there, savouring the procession of supplicants, counsellors and informants that traipsed through the door. The tavads cast her sidelong glances, probing and appraising, but none of them dared ask what she was doing in the king's rooms. They merely bowed and asked distantly after her health.

But Kubaza, officially appointed the king's amir-spaslari, treated her with new warmth, and she also grew to like the steward, Shota. She admired the quiet, humorous way he dealt with her father, convincing him to approve columns of the dullest numbers when it was plain he would rather have been doing anything else. He had a nice face, too, neither handsome nor the opposite, but so full of intelligence that you forgot to ask which.

Best of all was when the king, some time in the middle of the afternoon, would complain suddenly that the room was stifling him. He'd shove the table aside, abandoning whoever he was talking to, and stride down to the stables, Tamar chasing after him. Then they'd ride side by side through the long autumn shadows.

But that would all come to an end when the others returned. She sank lower into her chair and hoped an earth tremor or freakish early snowstorm might destroy the road. She was happily picturing her sister buried under a mountainside of rock, when hurried footsteps rattled down the corridor and somebody rapped at the door.

'Already,' her father said, a little surprised. 'I had not expected them until tomorrow at the earliest.'

Tamar gulped down a big lump of disappointment and stood up as the door opened.

'Gentleman to see you, my lord,' said the guard.

'Does he have a name, man?'

Before he could answer, the door opened wider and a tall, slender man strode inside. He was robed in the plainest possible travelling cloak, but something about the way the material fell and moved spoke of unimaginable wealth and privilege. Long fingers rested on the hilt of his sword, more shocking to Tamar than if he had marched into the king's presence naked. All men gave up their arms at the gatehouse – that was the law.

He had not even let his hood fall back before Giorgi bellowed an enormous welcome, seized him about the shoulders and embraced him. Most men would have buckled under the weight of so much affection, but although the stranger was not built on the same scale as her father, he withstood it with ease.

He was not a young man, maybe even as old as the king. But where her father's face was reddened and roughened, his hair a grizzled bedlam, pouches beneath his eyes, lines criss-crossing between his features, this man looked as if a sculptor had only that moment laid down his chisel. He was, she decided, spectacularly good-looking. His skin was a smooth, golden brown, his hair a dark, even grey and his face was beautiful – neither soft and boyish, nor brutal and sensuous, but regal, commanding. Maybe Theseus had looked like that as he sat on his throne in Athens. Or Hektor might have done – if Akilleus had not cut him down before the walls of Troy.

When he spoke, it was in such elegant Hellên that she knew she'd been right to think of the old heroes.

'Giorgi, my dear fellow, dearest of friends. It does me great good to see you once more.'

No *sir*, no *my lord*. Tamar was startled. It was the first time she had seen any man treat her father as an equal. It should have felt indecent – but from this man it was natural, and her father evidently felt the same way.

'And you are a welcome guest. You honour my house,' he replied in his inelegant, but serviceable Hellên. 'Your arrival is timely. We have finished dealing with a few little troubles and we can now entertain you fittingly.'

Tamar was shocked. The horrors of the rebellion *a few little troubles*? Something tiresome to be got out of the way before fun and feasting? She glanced at her father, perplexed and a little insulted. The stranger caught her look.

'This young woman appears not to be of your mind,' he remarked.

She had not thought he'd noticed her – still less that he could read her thoughts.

'Tis often thus, my friend,' the king laughed. 'Well, Tamar, do you disagree with me?'

'You put me in an impossible position,' she replied. 'It is a sin to disagree with the father, but it is a dishonour to disagree with the guest. You can wish me neither sinful nor dishonourable – so I shall remain silent.'

She smiled to herself. Those sorts of things sounded so much better in Hellên than in their own tongue. The man was delighted. His face, severe and almost cold at rest, brightened into a wonderful smile.

'So this is your daughter. She does you credit, Giorgi. Introduce us, I entreat you.'

For a moment, her father looked almost worried and the man chuckled.

'Forget the sins of my youth. My character is now blameless.'

'Forgive me. This is my firstborn child, the princess Tamar. Daughter, this is Andronikos Komnenos who should need no other introduction.'

He didn't. Andronikos Komnenos was first cousin to the basileus, the great emperor in Constantinople. He was a legend: a great general, a great adventurer and a great – she blushed – lover. She had overheard many tales of his affairs, not always understanding them, but repeating every word to her sister with glee.

'I see my reputation precedes me even to the nurseries of Tbilisi,' Andronikos said.

Tamar bristled. 'This, sir, as you can see, is the king's chamber, not a nursery.'

Her father looked as if he was about to order her from the room, but Andronikos stayed him.

'Nay, I am not offended. Forgive me, Tamar, any man can see that you are not a child and I was wrong to suggest it – even in jest.' He bowed and Tamar immediately forgot why she had been angry. 'And now there is somebody I would like you to meet. My love!'

He called through the door and a woman, lost under a thick, black cloak, entered. Only a pair of perfectly tiny silk slippers, the seams double-stitched in gold thread, told Tamar that she was a great lady. She turned and shrugged off her cloak, which fell into Andronikos's hands with the soft swish of silk.

It was the first time Tamar had seen a woman who could rival her sister in beauty. There was something so rich, so heady in the woman's face that Susa seemed almost brittle in comparison. And her shape. Even her modest travelling clothes could not disguise the swell and plunge of her body. Tamar was blushing again, although she couldn't have said why.

'Giorgi, Tamar, this is Theodora, my truest friend.'

But not his wife? Again, Tamar was amazed. If they were married he would have said so. She knew men had friends as well as wives, but she also knew that kings' daughters were not – ever – meant to meet them.

The king bowed over her hand. 'Your beauty brightens the day like a second sun.' Tamar blinked. Her father waxing poetical? She would sooner have expected him to grow wings and fly out the window.

After he had called for food and drink, they settled into chairs and began to exchange news. Tamar kept quiet, happy to observe these two magical new creatures. It seemed they were living on the southern shores of the sea, and although nobody mentioned it explicitly, she guessed they had been exiled from Constantinople. They talked of two young children, but also of their grown-up sons, who Tamar decided must belong to another woman because they didn't sound much younger than Theodora herself.

'In fact,' said Andronikos, 'I must own that although no man needs a reason to come to Tbilisi, we are here on behalf of my eldest son, Manuel.'

Tamar felt three pairs of eyes land on her.

'I understand. Say no more now,' her father replied. 'You do us great honour.'

Chapter Twelve

Sos and Zak wove past many other travellers on the road, who were ambling south in little knots or sprawling caravans until a party was already in full swing a day's ride from the city. People called out news to half-recognised friends, joined in snatches of famous songs, offered strangers peaches, walnuts or wine. Overexcited boys charged their ponies up and down the roadside, while the wagon coverings quivered and twitched as mothers and daughters kept watch for handsome knights. Some were under the same orders as Sos, but most were simply drawn by word of a great gathering at Tbilisi, the promise of food and drink, of games with magnificent prizes. Hadn't the king plundered Orbeli's vaults where the rubies were stacked high as tomatoes at market, the gold as thick as spring grass? Only a fool would miss it.

Sos and Zak planned their bright futures as they jogged through the rolling crowds. They agreed they were boys no longer.

'It's all about respect, I reckon,' said Sos.

'Respect,' agreed Zak.

'I mean, it was all very well having fun when we were young, but we're men now and we need to make sure we're treated like men.'

'Like men.'

'It's time to make our mark. Make sure we don't get left behind when the next war happens. We deserve our share. Seljuk gold – '

'More than we can carry – '

'Turkoman horses – '

'Great long strings of them – '

'Persian girls — '

'One for every day of the week — '

'But, Zak, we'll have to work hard. Make sure they can't ignore us.'

'Yes,' Zak frowned. 'They who?'

Tamar. The princess.

'You know. The tavads, the captains, the big men at court. The people who count.'

'Right.'

'That's what we'll do.'

'Right.'

The city opened up before them. Sos cupped its walls with his palms, brushed the tiny houses with outstretched fingers. That was where life happened. Down there, in the streets and courtyards, the halls and bedchambers of Tbilisi. Not in his muddy valley under the mountains.

They bought two fat chickens and a handful of radishes at jacked-up prices from a gaggle of women turning a quick profit from the throngs of travellers and made camp on a wooded bluff. No point wasting money on a flea-infested room in an inn. A happy haze settled on their talk as they drank the last of their young wine. Zak lay on his back, his hands under his head, eyes not quite open. Sos sat by the fire, poking the embers with his dagger point, lulled by the soft heat on his face and the dance of the tiny flames.

Mountain farmer. We'll see about that.

They rode into the city on the first day of the victory games. Sos didn't rate his chances wrestling or blunt-blade fencing. He'd never say it out loud, but he wasn't hefty enough to win empty-handed and the older men, the experienced soldiers, would probably disarm him in the first bout and he'd be on his back in the sand circle, staring at the sky with a sword-point at his throat. No. For now, he'd stick to his bow.

Zak shook his head in mock-horror when Sos asked if he was coming with him.

'You know damn well I'd miss a dead sheep with all those people watching. You go, Sos. I think I'll try my luck with wrestling.' He flexed his arms, knit his brows and growled.

'All right,' Sos laughed. 'Come back and find me here when they're done with you.'

'You suggesting I'll get knocked out before you do?'

'Not suggesting. Saying.'

'Fair point.' Zak grinned and bounced off through the crowds.

To win a place in the great hunt the next day, Sos first had to defeat scores of other men at target shooting. He marched up, chin high, and saw man-sized hay bales, swathed with rough linen, propped on wheeled carts halfway down long lists. Goga, the head of the king's stables, was daubing a splotch of bright red paint on each target, leaving a trail of drips behind him. Blue and green flags chattered in the tricky cross-wind.

Sos strode over to one cluster, ignoring the malicious little voice that whispered it had been months and they'd probably all have forgotten him.

'Where'd you disappear off to, Sos?'

'Decided to come back now the fighting's done?'

He'd been practising his reply, serious and nonchalant.

'I had to bury my father.'

Sympathetic nods, a hand or two clapped on his shoulder, mumbled prayers to heaven and that was it. They all understood a man's duty to his father's deathbed.

'What brought you back?'

'How long do you stay?'

That was easy. He cleared his throat.

'The king's messenger came to my lands not ten days ago. Said the king wanted me at the victory feast.' He shrugged. 'I thought my people would be well enough without me. I have a good steward.'

He relished the impressed faces of boys who still had to do whatever their fathers ordered and instinctively patted the small purse of silver strapped under his tunic as he did a hundred times a day.

Goga stuck two fingers in his mouth and blasted a guttural whistle, silencing them.

'Right gents. The rules are simple. Form up, six at a time. Hit the red and you're through. Miss and you're back with them rabble.' He jerked his head at the crowd, who booed him affectionately. 'Then me and my lads wheel these targets back ten paces and everyone who's in goes again till there's three of you left. Got it?'

'Yes, Goga, all right, Goga,' they chorused. He'd thrashed most of them for pilfering or cheek or idleness when they were small boys and was therefore a great favourite.

'And my word is final. No ifs. No buts. Or you'll have to take it up with this pair of lovelies.'

The city's two most successful blacksmiths, their muscles comically developed, stepped to his side, legs wide, arms folded.

'Right. First six. Let's have you.'

When Sos's turn came round, he twitched an arrow from his quiver and, still swapping news with the man behind him, buried it in the red. He hadn't taken aim, nor did he look to see where it struck. He sauntered to the back of the line, pausing to take a swig of cool pale wine from a barrel propped in the shade.

'Well, Con, it's easy for him,' said a voice in front of him.

'Why's that, Vardan?'

'All that practice scaring the wolves off his goats.'

Low laughter. Sos tensed, about to grab the one who had spoken first by his fancy cloak, swing him round, ask him what the hell he meant, but then he remembered the smiths and changed his mind. A brawl wouldn't help him now.

A scrawny flaxen-headed boy, younger even than Sos, had missed and was about to burst from the disappointment. He hopped from foot to foot in front of the stable master, gesticulating, stuttering protests, while the delighted spectators baited him.

'Go on, you tell him.'

'You were robbed.'

'Don't give up without a fight, lad.'

Goga rolled his eyes heavenwards and gave the smiths the

nod. Silently, the two giants planted themselves on either side of the boy, plucked him into the air and pitched him into the crowd.

'Bad luck, buck.'

'You nearly had them, son.'

'Never mind, have a pull on this.'

The day grew hotter, the crowd rowdier and one by one the archers were knocked out. By the time the targets were a hundred paces away, there were only four of them left. Sos, then a slight, serious boy, his face a knot of concentration, then the boy in the fancy cloak, then his friend Con.

At a signal from Goga they all lined up.

Sos was about to shoot when he saw the cloak-boy, Vardan, turn round and mouth something at the serious boy. Sos couldn't make out what was said, but the boy's face reddened and he let fly too fast and his arrow fell short, kicking up a tiny plume of dust. He blinked a couple of times and walked off without looking back. Vardan and his friend laughed and both fired straight and true.

Sos no longer had the nerve not to concentrate. He shut his ears, took a careful stand, clamped the rough red circle on to the back of his eyeballs and let fly. Flawless.

He turned to the two men he would have to deal with the next day. They were high-born Karts, Vardan tall and slender as Sos, the other more compact, with his features squashed together in the middle of his face. They had some sort of pomade in their hair that smelt like women's bedrooms, and moved with a studied elegance that was completely alien. They had never slept in a palace doss-room, that was plain.

Vardan's pale eyes fell on Sos and he smiled, showing two rows of unpleasantly small teeth. 'Rest well. Big day for you tomorrow, Osset. Come on, Con, let's go.'

'Rest?' Sos said to their retreating backs. 'Rest? Tonight is for wine, for feasting, big day or no. Are you off to your fathers' tents for milk warmed by your mothers?'

They halted and turned slowly round to face him. Sos dropped his bow. But before anyone could swing, the blacksmiths materialised.

'Well done, gents, well done all. Master Goga asks you be at the east gate an hour after sun-up tomorrow. Then we'll see what's what.'

Zak, rumpled and limping, ducked out of the crowd.

'Come on great-heart, I need a drink.' He took Sos by the arm, adding in an undertone, 'You don't know what they're like.'

And he pushed Sos through the crowds to where dozens of piglets lay nose to tail on long tables waiting to be eaten.

Sos woke up long minutes before he could open his eyes. He probed around inside his skull, searching for the reason why he seemed to be moments from death, why his brain seemed to be seeping from his ears, why his tongue no longer fitted inside his mouth. He staggered to his feet, thwacked his head before he got far and collapsed back.

'Godsake!' Somebody underneath him howled and kicked. He thrashed about, unwound himself from his cloak and saw Zak lying clutching his head. 'You idiot. Big Osset idiot.'

'Shuddup.'

'Where are we?'

'Tbilisi. Um . . . under a table.'

Of course. They had planned to camp out on the plain after they'd eaten and drunk a bit. But sunset and moonrise came and went and their cups always seemed to be full and then a couple of the captains were persuaded to tell the story of the battle all over and then there was a long debate about how best to kill Seljuks and then singing and then somebody suggested a swim in the river to perk them up. A cock crowed loud and enthusiastic.

'Zak! The hunt, the hunt. What time do you think it is?'

'Mmmph. Sleeptime. Shuddup.'

'Wake up! Zak! An hour after dawn. The hunt.'

Zak lurched to sitting and laughed at Sos through mangled hair. 'Rather you than me, friend. I couldn't stay sat on a horse.

Tell you what, borrow mine today, if you like. Yours isn't fit for hunting cows.'

They stumbled about, shaking off the night before, as the day lit up the city, nudging other bamboozled revellers awake. By the time they reached the eastern gate, they agreed they felt as robust as if they'd had ten hours between silk sheets.

A great fence ringed the plain, many days' work, and behind it stood the king's guard, each man five paces from the next, and behind them milled the first of the many thousands of people who would spill out of the city to watch the hunt. Overnight, workmen had built up a platform, a bank of earth beaten hard with shovels, covered with rugs and shaded by pale silks suspended from fresh-cut branches. The king would watch from there, high above the plain.

At the base of the platform Vardan and Con waited with fathers, uncles and brothers — all the Jakeli and Dadiani clans — looking fresh and smart as if the Virgin had dropped from heaven to stitch their tunics and comb their hair. Sos slouched to one side with Zak and pretended they weren't there.

The sun had boiled off any hint of dew or cloud and the wind's breath was already warm as a lion's. Every five minutes horns blasted the morning air, so nobody would stay in bed and miss the excitement. The crowds surged up against the soldiers, who crossed spears and beat them back cheerfully. Then a great cry cut across the babble.

'The king! The king!'

Sos turned with everyone else and saw Giorgi riding his black horse out of the gate, with Andronikos Komnenos, the guest of honour, keeping pace by his side. Then his eyes fastened on the girls behind them. They were both veiled and wearing droopy, rippling robes with gold at their wrists. But Sos knew which was Tamar from the careless way she sat her horse. Correction. His horse.

'What?'

Zak was nudging him. 'It's them. That's something you don't see every day. The princesses. If only we could see their

91

faces. Maybe we'd be struck blind or dumb or mad by their beauty.'

'Not if they take after their father.'

Zak was about to protest when the trumpets blared again and a courtier told the three huntsmen to make their way to the king. Sos didn't move. He tried to remind himself that if it weren't for him, there wouldn't be much to celebrate, but that didn't help much when nerves and undigested wine were doing battle in his guts.

'Get on with you,' hissed Zak, grabbing the reins from Sos and shoving him in the right direction. 'The king won't bite. Not today anyway.'

Sos stumbled into place behind the other two, who'd strutted up to the king like cockerels. Giorgi obviously knew all about them. He was shaking their hands, asking after their fathers, switching into Hellên to introduce them to Andronikos and then back into Kart to present his daughters.

Sos's mouth was dry. The sun was in his eyes. Sweat stung his neck. His mind was pebbles and scrub. His stomach wavered. Then the king motioned the other two to one side and rested his gaze on Sos.

'What's your story, lad?'

'I'm Sos. That is, they call me Sos. My name is Soslani. My father was Jadaron, lord of the Osset lands under the pass.' He finished. He'd forgotten something. 'Sir,' he added.

'Was?'

'Yes, sir. God called him at midsummer.'

'So my summons put an end to your mourning. Forgive me.' The king spoke grave and low. Sos hadn't expected that.

'It's not for me to forgive you, sir. I came willingly, gladly.' That was good. He'd surprised himself.

'Well, I am glad to see you're not wasting your time now you're here. My daughters and I wish you good fortune today.'

Sos backed away, refusing to seek out the black eyes behind the veil.

Chapter Thirteen

Tamar glowered through the prickly gauze in front of her face at the boy's retreating back. She wasn't going to be impressed by a bit of arrow play. Nor by him lisping up to her father. To hell with it. She swept off her veil.

'Who do you care to see victorious, sister?' Susa's words wafted towards her.

Tamar shrugged. 'It's all the same to me. Why, one of them caught your eye?'

She felt rather than saw Susa colour prettily – as she always did when men were mentioned.

'Why no, how can you say such a thing? But you were certainly interested in that boy. One does hear such remarkable things about Ossets and their horses.'

If Tamar were a lizard covered in green scales and chain mail, her sister would still know where to stick her pins. How did she do it? Susa knew nothing about what had happened with Sos, nobody did, but she could always make Tamar uncomfortable.

It had been the same ever since her mother and sister, mounted on little dappled ponies, had ridden back into the palace court-yard. Flanked by an escort a dozen men deep, Susa had looked smaller and even more vulnerable than usual, but the glow that surrounded her was bigger and hungrier, trapping anyone who ventured too close. Tamar had stared glumly as Sirchak, the duty guard captain, reached up and lifted her off her pony, looking guilty that he was setting something so precious on something so ordinary as the ground.

Her mother, by contrast, had faded. She'd touched her fingers gently to Tamar's cheek by way of greeting and drifted indoors

93

as if she did not know who she was or where she went. That morning, too, she'd sent word that she had a headache and would keep to her rooms, which Tamar thought was absurd. She wouldn't have missed the victory hunt for the world. She decided to put them both out of her mind and stood up to get a better view of the quarry pens.

'My word, Tamar,' came Susa's voice from behind her, 'but you've grown tall as a horse. You'll have to stop soon or there won't be a man you can look up to. And you're such a wonderful colour. You're like a lovely big brown horse.'

'Enough,' said the king. 'Our guest may not understand Kart, but I do. You are grown women. Do not squabble like servants.'

'Forgive us,' said Susa, lowering her eyes. 'Father, please tell us, you were always the hunt-victor in your youth. Who do you expect to win?'

Giorgi grunted. 'My youth.' A snort. 'Would you remind me that is long past? Eh, daughter?' He gestured at her veil. 'Come on, you'll see better without that thing.'

'But the sun, the dust . . .'

'Your sister doesn't mind.'

A soft sigh and Susa unswathed her face. A different kind of sigh as every man within a hundred paces swivelled his head and squinted up into the sun to marvel at the crystal face, the ruby lips, the jet eyelashes. It was unbearable. Even the three hunters, now on their horses, the start minutes away, twisted round to stare.

Giorgi laughed, not in a happy way. He turned to Andronikos, the only man apart from the king who did not appear moved.

'That's how her mother felled me, Andronikos. A sharp axe through my roots. And to answer your question, Susa, the winner will win. And we won't know who that is until the very end. But first, we must begin.'

He stood up and lifted his sword into the air. As it fell, the gamekeepers flung their corral gates wide and stags, goats, wild donkeys, leaping chamois, whole herds of animals, poured on to the plain.

The animals, trapped, terrified, thirsty, went berserk. The deer charged the fences and the front row of the crowd. A few leapt free, twisting and desperate, and darted for the woods beyond, but most swerved at the last minute and ploughed back into the melee. The donkeys chased each other nose to tail, round and round in a panicked ring, screaming, the dust from their hooves dancing in the rays of the sun. Here and there a goat stood, blank and alone, the sound of its bleating swallowed by the roar.

The three huntsmen fanned out, bareback, quivers packed with colour-tipped arrows. Red for Sos, blue for Vardan, green for Con.

Kill the most. The one rule. And there was no doubt who was winning. Everywhere Vardan and Con turned, Sos was ahead of them, a man-horse, slipping, sliding, weaving, writhing, his right arm a blur. The plain turned red.

All three were converging on a pair of deer when suddenly Sos slumped over his horse's neck. It stumbled, knocked off balance and nearly threw him headfirst to the ground. The crowd gasped – dead animals were one thing, but a dead man would be even better. But Sos heaved himself upright and – another gasp – wrenched an arrow out of his thigh. He flung it to the ground, kicked his horse's belly and chased after Vardan and Con. They were several strides ahead, trying to trap the deer against the corral before taking aim, but Sos fired past them and one, two, the deer dropped dead. Another moment and he'd crash into the fence, but at a squeeze of his thighs, his horse took off, tucked its legs and sailed clear. He span as it landed, sprang back into the field and looked to see what was left to kill.

The last beast was a milk-white goat, a determined tufted thing, hornless but defiant. It scuttled away from Vardan and Con, dipping in between the legs of the soldiers who, hooting amusement, tried to kick it back into the middle. The two boys snarled their frustration: no way they could risk an arrow so close to the king's guardsmen.

At the far end of the field, Sos accelerated into a mad, thundering gallop, pounding up the line, a handspan from the soldiers who all leapt backwards. He gripped his horse's mane, swung down, scooped up the goat as if he was picking a flower and cantered over to the king's platform, the startled creature perched in front him, to drop the royal family a breathless bow.

The crowd bellowed its approval. Giorgi chuckled and called for more wine, Susa clapped her hands and declared it was delightful as a howl of trumpets announced the end of the contest.

A band of stableboys scoured the plain, wading through the blood-soaked earth, plucking arrows from head, neck or chest. They dropped all they found at Goga's feet. He, solemn to his boots, split them into three piles and slowly, laboriously counted each one.

The three contestants panted, dripped and glowered. Sos was shockingly pale, Con beet-purple and Vardan pig-pink. Tamar saw a roly-poly boy race up to Sos and stop, bulge-eyed. Sos tried to shoo him away but his friend ignored him and fussed about bandaging the wound on his thigh. The goat dozed in his lap, kicking a little in its sleep.

Yet another trumpet blast. And the stable master strode up to their platform and dropped to one knee.

'Sir, the tally is complete.'

He held out a scrap of parchment covered with black marks. The king scanned it, smiled to himself and nodded for him to continue. Goga marched over to where the boys waited, pulled a heavy purse from his cloak, held it aloft, gave it a great shake so the coins jangled and then handed it to Sos.

The king was on his feet, clapping loudly and shouting for that man Soslani to come up here. Sos tumbled off his horse and walked lopsided towards the royal platform, his eyes bright and glassy. He bowed, keeping his right hand clamped to his thigh.

'Are you wounded, young man?'

'It's nothing, sir. A stray arrow. An accident. It'll mend.'

The king shook his head. 'How did an arrow end up in your leg?'

'I couldn't say, sir.'

'No, I suppose not.' He snapped his fingers and a servant appeared. 'Whistle up my physician and tell him to take care of Soslani here. We don't want his leg rotting off after he's entertained us all so handsomely today. Where are your quarters?'

'I . . . I only came to town yesterday.'

'And slept under the stars? Good for you. But we'll find you a room in the palace while you mend.'

Tamar, ears wide open, had been busy examining the more eye-catching sections of the city walls, but she took one greedy glance. Their eyes collided. She snatched hers away, feeling a stupid flush blossom across her cheeks. She could hear Sos mumbling his thanks – his accent atrocious – to Andronikos's congratulations, and when she looked again he was limping down the platform, waving away the arm of the servant.

'Why are you so red?' Her vulture sister, hovering in slow circles, missed nothing.

'You're red too. It's very hot.'

'You're a different kind of red. Why were you ignoring the Osset boy?'

'I wasn't ignoring him.'

'Yes, you were.'

Her father's cough intervened. Tamar saw the two losers traipsing towards them, shamefaced.

'So, Vardan, Constantine, which of you couldn't tell the difference between a man and a deer?'

Con looked to Vardan for guidance. Vardan dropped a wide bow, encompassing the king and his daughters.

'My lords, gracious ladies, the game-hunt has always been dangerous, has it not? That is why the people flock to see it, why the victor is so generously rewarded.'

He bowed again. Con blinked a couple of times and found his voice.

'That's right, sir. That Osset was damned lucky not to kill anyone with that charge of his. Damn lucky.'

'Watch your tongue, young man. This is not a barrack room.'

'Yessir. Sorry. Forgot myself. Apologies, ladies.'

'Now be off with you.'

Stepping to the front of the platform, the king lifted his arms into the air. Thousands of voices fell quiet, a few stray shouts collapsing into silence after they burst into the hush. All eyes were on the king, as if he'd pulled them to him with invisible threads. He did not move or speak until only the babies and the birds weren't paying full attention. Then, from deep within his chest, his battleground voice boomed.

'My people—'

Cheers swamped him.

'My people! Today is a day of celebration and of thanks. A day of victory and of peace. Our enemies are dirt under our feet.'

Even more enthusiastic yells and whistles. Tamar reflected that some of the white-brown dust swirling in the air, getting in everyone's eyes, was indeed the ash of burnt-up Orbeli soldiers.

'God guided my hand. He smiled on me and my family.'

Ecstatic shouts.

'And he showed us what happens to traitors.'

A confused noise had started among those closest to the city gates. The king was also looking that way. People turned to see what was going on, stretched up on tiptoe, shading their eyes, while boys leapt on to the shoulders of anyone bigger than them. Susa hid her face with a sob and a shudder.

Three men on horseback. Two soldiers flanking a third. Tamar stared. It was Demna. He was swaying from side to side as his horse stepped through the yawning gap left as people backed away, crossing themselves. The men on either side prodded him upright, stopped him falling off. But it was his face that was making the crowd melt away. The white-and-pink cheeks. The little bow of his lips. The red holes where his brown eyes had once been. And Tamar guessed that there was no longer anything between his legs but a cauterised mess.

A few boys started to hurl insults, pebbles.

'Enough,' roared the king. 'Let him go. No one shall harm him. He has been punished.'

A string of brown-robed monks fought to the front of the crowd and grasped the horse's leading rope. The soldiers looked up at the king, who nodded, and Demna, the boy who might have been king, disappeared.

Chapter Fourteen

'Did you have to do that?'

'Do what, daughter?'

'You defeated him. Was that not enough? Did you have to mutilate him as well – your own nephew, your own brother's son?'

'Yes, I did.'

'Why?'

'You do not have the right to ask,' he replied and walked over to the window. 'Now, leave me in peace.'

But Tamar did not move. Ever since she'd watched, horrified, as her cousin was paraded after the hunt, she'd woken every night, some time between midnight and dawn from the same dream. In it, Demna's face first became Dato's and then, somehow, it was her on the horse, blind, groping through the crowds, their jeers still screeching inside her head as her eyes jerked open.

'Where is Dato?'

'I was wondering when you would ask,' he said, his back still to her.

'So you know where he is.'

She hoped he would say that his body had been found on the battlefield, a simple fighting death, and tossed on one of the pyres. That, at least, would mean there was nothing more to think about.

'Yes, I know.'

'Where is he?'

'Where he belongs.'

'Is he dead?'

'No, not dead.'

'Then where is he?' Silence. 'Father?'

He sighed and turned to face her.

'He was found on the battlefield, near death. He is now locked in the dungeons.'

'I want to see him.'

'Never.'

His answer came hard and fast.

'Never,' he repeated, slower, firmer.

'Why not?'

'The dungeons are no place for a girl.'

'*No place for a girl.* You sound like Nino.'

'In this case she'd be right.'

To her surprise, she found the right words ready inside her head. 'It's too late. You can't undo the last months. I have lived them and even you do not have the power to change that. I have seen cruelty and blood and death. Take me to him. It is my right.' She paused. 'It is not only you he betrayed.'

He still looked doubtful, but she held his gaze, refusing to allow him to dismiss her. In the end, it was the king who looked away first.

'Very well. But daughter, heed my warning, you may not like what you see.'

They wound through tunnels hacked out of the rock beneath the palace, the way lit by greasy torch smoke. Angry draughts snaked around her ankles and a feather-light breath skimmed the nape of her neck. The floor scurried and Tamar had to stop herself wishing she was somewhere else.

'Father, how deep do these go?' Her voice was hoarse, the smoke's fault.

'We can go back any time you want.'

'I just asked how deep.'

'You'll see.'

He nodded to one of the guards who chose a long, thin key from his belt-loop and unlocked a low door to their left, kicking the frame hard to unjam the hinges. It grunted open. Her father took a torch and held it up so the flames spilled across the stone roof, turning the darkness dirty orange. A cloying butcher's smell enveloped them, then she saw a sack dangling from a giant hook in the middle of the cell. The door shut behind them. The king spoke unnaturally loud.

'This, daughter, is how we deal with traitors.'

From inside the sack a voice gurgled through blood and phlegm.

'Giorgi, for the love of God, don't.'

A pause, her father's breath rasped loud, and again she heard the same drowned sounds.

'Giorgi, don't.'

The king unsheathed his kinzhal. Tamar started, but the blade only sliced through the rope, dropping the sack to the floor. Like a corpse climbing out of the earth, Dato fought free and stood before her, blood oozing black through his shirt, his eyes punched shut, his right arm out of its socket, his fingers at odd angles, far away, indistinct, nothing to do with her. Then she remembered it was all her fault and she thought she was going to be sick.

Her father thrust the torch into Dato's face, the hiss of singed hair the only sound in the cell. Then he spoke through clenched teeth.

'Don't do what? Don't kill you?'

'No.' Dato's voice was stronger. 'Don't make Tamar see me like this.'

'Wrong, Dato. She asked – no, demanded – to see you. She is trying to understand why a man she looked up to, a man she adored like an older brother, set Orbeli's jackals on her. I tried to stop her, but she had that determined look on her face – you know the one. Now, go on, tell her why you did it.'

Dato twisted his head away from the flames and opened his mouth to speak, but Tamar broke in.

'He already told me in the mountains. He said he wanted peace.'

Her father laughed, a sharp humourless bark.

'And you believed him?'

102

'Yes. Why not?'

'Because it's a whoreson lie. Listen, daughter, you are not the only woman to want to see this man. Last night your mother came to my bed – a rare treat – and begged me to spare one of the prisoners. Whose life did she want? Whose?'

The torch flared, sending their shadows racing up the walls. Tamar stared at her father, then at Dato. Had she understood what he was saying? He spoke again into the silence, his voice tight, his face distorted.

'I will never forgive myself for being so blind. She loved him, that is plain, and I believe he loved her. Forget his fine talk of peace. It was revenge, cold and calculated, after years at my side.'

Tamar took a step towards him. 'Dato, is it true?'

He did not meet her eye. 'He thinks it is. What else matters?'

'Father, what are you going to do with him now?'

'Make him pay. Slowly. He will have many long nights down here to dream of death.'

Tamar saw Dato once again in the mountains, on the cliff edge, the sun in his eyes, his face eaten up by fear that she'd jump. *How can I make you pay?* Now she had her wish. He was going to die, one long day at a time, just like she'd wanted.

Her father pulled her towards him. 'Come, you've seen what you wanted to see. You have your answers. Now you can forget him.'

But how could she forget? He would be under her feet, in agony, while she lived in the light above. Deep inside, deeper than thought, she made a decision.

She wrenched the kinzhal from her father's belt, flung herself back across the cell and drove the point deep into Dato's chest. His hands shot out and clutched her shoulders, his breath hot on her face, then his grip loosened and he collapsed to the floor.

She sprang back, appalled. Her father would never forgive her. He would strike her, kill her too. It was all over. But he only nodded, once, as if agreeing with something she'd said, and

103

stood perfectly still, watching her. She wiped the blade on the sacking and held it out in the palm of her hand, but he shook his head and closed her fingers about the hilt.

'Keep it,' he said. 'It's yours.'

The torch crackled in the dead air.

'We can say he died of his wounds,' he continued. 'I will never speak of this. Nor shall you.'

Her hands were sticky with blood. She was running, desperate to escape, desperate to be alone before she vomited or fainted. The guards by her chamber stood aside as she fumbled with the door latch. She did not notice their strained faces nor taste the oiled smoke that filled the air. The thumping inside her head crowded out everything else. With the door safely shut behind her, she plunged her hands into the water basin and waited for her breathing to steady.

She had seen men die before. She had seen men killed before. Her father had sent numberless men to their deaths and slain many more in battle – joyfully, gleefully. She told herself that this was no different.

'I had to do it,' she whispered to herself, to Dato and to God. 'I didn't want to, but I had to. Believe me, please, please, believe me.'

The door clicked open. She spun round, knocking the basin to the floor. Nino stood at the threshold, ignoring the shards at Tamar's feet. She was shaking, her eyes bitten with tears.

'What in God's name—' Tamar gasped.

'Your mother is very sick.'

'She has been weak since the rebellion, hasn't she? It's one of her attacks, isn't it? Nerves, vapours . . .'

But Nino shook her head.

'No, Tamar. This time it's different. She refuses food and drink. She won't even talk. She has decided to leave us. The physicians say she will not last the night.'

'People don't die like that. They can't decide. Someone, something, has to kill them.'

104

'Not always. Sometimes people wither, like plants without water. You should go to her, Tamar.'

Tamar was suddenly frightened.

'What can I do?'

'Say goodbye, child.'

She forced herself to walk the few steps to her mother's chamber, tapped on the door and waited until the maid opened it.

'Why is it so dark in here?' Tamar whispered.

'My lady wills it. She cries out if I open the drapes.'

'Would not light and air help? Do her good?'

'We have tried. She turns her face away.'

The maid curtsied again and withdrew. Tamar lingered by the door. She did not want to approach the figure buried under the blankets.

'Mother?' she whispered. 'It's Tamar.'

No answer.

She knelt by the bed and looked down at her mother's face. Her eyes were open, glazed as if by fever although her hand was quite cool. Her face, scored only by the most delicate lines, looked drowned, bleached of colour, swollen and sunken as if the person inside had long since fled. Tamar was shocked. Normally, her mother looked wan and other-worldly when she was ill, but this was horribly different. She squeezed her hand.

'Mother, please, it's me, Tamar. What's wrong?'

The blank eyes swivelled in her direction and appeared to see her, but then they closed and her head turned away. Sorrow and anger struggled inside Tamar. What was she supposed to do? Beg? Plead? Surely the dying owed something to the living.

The gulf loomed between them – every conversation evaded, every confidence avoided. She had turned her back on her mother and now, at the end, her mother was doing the same to her. Tamar was furious. She wanted to storm from the room and slam the door, but instead her head fell forward and she found herself weeping uncontrollably.

A hand started to stroke her head, the fingers separating strands of her hair, combing, soothing. Her tears stopped, but she continued to kneel while she surrendered to her mother's touch. She only looked up when the hand stopped moving. Her mother's face was still, but her chest was moving slowly up and down. Tamar kissed her hand and kissed her lips and, not knowing what else to do, slipped quietly from the room.

Chapter Fifteen

Three days later Tamar squared her shoulders and walked into her father's chamber. He looked up quickly when she crossed the threshold. He looked older. His eyes were dull, puffy.

'Your mother . . .' he began.

'. . . is dead,' she finished for him, quickly. 'Soon after dawn. I know.'

'Do you grieve?'

'Do you, father?'

Silence.

'How is your sister?'

'Undone. She scratches her cheeks. Her clothes are ripped.'

He nodded. 'Very seemly.'

'Would you have me red-eyed, hysterical?'

'Maybe.' He tilted his head, weighing her on a giant pair of scales only he could see. 'Maybe not.'

She did not know what to say. There was so much she wanted to understand, but every question stuck on her tongue. So she asked the one thing that would be on the mind of every man and woman in the kingdom.

'Will you marry again? After you've mourned?'

'You would have me marry again? You wish for another mother?'

She ignored that. 'You still have time for a son.'

'A son. A boy. A prince. What a fine sight that would be. My heir chuckling in his crib. Where would we be now, I wonder, if you had been born a boy, Tamar? God knows how I cursed heaven for giving me a daughter. A staring, scowling girl.'

Tamar – mid-stare, mid-scowl – rearranged her face.

'But now I'm not so sure. Sons. If their fathers are strong

107

they resent them and long to supplant them. And if they are weak, they despise them and take their place all the same. Maybe there's something to be said for daughters after all.'

He stopped. Tamar wondered where this was leading.

'I could marry again, you say. Who would you have me marry? A hungry daughter of a hungry noble? A fine, ripe maiden a year or two older than you? And for what? So I can eke out my last years flopping about like a seal, rubbing potions on my prick to make it stand tall enough, long enough to squeeze a son out of some girl who'll wish me dead the minute the cord is cut so her son can rule my kingdom?'

His body vibrated with revulsion.

'No, daughter. I have some years left. And I do not plan to spend them creeping outside my lady's bedchamber, begging to know whether she swells, whether she bleeds.'

He towered above her.

'No, daughter, I have made my decision. I will not live for ever. Nor will I have a son. You, Tamar, you will be king when I am dead.'

King.

The word ripped through her like bright-white summer lightning.

King.

And in the silence that followed, as her father looked at her intently, a tiny voice, soft as a May morning breeze, whispered inside her head.

What is he doing? Dear God, what is he doing?

'Well? Speak, daughter.'

'Is this a jest?'

'No. Would I jest about such a thing? Come, are you not pleased?'

'Have you discussed this with the tavads?'

'No. There is nothing to discuss. A sovereign, not his subjects, chooses his heir.'

'But they will contest it.'

'You are my eldest child. Why should they?'

108

'Because, father,' she spoke slow as if she were talking to a child or a fool, 'because I am not a man.'

'So?'

'No woman has ever ruled Kartvelia.'

He shrugged.

'Half-wits, weaklings, pox-sodden maniacs have all ruled Kartvelia. My daughter is better than they.'

Why was he being so obstinate, so obtuse?

'Even a pox-sodden maniac is brought to kingship from birth. If you wanted me as your heir, you should not have kept me in the nursery all these years. I should have been by your side. Learning.'

'We can start tomorrow.'

'Tomorrow is ten years too late.'

'I thought you would be delighted,' he said, offended now. 'The daughter I thought I knew would be delighted.'

Delighted? What did he expect? Her gratitude? Her stammering thanks? She was suddenly very angry.

'Father, the day you die I will be left at the mercy of the same men who but a month since wanted both of us dead. But unlike you, I cannot don armour and force them to submit.'

'Kubaza will help you. You could not hope for a better commander.'

'How do you know he will outlive you?'

He slammed his hand on to the table.

'Enough. You sound like a marketplace rhetorician. If your courage fails you, if you do not have the stomach for it, then say so. Admit it and do not hide behind these arguments.'

He was being cruel, and that she would not tolerate. She raised her voice to match his and flung everything she had at him.

'This has nothing to do with my courage and everything to do with your pride. You are dreaming of the great glory of your blood—'

'And yours.'

'But they will laugh at you – and at me – and say my mother's death has turned you mad—'

109

'I said enough!' he roared.

For a moment he did look mad indeed and she was afraid of what he might do, but at that moment the door swung open. Andronikos stood on the threshold.

'You asked to see me, friend?'

The king span round.

'Yes, I did. You told me you desired the hand of this girl for your son. I said I required time for consideration. I have now considered and I give you my consent.' He turned from Andronikos and aimed his final sally at Tamar in their own language. 'They're welcome to you.'

Without waiting for a reply he marched from the room, slamming the door shut behind him. Neither of them moved. Tamar was too wounded to trust herself to speak. Andronikos was watching her, a wolf testing the night air.

'Shall we sit down?' he said mildly. 'You look tired.'

He chose a chair as far away from her as possible, crossed his long legs and rested his chin on his hands.

'What has occurred? The truth, if you please.'

She started.

'What do you mean?'

'Why has your father changed his mind? I was sure he was not ready to part with you. Every day since I arrived he has been praising your sister's virtues – although a man would need to be blind to miss them. He was going to ask me to alter my son's suit, and I was going to agree. But now he offers you, with spectacularly ill grace, and so I must ask – what has occurred?'

Tamar could think of no reason to lie to him.

'He wanted to name me his heir, but I refused. That is why he has changed his mind.'

'Will you be glad to marry my son instead?'

'My father orders it. What can I do but obey?'

Andronikos's expression cooled.

'There talks your pride. Answer me properly: would you like to marry my son?'

She shook her head. 'These are my lands, and I would not quit them for all the world. It is foolish, maybe, but I wanted things to remain as they were.' He opened his mouth to speak, but she cut him off. 'You do not need to tell me. I know that cannot be. If another man is named as my father's successor, he will see me as a threat. He will have me killed. Or wed me himself.'

'If you see it all so clearly, then why, in the name of God, did you refuse?'

Why did she refuse? Not for the reasons she had given her father. Andronikos's eyes were fixed on hers and she found herself wanting to tell him.

'I did something I am not proud of, something cruel and pitiless. I fear that is why he now thinks me fit to be king.'

He waited until she could make the words come.

'I killed a man.'

Before she had time to think, the whole story spilled out – Dato, his betrayal, his death at her hands. 'Afterwards, my father gave me his dagger. I do not want it. I am a monster.'

At that Andronikos smiled, so warm and kind she hardly knew him. He crouched down beside her, put one arm about her shoulders and drew her close.

'I do not believe you know what it means to be cruel, my child. That was not cruelty. That was a deed both brave and merciful. You gave peace to a man you loved. If your father judged you more fit to rule after this, he was right.'

'It was a sin.'

Andronikos shook his head.

'I am no bishop, but I know there is no blood on your hands. God sees all and he will judge you more kindly than you do yourself. Certainly, this is no reason to refuse the throne.'

She said nothing. More than anything, she wanted to believe him. They were silent for a while, then suddenly Tamar smiled.

'This must seem like a game to you, my lord. We are but a tiny kingdom compared with the great lands of your family. It must titillate you. The very idea of a girl king. I am a curio – a two-headed lamb.'

'Not at all. And don't simper. It doesn't suit you.'

She glared. She hadn't been simpering.

'That's better,' he laughed and stood up. 'Now, let me tell you something, Tamar. I have spent my entire life longing to hear those words your father spoke. *Be my heir.* You cannot imagine what it is like to be so close to an empire, only to have it denied you. It has blighted my life. I, who have been so blessed, have felt myself cursed.'

'What are you saying?'

'I am saying that I think you will regret your decision.'

She hesitated. 'But I have already refused. I said things I should not have said. My father does not forgive easily.'

'You he will forgive. Go to him. You are proud, but so is he – far too proud to beg you to reconsider.'

'It won't be easy.'

'Yes, but easy is dull. Easy is death. Easy will kill you, Tamar, quicker than any one of your hungry noblemen. Easy is not your future.' He bowed and kissed her hand. 'For myself, I am relieved. I think you will make these lands a great queen, but you would have made my poor son a terrible wife.'

Chapter Sixteen

The sun had already sunk behind the western hilltops and the eastern sky was thickening blue-purple as its beams drained away. The torches would soon be lit, but for now the great hall floated in its own twilight. A tiny bird had flown in through an arrow slit and was dancing unseen over the heads of Kartvelia's ruling families.

Giorgi brought his staff crashing down on the raised platform where he and Tamar stood side by side. The men froze like rabbits grazing near their burrows who suddenly sense the fox is upon them. Most had been drinking, and the intoxication made them brittle and bright. Although the rebels were dead or chained deep in the pits, no man was free from fear. Everyone was wary. Everyone mustered a frank gaze, a halo of devotion.

Giorgi's eyes narrowed as he drank in the atmosphere of the chamber.

'It is as I said, daughter. A cartload of market slaves would sooner defy me than these goslings. Only a brave man will speak up. Mark me well.'

That was said quietly. Those watching would only have been able to tell he spoke by the twitch of his moustache over his lips and the slight rise and fall of his throat. Then he spoke loud.

'My lords, even as we celebrate our victory, we mourn my wife.'

The faces below rearranged themselves into church images of respect.

'Her body lies entombed. The monks are preparing the way for her soul. Our Saviour will welcome her.'

The hush thickened. Tamar saw a servant enter the back of

the hall carrying a long taper to light the torches. He stopped short, his right foot hanging in the air. Slowly, he let it fall and edged backwards out of the room.

'But tonight, my lords, tonight belongs to the living, to us.'

And he stepped a little to his left and turned to look at Tamar. Few had noticed her. Her father blunted awareness of anyone else, so only the subtlest men would have asked themselves why the tall girl was waiting beside him in the shadows.

'Why are we huddled in darkness?' Giorgi demanded.

Men rushed in, weaving through the crowd, stretching up to fire the braziers that ringed the chamber, chasing away the cold twilight. Giorgi gave the room time to settle, but before the wait began to feel unnatural, he spoke again, almost conversationally, a man amongst men.

'The lion's cubs are equal, be they male or female.'

A ripple of movement as the faces of the men below her shifted. Blank confusion or sudden comprehension. The cleverest showed nothing at all, but an extra stillness gripped the hall.

'Some of you might be looking upon my daughter for the first time. Look well. Look long. Look hard. You are looking at my heir, my son that never was. Your king, my lords, your future king.'

Tamar could see the joy he took in exercising his power. He wielded it like a cudgel, like an unwrought stave, each word a killing blow. It frightened her and yet at the same time made something tighten in her belly, a seductive feeling, like balancing on a thin branch, high up a tall tree.

'My sun is setting, but a new moon is rising. Slender it may look to your eyes, accustomed to the glare of the sun. But, never forget, the full-grown moon can chase away the darkness and outshine the brightest of stars. Heed me well, my lords. Tamar is your king.'

A rustle sounded near the foot of the platform as Qutlu moved into the space between king and crowd, smoothing his moustache with long fingers.

'My lord, my lady,' he began, placing a careful emphasis on

each word. 'Every man truly has one peer, one equal. His child. Who amongst us has not heard of Tamar's deeds? Surprising, most surprising. But maybe no surprise in a child of yours. She has proved herself fearless, resourceful and under your guidance I am sure she will learn wisdom, justice, mercy.'

His words crackled in the air.

'But who, my lord, will lead our armies into battle? Forgive my vulgarity, but Tamar can no more cross swords with our enemies than Kubaza could suckle his children.'

Tamar spoke. She couldn't help herself.

'What are captains for, Qutlu?'

The weight of all those eyes was suddenly upon her. Blood swarmed to her cheeks and she filled her lungs.

'Yes, gentlemen, what are captains for? If heaven had decreed the only way a country could defend itself was for king to scrap with king like cocks in a pit, then I own I would make a poor ruler. The shah of Shirvan might peck me to pieces.'

A reluctant chuckle ran round the room. The shah was sixty-two, his harem the site of his only renowned exploits.

'Strength comes in many guises, my lords. Do we bow down and follow the circus giant?'

Another chuckle, warmer this time. Her father shot her a glance from under his brows. She lowered her eyes, gripping her hands in front of her to stop them shaking out of control.

Qutlu carried on speaking as if uninterrupted.

'And then, of course, there is the matter of a husband, or should I say consort? A man rules in his own house. That is the law. But the king rules over all men. That too is the law. Tamar cannot go unwed. She must bear children. The succession must be secured. But how can we bow and call her king when, forgive me, a man rules her?'

His eyes swam lazily over her. Tamar's heartbeats measured the silence as the men turned their heads, snickered, shared glances. Her father laid a reassuring hand on her shoulder.

'You make another worthy point, Qutlu,' he said. 'Let us give thanks that no man here has ever had cause to bend his will to that of his wife. Or perhaps I am mistaken? Maybe some of you have faltered in the face of some whim, some desire of a woman?'

Qutlu listened politely, patiently while around him a dozen faces turned red and rueful.

'Most droll, my lord, but would you not—'

To Tamar's surprise he broke off and without another word bowed and retreated into the crowd, a knuckle pressed to his lips as if he had remembered something crucial. She saw his eyes flick up to the right, once, twice, but when she followed them she saw nothing there.

Nobody else spoke.

'So,' said Giorgi, 'it is agreed.'

Sos watched as the king strode to the back of the hall and stepped aside, allowing Tamar to pass in front of him. She disappeared from view into the dark of the royal apartments. Before Giorgi followed her, he turned and gave the men gathered below one last lingering look, the corners of his mouth curling down in a strange triumphant half-smile. He raised one hand – a salute, a benediction, a warning, it was hard to tell – and then he was gone. His Kipchak guards crashed the doors shut behind him.

The hall stood locked in a still hush of astonishment. Then a hundred voices began to bubble and spit like cheap stew. Shouts burst above the hubbub. Menacing knots formed at the foot of the dais, taunting the soldiers, calling them goatboys and worse, wanting the Kipchaks to retaliate, to stoke their blood, to make them foolhardy, to make them charge.

Younger, drunker men made a show of following the king, shoulders squared, fists raised, but wiser friends pulled them back. Nasty scuffles broke out as some men tried to fight their way past those who were calling for calm. The doors opened and a dozen more guards tramped on to the platform. They stared out over the heads of the crowd, rigid and impassive, refusing eye contact, swords drawn. The room surged forward. Sos was caught up in the press, but before the two sides clashed, before the night turned ugly, Qutlu rose up between them.

116

'Do you think blood will wash the taste of cowardice from your mouths?'

His voice crushed them.

'Shall we ask the king to return now you all have so much to say? Well? Shall we call him? What say you?'

With each question, he poked one then another wild-eyed, well-born young man in the chest until their tempers were doused and their heads hung low. There was a smothered silence.

'You all seem so upset. Why did none of you speak before?'

He made the question sound kind and paternal. The men writhed, willing somebody else to speak. Of course, every man had a good reason why he had clung to the shadows. Maybe an elder brother in the room who should by rights have spoken first. Or a father in chains.

Qutlu shook his head.

'When dogs fight, the loser rolls over and waves its prick in the air. Men are different. The loser says the sun was in his eyes, a stone tripped him, a wasp distracted him, anything, so long as he does not have to admit he has been bettered. A simple truth, my lords, one you would do well to remember this night. You have lost. Accept it.'

The tension left the hall like air escaping an old wineskin. The guards' grip on their swords relaxed as the men started to file out. Sos, one of the last to leave, found himself in front of Qutlu who was talking low and earnest to two tavads. Sos recognised them as fathers or uncles to Con and Vardan.

'Why, Qutlu? Why did you rein them in? We could have been through that door in seconds and put a stop to this.'

As they stepped into the still night air, Qutlu pulled his hood over his head so Sos could no longer see his face, but his voice carried in the dark.

'Look, my lords. If I had delayed, we would all have been dead.'

Sos saw easily in the dark so he realised what Qutlu was talking about before the other two. He heard their sharp intake of breath when their eyes made out the row of ladders propped up against the stone walls of the great hall.

'Those slits let arrows in as well as out. The Kipchaks have vanished already but believe me, they were ready for us. I saw one head at the second window on the eastern wall. The king was leaving nothing to chance. I had no desire to join Kartvelia's finest in a bloodbath.'

The three men drew closer together.

'No, my lords, while the king rides high, while Kubaza commands, we must wait. The quick stroke often goes astray.'

'But the quick stroke is the Kart way,' muttered one of the lords. 'I have no love of plots. Leave that to the basileus and his half-men.'

'That is why we are what we are and basileus rules half the world,' Qutlu replied. 'Timing is everything. Orbeli timed it ill. We must not make that mistake again.'

Chapter Seventeen

Sos knocked on Shota's door and walked straight in before hearing an answer. The steward stood up to greet him, shoving a bundle of parchment under an accounts ledger.

'What's that you're writing? Love letters?'

'Mind your own business, Soslani.'

Sos snatched one of the leaves that was poking out of the pile on the table and started to read. Shota did not rise to the bait, but sat and listened, his head on one side.

'*There was in Arabia a king by the grace of God, happy, exalted ... When the flower on the rose blooms and withers ...* Shota, what is this?'

The steward leant over the table and deftly removed the sheet from Sos's hand. 'Something to occupy my few idle hours, young Sos. We can't all spend our spare time galloping after our great kingdom's fleetest-footed fauna.'

'It's a poem.'

'Yes, it's a poem.'

'Can I read it?'

'Not a chance. Now, what can I do for you?'

Sos grinned. This was the part he'd been looking forward to. 'As promised.'

He plucked two coins from the pouch at his waist and placed them side by side on the only corner of the table not covered in books. They vanished up Shota's sleeve.

'Thank you. I imagine those two have a bit of company now?'

'What? Oh, yes, I see what you mean. Things are a little – well, a lot – easier now.'

'I'm glad.'

Shota smiled, waiting for Sos to take his leave, but the young man wandered round the room, plucking books off the shelves at random. The steward sighed and sat down.

'What is it, Sos?'

He hesitated for a moment then grabbed a stool and pulled it so close to Shota that their knees were almost touching. When he spoke, it was in a half-whisper.

'I don't understand politics.'

'Nobody ever does – and don't believe the man who says otherwise.'

'But you understand everything. Everyone says you do.'

Shota shook his head. 'I listen. I watch. But I would never say I understand. Come, what is troubling you?'

Sos took a deep breath. 'Conversations.'

The steward nodded, encouraging. 'Go on.'

Sos changed tack. 'I thought the rebellion was over. I thought the king had won. The tavads bow and scrape to him. They've all sworn to follow Tamar when he dies. Yet I've been hearing strange talk. Vardan and Con, their fathers, they hate him – and her. I can tell. And I'd swear many of the other nobles feel the same way. Qutlu Arslan most of all.'

'You must understand, Sos, the forefathers of those great men once ruled over their little princedoms undisturbed. They were free and proud – but helpless before the Seljuks. Davit brought them together and scoured the plains. People could grow crops and raise livestock in peace. But peace came with a price – fealty to a king. And that was not to everyone's taste.'

Sos frowned. 'And Qutlu?'

'Qutlu is an ambitious man – and subtle. It took untold prescience for him to abandon the rebellion when he did. I am sure he was happy to see Orbeli broken, but that is all. His loyalty to the king goes no further.'

Sos blurted out what he had wanted to say.

'Shota, should I tell the king what I've heard?'

'No.'

That was not the answer he'd expected.

'No?'

'The king already knows.'

His surprise turned to incredulity.

'The king already knows?'

'Yes, Sos. The most powerful men in the kingdom are always plotting against the king. That's politics.'

Sos digested this.

'But if I told the king, wouldn't he think I was loyal? Reward me?'

'Maybe. But he'd ask himself how you heard and why you heard. He'd ask himself who else you were carrying tales to. And do you think you could tell him in private? What if someone heard you telling him and whispered it in Qutlu's ear? How do you think he would feel about it?'

Sos winced.

'So I say nothing?'

'If it's advice you're after, that's mine. The time will come when you'll have to choose which way to point your sword. But choose then, not now. It's easier to make the right decision with your sword still in its sheath.'

'It's confusing.'

'Go back to your mountains then.'

That hurt. Sos jumped up, knocking the stool over, his neck burnt a deep red, but when he was halfway across the room he stopped and turned round, his smile back on his face.

'That's what I plan to do, actually, now my leg's mended. I need to make sure nobody's plotting against me in my own great domains,' he said with a tiny twist to his lips.

Shota laughed. 'Forgive my bluntness, Sos, but that's the way it is at court. We must be thankful we weren't born in Constantinople — they are the masters of confusion there. They'd have you for breakfast, me for lunch and Qutlu for supper.'

Shota paused and looked at Sos speculatively.

'But why this sudden interest in the king's welfare? I know it can't only be because he gave you a bag of gold, however enormous it was.'

Before Sos could answer, the door burst open and a blast of cold air scattered the papers strewn on the steward's desk.

'Shota, are you busy? I've done with these, but forgive me, your work . . .'

Tamar knelt down to scoop the papers up, crawling on hands and knees to tug a couple of sheets from under a chest of drawers, talking all the time. She looked unkempt again, more like the boy-girl from the mountains than the lady Sos had grown used to seeing from a distance. A scent of spice and pine fire had followed her into the room. He could see the backs of her calves and the hollows of her knees.

'I want to know more about the Franks in the holy cities. Are they really as barbaric as everyone says?'

Tamar sprang back onto her feet and was about to dump her armful of scrolls on the table when she – finally – saw Shota motioning to where Sos was standing by the door. He probably should have ducked out while she wasn't looking, but he hadn't. She started – she really hadn't seen him – and gave him a nod that he decided was not altogether unfriendly.

'My apologies, Shota, I do not wish to trouble you if are engaged in business.'

Shota's eyes flicked back and forth between the two young people in his room. Sos was now staring at the floor. Tamar was staring at a point two fingers above Sos's head. Shota might claim not to understand politics, but he did understand people.

'My lady, may I beg leave to introduce the lord Soslani, son of Jadaron, the ruler of the Osset lands east of the great pass, south of the ice-river.'

Shota made a face at Sos, who was standing still as a fencing-post. He collected himself, smiled and mustered a respectable bow.

'I am honoured, my lady.'

Tamar laughed. 'No need to introduce us Shota, we are old friends.'

'You are?'

'We are?'

Both men spoke at once and Tamar laughed again.

'You were not there I think, Shota, but I saw my lord Soslani perform a great deed with much skill and daring. I was very struck by his courage.'

'Ah, yes, the victory hunt was the talk of Tbilisi,' Shota acknowledged.

'The lady Tamar does me a great honour to remember. I don't recall her being very impressed at the time,' Sos said.

A pounding silence engulfed the room, broken by Shota's delicate cough.

'My lord Soslani and I can finish our business another time if my lady has a mind to discuss the wars of the cross.'

'I am indeed so minded, Shota. But——' and she clapped her hand to her head, 'but I find I have forgotten the manuscripts we were studying. It would be such a great kindness if you could send for them. I shall wait for you here. And please,' she smiled, 'no need to hurry.'

Sos watched Shota hesitate. It wasn't exactly wrong for him to leave them alone together. But nor was it exactly right.

'As you wish, my lady,' he said after he'd given both of them a long – a very long – look.

Tamar wandered behind Shota's table and began leafing through the mess. Sos waited, wondering whether he was supposed to speak first.

'So you forgive me then?' she said, without looking up.

He widened his eyes. 'I must have missed something. When did you ask for my forgiveness?'

'I . . . You're right.' She moved to stand right in front of him and made a most serious face. 'My lord Soslani, will you forgive me the wrong I did you?'

He bowed. 'Willingly, my lady.'

They shared a small smile.

'Were you very angry with me?' she said in her normal voice.

'How could I be, my lady?' he said, a new look hovering about his eyes. 'You are my sovereign. You can do no wrong. My horse is your horse.'

123

He noticed that she had the grace to blush – a little. 'I was going to say – he's in the stables. I'll tell the grooms to prepare him for you.'

'No, keep him. A memento,' Sos found himself saying – although God knew it was hard to give up such a good animal. 'I was glad to help, truly. And I'm still glad.'

'Honestly? You've had little enough reward.'

'Honestly. I'd do it again.'

'You would?'

'Of course.' He cleared his throat. 'A man should help his friends.'

'Am I your friend?'

'Yes. Well, you were.'

'Were?'

'I was friends with a boy in the mountains. It's different now, isn't it?'

But before she could answer Shota was back in the room.

'That was quick,' Tamar said.

A nod. 'Naturally, my lady. One must hurry to do your bidding. Now – if you'll excuse us, Sos – we can turn our attention to Salah ad-Din and the men of Aegytpos.'

Sos could take a hint. 'Farewell, my lady.'

'I shall see you at my sister's farewell feast, my lord?'

He shook his head. 'Alas, no. I must return to the mountains.'

'Of course. You have your duties.' Something skimmed across her face. He hoped it was disappointment. 'Shota, forgive me, I find I have no desire for study after all. Goodbye, gentlemen.'

With that she was gone and Shota was shaking him hard by the shoulder.

'For the love of God, Sos, what on earth was all that about?'

'Politics, I think,' came Sos's pleased reply.

Chapter Eighteen

Susa had gone, bound west for Andronikos's son.

As the last cart, laden with clothes and gifts – a princess's dowry – swayed through the gate in her wake, the king nodded, mounted his horse and spurred it for home. The tavads, no longer arrayed in meticulous, ceremonial ranks, straggled behind him.

Tamar did not move immediately, but stood, staring after her. She had expected to feel relief, maybe even joy, but something about her sister's dignified departure – the two careful kisses, the lovely face empty of reproach – snatched at her conscience. Susa had probably fixed her eyes on the road ahead, but some impulse made Tamar lift her hand in a final farewell.

She wondered when Sos had left. He must have slipped away unnoticed. It had been days since she'd last glimpsed him crossing the courtyard, fast and light on his feet, as if his blood ran a little quicker than other men's.

'Forgive me, my lady, but you seem quiet – not your usual ebullient self.'

Qutlu had appeared on his horse behind her. She nodded a polite acknowledgement and beckoned to the groom to hand her up on to her saddle. But he was not to be brushed off so easily.

'Your sorrow is understandable and, if I may say so, commendable,' he continued in a voice she imagined was meant to be kindly. 'It speaks highly of the true tenderness that is only to be found in a woman's heart.'

'Indeed, Qutlu.' She pinched her lips together and kept her gaze fixed between her horse's ears. She didn't look at him for fear she wouldn't be able to keep the dislike off her face.

'So many of our finest young women must wed abroad, but I fear even the most sensible, the most obedient feel a certain resentment at what they, misguidedly, perceive as a form of banishment.'

She flashed an angry look at him. He raised his eyebrows.

'Of course, I do not refer to your sister. No, no. It is a great match. Your father did not cast his pearl – one of his pearls, I should say – before swine.'

She had to offer a few words in reply.

'A noble family indeed, my lord. We need not shame to call them kin.'

'Indeed not. I only hope your sister will not feel ashamed of us when she sits in the great palaces of Constantinople.'

He laughed lightly and Tamar jerked round.

'Constantinople, my lord?'

'Oh, forgive me. I speculate, that is all – think nothing of it. You do not wish to be troubled by my musings. I shall leave you in peace,' he said and made to ride off.

'Qutlu, what – Qutlu, pray tell me what you mean.'

His lips thinned into a smile.

'The basileus is ailing, my lady. His son is but a boy – young and inexperienced. And youth and inexperience are a perilous combination, as I'm sure you don't need me to tell you. The basileus will need to live many, many years if his son's position is to be assured.'

'And if he does not live long? If he dies soon? What becomes of his son then?'

'Andronikos will not wish to see the empire flounder. He will put himself forward as a suitable regent – maybe as a suitable alternative – and I am sure plenty of men will follow him.'

Tamar snapped.

'Qutlu, enough, I know what you are implying.'

He looked shocked.

'What do you mean? You cannot think . . . ? But no, today is a difficult day, an emotional—'

'You are threatening me. You say nothing plain, you never

126

do, but you do not deceive me. You would say that I, too, am young and inexperienced. You would say that I, too, will not last long upon my father's death. Do not shake your head and act innocent, I know very well—'

A hand seized her elbow. She turned sharply to see Shota at her side.

'Forgive me, my lady. Your father asks to speak to you. My lord, you must excuse us.'

And he set off for the palace at a fast trot with Tamar following, wondering what could be so urgent. She was even more surprised when Shota did not lead her to her father's chambers, but into his own small room.

'Shota, where's the king?'

'Not here. At least, I hope he's not.'

'But you—'

'I had to say something to stop you accusing one of the most powerful men in the kingdom of treachery, plotting, intrigue and the devil alone knows what else before several dozen witnesses.'

'But he was—'

'No, Tamar, he wasn't. I heard every word. He was condoling you over the loss of your sister and sharing his thoughts about developments in the internal political situation of one of our most important neighbours as befits – I repeat – one of the most powerful men in the kingdom.'

Tamar slumped into a chair and groaned, her head in her hands.

'You're right, you're right. I should have realised he was trying to provoke me. Why am I still such a fool?'

He gave her a wonky smile.

'Don't be too hard on yourself, Tamar. He's been playing this game for a lot longer than you. And he plays for pleasure as well as for profit.'

'He'll be laughing about it with Jakeli and Dadiani – how he played the silly princess like a dozy carp. He was testing me and I failed.'

He gave her shoulder a brief pat. 'Come, don't look so downcast. Next time you'll be better prepared. You wouldn't mind if Kubaza knocked you down in the sword pit. This is the same. You're learning. Every man was a novice once.'

Tamar chewed her lip. 'You're kind, Shota – too kind. Nobody will ever expect me to be able to win at arms, but at this, at words, I must be better than everyone. Qutlu's right. I am young and inexperienced.'

'Youth is not always a bad thing. The great Davit himself was younger than you when he replaced his father. And he did well enough, didn't he?'

Another wonky smile.

'But Shota,' said Tamar, exasperated, 'he was the greatest fighter our kingdom has ever known, a legend. And he faced the Seljuks, a real enemy, not a bunch of sniping, conniving tavads squirming about under his feet.'

'He is a legend now, but he was a man first. And he had to deal with the grandfathers of the same sniping, conniving tavads as you do.'

'Yes, but he had a sword to help him. And what do I have?' She opened her hands and held them palm up. 'Nothing.'

Shota flung his arms into the air.

'Swords, swords, everywhere this obsession with swords. A great swordsman is not the same as a great king, Tamar. The world is full – too full – of men who can thrust and parry. But men who inspire others? They are rare. You said as much the day the king made you his heir. You should pay better heed to yourself. You talk good sense – sometimes.'

'Only sometimes, Shota?'

'Sometimes is a good beginning.'

Part Two

Chapter Nineteen

Spring took Sos by surprise, as it always did. For days, he had been splashing through the crunch and slop of old snow, his toes clammy from the brown water, his head aching from the spiky gusts, with nothing to look forward to in the evening save another flavourless pot of bean stew. His steward grunted that the seven trumpets would sound before they saw the thaw and then the fires of hell might be a welcome enough treat. His sisters giggled and his mother tutted, spat and crossed herself.

But one morning, which had dawned no more promising than the last, a different air blew over the mountains and swallowed up the snow, leaving every stone glistening in weak, wet sunlight. Shutters cracked open and the new season raced into dank corners. Rugs and mouse-gnawed sheets reeking of fire-smoke were pulverised clean, flung over lines and left to snap and balloon in the stiff breeze. The wind still bit, but it carried a foretaste of summer, a faint promise of green leaves and golden evenings.

It was time. Sos readied what he ruefully thought of as his goat tax – the king's tribute – listened to his mother's never-ending shopping list, called for his horse, skittish and scrawny after the winter, and cantered away, the clouds streaking east over his head, weaving a complicated dance with the sun.

He had thought to return to Tbilisi that first spring after he met Tamar – and for five springs after that – but endless difficulties pinned him to his homeland. Nomad raiders from the north. Svan rustlers from the west. His young kinsmen had to be kept in line and the valleys' elders needed to understand he was now their lord. Not that he hadn't been successful. He was popular and his people prospered. Maybe that should have been enough. But news of Tbilisi – news of Tamar – trotted slowly up into the mountains, drawing his thoughts ever south.

He collapsed on to a bench-seat in an alcove off the common room of what the gatekeeper had sworn was still the best inn in town and swung his feet up onto the stool in front of him. The room was a rough oval in shape, about thirty paces across, with a large hearth in the middle and little half-circles scooped out of the walls, like petals on a flower. Noon had long passed, but evening was still some way off, so there were fewer than a dozen other men hunched in talk or sleeping off a meal.

A motherly sort of woman appeared, wearing a faded and patched butcher's apron and brown woollen leggings. She asked his pleasure and whether he minded keeping his muddy boots off her furniture. He grinned in apology.

'Forgive me, mistress, seems I forgot my manners on the road. Supper and a bed if you have them.'

She nodded and bustled back into her kitchen to be replaced by a girl, her daughter maybe – they shared the same square jaw and purposeful neck – with a bronze bowl brimming with warm, oily water. Without a word, she pulled off his boots and started to rub the dirt and tiredness from between his toes, cupping his heels and kneading the balls of his feet. Sos settled deeper into his seat, put his hands behind his head and leant back. He was soon asleep.

When he opened his eyes, evening was reddening the far wall. Someone had lit a fire, but not long ago as only the kindling had caught and the copper chimney had not yet started to draw. Soon it would be a brilliant blaze.

The inn had filled with the usual noisy mix of merchants, mercenaries and anonymous wayfarers, some in bright comfortable groups, others alone with their thoughts in the darker corners. His ears picked out a couple of mountain tongues, fighting Hellên, the desert language and others he did not recognise. The girl was weaving through the press with a basket of flatbreads under one arm and a tray and cups balanced on the other. Steam and the smell of meat fat clouded over the swing doors that led to the kitchen.

Sos smiled to himself, stretched and was about to call for something to eat and drink and join one of the communal tables, whichever looked likely to be most liberal with their talk, when he caught sight of two familiar faces through the crowd. Vardan and Con were heading his way. He groaned. Why did he have to run into them of all people on his first night back in town? But luckily they were mid-discussion and walked straight past him.

'Just one drink, remember, there's not time for anything else,' Vardan said, jabbing Con in the back.

'I know, I know, come on, sit down.'

He heard a yelp as they kicked a pair of drowsy long-eared dogs out of the way and settled into the alcove to Sos's left. He could see Vardan's slender ponyskin boots and Con's shoulder, but nothing more.

'Wine, your best,' Con bawled at the girl. 'And quick-smart, poppet.'

'What does yours say?' Vardan was on the far side and his voice did not carry as easily as Con's. Sos had to strain his ears to make out the words.

Con shrugged. 'Same as yours I expect. Very little.'

'Show me.'

Con reached forward and pulled a piece of dirty parchment out of his boot and handed it to Vardan. The girl appeared and dumped two cups on the table. There was a short silence and then Vardan said something that was too quiet to make out.

'I wonder what's happened.' That was Con.

Sos wriggled round to the other side of his alcove.

'. . . must have asked everyone,' Vardan was saying. 'I even saw Gamrekeli – not like him to come west so early in the year. He must be going.'

'I wonder's what happened.' Con again.

'Horn's teeth,' Vardan exclaimed, 'that's the hundredth time. The sun's nearly set – we'll know soon enough.'

'Why sunset?'

Vardan was back on his feet, draining his wine cup.

'Discretion, muttonhead. He must want us to arrive under cover of dark. Maybe we're going to move at last. Come on, time to go.'

Con stumbled to his feet, groped around for a couple of coins and flung them on the table, following Vardan who had already disappeared through the door. Sos stared after them, chewing his lip.

'Sir? Sir? What d'you want, sir?' The serving girl was standing by him, impatient.

'Oh, sorry, nothing. That is, not now. I've just remembered I have to . . . to go and see a friend. Here's for your trouble.'

'But your bed, your horse—'

'Later, I'll be back later.' He handed her another coin and hurried to the door.

The night was cold and black after the generous fug inside the inn and it took Sos a moment to work out which way they had gone. He picked out their footsteps heading towards the river, pulled his cloak over his head and followed. His stomach grumbled and he wondered briefly why he wasn't settling down to a bowlful of something hot and fatty, but there was a note of suppressed excitement in Vardan's voice that was too tantalising to ignore.

They crossed the bridge, left the belly of the town behind and started to climb the eastern bank. Only a handful of very rich men had houses up here, so there were fewer people about and Sos had to tread more cautiously. His scalp prickled. Another set of footsteps, firmer, was coming up behind him, fast. A second later and the others heard it too and stopped. Sos sank to the ground.

'Who's there?' asked Vardan, sharp.

'Zakari Mkhargrdzeli,' the reply floated through the night. 'And you?'

'Vardan Jakeli and Constantine Dadiani.'

134

'Are you going to – to the same place as me?'

'Evidently.'

Sos frowned. Zak? What was his friend doing with them?

He followed at a greater distance now – he had more respect for Zak's ears – until the path levelled out and they halted before a stone-built house, its front gate marked by a smouldering brazier. Sos could hear the rush of the river below and the stamp of guards pacing the darkness.

As Zak entered the pool of light, Sos stared. His roly-poly childhood friend had vanished. In his place stood a man at least two heads taller, with hands like spades and muscles bulging at the sides of his neck.

A creak and someone opened the gate a crack. Vardan and Con walked straight in, but whoever it was stopped Zak with a hand on his chest.

'Your name, my lord?'

'Mkhargrdzeli.'

'Zakari or Iovanni?'

'Zakari. My brother isn't coming.'

'Welcome.'

The gate closed behind him. Sos peered up at the high walls and wondered whether he had come far enough. He slipped down the hill, counted to three hundred, then ran back up at full pelt and arrived puffing and panting by the brazier. He hammered on the gate and the head appeared.

'Greetings,' Sos gasped. 'Sorry if I'm late. Mkhargrdzeli here.'

The man looked him over. 'Your brother said you weren't coming.'

'He left me puking and mewling like a baby in an inn south of Kojori. Some swine had fed me bad meat,' he shrugged, 'but I mend fast.'

'You don't look much like him.'

'It's a sore point. He got the brawn. I got the good looks and charm.'

The man snorted. 'You don't say. Follow me.'

Together they crossed a dim courtyard and entered a large

room, lit only by a fire at one end. It was windowless, like a cell. Inside were at least four dozen men, standing in little knots of three or four or leaning up against the walls, arms across their chests, eyes low and watchful. Whenever a face shifted and caught the glow of the fire, Sos found he recognised it. The room was full of men from the oldest, richest families in the kingdom.

Zak was standing alone near the doors. The gatekeeper tapped him on the shoulder. 'Your brother, Mkhargrdzeli.'

'But—'

Zak turned, caught sight of Sos and fell silent, his mouth slightly open.

'You should have known I'd make it.' Sos embraced him and the servant moved away to close the doors.

Zak threw him off and dragged him into a corner.

'God's love, Zak,' Sos gasped. 'What have you been eating? Goliath's got nothing on you.'

'Are you mad?' Zak hissed.

'No,' returned Sos, 'just curious. Where are we?'

'If you weren't asked, I'd get out now while you still can. He won't like intruders.'

'Who won't?'

Suddenly, Sos sensed a change in the room. All eyes were fixed on a tall man, silhouetted by the fire.

'Gentlemen.' It was Qutlu Arslan.

Some of the men started forward to shake his hand, but Qutlu waved them back.

'No, no ceremony. Thank you for coming so quickly.'

He turned to the fire, pulled off a pair of gloves and held his hands so close to the blaze that Sos wondered how he stood it. He could see his face in profile, the skin wax-white even in the glow of the flames, a charcoal pit under the arched bones of his cheeks, the sagging lower lip out of kilter with the mathematical nose and domed brow.

Qutlu spoke into the rapt silence.

'My lords. I have the gravest news. Much depends on the coming days.'

A pause.

'The king is dead.'

A silent snap of unseen fingers and everyone started speaking at once. Sos had not heard a whisper, a hint, a wink that Giorgi was even ailing and it was plain nobody else in the room had either.

'What did—?'

'When, Qutlu?'

'But how do you—?'

Qutlu silenced them with a half-raised finger.

'They had thought to conceal it from us, but I found out in time to summon you here.'

Qutlu placed his hands together in front of him as if he were going to pray and tapped his fingers together, pacing slowly in front of the fire.

Everyone waited.

'My lords, did we kneel before God and swear Tamar would be queen when Giorgi was gone?'

Gamrekeli, one of the oldest men in the room, his elegant good looks now faded, spoke first.

'I did. You did. We all did, for the love of God. What is it you are saying, Qutlu?'

'I am asking whether an oath made to satisfy a crazed whim of a power-mad king has any validity amongst men of honour?'

Sos's stomach tightened. So this was how a rebellion began. His father would have rejoiced at the news.

'But the girl is not alone,' Gamrekeli continued. 'What of Kubaza?'

'That will be taken care of.'

Every head snapped up.

'Meaning?'

'What it means, Gamrekeli. Soon we will have no need to fear the mighty Kipchak.'

'I do not fear him, Qutlu,' came the offended reply. 'I merely have a healthy respect for a proven fighter who loved the king like a brother and commands a thousand well-armed men.'

137

Grunts of agreement.

'As do I. However, I encountered an intriguing herbologist overwintering in the city. His plants, he claimed, can make the wisest mad with love – and many marvels besides. My lords, he also showed me certain weeds that cause seizure, followed by paralysis and death.'

The room rippled.

'How could you be sure he was no mountebank?'

Qutlu parted his lips and smiled. 'I am one slave the poorer. No great loss. But Tamar will not find Kubaza so easy to replace.'

Sos was astounded. When he had been a boy in the palace, Kubaza had been more myth than man. His death would change everything.

'And what will become of Tamar?' Gamrekeli demanded. 'I want no part in the death of a woman, whoever her father may be.'

Again a rumble of assent.

'No more do I. She may yet be useful to us. But she must be made to understand who she answers to.'

'And who is that, Qutlu?'

'Why, to us, Gamrekeli, to the first men of the kingdom, to the men in this room.'

'And she will agree to this?'

'You worry too much about what this girl thinks. She has no choice. Maybe she will even be relieved. It is time to end the charade that there will ever be a Kart queen.'

Vardan leapt forward. He looked like a boy on his first hunt who has heard the crash of a doe breaking cover – his bared teeth and eye-whites flashed in the firelight.

'Qutlu is right.'

A dozen voices joined his, a few cheers. Qutlu had carried the room with ease. Sos saw men's faces take on the deep flush or stark colourlessness of great excitement. Only Gamrekeli looked troubled – or maybe resigned. Beside him, Zak was clearly struggling to take it all in.

Qutlu was walking slowly through the crowd, shaking hands,

embracing, murmuring, 'So we are of one mind . . . Excellent, excellent . . . Tomorrow will be a great day.'

Sos's heart started to thump. He had been so intent on listening that he had completely forgotten he wasn't meant to be there. Qutlu was coming closer and he started to back away. He had his hand on the bolt, drew it across carefully and nudged the door. It would not budge: it was bolted on the other side. He turned round.

Qutlu's arm flashed out like a scorpion's tail and long fingers gripped him by the throat. Sos twisted to shake him off, but only felt his nails digging deeper into his windpipe. He stopped struggling.

'What have we here?' Qutlu asked, his blank eyes boring into Sos.

Zak was gabbling by his side, 'It's my brother, Qutlu, sir, he's been fighting long in the south—'

'He is no more your brother than I am. I repeat, who are you?'

Qutlu's eyes did not leave Sos's face, nor did his grip slacken. Sos tried to speak, but he could only gag, splutter, shake his head.

'I don't like anyone skulking in the shadows. How did you come here? Why were you listening, boy?'

His father's words formed in his head, although there was barely enough air in his throat to whisper them.

'It is time to say *No*. It is time to say *Enough*. We will rule ourselves.'

An unnerving, dry, hacking sound emanated from deep within Qutlu's chest and he unwound his fingers. Sos realised he was laughing, although it was like no laugh he had heard before, and he had to beat down a shameful urge to run as far and fast as his legs knew how.

'I couldn't have put it better myself. What's your name?' There was a wheeze at the back of Qutlu's voice as his attack of good humour ebbed.

'Soslani.'

That piqued Qutlu's interest.

'Jadaron's boy?'

'Yes.'

'Let me have a proper look at you.'

He pushed Sos into the firelight and ran his eyes back and forth as if he were scanning an accounts ledger. Sos stared back. Close up, he saw that Qutlu was older than he had thought. Thin lines ran between his nose and mouth and across his forehead, and there were creases around his eyes. He had seen fifty summers at least. When he spoke, his voice was warm and courteous.

'I admired your father – his independence and pride were an example to us all – but it was a shame he chose to cut himself off from like-minded men. In this at least I am glad you are not inclined to follow his example. You are welcome. I will not ask how you came to be here – let us put it down to youthful enthusiasm. A laudable quality.'

He turned to the others.

'My lords, come, let us eat,' he said and strode out of the room, followed by the tavads.

A few of them gave Sos a nod, a smile as they left, including him, making him one of them. Vardan even held out his hand.

'You're in luck. Qutlu doesn't often take a shine to people,' he said as he passed.

Soon Sos and Zak were the only ones left in the room.

'So, Zak, you got this letter, too?'

'Yes. Well, my father did. He sent me to find out what it was all about. Told me to decide what to do – on his behalf.'

Sos heard the pride in his voice at his father's faith in him and felt a twinge of envy.

'And what will you do?'

Zak paused.

'My father gave me a piece of advice before I left.'

'Let me guess. No dice? No loose women?'

Zak gave him a look.

'All right, sorry, what did he say?'

'He said Qutlu's always on the winning side.'

A steward was standing at the door, waiting to usher them through.

'My lords? Will you be so good as to follow me?' he called.

Sos glanced at Zak. The doors behind them were guarded.

'Seems we don't have much choice.'

Chapter Twenty

Tamar was marooned with her father's corpse in the cathedral. Her eyeballs were raw and inflamed. The sobs she had forced herself to swallow lay sick and heavy on her stomach. She had been kneeling, the flagstones grinding into her bones, since they brought him there at dawn, but she couldn't pray. Every time she tried to lift herself to heaven, the blackness inside her sucked her down towards the stone coffin.

She listened to the rise and fall of the monks' chant and watched the fingers of daylight walk around the altar until they lengthened and faded into nothing.

Night was easier. No sound but her breath, the dance of guttering candles, the world asleep at her feet. Night belonged to his world, to the dead. She unclasped her hands, flung herself full stretch and wept long and loud in the silence, in the dark, trying to blot out everything that had happened since the midwinter night when she realised she was losing him.

She had been nestled in her chair in his chamber, watching a new-lit fire leap from log to log in the grate. The kindling twigs glowed red, then white, then disappeared. She felt warm, sluggish and at peace, and snuggled deeper into her furs, reaching for the mug of weak, warm wine by her side.

The king dozed in his chair. He had been retelling the story of her great-grandfather and his victory over the invincible Seljuks at Didgori, but his voice had been growing quieter all through her favourite part – where Davit ordered boulders to be tipped into the Nichbisi gorge so that, whatever happened, his army would not be able to retreat – until it stopped altogether. Then his head lolled forward and he started to snore gently. Tamar smiled to herself. They'd had a long day talking spear levies with Kubaza. Why shouldn't a man sleep?

Giorgi woke with a start and carried on speaking as if nothing had happened. But his lyrical mood had changed to bitterness.

'Davit, the restorer, sword of the Messiah, king of the seven kingdoms. What did his children do? Fought and argued. My father, my uncle, my brother, me, we forgot everything he did for us and squabbled like milk-fat babies . . .'

He stopped speaking and Tamar felt much less comfortable. He stirred and looked surprised to see her sitting opposite him.

'Run along, child, run along and play with your sister.'

Her heart thumped. 'She married into the west, father. Years ago. You remember. She's grander than all of us now.'

Tamar tried to add a smile, but fear was snatching at her gullet. The king still looked confused.

'You asked me to spend the evening with you, father, you remember. Telling me stories that will help me when I am queen.'

That roused him. 'Queen! You want to be queen? You want to steal my kingdom from me! Viper. Vixen. Who are you?'

He jumped to his feet, eyes ablaze, more like her real father. Except something was missing. He was staring straight through her, shouting at ghosts in the fire.

'Father, father . . .' She tugged at his sleeve and stroked his arm and he quietened. She pushed him towards his chair and he sat down, meek as Jesus. Suddenly he grasped her hand and stared up at her, his eyes brimful of tears.

'My heart, my love, what do I have to do . . . tell me how to win you . . . give me a chance . . . I beg you . . . my heart, my own, my mountain flower, my Osset rose . . .'

Tamar ripped her hand away and bolted from the room, leaving him sobbing and mumbling, his face buried in his hands.

She had her own apartments now, but she didn't go there. She fled down the corridors, past startled guards, to the nursery. She burst through the door and flung herself on to the low divan in front of the fire, startling Nino from her sewing. Even then the tears did not come. She sat dumb and stricken, her back straight and her head up, twisting her hands in blind circles. When she spoke, it was to accuse.

'What's wrong with him?'

Nino came to her and put an arm round her shoulder.

'I thought you—'

Tamar shrugged her off.

'Tell me.'

'His soul is working loose.'

Tamar shook her head. 'No.'

'Forgive me, Tamar, but you must have seen it yourself. His face . . . his eyes . . . he's fading. I have seen it before.'

'You're wrong.' Tamar hurled the words with all the strength she possessed, but it wasn't enough to banish what she knew – had long known – but refused to admit.

The king had become quieter, stiller, rubbing his brow, staring out of the window. He ate less, pushing his plate aside, swearing at the cook, saying he'd eat later, ignoring his wine. She had started to feel sad and empty when she looked at him, whereas before he was invigorating. He had shrunk, like a leviathan washed up on a pebbled beach, choking on sunlight.

She swallowed. 'Does he know?'

'It is not an easy thing to know about oneself, my lady.'

'Who else?'

'My lady?'

'Who else knows?'

'The lord Kubaza came to me. I only confirmed what he had guessed. Nobody else sees enough of the king. We have made sure of that.'

'How long?'

'He may see Easter, but not midsummer, we cannot hope for that.'

'What do we do?'

'We can only pray, my lady.'

'Yes . . . I'll go to the bishops tomorrow. A mass, a great mass. God loves him. He will spare him.'

'No, child, that is not what I meant. We can only pray for a quick and easy death. There is no recovery.'

The candlelight in the cathedral paled and disappeared. The dawn would already be calling the tavads from their beds. Tamar wished she could grasp the sun in the palm of her hand, fling it back below the horizon and stay hidden in the half-dark, swaddled by the shadows.

A loud thud shook the double doors. So they had come. She grimaced – who indeed would stay in bed on a bright, kingless morning? She blew out the candles around her father's body, leant forward, touched his hand and closed the lid.

'Peto.' She turned to a pale, gangly monk. 'Call my guard.'

He scurried to the back of the cathedral, nearly tripping over his long brown robes, and disappeared behind a curtain. Before she had time to think, he came back at a run.

'My lady, my lady, your guards, they've gone.'

She blinked. Kubaza had told her it would be safe for her to spend time alone with her father and with God. If he had betrayed her, she was lost. She might as well cut her own throat and climb inside the coffin next to the king.

'Unbar the doors.' Her voice hit the domed ceiling and bounced back to her.

'My lady,' Peto stuttered, 'you can't go out there alone.'

'Can't?'

He blushed. 'That is to say, if the men have wandered, let me summon a fresh guard fitting for your majesty.'

'You are kind, brother Peto, but it is not fitting for a queen to hide under a monk's skirts. I think we both know the guards have not, as you say, wandered.' She smiled, trying to encourage him. 'Fear not, if they had decided to kill me, they would have done so already, God's house or no. I beg you, go forth and see who would disturb my prayers.'

The monk bowed and pulled his cowl over his head, crossed himself several times and set about working the great bolts free.

She turned to the corner where a red-and-gold Saint Giorgi,

the halo shimmering above his bare head, was captured in the middle of skewering a squirming green lizard. She traced the length of his lance with one finger and whispered, 'As you are my witness, I swear I will not die this day.'

She turned and walked out into the daylight. As she appeared on the threshold, the wind whipped round the cathedral and caught hold of her mourning cloak, sending it billowing, turning her into a black butterfly before it fell to her sides.

Qutlu stepped forward. His sword was hidden – a bad sign. If he meant her no ill he would not scruple to wear it openly, like a man. He bowed deep from his waist, supple as an acrobat.

'My lady. We come to offer you our most humble condolences. King Giorgi – may he rest in peace – was as a father to us all.'

'He'd rest more peacefully still if you weren't hammering down the door,' she replied.

'A father,' Qutlu repeated politely as if pretending not to have heard her, 'a far-sighted father who, were his end not so regrettably sudden, would surely have appointed a council to help you with the burden of assuming his regal mantle. We beg you to accept our guidance and enjoy the fruits of our experience after many, many long years in your father's service.'

'Your offer is as generous as it is considerate, my lord Qutlu. But happily my father did have time to make provision. The general Kubaza is to act as my right hand in all things. That was my father's wish – and mine.' She paused. 'As you would know had you called at the palace rather than blundering up here.'

Qutlu's face folded into an aspect of profound sorrow. 'But, my lady Tamar, that is precisely the problem. We called at the palace and heard from your steward that the general Kubaza has been struck down by a grievous malady. He is feared to be scant moments from following your father to God's heavenly kingdom.'

His eyes did not leave hers. A killing rage sped through her blood until her head roared and her fingertips twitched. If she held his gaze for a moment longer she feared she would break and fling herself at him. It was unthinkable. She wasn't a raw girl any longer. She mustn't, whatever it cost, she mustn't. She dropped her eyes and breathed hard and slow, the crisp air burning the back of her throat until she could match his level tone.

'A horrible coincidence, my lord. A double blow for my kingdom.'

'Indeed, my lady. But even as faithful dogs pine for their masters or grieving wives follow their husbands to the grave, so too can it be with soldiers and the lords they follow.'

Her eyes blazed and she marched straight down the steps, and before Qutlu knew what to expect, the point of her father's kinzhal, hidden from sight by the looping sleeves of her robe, pricked his groin.

'You go too far,' she whispered. 'Beware lest I do likewise.'

A dozen men leapt forward but Qutlu, his cheeks a sudden red, ordered them back with a quick twitch of his head.

'My lady is stricken with grief.' The black middles of his eyes had swollen with shock, but were now narrowing to little rapier points. 'Would she rest awhile?'

She gave a sharp jab and spoke for his hearing alone. 'Serve up your words as fine as you choose, but today you get mine plain and unadorned. What are your terms?'

'Terms, my lady?'

'Yes, my lord, your terms.'

She watched his Adam's apple bob up and down as he swallowed.

'Kubaza is dead. You have no friends. Give thanks to God that you are a girl – none of the men want a maiden's life on their conscience. So you may live. We may even decide to seat you on the throne. But you will rule no man here. We shall rule you.'

'We? You mean you. You will decide. You will rule.'

He ignored that. 'Those are my terms. Your life in exchange for your obedience.'

Death would be better. She could kill Qutlu. The tavads would cut her to pieces and it would be over. The wind would dry their blood on the steps. But that was a coward's choice. The dagger disappeared up her sleeve.

'What a relief,' a lilt leavened her voice as she spoke out for all to hear, 'to have such counsellors in this darkest of hours. What should I have done without you?'

She pretended to look about her.

'Now, forgive me, my lords, but my guards seem to have strayed. I beg you, would you do me the honour of escorting me back to the palace?'

She spread her arms wide as if to embrace every man before her and dropped a deep, respectful curtsey. As she rose she saw Sos for the first time. He was standing a little apart on the far left of the group, dressed in a sober black tunic, clasped with silver, nothing like the patched brown-grey gear he used to wear.

Her heart leapt. He was back. But then her face closed. He was with them. Qutlu was right. She had no friends.

She felt like a lamb being herded to the block by a pack of dogs, but the townspeople saw the king's daughter leading the first men of the kingdom through Tbilisi.

Qutlu and the tavads left her at the gates, promising to return the next day to see to the business of the kingdom. Small pockets of soldiers mustered outside the walls. She was, she realised, a prisoner in her own house. She crossed the courtyard, which was strangely bare without guards. No noise came from the smithy or kitchens. Most of the servants must have fled. She felt a small brush of relief when she saw Shota and Nino waiting for her.

'Oh thank the heavens you're safe.' Tears started in Nino's eyes and she buried her face in her hands. 'We've been so—'

'I know, Nino, I know. But I'm fine, really I am. Shota, tell me of Kubaza.'

The steward was shaking his head.

'The good Arab physician was nowhere to be found. No mystery about that. Nino and I could do very little for him apart from make him comfortable . . .'

'When did he die?'

'Die? But he's not dead.'

'Not – not dead?'

Hope flared.

'It was close, my lady, for long hours last night he walked in shadow. The poison was ruthless, but Kubaza is unlike other men. His body has failed – he is now no more a fighting man than I am. But he lives yet.'

'His mind?'

'Sharp as ever.'

She could have hugged him. 'Can I see him?'

'He should not be disturbed. He needs rest, absolute tranquillity.' The steward smiled. 'But of course he has been asking for the lady Tamar twice a minute since he awoke. Come, I'll take you to him. I've placed him in your father's chambers.'

'My father's?' Her voice was a little sharp.

'They are the easiest to guard, my lady,' Shota said gently.

Tamar put her hand on his arm. 'Thank you. I see you too are a fighting man – in your own way.'

She followed Shota down the familiar corridor, past a dozen Kipchaks, their faces grim, until they reached the door, guarded by still more of Kubaza's men. They neither made way for her nor blocked her path. They simply stood, unbending, unblinking.

'Come now, Sirchak, you know your master wishes to see the lady Tamar. Stand aside,' Shota said in his mildest voice.

The captain pushed open the door and slipped inside, pulling it firmly shut behind him before they could follow. They waited, edgy, until he reappeared.

'Very sick. You only, lady.' He gave Tamar a perfunctory nod, which she decided was soldierly brusqueness fitting to the times, not a calculated insult.

'Wait for me here,' she told Shota, and ducked under the door after the captain.

Kubaza lay on his back with bolsters packed around him on a rough tent bed in the middle of the room. His left arm lay inert, the large-knuckled fingers clenched into a claw. His face was lopsided: the left cheek had caved in and dragged his lower eyelid down with it. A thin line of spittle bubbled at the corner of his mouth.

Silently, Tamar cursed her luck as she sat cross-legged on the matting by the head of his bed and touched his arm.

'Greetings, Kubaza. I add my prayers to those of your kinsmen.'

He stirred and opened his eyes. 'I was dreaming that I lay under the stars and could hear my horses and smell the grass.'

It sounded as if someone had taken his voice in their hand and crushed it out of shape.

'Have something put under my head, my lady. I cannot talk like this.'

She shrugged off her cloak, rolled it up and took hold of his shoulders to prop him a little higher. He was heavy and it was a strain, but he looked pleased that she had done it herself.

'Qutlu?' The word slurred as it emerged from between his teeth, but there was no mistaking the enmity in his voice.

Tamar nodded. 'He came to the cathedral with the tavads at his back. He thinks you are dead. He thinks to rule through me.'

She sprang to her feet and paced around the room.

'Kubaza, tell me, why do they follow him? He's so . . . so . . .'

She couldn't find the word and kicked the wall instead. The right-hand side of Kubaza's face smiled.

'I understand. I have loathed him these many long years.'

'What do we do now?'

'That is hard. Were I my old self or if you were . . .'

He looked embarrassed and did not finish.

'If, if, if . . . It's all right, I know how different everything would be *if*. Kubaza, tell me the truth, is there any hope? Or is the convent at Gelati the best I can hope for? Shall I tell Nino to pack my bags?'

He shut his eyes and did not speak for many long moments. She listened to the fire and the sound of his breathing. At last, as if with great effort, Kubaza found the words.

'I do not see a woman. I see the rightful heir of Giorgi

150

Bagrationi, the man I followed from boyhood. I see the great-granddaughter of Davit who gave my people land and rewarded them with gold. I see the king of the seven kingdoms and if I but had the strength, I would kill any man who denied it.'

Tears sprang to her eyes and she turned away to hide them.

'Do not be ashamed to weep in front of me, Tamar. You forget that I also see the girl who has long gladdened a childless man's heart.'

She reached out and took both his hands in hers.

'You give me courage.'

He shook his head.

'I give you hope. Courage you already have.'

Chapter Twenty-one

Although the fingernail of new moon had long since ducked out of sight, the two young men carried no torches as they wound down the hill towards the riverbank. A cat hissed from a low wall and a dog whimpered as they passed. But nobody was abroad. The people of the city knew better than to stray outside after nightfall during the doubtful days when a dead king's heir was yet uncrowned.

Sos picked out a path between the mud walls of the poor houses, his ears picking up nothing but sleep-grunts behind the barred doors. Only once did somebody, bent on thievery or love-making, it was impossible to tell, cross their path, breaking into a shuffling run when he sensed two large shapes on the move in the dead of night.

A fresh breeze cut across the thick stench of the alleys like lemon juice through mutton fat and Sos realised the low hum in his ears was not excitement, but the river. They left the final huts behind them, stepping round knotted scrub and tree stumps, and came to the water's edge. Where they were, they could have leant over and touched the water, but on the far side, through some long-ago divine caprice, the bank rose steep and sheer, as tall as two tall trees, coloured like damp turmeric and pockmarked by sun and rain. And on top of it, a ghost shape under the brittle starlight, perched Qutlu's house.

'Remind me why we're doing this,' Zak muttered.

When her eyes had found him among the crowd of tavads Sos had been ashamed; worse — for the first time in his life he'd known what it was to feel like a coward. Even his father had

152

never made him feel so low. But at the same time there'd been something else, something that almost heartened him. Her anger had been directed at every man there. But the hurt – that was for him and him alone.

He and Zak had slowly fallen behind as the tavads followed Tamar to the palace. Then he stopped short, scuffing the dirt with his boots.

'What?' Zak asked.

'Fifty men with swords under their cloaks smirking while that man bullied her. Just because they were too chicken-scared to stand up to her father. It made me sick.'

'Me too, Sos, me too.'

'Then when I saw she had her knife at his prick. No whispering, no poison.'

'Straight, blunt.'

'I liked that, Zak.'

'Me too, Sos, me too.'

A pause. They'd looked at each other and grinned.

'What d'you say, Zak? Shall we see if we can find a way to even things up?'

The sentry torches loomed and vanished, a firefly dance, as Qutlu's men patrolled the perimeter. A little higher, one orange patch glowed, a Cyclops eye on the black face of the night.

'That must be his chamber,' Sos whispered, trying to sound confident, but his daylight certainties had sunk with the sun.

'How do you know?'

'Who else would be awake at this hour?'

'What if he's not alone?'

'Can you imagine that reptile coiled round a girl?'

'Maybe a guard at his door?'

'His walls are so close-guarded he'd have to be very jumpy to post one inside as well. And he's not jumpy – he reckons he's got it all neatly sewn up.'

'Can't we just kill him?' Zak said hopefully. 'It'd be a lot easier.'

'We've been through this: only as a last resort. Hostages are a lot more useful than corpses.'

Sos wished he would stop asking questions. Each one reminded him that their – his – plan was foolhardy to the point of lunacy. But Zak wasn't finished.

'Sos, honestly, do you really think this'll work?'

Sos took a deep breath and ordered the unpleasant writhing under his ribs to stop. 'No, perhaps not. But it's worth a shot. And,' his voice lightened, 'we'll certainly have surprise on our side.'

Zak snorted. 'He'll think two river demons have come to pay their respects.' He sighed, his mirth gone as fast as it came. 'Come on, if we really are going to do this, let's get it over with.'

They wriggled out of most of their clothes, scooped handfuls of wheel grease out of a small pot and started to slap it all over their bodies to stop the drowning-cramp stealing through their limbs.

'I'll go first—' Sos started, but Zak cut him off, suddenly firm and soldier-like.

'Don't be an idiot. We've been through that as well: your skinny sack of bones would sink before you got halfway. I've a much better chance. Rope me up.'

Relieved, Sos tied a bight of rope round Zak's waist, and gave his shoulder a squeeze.

'Good luck,' he whispered.

There was no answer, only a splash. The rope paid out fast, the neat coils flicking into the water with a whistle and a smack, rough against the palm of his hand. For a moment the sound of arms and legs thrashing through water reached Sos's ears as Zak was swept downstream, then the deeper swash of the river drowned it out.

He stood on the riverbank, unable to do anything except will his friend forward. Time billowed, the thump of his heart separated by a dead silence. Suddenly, a jerk nearly ripped the rope out of his hands, followed by a series of rhythmic tugs. Zak was over. Brilliant. Then he remembered it was his turn.

He made his end of the rope fast about the sturdiest trunk he could find, strapped a blanket roll stuffed with their weapons across his back and grasped the rope with both hands. Before he had time to wonder what might lurk in the deep, dark, fast-flowing water, he jumped.

The cold made a startling warmth bloom across his chest even as his skull prickled and shrank. He clung to the rope and, hand over hand, began to pull himself across. The current seized his legs, drove his head under, trying to tumble him, drown him, steal him for ever. His breath was coming in terrified, ragged bursts and sinking brown river smells clogged his nose. The muscles in his arms and shoulders quaked and roared. He could hardly feel his fingers. Were they still holding on or was he rolling down the river? Panic bubbled in his throat, but then Zak's voice reached his ears.

'Nearly there, water rat.'

The taunt did him good and the pull of the current was slackening closer to the bank. He kicked, hauled, spluttered and felt Zak's hands trying to get a hold on the back of his neck, under his arms, anywhere, and tug him on to the ledge where he was crouched.

'God, you're slippery. More like a frog than a rat.'

Sos couldn't speak. He was coughing up water, gagging, his eyes and nose streaming.

'How was the swim?' Sos croaked.

'Easy as kiss your hand.'

Sos felt mortified.

'But it's lucky you thought of the rope. We'd never have found each other otherwise,' Zak added kindly.

Sos emptied his lungs of the last of the water. 'Ready to go?'

They looked up. The bank — or cliff, now they were at the bottom of it — wasn't vertical, but it wasn't far off. It would have been hard enough in daylight, but in the dark, cold and numb, they would be lucky to make it to the top. But unless they could kill a score of Qutlu's guards apiece walk through his walls, there was no other way.

Sos went first, gingerly, feeling for handholds. The weather had been dry so the rock was easy to grip, but not so dry that it would crumble. He told himself he was climbing at home in the mountains – to retrieve a goat kid or for the fun of it, to outpace his cousins, to leave everyone behind. This was something he understood.

Cautiously, he lifted himself on to the narrow lip – no more than two handspans across – that separated the house from the cliff. He looked down. He couldn't see Zak, but he told himself that he would have made a lot of noise if he'd fallen. Untroubled footsteps sounded at the sides of the house, to and fro. Nobody had heard them.

Zak's head appeared, then his shoulders. Sos touched his arm. It was shuddering.

'You all right?' he mouthed in Zak's ear.

'Heights, not my thing.' His voice jerked. 'Glad that's over.'

'Not quite.'

There were no windows at ground level, but the first floor balconies were not far above their heads. Zak pressed himself against the wall and Sos used him as a ladder, scrambling up his back to kneel on his shoulders. Then, one foot at a time, Sos stood up, leaning into the wall to stop them both reeling over backwards into the water. He reached up and his fingertips found the bottom of a balcony. He took three deep breaths and hoisted himself up. Zak passed him up a sword. Now he was on his own.

He listened at the open window. No breathing: that room was empty. He cat-climbed on to the next balcony and put his ear to the shutters. He heard grumbling snorts – that didn't sound like Qutlu – then a few mumbled words. Two men at least – guards, housemen, people not important enough to sleep alone.

It was further to the next balcony. He felt his fingers out on to the wall, hunting a nook he could trust with his weight. He wedged two fingers and a thumb into a small gap between two stones and felt further with his right hand. There was a suspicion of a ledge. He rummaged for a foothold and then shifted his weight off the balcony. His left hand joined the right. Then he reached, blind, and grasped the balustrade of the next balcony. There were petals or leaves carved at the corners.

He waited until his breathing had stilled before he moved to the shutters. A low murmur drifted from the far corner of the room. Qutlu? There was no way he could be sure. Then, as if the sleeper could hear his thoughts, the sound stopped. The wind had dropped – the absolute calm that often comes before the sun returns. He waited for the breathing to start again, but it didn't. He heard a rustle, a stir, the slip of sheets sliding to the floor, then footsteps, slow, coming towards the window. The shutters opened outwards and he ghosted backwards to stop them touching his face. He felt rather than saw a long, thin blade emerge, followed by a head.

It looked left then right to where he stood, masked only by thin slats of wood. A glimmer of moon and he would have been lost. Sos did not think, did not fear. He emptied his mind. That was the only way not to be noticed. You had to become not worth noticing, an old bit of post.

The man leant over the balcony and shouted.

'Iakob!'

'My lord?' The voice, startled but alert, came back immediately from the side of the house.

'Rouse the second watch. And report to me in my chamber.'

It was Qutlu.

'Sir! Yes, sir.'

Sos heard the shout of orders as the guard captain, or whoever Iakob was, rounded up more men. Had some animal sense made Qutlu suspect? Or did he always tire of sleep before dawn? All Sos knew was that any ideas he'd had about knocking Qutlu out and tying him up were now useless. He had to act that second or not at all.

He put the point of his sword to Qutlu's neck.

'Jump.'

'You must be out of your mind.'

Qutlu sounded irritated, rather than surprised or angry, but there was no time to argue. Sos gritted his teeth and hurled himself into Qutlu's back. The balcony's rails splintered under their combined weight and they both tumbled over the edge.

I am going to die.

Then he hit the water hard and plunged deep down into the cold current. For a long dreadful moment, Sos didn't know where up was. He swam desperately one way then realised the pressure in his ears was getting worse, his head full of siren singing, the back of his eyes dancing red and black. He somersaulted and kicked as if he was trying to shake off the jaws of a million water snakes.

When he surfaced, the dark was unravelling fast. Shapes were disentangling themselves from the blackness. Sos squinted into the night, trying to blink the day into being. Where was Qutlu? Unconscious underwater? He swung this way and that. There – there he was, about twenty paces downstream.

The river was crawling with back-eddies, rips and little whirlpools and they were both being swept back to the palace side. Qutlu was swimming hard with the deliberate stroke of a much younger man.

'Oh no you don't,' Sos muttered and gave chase.

The current spat them into a little inlet, bristling with tangled nests of uprooted saplings that had been left high and dry when the flood waters dropped. Qutlu fought his way to the bank, grabbed an overhanging branch and hauled himself clear. Sos howled in frustration. He couldn't get away, not now. But then Zak came careering down the riverbank and cut him off. Qutlu tried to dodge, slipped, skidded and Zak crashed on top of him.

'What do you two think you're playing at?' Even face down in the mud, Qutlu still had a certain cold dignity.

Sos and Zak looked at each other. Sos's mind raced. He'd been so intent on snatching Qutlu that he'd not thought what he would say when he had him. Zak solved his dilemma. He swung

158

his fist in a neat hook and knocked Qutlu out, then flopped on to the ground, puffing like a spent stud-bull.

'Job done.'

Sos beamed.

'Now all we've got to do is rope the bastard up and carry him to the palace.'

Chapter Twenty-two

Tamar was bobbing in a dark doze that tasted of warmth and peace, her mind scrubbed clean. Her dreams raced away from her in little ripples. She tried to keep pace, but they danced ahead, just out of reach until sleep had gone where she could no longer follow. Then she felt the outline of a face and saw a hand shaking her shoulder.

'My lady, Tamar,' the voice whispered, then turned impatient. 'Come on, child, wake up!'

Nino, it was Nino and a candle and more light at the doorway. She swung her feet to the floor, her head a groggy stew of sleep and tried to rub some sense into her eyes. Nino already had a cloak about her back and was brushing at her hair as if she wanted to rip it out.

'What are you doing? What's happening? Stop that,' Tamar growled.

'Lady, please, come quick,' called a guard's voice from the doorway.

'Sirchak, is that you? What in the name of all that's holy are you doing in my bedchamber?' She shushed Nino, who was tutting automatically at the blasphemy. 'What's wrong?'

'Qutlu is here, lady.'

'What does he want in the middle of the night?' A fearful thought struck her. 'Are we under attack?'

'No, no, lady. Qutlu is seized.'

'Seized?'

Nino was trying to shove her feet into slippers, but she squirmed free and ran out into the corridor. Sirchak hadn't been long awake either – he had buckled his sword and had boots on, but sleep still crumpled one cheek and he was wearing what she could only imagine were his underclothes. He looked delighted, not at all like a man ripped from his bed in a night emergency.

'Seized, yes. In ropes, in hall. Very, very not happy man. Come see. Is very fine picture.'

Tamar raced down the passageway, remembered that her father never ran anywhere, and settled for a fast, purposeful walk. She snapped open the spyhole on the back of the door and looked inside. The hall, normally ablaze with light and crowds, was grey and cold; only one torch lit up the strange figure at the foot of the dais.

Qutlu was half naked, his body the colour of mud. Weed and hair straggled across his face and tight cord coils bound his arms and legs. He was shaking – whether from cold or anger it was impossible to tell – and flinging commands at six guards who stood as still as if they understood not one word of what he said.

Sirchak was right. It was one of finest things she'd ever seen.

She was about to congratulate him on a classic raid – brushing aside the piqued voice in her head that said Kubaza should have told her what he was planning to do – when hurried footsteps beat down the corridor and Shota emerged from the gloom, his hair springing up like fur on the back of a street cat.

'My lady, this is madness, total and utter madness,' he panted. He was trying to talk calmly, but his voice was cracking with agitation. She had never seen him so upset. 'What the devil is Kubaza playing at?' he demanded.

Sirchak waved his hands in front of him in quick denial – and maybe to protect himself, for Shota looked ready to spring at his throat.

'Not Kubaza. He sleep, deep sleep.'

'What do you mean not Kubaza? Who the hell was it?'

Sirchak shrugged. 'Two crazy boys do it.'

'Crazy? Crazy doesn't even begin to describe—'

'Quiet, Shota,' Tamar intervened. 'Which boys, Sirchak? Where are they?'

161

'They strangers to me. My boys give them little drink,' he winked, 'warm them up. Come see.'

The sky was blueing overhead as Tamar and Shota followed Sirchak to the guardroom where the men off-watch would doze or eat or play dice. She had never been inside before, but had often watched men emerge, rubbing their chins, for their next turn on the walls, smelling of stuffy air and horse-meat.

Sirchak thumped the door and shouted something in his own rippling language. After a tiny pause, it scraped open and two men wrapped in heavy horse blankets came out into the daylight. At first all Tamar could do was stare. Sos and the Mkhargrdzeli boy stood before her, one pale, the other flushed. But before she could say anything, Shota unloosed a spectacular tirade.

'Irresponsible young fools. There was never a worse time to show off. What — did you get drunk, dare each other to do it? This is not a game! You are not boys! This is serious! Serious!'

He had run out of words, but Sos already looked mortally disappointed. Even his curls were drooping.

'Come, Shota,' she asked, conciliating. 'Is it really that bad?'

'How can you even ask? The situation is delicate. Your life — all our lives — hang in the balance. Even Nino could tell you this was a reckless, dangerous, ill-advised, idiotic piece of bravado.'

'Nino would say the same about standing barefoot in the courtyard before breakfast.'

She caught Sos's quickly hidden smile and felt absurdly pleased.

'Tamar!' Shota was practically pleading. 'You must consider the consequences. The tavads say your father ruled with too heavy a hand. They whispered, called him tyrant.'

He breathed in deeply, gradually recovering his precise, careful voice.

'And now his daughter orders one of their number, their acknowledged leader, ripped from his bed in the dead of night — trussed up — half drowned — totally humiliated.'

'But I didn't order—'

162

'They will never believe that. They will see it as the first strike in a new war. And,' he threw another furious glance at Sos, 'I cannot say I blame them.'

The wave of elation that had washed over her when she saw Qutlu brought low, in her power, ebbed away leaving muddy reality. Shota was right.

A shrill warning whistle from the western wall, immediately echoed from all sides by shouts or quick horn blasts, made them look up. A guard tumbled down the gate-tower ladder and sprinted over.

'My lady, captain, sirs, many men, men on horses, bowmen. What do we do?'

Shota flung his hands into the air.

'What do we do?' the man repeated.

Bar the gates? Man the walls? Tamar searched frantically for the right answer, but then Kubaza's voice sounded behind her.

'We bar the gates. Man the walls. And ask who dares draw their sword against the sovereign.'

He was strapped to a chair with cords bound tight around his legs and across his chest and belly. His left hand was tucked inside his cloak and his head lurched from side to side as he fought to hold it upright. His skin was grey, the whites of his eyes an alarming pink, but his voice was undeniably stronger.

'I never yet heard of a battle where the odds weren't improved by having the leader of your enemies locked in your own dungeon. These young men have forced our hand, true, but I would rather fight the wolf at the door than shrink from the snake in the bushes.'

Everything felt better. That was the power of a great general, Tamar realised. Even though Kubaza could no more wield a sword than uproot an oak tree, he made everyone who heard him feel they were giants. Even Shota looked calmer.

'As for you two,' Kubaza turned to Sos and Zak, 'I look forward to hearing the tale of how you flushed Qutlu out of his hole, but now you must clear out through the kitchen gate while there is still time.'

They started to protest, but Kubaza silenced them.

'Of course you would rather stay, but two pairs of eyes and ears in the tavads' camp will be of more use than two extra swords here. Be off with you. Now, let me see what we are up against.'

He motioned to the men carrying him and they set off towards the walls. Shota nodded after him.

'The tavads won't like it one bit when they realise he's alive. Nobody has forgotten what happened when Orbeli rose against the king. It'll make them edgy – and you two can play on that. Come on, I'll find you some clothes. You can't go back to them looking like beggarmen.'

Zak followed Shota, but as if by some unspoken agreement, Sos did not move, instead he remained awkwardly by her side. There was a small silence.

'It's been a long time,' Tamar said finally.

Sos only nodded.

'I saw you with Qutlu,' she continued. 'I thought you were one of his men. How – why did you do it? Because you could? Because you wanted to?'

He looked embarrassed and when he spoke, he was looking at his feet, not at her.

'I swore an oath before God that you would be queen.'

She was disappointed. She had wanted to hear something else.

'So did Qutlu. So did every man else. Why did you keep yours?'

He opened his mouth to answer, then evidently changed his mind and asked a question instead.

'My lady, Tamar, tell me, forget Kubaza, forget Shota, are you glad I did what I did?'

He took a step towards her. She suddenly felt aware of her thin nightgown and bare legs and discovered his hands had closed over hers. Now it was she who could not meet his eyes.

'Yesterday, at the cathedral, Qutlu told me I had no friends and I believed him. But today, this morning, even with half the kingdom ranged against me, I feel happy.'

She forced herself to look up.

'I'd rather fight with true friends, than live at peace with men who despise me.'

She watched a glow spread across his cheeks. She wanted to stand there for ever, but she tugged her hands away and chased after Kubaza.

The tavads would not have expected to find the palace fully guarded, or so Tamar hoped. Nor would they have thought to hear the Kipchak's unmistakable voice bark from behind the walls that he would turn swineherd before he handed over Qutlu – poison-monger, oath-breaker, traitorous half-man. She smiled as he added that the lady Tamar would welcome the first men of her kingdom through her gates when – and only when – they had sent their mange-bit soldiers back to the fields where they belonged. Silence. Then Gamrekeli's voice entreated Kubaza to come out, to talk face to face. The younger men catcalled, jeered, but Gamrekeli quieted them and spoke again.

'Very well. If Qutlu does not walk out of the gate – unharmed – by noon on the morrow, you will have a battle on your hands, general. One you and I both know you cannot win. And when you lose, when every one of your Kipchaks is dead, I will not answer for the women, the children inside those walls. No, nor for the lady Tamar. Think on it.'

Tamar glanced at Kubaza, but he smiled reassuringly.

'Talk, my lady, nothing more. Once you've seen a few more battles, you'll learn to ignore it.'

When Sos and Zak slunk back into the camp, they found it awash with speculation. *How had the Kipchaks got to Qutlu?* Rumours leapt from man to man like red-itching fleas. Some suggested treachery – a faithless servant, a worthless guard – but nobody was reported missing from Qutlu's household. Stranger still, the men who slept near their lord's chamber swore they'd heard no sound of a struggle, only a ghoulish sort of cry that pinned them to their beds and chilled their blood. Older men whispered to flushed boys that Kubaza knew northern magic from beyond the mountains, magic that could lift a man out of his bed, hide him in the winds and hand him over to his enemies.

Sos lapped up every word – and added a few of his own.

'We know all about Kipchaks in Osset country,' he told a ring of slack-mouthed faces. 'My grandfathers held them back for years. They sent snowslides down on our heads, talked to the wolves in their own tongue and,' he added in hushed tones, 'whistled our womenfolk clean into their beds.'

The captains tried to stamp out the stories snaking through the camp, but dark tales wriggled free, like tiny eels through clenched fists, until by nightfall even grown men were refusing to leave the safety of the sentry fires.

This would not be the quick and easy strike they'd been promised.

Chapter Twenty-three

Tamar blew out her candle long after midnight, but sleep was not waiting. She stared at the blackness in her room until she could bear it no longer and slipped down to the guardhouse. She found Sirchak sharpening his sword, small sparks cascading on to his feet, a lifetime of shooting stars. He looked up at the sound of her footfall.

'Not sleeping, Sirchak?'

'No, lady. Not good night for sleep.'

'Will you bear me company? I am sick of imagining what is beyond the walls — I would rather take a look at them.'

Sirchak did not reply, but reached up and tugged a padded jerkin off a hook and handed it to her.

'Wear this. Warm — protect against unlucky arrow. This too,' he added, holding out a metal-rimmed leather cap.

Both were several sizes too big for her, but the sense of anonymity was almost as comforting as the thick quilting. The air, still untouched by the promise of sun, chilled her face. Along the walls, about twenty paces apart, the Kipchak guards stood sentry, their heads muffled against the cold. They looked like pillars, indistinct, no shuffle, no stamp of feet.

She looked out. It was quiet enough to hear the birds starting to call up the day. The watchfires had burned to small pools of red, pulsating at her feet, blurred by invisible mist. There was a brief stir of movement as the last night watch handed over to the men who would see in the dawn, shapes passing back and forth in front of the fires as men shook out their cold, stiff joints and others took their place. The tavads would sleep still in their tents.

'Do you think they really will attack or try to starve us out?' she whispered to Sirchak.

'Hunger very slow. Too slow for them. If we do not give Qutlu today, yes, I think they attack at noon like they say.'

'And then?'

'Kubaza says they not to have Qutlu. He says we fight. That is what happen.'

Tamar waited, but he said no more. She was quiet for a moment. She found it hard – almost impossible – to believe that in a few hours the world would be unbearably awake, the sleeping air alive with screaming horses and hungry arrows. The wall where she walked would be slippery with blood. Some of the men she had passed would be dead. Maybe she would be dead. Demna's eyeless face swam before her. Might it come to that?

The palace cock crowed, exultant to be the first, answered straight away by others in the city, like the bells of a dozen churches. The grey on the eastern horizon had thinned.

'You know what Qutlu told me, Sirchak? He said you would not fight. He said you were only mercenaries.'

'Lady, please, what is mercenaries?'

'Men who fight for money – not for home.'

Sirchak sniffed a couple of times and chewed his lips. 'Home, always with Karts is this home. Home is blue sky and horses, sun and tall clouds. Home is blood too – and your blood is good to us.' The lugubrious tone vanished. 'And, remember, we like to fight. We not need your whys.'

He paused.

'Why you fight, Tamar?'

She did not need to stop to think. 'For my father's kingdom, of course.'

'Maybe that is what the Kart blood say. But you also have Kipchak blood, no? Wife of Davit, she was Kipchak. Maybe you too like to fight?'

Before she could answer, a strange sound reached their ears, a silvery sound of peace and girlhood, so unexpected, so blithe and bright that it took her a moment to place it. It was the jangle of ceremonial saddle bells. She stared, wondering if the haze or sleeplessness had confused her eyes.

A covered carriage, a shock of crimson and gold, was plunging, breakneck, through the tavads' camp. The coachman stood tall, whirling the longest whip she had ever seen above his head, crying his horses on and on, lashing blood from their backs. They were galloping, mad and snorting, as his voice and the pain drove them into a nightmare stampede. She did not know who was in the carriage – only that they placed more value on reaching the palace than they did on their lives.

'Open the gates! Open the gates!' Tamar yelled.

The carriage shot up in the air, crashed down, reeled to one side. Tamar gasped, a wheel must surely come off, but no, it was halfway through the besiegers, sending men diving out of the way. One brave soldier leapt for the reins – but they ripped through his grasp and he was tossed under the wheels. A salvo of arrows gave chase. The carriage had made the clear ground before the walls and was careering towards the gates, which were grinding open. A dozen mounted men had jumped on their horses and were gaining fast, but the driver's confidence was breathtaking. He did not check the horses but flung them at the widening gap, a handful of air between safety and splintering ruin.

They shot through. The guards grunted their shoulders into the back of the gates and slammed them shut, forcing the tavads' men to swerve their horses. Tamar watched as one lost its footing, keeled over and pitched its rider headlong into the wall, before stumbling to its feet, shaking. The man on the ground did not get up.

She raced down the ladder to the courtyard.

The coachman had stilled his horses, their coats sweat-dulled to a dirty grey, yellowish froth dripping from their mouths. He removed his turban, revealing a ridged scalp that was turning blue with stubble, and sat coiling his whip, indifferent to what lay about him.

A voice, deep-grained and sure, came from behind the brocade.

'Is this all the welcome I can expect?'

A hand swept aside the drapes.

'If so, I'll turn straight round and head back to the desert where the people at least have manners.'

A large woman, her body spreading comfortably under voluminous robes emerged, moving with difficulty. She had alarming eyebrows etched high up on her brow and dark-stained lips. Her features were hidden beneath a thick layer of some opaque, fatty ointment so her face was the colour and texture of the freshest cream, no lines, no blemishes, plump and inviting. Tamar, agog, felt a pair of brown eyes – at once sharp and limpid – travel slowly over her.

'Who are you? No, tell me not. My brother sired you, that much is plain. He is staring at me from under those quizzical little brows. But who is your mother?' she asked in a voice that never quite delivered on its promise to break into true Kart.

'My father's wife.'

She guffawed and prodded Tamar's jacket with the point of the carved stick she had grasped in one hand.

'Then you are the elder one – I know the famous beauty married into the west. But why are you dressed like a camp boy? Tis an unconscionable fashion – even under siege this is too much.'

She reached out – a cache of gold bracelets, each two fingers thick, wedged about both arms – and engulfed Tamar in a smothering embrace. She smelt sweet and tart and sticky, like perfectly ripe fruit. Tamar felt a little faint when she was finally released.

'But who – who are you?'

'Why, child, I am your father's sister. I am your aunt Rusudan.'

Rusudan insisted on bathing before talking, saying her mind would serve them poorly unless it had been submerged in scalding water; that riled Tamar, who could not believe anyone cared that much about being clean. Then, with a bare two hours until noon, Rusudan waddled into the king's chamber, sat down and ordered – *ordered* – Kubaza to tell her what was going on.

The Kipchak scarcely looked at Tamar as he gave an account

of everything that had happened since the king's death. Her aunt's eyes narrowed all the while he spoke and she started to shake her head very, very slowly, scratching at the floor between her feet with her stick. When Kubaza finished, she asked in a voice of undiluted vinegar whether that was the best plan they could come up with.

'We must take control of the kingdom, or lose it for ever. That is what Kubaza thinks – and I agree with him,' Tamar said firmly.

'You think an afternoon's swordplay will solve your problems?' Rusudan asked. 'Child, you are dreaming.'

'Don't call me child,' Tamar growled.

'No? And what should I call you?' Rusudan asked. 'Sir? Your majesty?' She chuckled comfortably. 'That would be most precipitous.'

Tamar leapt to her feet.

'What would you have me do? Give up? Put on sackcloth and beg for mercy? I am no coward.'

She glowered at Rusudan, but her aunt was immune to that flat, black stare. Instead it acted on her like a tonic. She beamed.

'My dear, now I feel quite home-like again. Your father used to beetle his brows at me in just the same way when he was out of sorts. Quite unnerving.'

'And my father would fight.'

'Yes. When Giorgi and Kubaza were at the height of their powers they would have fought and they might have won. But your father is dead and Kubaza – forgive me – is little better. You might win this day. You might survive till the next moon, till the season's turn – but in the end you will lose.'

She dragged herself to her feet and advanced on Tamar.

'Do you think your enemies about your borders will watch like indulgent parents while you squabble? Rumours already stalk the roads. Panic and strife shadow your lands. Do you not know what happens when Kart fights Kart? Turkomen swoop from the east. Seljuk jackals harry from the south. And in the west, the lion in Constantinople flicks his tail. You are already a tempting dish. Why season your lands with civil war? Would you have the Seljuks come here and plunder?'

She crashed her stick on the floor.

'Rape?'

Crash.

'Kill?'

Crash.

Her voice dropped and she spoke kindly, wearily.

'Child, you think being king is about destroying your enemies – or dying brave and bold in the attempt. That is the mistake many men make, but they are wrong. Being king is about preserving your kingdom. So, I beg you, make peace. Some things you must needs concede, yes, but it will be better than plunging this land – the land I have loved and longed for these thirty years – into wilful ruin.'

Her aunt's words slowly leached the dreadful certainty of battle from Tamar's limbs, and her spirits sank. She looked to Kubaza. Surely the Kipchak would argue for all-out war? But he shook his head.

'Rusudan is right – and not for the first time. Tamar, my lady, forgive me. A dying man is maybe too eager for peril. He knows he will not live long enough to reap what he has sowed.'

A look of great sorrow swept across his face as if an east wind had torn the last leaves from the branches of a great tree, leaving it bare and black against the sky. Tamar wanted to reach out, touch his arm, but she stopped herself in time. He was better than her pity.

'Aunt, you say *make peace*. Will it be that easy?'

'For you, maybe not, but it is different for me. I have known those men since they were boys, younger than you. They will not have forgotten me.'

'Thank God you're here. But, tell me, how did you know to come now?'

Rusudan reached down and plucked a parchment roll from somewhere deep in her bosom.

'I had word. Read this.'

Tamar walked over to where sunlight streamed through the window and unrolled a message in her father's hand.

To my much-honoured sister. Greetings. I wake and know not where I am. I fear to sleep for fear I do wake not again. Forgive the past. Come home. You will find me gone. Help my daughter. I send this now before darkness returns. Your brother, who always loved you.

Tamar gripped the letter as tight as if she held her father's hand in hers and stayed staring out the window. She heard a rustle behind her and then her aunt was at her side, stroking her hair and rubbing her back like Nino used to do.

'Together we shall make him proud. I swear it.'

Chapter Twenty-four

The tent was crammed with men shouting, jabbing fingers and flinging their hands in the air. It was hard to work out what anyone wanted since any pretence of discussion had collapsed into dirty name-calling. Gamrekeli stood in the centre, demanding silence, but he did not have the strength to swim against the roaring tide of hot blood. It would take very little for this to tip into an out-and-out brawl.

'To hell with this. I don't give a damn if Kubaza is alive or dead. We should storm the palace.' That was Vardan.

'Storm? How d'you storm walls that high without siege engines? Shows you've never fought in a real war,' Zak shouted, giving Sos a wink.

'Neither've you, coward,' Con spluttered and lunged for Zak. Zak went down, dragging Con after him and Sos jumped on top, not minding that he was soon buried in a mess of fists and elbows.

A blast of trumpets from the direction of the palace restored order. Everyone crowded to the door of the tent and watched as a lone figure emerged from the gates on foot.

'Who is it?'

'Qutlu?'

'No, no, can you not see?'

'Some old woman . . .'

Sos was as puzzled as the rest as the strange envoy sailed into the tent. She looked about her, unabashed and unimpressed, like a nurse inspecting a group of filthy children.

'You gentlemen may be happy standing, but I need a chair. Boy,' she snapped at Vardan, 'would you leave your grandmother standing about in this manner?' She paused. 'Still less the grand-daughter of Davit?'

Half a dozen of the older men laughed or gasped in recognition.

'The princess Rusudan?'

'Good God!'

'Vardan, for pity's sake, get the lady something to sit on,' Gamrekeli ordered, a sudden smile lighting his lined face.

'I see you're a good man still, Gamrekeli. I am surprised to find you mixed up in this.' She might as well have chucked him under the chin.

The chair arrived and Rusudan settled herself down and held up her hand for silence.

'The boys amongst you are too young to know me – let me enlighten you. They call me Rusudan. I am sister to Giorgi, aunt to Tamar. I have outlived two husbands, great men whose kingdoms lay far beyond the borders of these lands. Now I am come to end this foolishness, and I will not – as those of you witnessed my arrival this morning will agree – be trifled with. Now, gentlemen, did you not swear before God that Tamar would rule upon my brother's death? And we are famed, are we not, as a God-fearing nation? Why then do I return home to find you running amok atop the palace doorstep?'

Everyone spoke at once.

'A girl—'

'Qutlu said—'

'Tyranny—'

'Tyranny?' Rusudan brandished her stick as if beating back a swarm of bats in a cave. 'Where is this tyranny? Tyrannised men do not behave as you do, serried before their sovereign's gates.' The stick traced a thoughtful circle before her. 'Ah! It was my brother who was a tyrant, you would say? But death has already conquered him. Death, I repeat, gentlemen, not you. Defeating his daughter – a girl, a defenceless girl – would be a pitiful recompense, would it not?'

'Tamar is not defenceless, Rusudan,' replied Gamrekeli. 'She has the backing of Kubaza and his band of Kipchaks.'

'Is that all that troubles you? What if he stands aside? Removes

175

himself from court? From the city itself? What if you could appoint a new commander? What then, gentlemen?'

The tavads looked stunned – stunned and delighted.

'You speak for Tamar?' Gamrekeli looked doubtful.

Rusudan did not reply. One firm nod, that was all. Only Sos and Zak knew how small a concession it really was.

'I see a new generation before me,' she continued. 'A collection of fine, proud young men. The sort of men who fought beside Davit at Didgori. The sort who can kill a Seljuk or two.'

She ran her eyes around the tent.

'Young men, tell me, were you honestly content to play sergeant to Qutlu's ambitions? Who is Qutlu, after all? What has he done to deserve your devotion? He promised you he would remove the king's yoke from your shoulders, did he not? But he was fashioning one of his own to replace it. He was planning to rule you all through Tamar. You wish to bend your knee to him? Raise him up as king? Is that what you wanted? Is that what you want?'

Sos had to shake his head to clear it. Her voice was captivating. She had the same power as the old king, but while Giorgi's words had landed like blows, hers drifted about a man's ears like a caress. Sos wondered what she'd been like when she was young. The older men's rapt faces suggested they all shared some vivid memories.

'No man here wants Qutlu as king,' said Gamrekeli.

'But you need a king, do you not, my lords?' she answered quickly. 'But who? There is not a man alive with Davit's blood in his veins. But there is Tamar.'

She struck an attitude of profoundest contemplation.

'It is strange, is it not, that Tamar is unwed? She needs a husband – a consort – a man to sit by her side. That man must be strong and courageous, well born and well respected. He would have to be. That man would become the most powerful man in the kingdom. Not a king, no, not quite. He would not rule in his own name – but his son . . .'

Sos frowned to himself as she let the idea dangle over their heads. He'd never thought about Tamar with a husband. What had happened in the hours since he'd last seen her? She hadn't been husband-hunting then.

The atmosphere was changing fast. Vardan – who had been trying to look tough and menacing – was now smoothing out his hair. And he wasn't the only one. Older men were eyeing their sons or nephews appreciatively, while the sons and nephews looked self-consciously regal. Temptation was the devil's oldest trick. And it was working.

'Come gentlemen,' Gamrekeli intervened, 'let us discuss this in private. If you will excuse us, my lady?'

'You would send an old woman to shiver in the cold while you talk?'

It was a mild, dry day and Rusudan was swathed in a black wrap big enough to keep a family of bears warm in winter. Gamrekeli arched one eyebrow.

'Cold?'

Rusudan coughed. 'I am used to the climate of the desert cities. If we are to forgo small matters of courtesy, then we really are doomed.'

Gamrekeli touched his thumb and forefinger to his temples and rubbed his eyes.

'Ah, Rusudan, dear Rusudan. I see the years have not mellowed you. Follow me, my lords. We shall talk outside.'

Tamar was waiting at the gate as her aunt returned amid the cheers of hundreds of men, all overjoyed that they would live to see their families once more.

'Well?'

Rusudan nodded. 'It is as I said.'

'You mean they have backed down? They will put up their swords?'

'As I said they would.'

'You are a marvel. A wonder. How did you know it would turn out so well?' she asked.

'I didn't.'

177

'But you were so certain.'

'Sometimes certainty is enough. The rest follows. I learned that from your father. And sometimes men long to be pulled back from the brink. That I learned from being sister to two brothers.'

The gates closed behind them.

'What,' asked Tamar, 'do they ask in return?'

'Nothing that is not easy to give.'

'But what?'

'Kubaza must leave Tbilisi and swear never again to bear arms – or his life shall be forfeit.'

'But he was my father's right hand. He is my friend. He—'

'A queen must be flexible in her choice of friends, my dear. They are willing to be flexible with Qutlu.'

'You mean . . .'

'Yes. Qutlu always was very persuasive, but love, trust, loyalty – those things he never understood. We can dispatch him without delay.'

'Dispatch? We're going to kill him?'

'I hope so. Does the idea agitate you? You won't last long if you're squeamish.'

Tamar had wished Qutlu dead often enough, but now he was in her power, she found she had no desire to kill him.

'I am not squeamish, but I want no unnecessary slaughter.'

'But this is necessary, believe me. Very necessary.'

'So that's it? Kubaza's banishment in exchange for Qutlu's death?'

Rusudan shook her head. 'Not quite. There is one more thing. After a suitable period of mourning, they will propose a candidate. You will swear an oath on your father's memory not to gainsay them.'

'A candidate? The commander to succeed Kubaza?'

Rusudan walked a few steps in silence.

'No, child, you misunderstand me. They choose the man who is to be your husband.'

Tamar stopped as suddenly as if an unseen enemy had sliced a sharp blade across the backs of her knees.

'My what?'

'Your husband. They will choose who you are to marry.'

Tamar's heart was pounding.

'We never discussed that. I will never agree to that. And I shall tell them so now.'

She spun round and would have marched out of the gates and into the tavads' camp, but her aunt's plump, white fingers closed round her wrist in a grip that would have choked the life out of a goose.

'Tamar, I was not under the impression you were a fool, so don't behave like one.'

'Nor am I something to haggle over. What if I don't like the man they choose?'

'That, as you should know, is irrelevant.'

'My father would never—'

'Your father indulged you, that much is plain. Do you think I wanted to marry either of my husbands? No. Did your sister want to marry Andronikos's boy? Come now, did she?'

'That's different.'

'Different why? Different how? She had no choice. And nor do you – not if you value your kingdom. Do you want to give up the throne? Is that what you want?'

Now it was her aunt who took a few steps back to the camp.

'Is that what you want?' she repeated.

Tamar shook her head.

'Good,' said her aunt. 'I thought I had perhaps misunderstood you.'

Chapter Twenty-five

Sos and Zak let their horses breathe and nibble the small shoots on the scrubby, snowless pass that marked the boundary between the east and west kingdoms. The wind swirled about them while they shaded their eyes and gazed north to where the slopes of the Kavkaz were swathed in grey cloud. Here and there a sharp, white peak jutted free and caught the morning sun.

'Hope it's not too wet at home,' Sos said.

'What word since you left?' Zak asked.

'All alive, all well. My mother's thankful there's to be no war and tells me I'm to remember to eat. My sisters ask for handsome husbands. And the steward has a fair litany of complaints, so that means he's happy as a pig in new straw.'

Zak grinned. 'Sounds about right.'

And they clicked their horses on again, jogging side by side at the rear of the sprawling, colourful train that was following the queen down into the woodlands of the west, the great hunting grounds of the Rioni plain. It was summer, a time of long evenings and lazy pleasures, time too for the queen and her court to unbend after the feverish days of spring.

The little mountain streams no longer ran wild, the cloudy, thick-brown of mud and meltwater, but bubbled bright and clear. Splashes of rainbows flashed into life where the current sprang over rocks, scattering water into the steepening shafts of sunlight. Fat bees skipped between the knee-high flowers that fought for space under the ancient trees, while the tiny beech leaves twisted and spun in the breeze like rags on a scarecrow.

'It makes you sick, doesn't it?' Sos ventured at last, ducking under a low bough that hung across their path.

'What does?'

'All this.'

'An easy ride on a sunny day?'

'No, the way they all hop about her.'

In the middle distance a shifting swarm of young and not-so-young men stuck close to a rider on a yellow horse.

'Who . . . oh, the queen, you mean?'

'Yes. Doesn't it make you sick?'

Zak considered. 'No,' he said. 'No, not really. It's what you'd expect.'

'But the moon's barely turned twice since they were baying for her blood and now they're bouncing up and down like frogs on heat. They look like morons.'

'They are morons,' said Zak, 'but practical morons. Don't forget there's a kingdom in it.' He leant over and nudged Sos hard in the ribs with his elbow. 'Why not join in? Her father married an Osset after all.'

'Very funny,' said Sos. 'We all know how well that turned out.'

Zak made a fair-enough face.

'Anyway,' Sos continued, 'I don't see you up there in your best tunic. Your chances must be at least a thousand times better than mine. Look at you. The son of our exalted commander-in-chief.'

Zak beamed. His father, Sargis Mkhargrdzeli, had been the tavads' unanimous choice to follow Kubaza as amir-spaslari and Sos liked to watch his friend try to pretend he wasn't still aching with pride whenever it was mentioned.

'Well, yes, Sos, there is that, but come on, you know me, I don't really have a best tunic. And I'm the youngest. And . . .' but he didn't finish.

'Go on. And what?'

Zak screwed up his face. 'Tell you the truth, I find her a bit, well, a bit much.'

'A bit much?'

'I couldn't feel easy with a wife who kept a dagger about her,' Zak said in a rush.

That cheered Sos up. He laughed so hard he nearly fell off his horse.

'Laugh all you like, my friend. Women,' said Zak, adopting a worldly air, 'are trouble. And well-born women are worse.'

'What about queens?'

Zak bulged his eyes, stuck his tongue out and pretended to strangle himself, making Sos laugh even more.

'We're sensible men, Sos. If we ever meet girls we want to marry, we'll strap on our swords and go and ask their fathers – and if they say no, we'll take them anyway. I say we leave the queen to Vardan and the rest of them.'

'All right, let's,' Sos agreed quickly. 'After all, who wants to be the only man in the kingdom worth less than his wife?'

But, unbidden, his thoughts floated downhill towards the red figure bobbing astride her horse. The long, full skirts of her gold-edged robes let her sit like a man, one leg gripping each flank. She looked good, natural, as if she was in control.

Sos shifted uneasily in his saddle and asked himself exactly who he was trying to fool – Zak or himself?

Despite the beautiful weather, Tamar's temper was souring faster than a noonday pitcher of cream. They were trying so hard it made her neck ache: her father would never have made her put up with it. He had boiled over fast when some of the tavads had tentatively suggested that the time was ripe for her to wed.

Don't be absurd! I don't want a hungry husband prowling about my palace scheming to poison my stew. And we can't have Tamar thick with child, her head full of mother love and backache and the Virgin only knows what else. Time for all that later.

Nobody had dared mention it again. He even used to joke with her over the exploratory letters that arrived from supposedly lovelorn neighbours. He'd read them out, putting on accents if he was in an especially good mood.

Impudent pups. Listen to this. Most honoured Giorgi, sovereign of the seven kingdoms, bright sun of . . . for the love of God get to the point . . . ebullient health . . . dove of peace . . . ah, here, we go . . . The wings of dawn carry tidings to our humble lands of the fair beauty of your thrice-honoured daughter Tamar, scion of your glorious and of-Jesus-so-beloved house. We do humbly beg audience with her who outshines the dewdrops of morning-tide and herewith admit of our desire to meekly swear our tall and true love before her so-dainty feet.

Tamar grinned: *so-dainty* – that had made them laugh.

Suddenly, Vardan's face swam into focus. Lost in her thoughts she had been looking at him without meaning to and his face had resolved itself into a pleasant, becoming smile, one eyebrow up to ask how he could serve his lady. He was everything that was courteous, limber, with a handsome aquiline nose, but she could not warm to him. She smiled, shook her head a little – and did not let his pale eyes hold hers. Even so, she could not miss the pleased flare of his nostrils and the conscious lift of his chin. He actually thought he was beguiling her.

She heard a cough behind her and saw Vardan's sidekick, Con. He was trying to hold his untidy face in a gentle smile, but the result was midway between a simper and a snarl. Clasped between his knuckles were three tiny, purple flowers. She bit her lips and held out her hand to take them.

'Constantine, that was very thoughtful of you,' she said with all due gravity and threaded them into her horse's mane.

'Saw them back on the crest, milady,' he blushed. 'Rare . . . um . . . beauty.'

He trotted next to her, searching for his next gambit. She did not feel inclined to help.

In a grove up ahead the servants had arranged rugs and sheepskins and shade now that the sun was high. The company halted to eat and wait out the middle of the day. The men hovered, waiting to see where Tamar sat, not wanting to commit themselves before she did. Vardan was bolder.

'My lady, do me the honour.'

He handed her down to a clump of cushions and snapped his fingers for orange water. The others swooped like starlings and she found herself surrounded once more. None of them talked to her properly. They talked at her, near her, around her, above her, below her, but not one of them looked her in the face. At the edge of the group, Sos lay on his front, stripping leaves off a twig, while Zak dozed on his back beside him, drying off after a dip in the stream beyond the trees. They looked cheerful and refreshed. She sighed, restless and resentful.

Vardan – ever alert – jumped to his feet.

'Come, we have no musicians, so we must make our own entertainment. I propose a battle of words, of wits if you will, to accompany our wine – who can propose the finest toast in praise of the beauty of our lady Tamar?'

The girls laughed in jealous delight. The men whooped and emptied their glasses. Con turned a little green and Zak, suddenly awake, slunk away from the circle to check on his horse.

'My lady,' Vardan turned to her, 'will it please you to confer some token of honour on he who pleases you most? Perhaps you shall permit him to sit by your side when we feast at Geguti?'

Tamar jutted her jaw and wished Vardan – and the rest of them – to hell. No man whose job wasn't to invent pretty words would call her beautiful. The noble boys of Tbilisi had never sighed over her until they realised she would rule them all. Fine words would dance too close to mockery, but there was nothing she could do. Vardan was practising good court manners, longer established than the trees overhead. It would be rude, impossible, to tell them to keep quiet so she could close her eyes and savour the blue sky on her face. Instead she inclined her head.

'Begin, gentlemen.'

A harmless boy called Toma had jumped to his feet and was hacking through a wild thicket of words that promised to compare her to a nightingale if he ever found his way to the end. It was pitiful stuff, but he'd been bold enough to go first, so his audience was gentle and he sat down to applause and slaps on his back.

And so it went on. Her face bedazzled the morning star, her eyes cast shame on sixty colours, her sweet voice stilled the tempest, her hair outdid the midnight waterfall. She squirmed and stared about her, wishing some of the older men were journeying with them – she could not imagine that the lord Mkhargrdzeli or even Gamrekeli would have much time for

184

impromptu verses. Her aunt had arranged herself a little outside the circle and Tamar tried to catch her eye, seeking a way out or at least some sympathy, but Rusudan offered nothing but a bland and benevolent smile.

Vardan was talking again. 'Let us hear from our Osset friend. We'd love to hear one of the lord Soslani's pastoral verses, wouldn't we, friends? How do your shepherds mark their admiration for their mountain maidens?'

'With deeds not words, plainsman.'

The group in the grove lapped that up. The girls' hands flew to their mouths and the men thumped the ground with their fists, hooting.

'But, my lord,' Vardan replied, 'it's too hot for great deeds. You must indulge us – play our games.'

'Go on, Sos—'

'Let's have a line—'

'Don't be shy!'

Sos did not look shy – unlike some of the men who had refused to take part – but he stood his ground.

'No, no, my lords and ladies, I am a simple man. I do not understand the rules.'

Tamar's head felt light and she knew she wanted him to speak.

'But my lord Soslani, it's very easy, I promise. All you need to do is compare me to a bird, a flower, I am sure anything of that sort will do.'

Everyone laughed. Everyone except Sos.

'Very well, if you will.' He looked her full in the eyes, a grave smile on his face. 'But my lady must promise to forgive a mountain farmer's clumsy way with words.'

He stood for a moment, head down, arms folded, then he looked up and spoke straight to her.

'You are like to a panther on the edge of a rock, its face flashing fury.'

He understood. For the first time in her life, the wild roar in her head had nothing to do with anger. Vardan stepped forward to deliver his own tribute. No doubt it was brilliant. But Tamar, although she saw his well-wrought lips moving, heard not a word.

Three nights later there was feasting in the courtyard at the great hunting lodge of Geguti. Six chestnut trees ringed the walls, forming a canopy that rippled back and forth in the night breezes that rolled down from the hills. Servants had shinned up the trunks and edged out along the branches to scatter the candles that now danced overhead, while a great fire in the middle of the ring of tables painted faces orange and black.

'Why are they staring at me, aunt?'

'You look well, my dear. The firelight, the forest – they become you. No, do not look doubtful. Enjoy their admiration. Men will look at you otherwise once you are wed. Come, they are waiting for you to choose your companion for the evening. Let me see. Vardan expects you to name him and I believe that would—'

Tamar turned her back before Rusudan could finish. She knew who she wanted and she was at his side before prudence – or her aunt – could make her change her mind.

'Will you honour me with your company, my lord?'

She did not wait to see Sos's reaction – or anyone else's – but settled herself in her chair and smiled a thank-you at the servant who poured her wine. She felt rather than saw him seat himself beside her.

'Again you are victorious, my lord.' It had been an effort to make herself turn to face him, but she was pleased with how calm her voice sounded. 'You are as skilled with words as you are with your bow.'

He laughed. 'I was worried I'd offended you. You gave me such a strange look after I spoke that I thought – well, I thought that perhaps I should have stuck to flowers after all.'

'No. Men make too much of flowers. And you were right – I was furious.'

'But why? You are the crowned queen of these lands. The tavads make no trouble.' He paused. 'And all men pay you suit.'

186

'Not all men.' Her glass was halfway to her lips. She fixed her eyes on his. 'Not you.'

He shook his head. 'No. Not me.'

'Why not? I am a great prize. You have no desire to win?'

'The odds are stacked too high against me.'

She was silent for a moment.

'I had thought you would be too bold to play the odds.'

'Do you wish me to be bold?'

The question was so direct that at first she could not answer.

He stood up. 'Do you?' he repeated.

'I do.'

He slipped from her side, and with a little lurch Tamar realised that everyone else had fallen silent. The tamada was on his feet, his glass raised, waiting for her attention before delivering the first toast. She swallowed and nodded her head for him to begin, uncomfortably aware that every eye must have been on her — and Sos.

The tamada's words boomed above the throng, as familiar as prayers whispered before sleep. Toasts to holy places in the hills, Saint Nino who brought them faith, Saint Giorgi who gave them strength, Davit who made them one, the good men who had died, the good women yet to be born. The men tossed back wine in great gulps, biting into tart greens and charred mutton, white teeth set in dark faces.

The wind began to blow harder, in confused circles, like a dog chasing its tail, buffeting the fire, punching it high, then flattening it. A stronger gust drove it hard to one side, making it roar like a fire monster, and for a moment she saw Sos laughing hard at some joke at the far end of the courtyard. Then the flames swept back and he was gone. The heat was making her dizzy, but the night air set her shivering.

The wind was driving the trees wild, their twigs scrabbling at the empty air, the leaves hissing. The tamada had to shout louder and louder to make himself heard. People spilled from the benches, coiled into new groups or vanished into the gloom under the trees. Tamar tried to concentrate on the string of young lords who surrounded her, talking, joking, jockeying. Then a quarrel broke out between two men, a table was upended, plates smashing to the ground. She saw a flash of dagger, one leapt for the other's throat, but missed and pitched forwards and a morass of people fell on them to rip them apart. No one was hurt. Hoots of laughter and her aunt marched over to adjudicate.

Tamar stood up and walked out of the noisy ring of light. She wanted to fill her lungs with clean air, clear the smoke from her eyes and the wine from her head. She ran to the steep, crumbling steps that led up on to the walls. Up there, she could feel the full force of the wind in her face, a real gale rising up off the sea, and she could breathe again.

She didn't hear him come, but suddenly she knew somebody was beside her. She whipped round and there he was, a dark shape in the darkness, then she reached up and he reached down and she felt his fingers running through her hair and her hands were on the warmth of his neck and he pulled her in tight and he was shaking and she realised she was too and she tried to speak but her throat was too dry.

Then their mouths found each other.

'Tamar!' A voice drifted up from the ground. 'Tamar!' Louder, more insistent.

She looked down and saw her aunt silhouetted by the fire.

'My aunt,' she whispered. 'I must go.'

She turned, but he found her arm and pulled her back and kissed her again, harder.

'Tamar!'

Her aunt was at the bottom of the steps. She had to go. She tore herself away and scrambled down.

'I'm here, I'm here. What's the matter?'

'What on earth were you doing up there?'

'Nothing, aunt, nothing. At least, I wanted some air. The wine—'

'Did that young man need air as well?'

Although the midsummer night was waning, it was too dark

to make out the expression on her face, but her words were drier than the dust that spiralled about them.

'Which young man, aunt? There are so very many. All drinking. All no doubt in need of air. Now – let me pass.'

She stepped round her and hurried indoors without looking back. The servants had readied her chamber for what remained of the night. Stones baked in the red-hot kitchen embers had been wrapped in wool and tucked under the bedclothes. A bowl of milk stood by the low fire.

A maid called Mzia was waiting with a hairbrush and a basin of mustard-water. She stood up uncertainly when Tamar came in, her arms bolted to her sides, her toes squirming in her slippers. She was new, little more than a child.

'I'll see to myself, thank you, Mzia. You go to bed.'

'Yes m'lady thank you m'lady,' she spoke fast, swallowing the words, then bobbed and scuttled out of the room.

Tamar sat down, took a sip of her milk, winced and put it aside to cool.

He kissed me.

A delicious smile licked up the side of her face.

Chapter Twenty-six

Whenever she shut her eyes, his face pounced and her insides wound tighter and tighter, a sweet and unbearable sensation. It alarmed – and excited – her how much she thought about him. The deep red-brown, like the very best soil, that glowed through his curls when the sun shone. The lighter-coloured hairs, so many snippets of golden thread, on the backs of his brown fore-arms. The lines that sprang to life around his mouth when he smiled. The downward sweep of his black eyelashes . . . a voice intruded and Sos vanished.

'My lady? I have the inescapable impression that my ledgers are failing to hold your interest as they were wont to do.'

'I'm sorry, Shota.'

'Should I perhaps embellish them a little? Recite them in quat-rains? Set them to the music of the harp?'

'Have pity. Am I not normally your most assiduous student?'

At that he smiled and nodded.

'That you are. I am sure your father never had so good a grasp of matters of money when he was your age – or maybe at any age. He thought them dull and did not scruple to show it. You at least have feigned a convincing – and flattering – interest.'

'I cannot squander merry hours hunting, sword-fighting and carousing. I must busy myself somehow,' said Tamar, more pleased than she was willing to show.

'And the guildsmen, the merchants, the churchmen, they all appreciate it.'

He shuffled a pile of documents together and stacked them carefully on one side of his desk.

'But,' he continued, shifting his tone emphatically, 'that makes your inattention the more surprising. You are here in body,

Tamar, that I cannot deny, but your mind appears to have strayed to pleasanter pastures. I admit that remodelling the tariff scale for the metalworkers of the city does not provide the same thrill as quashing bloody rebellion at your own gates—'

'Thrilling? I never—'

A sidelong look from Shota made her twist her mouth closed. It had been thrilling.

'—but we must take advantage of peace. Your father spent – I am tempted to say wasted – most of his prime trying to batter down the gates of Ani, mired in one battle after another. But there is so much else that we can do.'

'Roads and bridges, Shota, roads and bridges,' Tamar intervened. 'I know, I know – and I am as faithful to this vision as you are. Secure our borders,' she said as if reciting a well-worn prayer, 'and make travel safe. Bring trade to Tbilisi and our treasury will prosper. Thinkers and craftsmen will follow. Beauty and wisdom will take root and the glory of my kingdom will grow,' she finished. 'We think alike in this – I do not want endless rounds of campaigning in which I can play no part.'

She paused, reflective.

'But many of the tavads think otherwise. Battle-love seeps into their blood with their mothers' milk. They need a king, a fighting man. I am not enough for them.'

Both were still for a few moments. Shota pulled a new stack of papers towards him and started scratching with his quill, moving figures from one column to another.

'How are your matrimonial prospects, Tamar?' he asked, without looking up.

'I am spoilt for choice. I have driven every bachelor between the two seas into a frenzy of passion. Or so they would have me believe.'

'Show a little compassion, my lady, love has a powerful effect on young men.'

'Love,' Tamar snorted. 'If the pox had stolen away my nose, they'd still be in raptures over my beauty. You know what they love.'

'Thrones are lovable,' Shota agreed. 'Whoever sits on them.'

Tamar pictured her arms and legs fusing with the wood of a great chair until her whole body disappeared . . . She shuddered and stood up. It might be easier to say what she wanted with a little distance between them.

'The tavads have yet to choose my husband. I am a big prize and they are quarrelling too much amongst themselves to decide. But I have a good idea. At least, I think it's a good idea.' That was a feeble beginning – not at all how she meant to sound. She firmed up her voice. 'I would be grateful, Shota, if you would give me your opinion.'

Shota pushed his papers away and looked her full in the face. 'An idea, you say.'

She flushed. Saying his name out loud was not as easy as she had hoped. But if she was going to propose what she had in mind to her aunt, let alone to the tavads, she would have to persevere. *Would not the lord Soslani be a fitting match?* No, the words refused to come. She would approach from a different angle.

'How was my mother chosen for my father?'

'He chose her. He willed it.'

'He married for love, you mean.'

'Some would say that. Some did say that. But many more said that he married foolishly, selfishly. In my experience, it often comes to the same thing.'

'You have a hard heart, Shota.'

'No, Tamar, you cannot accuse me of that. My head is hard, but my heart is soft as butter. But that is my privilege because I am a steward, not a king. Or a queen.' He looked hard at her. 'But this is the past. What of the present?'

'Would not the lord Soslani be a fitting match?'

She'd said it. Shota's face did not move.

'Have you spoken of this to any man?'

She shook her head.

'To your aunt?'

'No, Shota. I came to you first.'

'And you want my advice?'

'Of course. That's what I said.'

'Often people do not want to be told what they do not want to hear. The teller then regrets his honesty.'

'That you shall never regret, Shota.'

'Very well. Then hear me. Never mention his name again. That is my counsel.'

Tamar paled. 'Why? He is well born and well thought of. He is close to the Mkhargrdzeli family. He is a good fighter.'

She had arranged the arguments like kindling inside her head, cosseting them until they blazed consolingly. Shota doused them fast.

'The same would apply to a dozen young men. Why him? Why not Vardan? Why not Zakari for that matter?'

'Because . . . because I like him. Because I would rather have him than Vardan or Zakari. Is that not reason enough?'

'No.'

'No?'

'No, it is not and you know it. You know it because you kept this idea secret. You know it because you told me first, in private. You know it because you are standing there, waiting for me to dissuade you.'

Tamar was about to protest, but he cut her off.

'Don't deny it. Listen, let us say you and young Sos love one another—'

'I never said—'

'No matter. Say you did. Say you propose him as a husband. What would happen if the tavads refused even to consider him?'

'I would look weak,' she replied, reluctant.

'Weak and foolish. And what if you demanded him as your consort? Swore you would take no man else? Worse – what if they agreed?'

Suddenly, Tamar resented Shota's patient good sense, and she answered childishly.

'I don't know, Shota. You tell me.'

'Yes, you do know.'

'No, I don't. I have to live this. I can't watch from a distance and reckon it all up on a counting frame.'

But Shota was not to be provoked.

'Very well, my lady, I shall tell you myself. Sos is brave and true. I would be happy to swear that no man has a better heart. And he has promise. But he is still more than half a boy. Were he ten years, fifteen years older, scarred from a dozen campaigns, wise after years of court manoeuvres, then it might be different. But if you wed him now, you sign his death warrant. Maybe yours as well.'

'You exaggerate.'

'Believe that if you will, but such a marriage could not last long. He would have too many enemies, too many powerful men, bitter and resentful, determined to depose him. And you, my lady, are not yet strong enough to protect him. He would be killed. And his killers would toss his body into the river and throw his head to the pigs. Is that what you want?'

The bell tolled for the guards' evening meal. Tamar spoke into the silence that followed.

'There has already been talk of this . . . of Sos? About the court?'

'Yes, Tamar. A little. Maybe more than a little. You showed him too much distinction at Geguti – and you still do.'

Tamar closed her eyes. The warm sun, enticing, a little soporific, that she had felt was shining on her, vanished.

Chapter Twenty-seven

'Gentlemen, I admit I am sore disappointed.'

Sargis and Gamrekeli looked up sharply and Tamar smiled to herself. Whatever they had been expecting when she summoned them, it was not a scolding.

'You had undertaken to procure a suitable husband for me,' she continued, allowing her voice to wax stern.

'My lady, we—' Gamrekeli spoke up first, but she rode over him.

'No, no apologies, no explanations. You have erred, but I forgive you. I tire, however, of being the target for so much speculation. It is as undignified, my lords, as it is dangerous. This waiting must cease.'

Tamar thought she saw an amused light flicker in her aunt's eyes, but Rusudan dropped her gaze before she could be sure.

'There is an unseemly glut of foreign princes in Tbilisi,' she continued. 'Some, I am sure, are genuine suitors, but too many are mingling their lovemaking with a little spying. The tavads and their sons also need something else to occupy their minds. There is too much uncertainty. And uncertainty, my lords, is dangerous.'

Gamrekeli had placed his hands together under his chin and was nodding attentively. Sargis was scratching his beard.

'What is more,' and here she allowed herself a small smile, 'Nino is grievously under-occupied. She nags, gentlemen. We must put a great-great-grandson of Davit in the crib if she is ever to grant me a moment's peace.'

They laughed – and she didn't care whether it was only from politeness. She was pleased with her speech, carefully prepared and casually delivered, and even more pleased with its effect.

'We thought you had your own ideas about who you would wed,' Sargis said, looking her square in the eye.

'Did you? What on earth made you think that?' she returned, bright and even.

She could almost see the possible replies roving across the general's face as he searched, helpless, for an answer. He was no diplomat and immediately she liked him better for it.

'What my lord Mkhargrdzeli means,' Gamrekeli intervened smoothly, 'is that we were waiting only for an auspicious moment to consult you before submitting a candidate for your approval.'

Sargis shot him a glance that was both grateful and disdainful.

'I am relieved to hear that you have not been idle. So, consult me. I am, as you see, quite at leisure.'

Sargis nodded. 'Many wanted to place Vardan at your side—'

'He's a conceited—'

'Yes, I said you'd have none of him. And you'd be right. Rich, for sure, a good age, high-born, a fair fighter, he is all that, but—'

'—but it would be gross foolishness to choose a husband from within the seven kingdoms,' Tamar finished for him. 'The tavads need a man they can unite behind. A man with no roots here. No ties. A man who owns everything and yet nothing. An outsider, in fact,' she added with a smile – which Sargis returned warmly.

The Mkhargrdzeli family were relative newcomers, their blood a mishmash drawn from the deep well of lands that stretched south and west from the Kart kingdom. They even professed the Armenian faith. Vardan and his cabal doubtless looked down on Sargis, resenting his position, but they weren't foolish enough to contest it.

'My thoughts precisely, my lady,' Sargis said, his face approximating approval for the first time she could remember.

Gamrekeli, who she suspected might have been open to an unimaginative choice such as Vardan, clearly felt he was not saying enough and broke in piously.

'Your husband must be of our faith—'

Tamar nodded. 'Of course. Although, please spare me one of those hairy, man-eating Franks we hear so much about.'

'My lady, we'd never—' Gamrekeli began.

'She's joking, man,' Sargis said.

'Ah, yes, of course. Davit's Kipchak bride was a wise choice in his day, but the memory of Kubaza is too strong for such an alliance to be accepted today.'

'So?' Tamar prompted.

'So you see the only place to turn is north, my lady. We must look beyond the mountains – to the Rus.'

That was when Tamar realised she was not the only person who had entered the room with an agenda.

'Who is he, then?'

'My lady?'

'It is clear you have somebody in mind. Who is he?'

'Tell her,' Rusudan said, quietly.

Gamrekeli climbed to his feet and expanded his chest like a Roman orator.

'His name is Yuri Bogoliubsky.'

'I know him not. What are his lands?'

'By rights he should rule Vladimir, Suzdal, Rostov – the great cities north of Kiev – but his uncle usurped them when he was a boy.'

'An obscure, penniless north-man? Is that all the Kart queen deserves? I was expecting better, gentlemen.'

'My lady, it speaks well of his luck and skill that he yet lives,' Sargis said quietly. 'He is a fighter who has lived rough, yes, but he grew up in the ways of a court and hungers for a place in a great kingdom. He will owe his good fortune to you – and you can be sure he will be grateful for it. And his kin are far away. We need not fear that the Rus princes will ever venture south of the mountains to trouble us here.'

'How came you to hear of him?'

Both Sargis and Gamrekeli turned to look at Rusudan. She cleared her throat.

'A merchant I use for delicate little missions—'

'One of your spies—' said Tamar.

'Very well. One of my spies,' her aunt spoke the word as if it prickled the inside of her mouth, 'brought me word of him. We have corresponded. I have made other enquiries. He is ostentatiously suitable. His lineage is impeccable. His qualities are manifold.'

Tamar met her aunt's level gaze. Not one word had she spoken of this. It hurt. It was too much like a betrayal.

'Very well. I am grateful to you all for your efforts. I take it all the tavads are in agreement?'

Three heads nodded.

'Then send for him. Let us have a look at him.'

Nobody spoke. Gamrekeli looked absent, Sargis profoundly uncomfortable.

'My lady, we have already done so,' he muttered at last.

'I see,' she said, slowly. 'When were you planning to tell me, I wonder?' She drew breath. 'No, no matter. You have told me and that is what counts. I am impatient to meet him.'

She nodded a dismissal and the two men prepared to go.

'Gentlemen,' she called before they reached the door, 'in future we shall keep matters in the open where we can all see them. Nothing of merit grows in darkness. Sunlight and fresh air are required. You understand me?'

Each man offered her a deep, final bow and left. Tamar was alone with her aunt.

'Well done,' said Rusudan.

'Well done?'

'I anticipated our little meeting would go differently. I was preparing myself for one of your charming tirades. Or at least a touching, heartfelt appeal. But I see you were one step ahead. So, I say again, well done. I believe they were impressed.'

'No thanks to you,' said Tamar.

'Niece, let us not be crude.'

'Was it not a little crude, aunt, to contrive this marriage behind my back? Do we see so little of one another, you and I, that you could not find an opportunity to mention this Yuri to me?'

'I feared you would not listen. You've been distracted.'

'Distracted?' Tamar was incensed, especially as she knew it was true. Her aunt smiled – she knew it was true as well.

'Yes, distracted. Preoccupied. Absent-minded. Elsewhere. Call it what you will, my dear, but your head has been floating in some pearly clouds of your own devising. I didn't want to be the one to wrench you back down to earth.'

'No, that might not have suited you so well.'

'Nonsense.' Rusudan batted the accusation aside. 'I am of course only too delighted that your mind is now fully girded for business.' She clamped her arms across her bosom. 'And now, while we wait for the lord Bogoliubsky to arrive, you must steer clear of that boy.'

A crack, and a log toppled over and tumbled into the grate. Tamar leapt up, grabbed the tongs and thrust it back on to the pile.

'Which boy, aunt?'

'Please, Tamar, you are not a naughty child caught with its hand in the honeypot. This is serious. You should not have been amusing yourself with—' she wrinkled her nose, 'that Sos.'

'The lord Soslani – as he deserves to be called – is an Osset lord from an ancient family. He is, moreover, a trusted servant who has proved himself loyal to our family. And there ends the tale. Only your eyes could possibly find anything ill.'

'Don't play the innocent – you give a pitiful performance,' Rusudan snapped. 'Listen child, your mother bewitched your father, blinded him to all else. He suffered – I cannot tell you how much. But love, mark me well, love is a game at which only men can play – men or girls with nothing to lose. A woman has to be practical. Love is not practical. Osset boys with big brown eyes are not practical.'

'I do not love him.'

'There is a saying from my youth: if you have not eaten pepper then why does your mouth burn? For burn it does, my girl. Any woman with eyes can see it – and it won't do. The tavads need to think of you as their beloved sister, their untouched daughter – as the Virgin Mary herself. They won't respect you if you're being fucked behind their backs by a boy half their age.'

'That is too much, even for you, aunt.'

'I said if.' Her aunt came closer. 'By the saints, Tamar, I don't blame you. I'm not made of granite.' The new tone – conspiratorial, intimate – was infinitely worse, like a snail edging across her bare arm. 'The boy's a picture—'

'Stop. None of this is necessary,' Tamar broke her off. 'I know what I must do.'

Rusudan drew back and her face closed.

'Very well. If you say so. But do not fail me.'

Tamar smiled softly. For once, her aunt's subtlety had deserted her.

'An interesting choice of words, aunt. Surely, it is you who should worry about failing me. Should I remind you which of us is queen?'

'How can you say such a thing,' Rusudan spluttered, 'when I am devoting the last years of my life to you – you ungrateful—'

'You? Devote yourself to me? Tell yourself that if you like, but we both know how far it is from the truth. Your jealousy follows you close as your own shadow. You were the oldest child, were you not? You think you should have sat on this throne – Queen Rusudan—'

'Cease these foolish imaginings.'

'No, every word is true. You can deceive yourself, but you cannot deceive me, not any longer. Is it my fault you had brothers and I did not? Is it my fault you were twice sold in marriage while I remained at home? Is it my fault that I am queen and you—'

'Enough. You fantasise.'

But Tamar knew she was right. Rusudan was beginning to sweat through her face paint, her eyes were melting, her lips smeared.

'You are the one with fantasies, aunt. Fantasies that you can rule through me.' She drew breath and finished as deliberate and provocative as she could. 'You are nothing but a leech. A mud-gorged worm.'

Rusudan lashed out, slapping Tamar with the back of her right hand. The blow was wild rather than hard, but her giant, rough-carved emerald ring caught on Tamar's cheek. She put her hand to her face and found it was wet with blood.

'Now look what you made me do,' Rusudan muttered.

It was the first time she had seen her aunt lose control. She was often angry, true, but it was normally deliberate, carefully judged for effect.

'I made you do nothing,' Tamar said, her voice cold. 'But I am glad that finally we understand one another. And now I have an errand for you.'

With a curt nod she handed her aunt a packet of dispatches, bound in red and white ribbons and closed with her seal.

'What is this?' Rusudan demanded.

'State business, aunt. Please inform the lord Soslani and Mkhargrdzeli's boy that they have been chosen for this winter's embassy to Shirvan. I imagine they will be gone for some months. They are to conduct my greetings to the shah. All other matters are detailed herein. They may go to Shota for clarification of any of the stickier points.'

Her aunt's eyes had been widening all the while she spoke.

'Surely they would prefer to hear about so singular an honour from you in person?'

'No, aunt. I believe you shall do very well in my stead.'

Rusudan smiled.

'Something amuses you, aunt?'

'Why ever was I worried? You learn fast, my dear, faster than I had hoped.'

She left and a snake of colder air chased around the room.

'Or feared,' said Tamar to herself.

Part Three

Chapter Twenty-eight

'Why lions for the love of God?' Sos groaned. 'What's she going to do with a pair of lions? What's wrong with silver and diamonds? Why did he have to be original? Why, Zak, why?'

'It's all your fault, Sos, and you know it. I bet he was planning to give us a thumping great box of rubies when you cracked one joke too many and he thought, I know what'll serve that young squab right, a pair of my finest lions. You aren't cut out to be an ambassador.'

Zak was right. Sos had fought a feeble battle to keep a straight face as the shah of Shirvan, soft and corpulent after decades of easy living by the shores of the Caspian, outlined a grandiose scheme whereby he would wed Tamar and sire a glorious dynasty to rule all the lands that lay, as he put it, twixt the oceans twain.

Some men wrinkle, wizen and wither as the years pass. But the shah beamed from behind the same unlined, innocent face he must have showed the world when he first entered it. His worldly appetites, too, had not left him. He could no longer chew meat or bread because his teeth had long rotted away; instead he ate mulched fruit and honeyed sweetmeats, primping and preening on his daybed under a fluttering canopy of gold-stitched damask. He had been charming and infuriating, his flowery, soporific phrases twining about them like silken bindweed.

'Does he honestly want to marry the queen? I think he just enjoys playing the lover,' Sos asked Zak after they'd bade a final farewell.

'Well he hasn't a hope in hell,' Zak replied. 'My father said they'll choose a great warrior.'

'I can't imagine the shah getting the better of a bowl of jelly. He couldn't lift a sword – let alone, you know . . .'

Sos was in the middle of a graphic mime of what the shah wouldn't be able to do when his subject emerged from behind a pillar, clapping.

'Dear boys. So vivacious. I am so glad we ran into each other before you left because it suddenly strikes me, I forgot one tiny little thing. A gift. The queen needs proof of my sincere adoration.' He paused and a beatific smile unfolded across his face. 'Living proof, I believe you call it.'

With a chuckle and a rare bounce in his step, he led them to his lion pen.

'And boys, I shall be most displeased, nay vexed, if my beauties do not arrive safely. I shall send to learn how they do, I shall certainly send. Now, be off with you. Dear, dear boys.'

Sos sighed. It was all his fault.

Manhandling the wheels round every lump and bump between Shamakha and Tbilisi under the yellow desert sky was grim work. On the way to the shah's court, he and Zak had barely noticed how rutted and uneven the roads were. But now they had to travel with a lioness and her cub in a cage on top of a hefty hay-cart, they grew to hate the fractured flood-grooves and landslide boulders. Whenever they passed one of the little pools where the herders gathered, gaggles of grievously overexcited boys capered after them, trying to poke the lioness with sticks or feed pebbles to her cub, dodging Zak's fists and laughing off Sos's grisly threats.

The lioness's temper matched Sos's – overheated and sour. But her son was as good-natured as a hand-fed houndpup, somersaulting from one end of the cage to the other as the cart joggled west, chasing invisible butterflies, playing some enthralling game with himself – until his mother batted him down with a forepaw and closed her jaw around his neck. Chastised, he lay meek for a mile or two, until something new excited him and the gambolling began once more.

Sos might have found it funny if he hadn't been worried about finding enough meat to keep the lions alive. Both mother and son had been reared in the shah's shady courtyards, but they still needed stupefying amounts of flesh, preferably dripping hunks of mutton hacked straight from the corpse.

Zak was more phlegmatic, but that was because he – still, after half a year away – was pink-eared with pride at the honour of having been sent to Shirvan. He thought they had been chosen because of his father, because they were somebodies. But Sos, although he couldn't bear to tell his friend, knew there was another reason. The embassy had been Rusudan's ruse to get him out of the way.

She had called them both into her chamber, oozing smiles and praise about how they had conducted themselves in the days after the death of the king. Nothing specific, no mention of night raids, but she said she was pleased with them. It was only when they were leaving, clutching gold and sealed messages for the shah, that Rusudan called him back – only him.

Her eyes swept over him, lingering in unexpected places. Her scrutiny was puzzling rather than unnerving and he bore it without flinching – even when she stalked around him in an excruciatingly slow circle. Eventually, she gave up and spoke in her most magisterial voice.

'You have a great future ahead of you. The lord Mkhargrdzeli is in raptures about your skill in the saddle, your prowess with the bow. He would be as loath as I to see a promising young man jeopardise his prospects on account of a piece of youthful folly.'

She stopped and waited for him to respond, but he said nothing. He didn't know what she knew, what she guessed, and he wasn't going to help her. Her eyes narrowed and she resumed.

'The road to Shirvan is long, my boy. You will have ample time for contemplation. I trust I make myself clear?'

It was clear. He was being warned off. Looked at in a certain light, that was quite a compliment.

He wished Tamar had at least tried to see him before he left, but he knew it would have been hard for her. Her aunt must have been watching her like a hawk. Although, Sos reflected, Rusudan wasn't much like a bird of prey, more like a bullock, munching, swishing its tail, dark eyes fixed on whatever was crossing its field. Placid but dangerous. Sos wondered whether Tamar would turn out like her when she was older, but dismissed the thought as soon as it appeared. It was too alarming.

He'd tried not to think about her while he'd been away, but the closer they came to Tbilisi, the harder it was to pretend. Behind every taste of food and drink, every joke with Zak, was the slow, steady drumbeat of her: her black eyes, her quick voice, the memory of her standing on the walls on midsummer's eve, blocking out the stars.

They were a few hours' ride from Tbilisi, see-sawing at the same frustrating pace as the sleepy packhorses, the mules and bleating goats, the beggars and monks. Sos was trying to amuse himself thinking up names for the cub when the pounding of many hooves pulsed in the soles of his feet. A pack of riders already filled the road ahead of them, kicking up a thick cloud of dust. They were enormous – more like giants than everyday men – and driving their horses hard.

Sos swore and tried to drag the cart to the side of the road, but the riders were upon them too fast. One of the horses spooked and blundered left, then right. The cart jackknifed and, slow as tree sap, overturned. Sos seized the maddened horse's head as it jerked back and forth, blew into its nostrils, scratched its cheeks and muttered and sang in his own language until it quietened.

'Sos, Sos!' Zak was shouting now. 'The cage's split. She's gone.'

The bars had buckled when the cage tumbled off the cart. The cub was frisking about the wreckage, delighted to be free, but his mother was nowhere to be seen.

'We've got to find her. Where can she—'

Sos was interrupted by a loud burst of laughter. The riders, their haste forgotten, were idling on their horses, admiring the chaos.

'Be on your way – or get down and help,' Sos called to them.

'Nay, mister, more merry to watch your sport. Mind us not,' said one, his accent strange.

He turned his words into whatever tongue his companions spoke. They sniggered and then the biggest of them said something that made them all laugh louder.

'My lord would ask whether lion-farming is here a tradition? 'Tis outlandish indeed. Do your women suckle griffins and ride river-pigs to church to say their prayers?'

That was too much. Sos's sword was out of his scabbard, its tip directed at each man's throat in turn.

'You. The tongue-smith. Tell me your lord's name and business and I will teach him some manners.'

'Sos, what the hell are you doing?' muttered Zak. 'There's six of them.'

'Three each. Get your sword out,' Sos hissed back.

'I am called Gleb,' the stranger began, 'and my master is—' but the big man silenced him with a wave of his hand before he could finish. Looking delighted at the challenge, he dismounted and advanced on Sos, sword drawn. He stopped a few paces away and nodded his head in a contemptuous bow. There was a bare streak across his scalp where no hair grew, an old wound, badly healed.

'My name – Yuri Bogoliubsky. My business – my own.' He pushed his sleeves up. His forearms were broader than a normal man's calves. 'Who you, boy?'

Sos swallowed hard and squared his shoulders.

'I am Soslani, lord of the Osset lands east of the great pass, south of the ice-river. You will regret your insolence.'

'Pretty talk. You fight pretty, too?'

Yuri's blade sketched a mocking little flurry of jabs and parries, then he crooked his left forefinger and beckoned. Sos didn't want to do what he was told, but it would be far worse to appear scared, so he stepped forwards, trying to keep his eyes on both Yuri's face and his sword arm.

Suddenly, something on the edge of his vision distracted him. He glanced down. The cub was romping around his feet jumping for the tassels on his scabbard, nipping the toes of his boots. He tried to shoo it away, but it thought he was playing a game and

209

pranced out of reach, before bouncing over to Yuri to invite him to join them.

Yuri drew his boot back and aimed a bone-breaking kick at the cub's head. Mercifully, the blow landed askew and the cub rolled, squealing and cringing, to the side of the road. Sos's face had suddenly sobered.

'You shouldn't have done that.'

The lioness pounced, and Yuri disappeared. Within seconds she would have torn his throat open, but Sos sprang forwards and buried his sword in her neck. She tossed her head from side to side, her paws scrabbling, until he lost his grip and rolled clear. But the sword stayed lodged in her flesh, and with a choking, gargling snarl, she collapsed, dead.

Yuri stumbled out from underneath her, blood streaming from the long gashes her claws had ripped down his neck. Dazed, he stepped backwards, shaking his long, yellow hair away from his face. Gleb and the others were running towards him, shouting. They dragged him away, bundled him into his saddle and together they galloped away into the haze, leaving only dust hanging in the air.

It had all happened very fast.

'Gone.' Sos sniffed. 'Ungrateful bastard. Cowards.'

Zak snorted. 'Come off it, Sos, we were outnumbered and they were massive. I wonder where they make men like that?'

'God only knows. In the north, maybe. The Rus grow big, I've heard.'

He reached down and picked up the cub, which was still whimpering, and rubbed its belly softly.

'A vicious brute as well as a coward.'

'Brute he may be, but I don't think he was scared of a fight. We might have had our hands full if she hadn't jumped him.'

'And then I killed her for it. I should have left him to die.'

Chapter Twenty-nine

Sos tipped a groom at the inn a week's pay to douse the cub in warm, soapy water until he was as fluffy and charming as a chick. Then he and Zak sauntered across the river to the palace, grinning at each other as a merchant shrank away when he realised the creature on the end of the chain wasn't a big-pawed mongrel pup. They found the palace gates barred, the noonday sun glinting off the heavy iron crossbeams.

'The queen's ambassadors to Shirvan have returned and desire speech with her,' Sos called up to the gate-tower.

Silence.

'Hey,' he yelled, 'open up.'

He was about to bellow once more, ruder, when Sirchak's head appeared high above them.

'Sos, Zak – I heard you back. Is good.'

'Sirchak, come on, let us in, we're parched down here.'

The Kipchak disappeared and a few moments later the gates heaved open and they were beckoned inside.

'Hey, crazy boys,' Sirchak gaped, 'why you have big cat on rope?'

Sos picked up the cub. 'You like him? He's a present for the queen – from the shah of Shirvan. A love token.'

Sirchak's face crinkled with amusement.

'Is good present. Girl bring me big cat – I marry her, no question.'

'You haven't met the shah, my friend. It's going to take more than a big cat to swing it for him. Hey—' Sos took in the near empty courtyard, 'where is everyone? They can't all be asleep, it's not that hot.'

The Kipchak shook his head and pointed towards the sun-struck heights that rose above the city to the west.

211

'They take new man to hawk hunt. Left early.'

'What new man?'

'North-man. Stranger.'

Sos and Zak exchanged glances.

'Who is he? What's his name?'

'Fine man, stupid name. Yoo-ree Bokho . . . Bolosk . . . Tyach, still I cannot say it.'

Sos frowned.

'Yuri? Big? Hair like straw? White as mushroom?'

'Yes,' Sirchak nodded vigorously. 'You boys know him?'

'We met on the road. I was hoping I'd see him again. We've got unfinished business.' Sos fingered his sword. 'Important business.'

'Stop, Sos,' said the Kipchak, suddenly serious, 'I think is man who knows much about business. You see size of him?'

Sos shrugged. 'Big men are slow in a fight.'

But Sirchak disagreed. 'Not Yoo-ree. My best boys try two-three passes with him yesternight. Little sport. Lady Rusudan suggest. He move like cat, like snake. Fight good. Lady Rusudan like very much. All man like very much.'

Sos was about to say that cats were shifty charlatans and snakes were skulking cowards when Zak took his shoulder and gave him a friendly shake.

'C'mon, take it easy, Sos.'

'I know, I know,' Sos grumbled. 'But why the hell he's pitched up here?'

'He's passing through. Plenty enough people do. Let's fetch our horses and go and find the party. It'll be good to see everyone again.'

The heat was fading from white to gold when they came upon the ring of awnings suspended between the trees. A dozen or so women had settled in the shade while their husbands and brothers were hunting on the ridges above. Musicians were strumming lyres somewhere out of sight and an amiable lethargy hung in the air.

At the sight of Sos and Zak those who were still awake called out friendly hellos and begged them not to go a step further. They wanted to pet the cub, which was drowsy and docile from the heat, and hear tales of their time with the shah. But the talk soon returned to Tbilisi and quickly settled on the new man, the Rus.

'He deserves one's pity, does he not?' said one woman, her voice drooping under the weight of her compassion. 'He was but ten, a little boy, when the monsters came and killed his father.'

'Not that he speaks of it,' added another.

'No, no, I only heard of it from the lady Rusudan. Imagine, my lords,' she turned to Sos and Zak, 'his father was hacked to pieces by his closest companions in his own bedchamber. With axes, like some wild beast. Yuri had to watch it all, every blow, but he escaped and grew to manhood in exile. Only imagine!'

'Imagine!' echoed the other women.

'A wretched start, and yet he has lost none of his nobility.'

'Quite the reverse.'

'How long's he been here?' asked Zak when Sos remained silent.

'He arrived after the snows – a month or two since, but it feels so much longer, as if he really belonged.'

Sos frowned. 'And when's he going?'

'Why, my lord Soslani, I beg you, do not wish him away. None of us would thank you for that – the queen least of all,' said the first woman, to scattered giggles.

At that moment, servants ran into the glade ahead of the main party and started preparing cups and plates, a signal for the women to turn away to touch and rearrange their hair.

'Sos, be sensible, all right?' Zak muttered.

Before Sos could answer – or even ask what being sensible might mean – an absurd litter swayed into view. The bearers, glistening with effort, dropped to their knees, laid it on the ground and Rusudan emerged. She noticed them immediately. Irritation, maybe even anger, rippled across her face, but by the time she had advanced across the clearing to greet them, her

213

arms swept wide, she could hardly have looked more thrilled if they'd been her own beloved eldest sons.

'Gentlemen, welcome home. The court has sore missed two of its very greatest favourites.'

Sos and Zak bowed low and correct and kissed her outstretched hands. The strong scent on her fingers tickled the inside of Sos's nose and suddenly, despite everything, he felt very young again.

'Tell me, how fares the shah?'

'The shah's health is excellent, my lady, and his hospitality was incomparable.'

'Truly unique, my lady,' added Zak.

'Splendid, splendid,' she replied, but it was plain she wasn't really listening. 'You shall tell us all about it in due course. Now, let me see, have you met our dearest, newest friend? He's a real hit, as you young people would say. Vardan was telling me he'd never seen anyone so skilled with a falcon. And you know how Vardan loathes to compliment another man. Come, come, let us find him. Don't be shy.'

Don't be shy? Sos mouthed at Zak in horror.

Rusudan propelled them through the crowds, too fast for them to do anything but nod quickly in reply to friends' greetings.

'Yuri, Yuri!'

He turned and smiled. Four fresh welts, puffy and pink-edged, ran down both sides of his neck. The sight of Sos and Zak did not unnerve him. In fact, Sos saw nothing but the briefest bemusement followed by delighted recognition. Before he knew what was happening, the Rus was clapping him on the back and talking fast and light in his own tongue, a slurred sing-song like the swash of waves on a shore. Rusudan nodded along, interjecting a few strange syllables here and there.

'What a coincidence,' Rusudan exclaimed. 'So you gentlemen have already met. The lord Soslani had lost control of a lion – really, my lord, a lion you say? – but Yuri beat it off, he tells me, and slew it. He now begs me to assure you that he bears you no ill will for endangering his life. How generous is the lord Bogoliubsky. You shall thank him.'

214

Sos longed to contradict every word but he could hear in his head how it would sound. *He's lying, ma'am. That's not true. Ask Zak. He's a liar. Liar.* A little boy whining, bearing tales to a schoolmistress. No, that would not do. Instead, Sos matched the Rus's broad smile and shook his outstretched hand.

'I am happy to meet you again, my lord.'

'Where,' said Yuri, switching to Kart. 'Where is little beast?' He made an impression of claws and a snarl that set Rusudan and everyone about them laughing.

'Enchanting. What, what is this? Another lion? What I wonder are you doing with all these lions, my dear lord Soslani?'

Sos gestured for them to wait and retrieved the cub from under its bush. It pushed itself back on its hind legs and yawned, its mouth open wide in what would one day be a mighty roar, but for now was merely an appealing squeak.

'The shah made a present of a lioness and her cub to the queen Tamar. The lord Bogoliubsky has already told you the fate of the mother, but her son is here and is eager to meet his new mistress. Where is she?'

'I am here.'

He was totally unprepared for how those three simple words tore into the back of his skull. He turned to where her voice had come from and knelt before her, his head bowed.

'My lady, the shah begs you to accept this as proof of the great love he bears you.'

He found he could not look up, but then her face appeared in front of his, her nose barely a handspan away. She reached out to touch the cub's ears.

'Thank you. He's beautiful. I shall treasure him. I only hope the shah will not be too disappointed.'

They were left staring at one another until the cub wrenched free from Sos and began questing along the ground. It came upon Yuri's boots, sniffed, then its hackles rose and it hunched ready to pounce, but Yuri reached down and picked it up by the scruff of its neck. It hung, helpless, in his hand while Yuri stroked its head and gently pulled its tail.

'Why, Yuri, even the wild beasts love you,' Rusudan chuckled. 'Now, what are the servants thinking of? Food, food and drink!'

She plucked at Tamar's sleeve and together they withdrew to where seats had been arranged under one of the awnings. Gamrekeli materialised at Yuri's shoulder and, with barely a nod in Sos's direction, steered the Rus firmly in their wake. Sargis was already sitting next to the queen, but when he saw Yuri approaching he stood up to make way. A row of backs blocked Sos's view, but not before he had seen Tamar turn and smile up at the Rus as he settled himself beside her.

He waited until they were riding back down into the city at dusk, then jogged his horse up fast beside the queen's and called loud.

'My lady, your horse's girth is loose.'

It was a feeble enough ruse, but it was the best he could do in the circumstances. He jumped down and set about loosening and tightening the buckle under her horse's belly while the others rode past. He wouldn't have long.

'Greetings, my lord—'

It was only then that he realised how angry he was. Her formality was mockery to him. He cut her off.

'When were you going to tell me, Tamar?'

'Tell you what?'

'That you are betrothed.'

'I am not betrothed.'

His heart leapt. Had he been mistaken? But then he looked at her more closely. Her face was set, her lips were unusually thin and her clear eyes were clouded. Also, she was gripping her reins too tight.

'No? You are not going to marry that man? That Rus?'

He turned away, picked up her horse's front hoof and pretended to be working at a stone lodged there. He heard her voice above him.

'You should not talk to me like this. You have no right to—'

'No? Do I not? You told me to hope. Do not dare deny it.'

Her face was impregnable.

'I can and do deny it. It is not my fault you were so presumptuous as to force your attentions on me. You are lucky I did not
have you punished.'

'Don't lie to me, Tamar. It is not like you. *Be bold.* Those were
your words. I remember them well – even if you want to pretend
you don't.'

He dropped the hoof and, on cue, Rusudan's voice floated up
to them from further down the hill.

'My dear, is your horse lamed?'

'A stone, aunt, nothing more. The lord Soslani is attending to
it.' Then the wall crumbled a little and she spoke fast to him. 'We
made no promises, you and I. Not one. Not ever. Leave me be.'

She gathered her horse's reins to leave, but he seized them.

'Do you want to marry him? Tell me. Have you fallen in love
with him?'

He had to know. It mattered more than anything. For a
moment she said nothing. Then her hand reached down and
touched the bare skin at the side of his neck. In his surprise, he
dropped the reins and put his fingers to hers.

'Please. It's no good, Sos. It's been decided. Soon, the whole
world will know.'

They stood, locked in a daze in the fading light. Then she
shook her head, wheeled her horse round and cantered fast
downhill after the others.

217

Chapter Thirty

'My lady?'

'Mmmm?'

'Come out. You'll get cold.'

'Two more minutes. Rub my shoulders?'

Nino had already scrubbed her red as a newborn, scouring away the dust and grime with a chunk of scorched pumice until the water stung her limbs. And now the scent of almond oil filled her nose as the nurse's thumbs sank into the tight spots around the base of her neck.

'Tamar, are you properly prepared for tomorrow?'

'Shota's worked harder than fifty oxen – everything will be perfect, I'm sure. And anyway, all a bride needs to do is turn up looking presentable.'

The thumbs paused for an instant. 'I meant tomorrow night, my love.'

Tamar twisted round so suddenly that water sloshed over the rim of the bronze tub and sluiced across the floor.

'Nino, please don't tell me we're about to have a little talk?'

'Well,' the nurse replied, resolutely matter-of-fact, 'seeing as your mother and your sister aren't here, I thought somebody ought to—'

'—lecture me about things I know more than enough about already?'

'Have it your own way. Come on, child, out,' she said, holding up a towel.

Tamar heaved herself upright and water washed down her limbs. Nino started to rub her dry.

'All I can say is, Tamar, it could be a lot worse. He's young, handsome too. Mzia was saying to me just this morning that half of the girls in the palace would give their best teeth to trade places with you. And the men think a great deal of him, that's for sure. He's perhaps a little too foreign for my tastes, but even I can't deny—'

'Nino. Stop it. Please.'

The clang and clatter of the wedding preparations suddenly sounded very loud in the rooms below. Nino turned away and busied herself arranging hairbrushes on the sideboard. For a long moment Tamar stood there, staring down at her naked body.

'You don't always marry the man you love, Tamar, or the man who loves you. Life doesn't always work that way. Here, put this on.' Nino bundled a plain-weave dress over Tamar's head and then put a hand quickly, lightly on her cheek. 'I know how you hate it when you can't have what you want.'

Tamar reached up and took the nurse's hand in hers. 'You're right, Nino. I do hate it. But maybe there's something I can do about it.' She crossed over to the table, scratched a couple of words on a scrap of paper and held it out.

'Here.'

'What's this?'

'What I want.'

Nino turned the note over in her hands. 'I can't do this, Tamar. And neither should you.'

Tamar nodded. 'I know. But I don't care. Please, Nino.'

Sos took refuge in Mother Crow's, one of the vilest drinking dens in the city, dank and violent, to drink himself stupid in peace. But even there, in a place rarely pierced by reality, everyone was obsessed with the wedding that would follow the next day. A lucid drunk was spinning stories to a rapt and unusually orderly audience.

'The Rus princes are wild men, I tell you. It wasn't so long ago that they crept out of the black forests where snow lies up to your chin the year round, where witches hide, and worse – dark shapes that swallow children whole, lure maidens into the shadows and drive good men mad. That's why the Rus are so

219

pale, you know. They lived so long under the tall trees, starved of light and laughter.'

The serving girl slammed another jug of wine on the counter. 'Well all I know is the woman I buy my bread off has a niece who says he's the spit of a hero from the old world.'

Most of the drinkers then said they too had laid eyes on Yuri – or the Rus, as everyone called him because it was easier to say than his name – or at least they knew somebody who had. The queen was lucky to have such a husband, they agreed, a real man, not some wizened stump or puffed-up princeling with Hellên airs.

'And you, sir,' called the drunk to Sos, 'who might you be? You look like quality. What say the tavads to this match? A great day, no?'

Sos lurched off his stool, fought his way outside and stood glaring up at the crescent moon that hung over the hills.

Somebody called out. He turned and saw a woman hastening towards him. She was dressed for midwinter, not a balmy summer's night, thickly swaddled with cloaks and scarves so that he could not see the outline of her body, let alone her face. For a moment, he thought she might be a madwoman, a fool, but she was too well fed for insanity or poverty. When she spoke, she was severely short of breath.

'My lord Soslani, you've led me a fine chase all over the city. Why will young men never be content to stop at home in the evenings? Why are you mooning about up here? No, no, it's not for me to know, although I'm sure I can . . . no, never mind. Now, where is it, where is it . . .'

Sos's head had cleared a little, but he still couldn't work out why this woman was standing in front of him, patting her dress down, rummaging through the myriad folds and pouches of material.

'Ah, here we are.'

She produced a letter triumphantly and held it out for him.

'From my lady.'

'From who?'

'From my mistress. Come now, don't goggle at it, read it.'

Sos took it from her, nodded a vague thank-you, and turned to go.

'No, no, read it now. I am to take your answer.'

'What answer?'

'The answer to the question in the letter. My word, has some sprite robbed you of your senses?'

He swallowed and read.

Come to me tonight.

He read it again. He read each word twice and read it backwards. It still said the same thing. It was unambiguous. But he had no idea what it meant.

'Well?' The question was impatient.

'Forgive me. I am at a loss. You see, you haven't told me who your mistress is.'

A snort, disgusted and amused, emerged from behind the woman's headscarf.

'I fancy you're drunk. You'll have to do something about that, sharp. Or perhaps you get messages of this sort all the time? That won't do either, my boy. No, I will not speak her name aloud here, but I will tell you mine. I am Nino.'

Nino. Nino? Wasn't every third woman from here to the sea called Nino? Then, at last, with a jerk that he could almost feel, his mind woke up.

'Mistress Nino! You come from—'

'Shush. Keep your voice down. Nobody – nobody – must know I am here, do you understand? You realise what an absurd risk she has set herself on running. I told her I should never countenance it, but she threatened to come and find you herself if I didn't . . .'

But Sos was no longer listening to her. He was staring at the torn-off scrap of paper in front of him.

Come to me tonight.

It couldn't mean anything else. Could it? Was he missing something? Was he being presumptuous? He looked up. Nino had stopped talking and was looking at him.

'Well?' she demanded.

'The queen weds on the morrow?'

'As every child knows.'

'And she . . . and your mistress wants me to come to see her?'

'If that's what the letter says. Of course I have not read it.'

'But – but why?'

'I could not say. That's a matter for you and she.'

Sos nodded a couple of times. 'I understand, it's just a . . . a surprise.' He grinned. 'A wonderful surprise. Please tell your mistress that I shall be glad to wait upon her this night.'

He turned and set off at a run.

'My lord!' Nino called after him.

He stopped. She waved him back.

'How will you get in?'

'Oh, yes, I had forgotten.' He thought for a moment. 'How will I get in?'

She smiled. 'Come to the kitchen gate after the bell sounds for the middle night watch, not a moment later. I shall be there.'

Sos nodded. 'Until later then.' He squeezed her hand again and bounded away, his mind a carnival riot.

I knew it. I knew it.

Tonight! Tonight!

I need to sober up.

He plunged his head into a horse trough, staying underwater while he counted slowly to twenty, then blundered back to the inn to find a fresher shirt. How to make the hours pass? He thought he might eat, but the smell of food made his insides turn over. Wandering through the city, he gulped down the night air, sweet as wine, the rest of the world a bright blur floating nearby. He imagined everything that could go wrong. He imagined everything that could go right. His stomach swooped and dived under his ribs as if on some crazed mission of its own.

But as the hour approached, he grew calm. He skirted the palace outbuildings and crouched by the kitchen entrance. The air was thick with burnt oil and mouldering vegetables. The cooks were up late preparing for the wedding feast and he saw that it would be easy for Nino to slip through and let him in. Everybody would be too rushed and flustered to notice. He heard her pointed cough and left the shadows.

'Don't look left or right. Don't look worried. Just keep your head down and walk right behind me. Here.'

She handed him a giant clothes basket that hid his face when he held it in his arms.

'That's good. Nobody'll think to give you a second glance. Ready?'

Sos nodded. Hiding in plain sight. It might work.

They wove through the kitchens, a haze of steam and shouting, then through the hall where tables were being set. He heard Shota giving orders. He shrunk deeper into his bones, trying to hide under his own skin. Nino stamped up on to the dais and had her hand on the door to the royal apartments when Shota called out.

'Nino! Nino!'

Sos did not move. He clung to the basket, his back to the hall. Nino turned and called down.

'Yes, Shota, what is it?'

'What have you got in that basket there?'

'My lady would cast her eye over some silks for tomorrow. Gifts.'

'Is that really necessary?'

The edge to Shota's voice told Sos he had been recognised. He tensed.

'I believe it is, Shota,' said Nino.

Sos could not see their faces but they were obviously locked in a silent battle, each waiting for the other to give way. They could not argue out loud. He did not breathe until he heard Shota's voice.

'Very well, Nino, bid my lady goodnight.'

'That's kind, Shota,' Nino called. 'Of course I shall.'

Then they were winding down a long dark corridor, to a part

of the palace where Sos had never yet been. They must be nearly there. What was he going to say? What was going to happen? He had spent so many hours longing for time to hurry up that he was unnerved to discover that he now wanted it to stop altogether. He was terrified.

'You can put that down now.'

Nino had stopped outside a door. Sos placed the basket carefully on the floor and stood, unsure what to do next.

'Go on. In there.' Nino gave the door a little push and stuck her head round. 'He's here, my lady.'

When Sos did not move, she put a hand on the small of his back and propelled him through the door.

The room was very dark. It was too warm, even at night, for fires to be lit. The only light came from a pair of candles, burning low by the window where Tamar was standing, her throat white against her loose hair. She looked defensive and didn't move towards him when he came in. They stayed like that, at either side of the room, for a long time.

'Tamar—'

'I'm glad—'

They had both spoken at once, which made them laugh, and suddenly it was a little easier. Tamar took him by the hand — hers felt cool, his was fevered — and they sat together by the empty hearth. He didn't know what to say.

'How's the cub getting on?' he said at last.

She smiled. 'He likes me, I think. He took a nip out of Goga's leg. Goga's furious that he's had to give up a stall to a wild beast . . .'

The words started to flow, easy and natural. They talked simply of a hundred things. But all the while Sos could feel the night passing. The stars were sweeping overhead, falling out of sight to wherever the sun waited, ready to send dawn ahead. They did not have much time.

He could no longer hear what Tamar was saying. Thick blood droned in his ears as he discarded a hundred different ways to take her in his arms. Each time he was ready, he suddenly doubted it was what she wanted. He counted to ten, then slipped out of his seat and crossed to the low chair where she sat. He knelt at her feet, taking her hands in his. He held them to his face, breathed in deep and kissed their palms. She had stopped talking and there was a look on her face that made his heart speed faster. Then her eyes clouded over and she closed them tight. When she spoke, her voice was taut.

'I don't want to marry him, Sos.'

He gripped her hands tighter.

'Then don't do it, Tamar, I beg you. There's something dangerous about him – like the high ice fields in winter. The way ahead can look firm, but you know from the smell, the sound, the feel that the ice will betray you. One foot wrong and it will boom, crack and swallow you up.'

'You can't prove that.'

'I don't have to. You're the queen. You don't have to do anything you don't want to. Isn't that the whole point?'

She shook her head. 'It's too late. I asked for this marriage. We've debated it. The tavads – Rusudan – everyone is in favour. I can't go against them all. Everything's prepared. I can't stop it. I can't.'

'You can.'

Again she shook her head. 'I dare not.'

'I've seen you dare more. You're the bravest person I've ever met.'

That did make her smile, but only for a moment.

'I like hearing you say that, but it isn't true. I've been many things – bold, rash maybe, and lucky – but I don't think I've ever been really brave. Doing what you want, even if it's difficult or painful, that isn't brave. Doing what you have to do – however much it hurts, however much you hate it – that's courage.'

She paused and her eyes, which had been half closed, suddenly landed on his.

'You know who I'd want if I were free.'

'Say it.'

'No, Sos, I can't.'

'Why not?'

'Because I have tried so hard to forget. Because if I tell you my courage will fail me and I will not be able to wed Yuri Bogoliubsky tomorrow.'

The watch change sounded below, a bell, quick shouts, the tramp of boots on the courtyard stones. In the quiet that followed, Sos stood up and walked over to the window where ribbons of night air swirled into the room. The candles had burned down to small stumps, the flames swimming above pools of wax. One by one, they sank and disappeared. He spoke with his back to her.

'Then why did you ask me here?'

She did not reply at once, but he heard her dress rustle as she rose and came to him. She wrapped both arms about his chest, just below his heart, and pressed her face between his shoulder blades. They stayed like that for a while, breathing together, two saplings in the wind, and then they turned to each other. He felt her fingers, soft on the back of his neck.

'I wanted to say I was sorry. I wanted to say goodbye.'

'And?' There was something else.

'And, tomorrow night, afterwards, I don't want him to be the—'

She broke off. But it didn't matter. He understood. He took her hand and together they walked over to her bed.

Chapter Thirty-one

In her sleep she had stood atop a mountain, all Kartvelia spread before her. She raised her hands and stretched them out over her lands, silver rivers and golden cities glinting between her fingers. Her skirts swirled around her legs, her hair whipped about her face and she felt strong – stronger than she had ever felt in her life.

She woke to find Sos smiling in his sleep and the taste of her dream lingered, happy and inchoate. There was no time for words. One kiss, another, then Nino – too soon – tapped at the door and he followed her away down the corridor. Tamar buried her head in her pillow, breathing in deep where his head had lain, trying to hold on to him.

Nino returned and settled a tray of hot bread and honey on the table. She stood at the side of the bed, leant down and touched Tamar's shoulder.

'My lady?' Her voice was wary.

Tamar rolled over and sat up, her hair tangled in extravagant spirals, spiky as a fighting cock.

'Nino, dear Nino, no need to look like that. It is my marriage morning, not my funeral. I remember my mother telling me this was the happiest day in a woman's life – or the most important. I forget which.'

'Tamar, please, it breaks my heart to see you distraught.'

'Distraught? Who says I'm distraught? I'm not distraught. I marry a great prince today. I secure the future of my lands today. I make my father proud today. I . . .'

But it was no good. The damp, grey feeling buried under her ribs fought its way up her throat, choking her, wringing tears from her eyes as the sobs of a much younger girl threatened to overpower her. She clasped her head in both hands and shook herself.

'I won't, I won't. Not even in front of you, Nino. I mustn't. You see that, don't you? I must bear it.'

She gripped her lower lip between her teeth and mastered herself. The tears stopped. She looked up at Nino with pink-rimmed eyes.

'Don't let me be weak. As you love God, as you love me, forget that I can cry – and I will forget it too. No man will be able to say my eyes were downcast today, no, nor flashing angry. They will see nothing. Nothing, I tell you. I will look glad, and every man will say there goes Tamar, the happiest woman in the world.'

She rode through the streets of the capital of her kingdom, cheers breaking over her head, a sea of open mouths and upturned faces, flowers and ribbons swooping through the morning air while forty-eight Kipchak guards kept step by her side.

Tbilisi was beside itself. The palace coffers had opened – there would be bounty for everyone – and at last a king was to mount the throne. It was the happy ending everyone had dreamt of: marriage, children and peace. The hopes and prayers of hundreds upon hundreds of people attached themselves to her like briers as she passed.

Every man was as proud as if his own youngest daughter were to wed, every woman as fascinated as if the love tales of Ramin and Vis, David and Bathsheba, Pelops and Hippodameia had come alive before her eyes. Even the children were swept up in the excitement. *Mother, isn't he handsome? Father, isn't he brave?*

Tamar was cocooned behind a thick fog, in hiding. It was the only way she could stop herself ripping off her headdress, wheeling her horse round and charging back to the palace. But the walls of the cathedral loomed ever larger until – too soon – she stood in their shadow. The same men who little more than a year earlier had come to steal her kingdom after her father's death now lined the steps to bow her to her marriage.

The walls muffled the sound of the people outside as if she had climbed inside a giant shell deep underwater. Waiting for her under the icons, she saw Rusudan, Gamrekeli and Mkhargrdzeli, decked out fine, as pleased as parents, as watchful as the Kipchak guards. And there, in the middle, was Yuri, bulging out of his new black breeches and finespun tunic. He had been shaven close and somebody had combed out his hair, oiling it so it lay meek against his head. His eyes, cold as the palest blue snow flowers, travelled slowly over her.

She did not look for Sos. She knew he would be there, standing in one of the alcoves. She could feel his eyes on her. For a moment, Yuri vanished and in his place Sos stood, dark and slender, warm and alive. But then there was only Yuri. She forced the muscles in her face and shoulders to relax and her feet carried her to his side. He took her hand, rubbed his thumb across her palm and smiled with his mouth.

Then the bishop was before them, dressed in the gold and silver and red of God and finality. His voice cracking like old leather, he told the empty air above their heads of God's will, God's joy and God's truth, spinning a net of divine approval around her, drawing it tighter and tighter until Tamar found it hard to breathe.

Twin crowns were raised above their heads and together they walked about the altar, their footsteps lost as voices behind the iconostasis cried out to God's glory. The saints stared down at her, sorrowful, pleased, indifferent, it was hard to tell, while the tavads watched like horse traders eyeing colts trotting round a paddock. Once, twice, a final turn, and they returned to the bishop, his fingers aloft, ready for the benediction.

And then it was over. She was married.

She unpeeled her tongue from the roof of her mouth, dry as the parched fields, and opened her eyes. Dawn was at the window, the late summer light thin and tired. Her husband was sprawled next to her, his hunched shoulders and wild-boar arms above a ruck of sheets. His foot, its heel thick and yellowed, was rubbing against the bedpost. The daylight picked out rough, reddened patches of skin around his mouth and white flakes at the corners of the eyes. Unnaturally straight lines ran across his forehead and between his nose and mouth. His nostrils let the light through them like eyelids. He stirred a little and she froze as his eyes opened, but they did not focus. He grunted and rolled away. But then she heard his breathing change and she knew he was coming to. Suddenly, he rolled off the bed, on to his feet and stood, naked, looking down at her.

His manner had changed.

'Not first time.'

'What do you mean?' She pulled the sheets up around her.

He repeated the words – with gestures – and she understood.

'How dare you?' she gasped, but the pitch of her voice was wrong, and she could see from his face that he knew he was right.

He nodded a couple of times, rubbing the stubble under his chin.

'No problem. No problem for you, no problem for me. But big, big problem for him.'

'Him?'

'Yes, him. I ask. I find who. I kill. Understand?'

She ignored him and put her hand on the bell to call Mzia, but in two fluid movements Yuri took it from her and plucked the sheet away.

'Not yet.'

He traced his hand across her breasts.

'Maybe too thin. I like more here . . .'

He shrugged.

'Now we do again.'

He climbed on top of her. She didn't know how to stop him. She couldn't stop him. Panic swarmed up inside her. She was about to try to fight her way out from underneath him when a series of sharp knocks and a man's voice sounded at the door.

'My lord, my lady. Forgive me for disturbing you, but my lord Mkhargrdzeli would speak to the king.'

'What is it?'

'My lord, there is word that Turkomen raiders, in large numbers, have crossed our southern borders.'

She was so relieved watching him dress that it was only after he had gone, when she was alone, that the word the guard had used rang again in her ears.

King.

Chapter Thirty-two

Sos gutted a Turkoman with an efficient sideswipe from his heavy-bladed sword, turned, slammed his fist into the face of another and ran him through. The body slumped to the ground and he span his horse around, looking for his next target.

But there was nobody left to kill. It had been a rout. The raiders had not expected to meet so many mounted men in Kartvelia's underbelly and had melted below the horizon, galloping back towards the empty lands in the east when they realised they faced a serious fight. Only a fine brown mist of dust falling through the air remained.

The Rus let out an enormous roar, echoed by the Kart fighters who thronged to honour their king and his victory.

The land about them was spoiled and scorched. The Turkomen, not burdened by women or livestock, had come to plunder, not conquer. What they could not take with them they burned, despising men who died in the same place they were born.

At Sos's side, Zak was beaming, exultant. He never looked entirely comfortable at court. His body was too big for peaceful places – he stumbled and bumbled, like a waterbird on land, shuffling and apologetic. But on the battlefield he had soared, diving and swooping, and Sos had counted himself lucky to fight next to him. Zak wasn't bloodthirsty – he never killed with the savage glee Sos had seen on other men's faces – but he was unstoppable, always a little surprised when each enemy collapsed so easily on to his sword, always ready for the next man, and the next.

Sos, too, should have been exultant. He'd traded enough grimy, sweaty bear hugs to know he'd fought well – better than well.

As a boy, he'd spent his most private hours picturing himself standing triumphant in the middle of the king's army, having proved himself as good as any man there. But now that day had finally come, he could not enjoy it. The deep-throated cheers, the mindless solidarity, it all grated. His dreams, he realised, had changed.

Beneath an oppressive twilight sky, pregnant with rain and thunder, the victorious soldiers were already deep in drink, their voices and faces bleared by the wine. Sos was reeling. Time darted forward in bursts, then lulled and wallowed. Normally, drink fired him, made him wild and funny, made him love every man he spoke to, made every man love him. Not tonight. Tonight two black rats had settled in his stomach and were running round and round in circles, faster and faster, while wasps beat against the inside of his skull, stinging, buzzing, trying to escape. He drank on, waiting for the lightness and ebullience to find him, but the more he drank the darker his thoughts became.

He no longer doubted that his loathing of the king was mutual. Ever since the levy before the city walls, he'd been sure.

It was the last time he'd seen Tamar. Pale, stately, distant, somehow unlike herself, she'd walked amongst them, wishing them goodbye and good luck. She approached him, Yuri hulking at her side, and looked straight at him, but her eyes settled beyond him, as if he were empty air, not blood and bone. The starlings, chattering and cleaning their wings in the trees, might have taken more notice. Her polite questions – his mother, his sisters – still smarted. She said much the same things to the men beside him, but they enjoyed her courtesies and shuffled and glowed. It was different for them.

The king and queen moved on. Sos hadn't realised he was scowling at their backs until Yuri looked round and their eyes met. He'd tried to banish whatever was on his face, but it was too late. The Rus gave him an infinitesimal shake of his head and followed the queen, putting one arm lazily about her shoulder.

Then came the call to mount. Yuri clamped his helmet on his head, leapt on to his huge, black horse, bent down and caught Tamar's chin in his hand to kiss her farewell. The soldiers cheered. The brave young king and his devoted queen – perfect. And now Yuri would return to her, to her bed, covered in glory after one pitifully easy fight. Sos almost wished they had lost. He drained what wine he had and called for another skin.

A gang of music-players – the sort that spring up wherever there are soldiers – struck up somewhere outside the light of the fire, a barrage of pipes and drums and cymbals and whooping, then danced into the ring of men to roars and claps. Many were dressed as women, with enormous red lips and sagging padded chests. Others cantered on broom-horses, waving stick-swords, aping the king's troops who lay sodden, gurgling, shouting encouragement, abuse, trying to grab the horses' tails or pull the men-women on to their laps. They started up a song with crashing rhymes banged out on cymbals about the women who were waiting at home. Everyone soon caught the refrain, shouting it louder and louder.

The song ended and a young man, all soft flesh and big eyes, swathed in tattered red silk pranced over to the king and slopped on to his lap, pecking kisses all over his face, squeezing his arms and making pouting Os of admiration. Yuri, blood still smeared across his face, shoved his hand under the man's skirts and he squealed and whisked away.

A bang of thunder and then the rain started to fall overhead, fat drops, tapping the leaves, hissing in the flames, but nobody noticed. The men thumped the ground, whistled and bellowed for more.

'Come, lady, come,' the king called.

The boy-queen tiptoed back to him, smoothing his wig, waggling his hips. Yuri grabbed him, spun him round, bent him over and flipped his skirts over his head, then paused and deliberately let his eyes land on Sos with a drunken leer.

'Queen like much.'

Sos snapped. He ripped his dagger from his belt and sprang

across the circle, knocking the boy out of the way and tumbling Yuri to the floor. He meant his blade to skewer a killing hole through the king's throat before anyone could break them apart.

But Yuri was waiting for him, viciously sober. His hands flew up and caught Sos's right arm before the blow landed. Sos tried to drive the dagger down, his left hand helping now, but the king was stronger and was already twisting the blade so it was pointing back at Sos. Sos rolled hard to one side, hoping to break Yuri's grip. Again the Rus was ready for him and rolled with him, on top of him, crushing him. Sos struggled to break free. It was taking all his strength to stop the dagger plunging into his face, but he had a horrible feeling Yuri wasn't trying as hard as he could. He was in control, while Sos's limbs wouldn't do what he wanted.

Suddenly, the king scrambled to his feet, beckoned Sos up, laughing, a smile on his face. Sos clambered upright, the ground see-sawing underneath him. Far away he could hear Zak telling him to stop. Sargis was shouting something, but Sos lurched and lost sight of him. He could only see Yuri walking round him, talking to him in his own language, mocking him, toying with him. He had to turn as Yuri circled and it was making him dizzy. The earth slid under him and he slipped in the mud.

Yuri put his fists up, grinning, play-fighting. Sos pounced, but the king punched him away with a blow that curled up out of nowhere. It knocked Sos off his feet and he thumped hard on to his back, the air knocked out of him. Yuri did not come after him, but stepped back and waited while Sos struggled to lift himself off the ground.

Thunder rumbled overhead and dread, colder than fear, darker than anger, iced his limbs. What was he doing? What had he started? Why was he reeling, bare-fisted, trying to kill the king? He leapt again. And again Yuri's fists were faster. One blow to the head, another to the stomach. He dropped to his knees.

'Up.' The word cracked above him.

He could see nothing but red shadows. He was standing, but not for long. A flowering of pain told him he had been knocked down again, and this time Yuri was on top of him, his fists everywhere. Blackness.

He woke, coughing up scalding vomit.

'You're an idiot, Sos.'

Zak. Zak?

He tried to speak, but all he heard in his ears was a gargling groan.

'Careful, be still.'

He felt a cloth near his eyes, then fingers walking up his ribs. He winced, nearly cried out.

'Don't try to open your eyes any further. You'll struggle to see for a day at least. And keep your fingers still until I've splinted them. You're lucky to be alive.'

I wish I was dead.

'He was about to rip your belly open – but my father stopped him. It was close. He wanted to kill you. My father laughed, said you were drunk, hot-headed, said it loud, the others laughed, called on Yuri to let you go. He did. He didn't want to. You're lucky that people like you. Sos, why'd you do it?'

He could hear the shock in his friend's voice. He hawked, spat and emptied his throat.

'Where's your honour?' A pulverised whisper. 'Insult like that. About Tamar. About the queen.'

'Sos,' Zak began, gently, 'amongst men, after a fight, that was nothing. I didn't admire it either, nor did my father, but you didn't need to fling yourself on him like a madman.'

Zak dipped his cloth into a bucket of water and rinsed it out, then opened the pouch at his side and drew out a needle.

'Your lip needs a stitch or two or it'll never heal.'

Sos tried to block out the snaking feeling of the thread sliding through his face – along with everything else. He was a fool.

'There you go. You'll live,' Zak said. 'Have a drink.'

'Last thing I need.'

'Of water.'

'Oh.'

Zak tipped some down Sos's throat, making him splutter.

'He did it on purpose, Sos.'

'What d'you mean?'

'I could see the way he was looking at you, all the time. He wasn't drinking – not much. He knew what he was doing. He wanted you to do what you did. To make you attack him.'

Zak shook his head and his voice grew quieter – and maybe a little angry.

'You told me you were going to steer clear. What was it you said? *Who wants to be worth less than his wife?*'

'I'm sorry. I couldn't help it. I should have told you.'

'You're an idiot,' Zak said, but his voice was already kinder.

'I know. Worse than an idiot. I wish Yuri had killed me.'

Footsteps closed on them through the dark. Zak picked up his sword, but it was Sargis who spoke.

'No you don't – because then you'd be dead. And believe me, even fools are better off alive.'

He crouched down slowly, his knees cracking.

'You can't stay here, Sos. You know that, don't you?'

'Of course. I tried to kill the king, didn't I?' Sos smiled a little – the words sounded strange and dramatic in his ears, as if they belonged to somebody else's life. 'I'll go home. Keep out of the way.'

Sargis shook his head.

'That won't do either, Sos. I spoke to Yuri – exile or death, that's what he wants. I don't know what this is about and I don't want to know, but he is the king, so you must go. I'm sorry.'

'I won't run away. My lands are mine. He can come and find me there if he wants.'

Sargis put a hand on Sos's shoulder.

'You speak right, lad, but it won't just be you he comes and finds. Think of your family – your people. He could send an army to find you. You could hide out in the mountains. But you know what angry men do when they can't find what they seek.' He paused. 'I'm sorry, Sos.'

'But where am I to go?'

'West to Constantinople. That's where men always go if there's been trouble. The imperial armies are the best place for young men who can't go home. I have friends there, kin too. I can write you an introduction. And the queen's sister is there. She might be able to help.'

'I sell my sword to the basileus?'

'You have no choice.'

Chapter Thirty-three

Tamar woke to the thud of Yuri working his way up the corridor. She sat up in bed and hoped he would trip, knock himself out and forget where he was. Then she heard Nino's firm voice.

'My lord, the lady Tamar has long been abed. I heard the guards calling the third watch. Must you disturb her rest now?'

Yuri laughed. 'Stand clear, woman.'

He entered the bedroom. Tamar nearly pretended to be asleep, but decided that would be cowardly. Instead, she stood up and lit a candle from the embers of the fire.

'I am glad you are safe returned, my lord. Shall I call for wine, something to eat, perhaps? Would you like to sit down?'

He knew what she was doing. He wasn't stupid.

'No. No wine. I already eat. I come to see my wife.'

He threw the candle into the grate, took hold of her and ground his mouth against hers, his hands swarming all over her back. Every muscle tensed up. She was suffocating. He was unwashed, sodden with drink. His breath heaved and panted in her ears. He spun her round and grabbed at her breasts, while he started to kick off his boots. He let go of her and wrestled with his leg coverings.

'Bed,' he said.

She waited in the dark while he groped towards her and started to pat the bedcovers trying to find her. Suddenly, she knew she couldn't stomach it – not tonight, not ever again. She reached under her pillow, took hold of her kinzhal and held it out in front of her. His hand stopped when it touched the blade.

'Get out, Yuri,' she whispered.

She expected him to back away – maybe shout and curse. But he sat at the other end of the bed and spoke in the darkness.

239

'Little sword not help you. You need son. I need son. Kingdom needs son. Your men – every man – want son. If you lie with little sword – that not happen. So you lie with me. Understand?'

'No. You disgust me. Do not touch me.'

Yuri laughed. 'You not like to lie with me?'

'No.'

'You like to lie with other man?'

A snarl warped the edge of his voice.

'No,' she replied, teeth set.

'Maybe that boy? Little pretty boy. I like to fuck him too – find out why so good.' He laughed again, pleased. 'But I can't. He gone now, gone far. You not fuck him no more.'

'Get out.'

Yuri was heavyset, but he could move fast. He grabbed her wrist, smashed it against the bedpost, making her drop the blade and clamped both hands about her throat. His fingers started to move slowly, massaging, rubbing each bone in her windpipe, squeezing the flesh underneath her jaw.

'No. I stay.'

She ripped her head away.

'I'll shout. Call the guard.'

'And say what? My husband wish to lie with me? *Help! Help!*' he parroted in a high-pitched voice. 'No. I think is not good idea. I think they laugh at you. Queen or not queen, woman has duty.'

She blanched. The tavads would probably agree with him.

'Husband has duty too. I fuck until we have two sons. Then I never touch you again. That is – what you call it? – that is promise.'

Tamar tried to hide deep inside her head while he jerked and grunted and finally flopped to a standstill at her side. She waited for him to go, but he rolled on his back and started to snore. Her body writhed. The mulch of meat grease, sweat and dirt that clung to him was now all over her. She edged off the bed, dressed herself slowly and tapped on the door to Nino's room. Her nurse was awake and was by her side immediately.

'What is it, child?'

'I need to bathe.'

Nino asked no questions.

'Of course, of course. I will ready everything myself. No need to wake Mzia or the others. Wait in my room – I'll put a log on the fire.'

Nino nudged her inside, sat her down and left. Tamar's head sank into her hands. The tavads would soon be snatching glances at her belly, waiting for the first hint to come creeping down the palace corridors from her quarters.

The lady Tamar is a little sick. The lady Tamar kept her bed till mid-morning. The lady Tamar ordered new clothes to be sewn.

Tamar feared they would not have to wait long. She pulled her shawl tight around her and stared at the dark spaces in the hearth where the red heat had burned itself out.

Chapter Thirty-four

Sos stared out across the roll and shimmer of the waves, his eyes flinching as they found the yellower patch behind the clouds where the sun must be. The salt breeze in his face tasted of strange places and new people: the west. It was warm and energetic, different from his empty mountain air that asked nothing and made no promises.

Ahead of him lay Constantinople, the home of the basileus, the centre of the world. But he could not find any excitement, only a bleak awareness that beyond its palaces and churches lay another sea, bigger than the one under his feet, and beyond that, so they said, rolled an ocean of storms and monsters that only had one shore. Everything and everyone he had ever known lay behind him.

A friendly shout called him to stop mooning and come and eat.

He had taken ship at Trebizond with a party of merchants. At first he could barely follow their talk. Sos wasn't over-proud of his Hellên, but he knew when it was spoken well. Their version was a crazed patois, both guttural and lisping, with words culled from every tongue spoken wherever a harbour stood on the shores of the sea. They'd made fun of his bafflement with great good nature, repeating themselves in woefully exaggerated court-speak, booming every schoolboy cliché from the old poems until he understood. He'd laughed so hard that for a moment his own troubles had lightened.

The merchants had left one of their trading posts on the southern shores of Kirim – although they called it Taurica – laden with goods that the north-men had floated down the Don.

242

Furs, amber and honey were stuffed in the hold, while a few beautiful, angry girls bound for the slave markets had been penned on deck.

After four days at sea, a northerly wind had licked up out of nowhere and driven them across the whole breadth of the sea, howling destruction at their backs, until they could see the waves breaking under the steep cliffs of Trebizond. But God, they told him, who loves seafaring men, heard their prayers and stilled the tempest, although not before half a dozen other ships, less blessed – or with less sea room – had splintered on the rocks.

They needed a few days to re-step their mast, strained close to breaking in the storm – and to see whether anything of interest had come up overland from Tabriz – but then they'd bear him west if he had gold enough. Sos only had to show them a few of the coins in Sargis's purse for them to wave him up the gangplank, telling him to find a patch of deck and keep clear of the bosun whose rod knew no difference between passenger and crew.

Sos had hoped for dolphins dancing on silvered crests, but the sea was like a tureen of bad soup, grey and lumpy, the same colour as the sky. There was no true wind, only reluctant gusts that squalled down off the mountains to the south, setting the boat racing before vanishing as fast as they had come. He had nothing to do but lean over the side and watch the swell march past or lie on his back and listen to the slop of the water, the thud and crack of the sails. Nothing to do but think.

So he was oddly relieved that one boy, about the age of his cousin Niko, was always keen to talk. He told Sos in a great rush that his name was Vasilis, that his family was originally from Miletus and that this was already his third trip.

'When we slipped Constantinople two years ago they'd just offed the old emperor's little boy. His mother loved the Latins. Latin bitch. She wanted her kin to have everything. She deserved to die, her and the boy. Everyone was glad to see Andronikos take the throne. He's the real thing.'

'I know. I met him.'

Vasilis stopped short. 'You met—? You mean you saw him once. From a distance, right?' He sounded as doubtful as if Sos had claimed to have been sired by a green sea serpent.

Sos shook his head. 'No. He was a guest in Tbilisi. I kissed his hand. I'd won a hunt game – he congratulated me.'

The boy's face fell and Sos was sorry he'd needed to show off.

'It was only quick – and I hardly dared say a word. Go on,' Sos nudged him, 'tell me more of the city. You know I've never seen it.'

'Haven't you?' said Vasilis, cheering up immediately. 'Some men faint when they first set eyes on it – or cry like babies. And I bet the Church of Wisdom would make anything you've got in Tbilisi look small as a beetle. If I was purple-born I'd live my whole life in the city and never leave. I'd have birds of gold singing in the trees in my garden. And my fountains would flow with wine and honey, not water, no way. That's how they live . . .'

Sos let Vasilis chatter on until he had to scamper away to work. He knew the boy took him for a nobody, travelling as he was without servants, without baggage. He fingered the letters Sargis had written him. One of them was addressed to Susa, and he smiled briefly as he imagined Vasilis's face if he told him he had an introduction to the great emperor Andronikos Komnenos's daughter-in-law in his pocket. But the more he thought about it, the less inclined he was to seek her out. She was too close to Tamar, too close to Yuri, too close to everything he had to leave behind. No, he would steer clear of court and become a plain soldier. He would go and fight the Normans, the Sicilians, whoever it was the empire was at war with. He did not care.

The nose of the boat hefted to the left and the heavy sail flogged overhead. Blocks thunked and ropes squealed. Something was happening. Vasilis popped up next to him, red-faced from heaving.

'Are we there?' Sos asked.

'No way – there's miles to go yet. You'll know right enough when we're closing the city. This is only Amisos. We're putting in for a day or two, my uncle says. He's got some business here.'

The wind had died altogether so the sailors untied long sweeps and paddled the boat towards shore. They squeezed into a gap against the harbour wall and immediately friends and compet-itors, agents and money-changers – Sos couldn't work out which was which – charged on board before the warps had even been made fast. Dozens of men were jabbering at each other in a language he only half understood, about people he did not know and places he hadn't heard of. He was about to slip ashore and start exploring when Vasilis skidded to his side.

'You hear that, Sos, you hear that?'

'Yes – no. I cannot understand when they all talk at once. What are they saying?'

Vasilis rolled his eyes. 'It's incredible, Sos, listen, word only got here three days ago, on a fast ship out of the city, listen, the emperor is overthrown – Andronikos he's dead, completely dead. He got torn to pieces in the hippodrome. Limb from limb – '

Sos must have looked sceptical. The man he had last seen lounging cool and elegant at Giorgi's side – ripped apart? But Vasilis wasn't going to let him doubt it, not for a moment.

'It's true, Sos, I swear it's true. Everyone knows. Ask anyone.' He lowered his voice to a dark whisper. 'He went mad, Sos, mad as a thousand devils, killing everyone, anyone. His death was agony. God, I can't believe we missed it. It must have been amazing.' He shook his head sadly. 'Isaak the Angel rules now, and there's war coming, and the city's in chaos—'

'But what does this mean for us?' Sos interrupted. 'For the ship?'

'My uncle's not going to be worried,' said Vasilis, as non-chalant as a boy bouncing with excitement could hope to look.

'He'll still risk putting in at Constantinople?'

'People always need goods, Sos, that's our secret. We make our best trades when other people are too scared to leave their houses, let alone buy or sell. We'll make a killing,' he beamed.

245

Sos nodded. A good time for merchants, but not for a man bound for a strange city, a city turned upside down. His introductions would be worthless; worse, he suddenly realised, they might even be dangerous. He took the letters out of his pocket, chucked them over the side and watched them sink.

'Thanks, Vasilis. I think I'll take a walk.'

He wandered along the docks, one hand on his sword hilt, the other on his purse. He needn't have worried. He was scowling and muttering so much that everyone gave him a wide berth, knowing that young men in strange moods could be dangerous.

Now he was by himself, he tasted the humiliation of his defeat like yellow bile in his mouth. What would Tamar be thinking? She must be disappointed, ashamed of him. As she should be. A man who couldn't win a fight was no kind of a man. If only he hadn't drunk so much. But maybe it wouldn't have made any difference. Yuri had guessed something. He would have waited for another chance. And he was stronger, much stronger. The shame bubbled once more in Sos's throat and he stopped, cursing himself.

Somebody barged into his back.

'Hey,' Sos called, his voice belligerent, 'watch where you're going.'

The man didn't look round. Sos saw a bull neck and a broad forearm clamped round a woman. He was pushing her hard through the crowds. A second man, scrawny in comparison, was hurrying after them with a very young boy tucked under his arm like a sack. The boy was howling, raw and pitiful, and the woman was stumbling, tripping over her cloak, her arm bent at an awkward angle. She craned her neck around. Her veil had fallen back and gold-brown hair was tumbling about her face – a beautiful face. Sos stared into a pair of panic-struck eyes, then the man wrenched her onwards and the crowds swallowed them up.

Gulls screamed overhead.

Then it hit him.

Susa.

'Susa!'

It was too late. She had disappeared. He blundered after them. What the hell was she doing there? Who were the men? What did they want with her? His mind galloped through a hundred questions. She must have escaped from Constantinople. The boy. He must be her son. Of course. A man could make a fortune if he delivered him to the new emperor. The dead emperor's grandson. Dead or alive.

Sos increased his pace, weaving, dodging, scanning the morass of people that filled the waterfront. *There.* He saw the men ducking into an alleyway and chased after them. It was darker, the shadows dirty, the air greasy. They'd come to a halt and Susa was pleading with them, showing them a necklace, gold and red. They were laughing at her, gross and leering. With a jolt, he realised one of her hands was cradling the head of a tiny baby strapped across her chest.

Sos drew his sword.

'Back up. That's my sister.'

The men turned fast.

'And I'm the queen of Sheba,' said the big one. 'We know who she is and we know she's got no brothers. Get lost. She's ours.'

'How much?' Sos demanded. 'I'll make it worth your while.'

'You haven't got near enough. Clear out or you'll be sorry.'

Sos looked from one man to the other. They weren't soldiers. The one holding Susa had a giant meat cleaver tucked in his belt and the other, seedy and pockmarked, was holding a long, rusty knife. They couldn't fight, not without letting Susa or the boy go, but nor could Sos attack them. He held his hands open, appealing.

'Listen, how are you going to get them to Constantinople? How do you know somebody else won't take them off you? How do you know the emperor's men will pay up? I can offer you good money for her, up front, right now. How about it?'

He jangled his purse meaningfully. The men glanced at each other. The butcher was obviously calculating how he could get the money and keep Susa, but the rat-faced one looked keen. He took a step forward, his hand over the boy's mouth to keep him quiet.

'How much you got there?'

'Come and have a look.'

'No, show us.'

Sos shook a couple of coins on to the dirt.

'There's a lot more where that comes from.'

The man gawped. 'He's loaded.'

Entranced by the gold, he made a mistake. He loosened his grip and the boy sank his milk teeth into his fingers. He yowled, startled, and dropped him. Sos darted forward, swept the child behind him and back-handed his sword deep into the man's thigh. He crashed to the ground, screeching with pain. Sos swung to face the butcher who was edging backwards, trying to pull his cleaver free.

'I'll kill her. Kill the kid, too. I mean it.'

'No you won't,' said Sos, calm and reasonable, holding his gaze. 'Because then I'll kill you. And you don't want to die. Nobody does. Not when you can pick up those coins there. And these—' he shook three more on to the ground, 'and get the hell out of here. Easy money. Go on. Let her go. Go on.'

'Let them go, God's sake, my leg, help, let them go . . .' the wounded man moaned up at him.

Sos could see the butcher was wavering, but he still had a tight grip on Susa.

'Hit him where it hurts,' Sos said urgently in Kart. 'Now, Susa, now.'

For a moment, she looked blank and he cursed well-born women, but then her eyes widened in comprehension and she elbowed her captor hard between the legs. He doubled over and she tore herself free. Sos scooped the boy up, grabbed her and together they raced down the alley and back on to the waterfront.

'Quick,' he said. 'We need to get out of here, fast. Sorry, but can you run? You must run, come on.'

He looked up and down the long line of boats. How was he to know which one might be going east? 'Trebizond? Trebizond?' He darted up to the longshoremen hulking goods on and off boats. Most shrugged, some shoved him out of the way. He swore under his breath.

Then he heard somebody shouting his name. 'Sos? Sos!' It was Vasilis, his face nearly invisible behind the coil of frayed hawser in his arms. 'What you doing, Sos? Who's she?'

'She's – she's my sister. Long story, Vasilis. Look, you've got to find us a ship going back east.'

'But I thought you were—'

'I was, but now I'm not. Come on, we've not got much time.'

'What's the rush?' Vasilis looked at Sos, then at Susa, bewildered.

'Please,' said Susa. 'I'm in great danger.' Vasilis flushed as she turned her gaze on him and he suddenly became very purposeful.

'Right. Say no more. I'll find you a ship. Follow me.'

'Wait, Vasilis,' Sos said. 'We need to keep out of sight.'

'There's my uncle's warehouse,' he replied quickly. 'You can stay there safe till I'm back. We're not shifting more till morning. Over here. This way. Come on.'

He hustled them down another alleyway, pushed them through a small side door, dumped his mound of rope and disappeared at a run. Sos pulled the door shut and barred it. The last of the afternoon light shone through a row of windows set high in the gables.

'How did those men recognise you? Could there be more of them?' Sos demanded.

Susa was soothing the boy, who was hiccuping and whimpering quietly, both hands gripping the hem of her dress. The baby lolled silent at her chest.

'Before Andronikos became emperor we lived on a big estate not far from here. They must have known me from there. It was bad luck, I think, nothing more. I'd noticed them staring at me as soon as I got off the ship. If it hadn't been for you . . .' She trailed off. 'I haven't asked – who are you? Why did you—' She stopped, gasped.

'But I do know you. You're the boy from the hunt. The one my sister kept looking at. Forgive me, I can't remember your name.'

'That's all right – it's a long time ago now. I'm Sos. Lord Soslani. Well, I was.'

'Was?'

'I've been exiled. Royal decree. I'm not sure you can still call yourself a lord if you can't set foot on your own lands.'

Susa looked worried. 'Oh . . .' she said, then fell silent.

'What is it?'

'I'd assumed you'd be bound the same way as us. I was hoping – but I'll manage somehow.'

Sos smiled. 'Don't worry. I'll get you back to Tbilisi. I can hardly abandon the queen's sister out here, can I? Not when you've got this far. I really would deserve exile then.'

'Thank God.' Tears started in her eyes, but she brushed them away. 'Sorry. I'm just so relieved. The past weeks . . . they've been . . .' She paused. 'But what'll you do after we get back? You can't just leave again. Not after what you've done. I could talk to my sister—'

'No,' Sos shook his head, 'don't. Never say a word about me.'

'But why not? Whatever you did, I'm sure she'll forgive you. She's just quick-tempered, like our father—'

'No, you mustn't.' He'd spoken much louder than he'd meant to, startling the boy.

'Where's father? I want my father,' he muttered, half asleep.

At that moment somebody rattled the door, then thumped it hard.

'It's me!' They both relaxed at the sound of Vasilis's voice and Sos hurried to let him in.

'You're in luck,' he panted, his eyes beaming with self-importance. 'There's a ship leaving before sundown. The captain'll take you – he's a countryman of yours. Triple rates, though, he knows men are looking for you.'

'Fine. When can we board?'

'Now. It's not far.'

Sos nodded and knelt beside Susa's boy.

'What's your name?'

Silence. 'Alexeios,' Susa supplied.

'Do you have a horse, Alexeios?' Sos asked in the gentlest voice he could muster. 'I bet you do. A handsome white pony?'

A nod.

'What's it called?'

A sniff.

'Bucephalus.'

'Well, let's pretend I'm Bucephalus. Jump on my back and we'll hide you under my cloak. And don't worry – we'll soon be safe in Tbilisi.'

'What's Tbilisi?'

'Home, Alexeios, it's home.'

Chapter Thirty-five

The two sisters embraced cautiously. Tamar was wary, on the defensive, waiting for Susa to winkle out how defeated she was. Her heart quailed. Everything would be a hundred times worse once her sister knew how she had failed.

'You're very thin, Susa,' she said eventually. She could feel her sister's ribs through her dress, see the blades of her collarbone.

'I've been too scared to eat much. And I've been feeding Davit. With Alexeios I had a wet-nurse, but now . . .'

Her voice faded. Susa's voice never used to fade. It used to build to a screeching pitch until you wanted to throttle her. There was a great deal about her that Tamar was struggling to recognise. Her features were firmer, more defined – she no longer looked like a piece of fruit that would bruise if you breathed too close it, but the set of her eyes had softened. Tamar expected to find reproach or resentment in them, but instead saw sympathy and unspoken questions.

She began again. 'You had my letter about father?'

Susa nodded.

'It was strange. It all seemed so far away. Another life.'

She fell silent for a moment, then looked quickly at Tamar.

'And it was hard to feel sorrow for a man who felt no love for me.'

'How can you say that?'

'Because it's true. I do not blame him. I did before, but not now. After he realised mother could never love him, he poured his heart into you. There was none left for me. It might have been different if I did not remind him of her, but as it turned out . . .'

Tamar nodded. She could not deny it. Susa was a gossamer

version of their mother, a copy in down and feathers. Suddenly, Tamar knew something else that was true.

'I felt the same when mother died. She always looked at me as if I was strange to her, like she was bewildered I existed.'

They were silent, surprised and pleased to have spoken so openly.

'What was Constantinople like?'

An easy question and Susa answered in a great gulp.

'Big. Beautiful. I didn't see much. They kept me close to the palace – it was a dangerous time. My boys made it easier. I knew that so long as they were well, I could be happy – happy enough, anyway – and my husband was a good man in his way. Of course, he was terrified of his father, but by then so was half the world. Andronikos changed so much, Tamar. Becoming emperor warped him. It was terrible to watch. Terrible. Maybe he even deserved to die like he did.'

'You didn't see—'

'No, thank God. The mob tore him apart. Nobody on the road here talked of anything else.'

'But what happened to your husband?'

'They seized him and put his eyes out. The wounds soured and he died. That is what I heard – thank God I did not see it. He was not a bad man – he was kind to me, kind to the boys – but he was his father's son and so they hated him.' A moan suddenly escaped her throat. 'What would they have done to my boys . . . to the baby . . . ?'

She was rocking backwards and forwards as she spoke, her arms clasped across her chest, cradling an invisible child. Tamar put a hand out and stilled her.

'Don't think about what might have been, sister. They are safe now and they will grow into fine young men – a joy to their mother. I promise.'

Susa nodded and rubbed away the tears that stood in her eyes.

'Yes. It's a miracle we're alive.'

'It is astounding. How in heaven's name did you escape that madness?'

Her sister looked down at her hands and did not answer straight away.

'Forgive me,' said Tamar. 'We do not need to talk about it if you would rather forget.'

'No, it's all right. At first I didn't realise what was happening. The baby was so tiny and I was still recovering from his birth – I had little thought of anything else. My servants must have been ordered to keep all news from me – not to worry me. But their faces – it was impossible not to realise something was terribly wrong. Then a half-man, one of eunuchs – he was my friend – he told me I would be killed if I went with my husband. He persuaded me to let him hide us, then he smuggled us on to a ship. Simple, really.'

Tamar smiled. 'One thing at least has not changed. The effect you have on men. Even a man with no manhood rushes to your rescue.'

She'd meant it as a joke but Susa's face fell.

'Sorry, sister. I am not mocking you. I admire you. It was a huge risk you ran. Brave too.'

Susa shook her head. 'I thought of you – how you escaped from Orbeli's men in the mountains. I thought that if you could return home safe, so could I. And my boys gave me strength. I could not let any harm come to them.'

A slight pause.

'I'm sure you'll feel the same when your child is born.'

Tamar's hands went to her belly. She hadn't realised it was so obvious already. She nodded, but said nothing and Susa did not press her further.

'Tamar, tell me, how are things here?'

She could not answer.

'Not good?'

She shook her head, not trusting herself to speak.

'But you are queen. The tavads crowned you. We heard that in Constantinople. I was proud – truly.'

There was nothing but kindness and concern in her voice. It was dreadful. Vindictiveness would have been easier to bear.

At that moment, Mzia entered the room and stood, gaping at Susa.

'Yes, Mzia, what you've heard is true. Here's my sister, back safe with us from the west. Please prepare our old nursery for her and her boys.' The girl nodded, but did not leave. 'Is there something else?'

'Please, my lady, Shota said to say a scout's come ahead, says the king will be here by sundown.'

Tamar blinked. She had not expected him for another day at least. She answered as calmly as she could.

'Thank you, Mzia, please ask Shota to get everything ready.'

'Yes, my lady,' she replied and hurried out.

Susa had a puzzled frown on her face.

'What is it, sister?'

'Forgive me, Tamar, maybe it isn't important, but I thought the women who served you were all unwed.'

Tamar nodded. 'They are. Why do you ask?'

'Maybe you already know, but that girl is at least four months gone with child, I am sure of it.'

Tamar hesitated, but then shouted for Mzia to come back. Her head appeared round the door.

'My lady?'

'Come inside, Mzia, and shut the door behind you.'

'Yes, my lady.'

'How long, Mzia?'

The girl stared at her, horrified.

'Don't worry, I am not angry.'

'You're not?'

'Of course not. Come, is it a boy from the city? One of the soldiers? Who? I can make him help you.'

Mzia squirmed, chewed her lip, twisted at her dress, went very red, then very white, but did not utter a word. Tamar sighed and went over to her, took her by both shoulders and asked again, gently.

'Who?'

The girl's face puckered and she burst into tears. 'Don't make me say, my lady, I don't want to say, my lady, I'll go away, right away, only don't make me say.'

Tamar ran out of patience. 'His name, Mzia, or I'll hand you over to the monks for penance.'

Mzia made a mangled sort of noise, gulped down another sob and then whispered, 'The king, my lady, the king.'

Tamar listened in silence while Mzia stumbled through what had happened. First it had been Gleb, one of Yuri's Rus friends, who'd eyed her up while she waited on the queen, snatching at her dress, leering at her. Then he'd waylaid her in a corridor. The first time she'd managed to kick him and duck out of the way. The second time a couple of guards had appeared and he'd had to let her go. But the third time she couldn't fight him off and he'd bundled her into a storeroom and – but at that point Mzia was crying too hard to make any sense.

'Why didn't you tell me, Mzia? Or Nino? We could have put a stop to it.'

'I told him I would tell you, my lady, that's what I said, I said you wouldn't stand for it, but then the next time he found me, he had the king with him as well and they both, they both . . . and the king said that if I told you, you wouldn't believe me, and anyway if I did tell you, he'd make sure I disappeared and my mother too and . . . and . . .'

The tears overwhelmed her again and she collapsed. Tamar was still. It was Susa, very white, who scooped Mzia up off the floor and kissed her cheeks.

'Go to your room, my love. We'll send Nino to you. She'll stay with you until you can sleep. Don't worry. The queen will look after you now.'

Mzia stumbled out of the room.

'You don't seem that surprised, sister,' Susa murmured.

'It's not just Mzia,' Tamar said.

'What do you mean?'

'Girls from town. Kitchen girls. Even stableboys. Shota hardly knew how to tell me. I know kings are no more angels than other men. Away from home, after a battle, that I could understand. But this never stops. And the violence. If one of his horses sickens or does not run as fast as he would like, he beats the groom until he's blood and mulch, nothing more. If one of the table-servers drops a cup, it's a blow to the side of the head, enough to fell an ox.'

'But what do the tavads say about this?' Susa asked.

'He isn't stupid. He only does it before his own men – or before men of no account. I hear things and try to make amends, but the tavads admire him still. They see a warrior, a king, ruthless, hardy, battle-hungry. Even Gamrekeli – who, God knows, is not a cruel man – told me he admired Yuri's appetite for life. *Appetite for life.*' The words escaped between her teeth like a sigh. 'And, what's worse, Rusudan adores him.'

'Rusudan? You mean—'

'Yes, our aunt. She turned up right after father died. I wouldn't be where I am without her. At first I thought heaven had sent her, but now . . .'

Tamar swallowed the ball of sickness that refused to leave her throat.

'I think she knows Yuri is bad, but she refuses to admit it, even to herself. She took a lot of credit for finding him, you see, for making the match. And of course he's charming to her – or I imagine he's being charming. They talk in his language and I can't understand a word they're saying. She simpers and bats her sticky eyelashes at him. Hints I am lucky to be wed to such – you know what she says? – such a *stallion.*'

Susa wrinkled her nose. 'She sounds horrific.'

'She is.' She jumped up. 'It makes me so angry, Susa.'

'Then do something about it.'

'What?'

'I don't know. But the sister I left behind never would have suffered these insults, never.'

'The sister who left never would have spoken so true.'

'A lot has happened. I have changed.'

'We have both changed. But I have changed for the worse. There is a coward skulking under my ribs, whispering, gnawing, whining and I can't shut him out. Father made a mistake. I can't do this. I'm not who he thought I was. I'm not like him.'

'Of course you're not. The sun is yellow, the grass is green – and you are a woman. You can never be as father was, roaring about the palace, stamping and shouting. And thank God for that.'

'Thank God? How can you – he was a great king.'

'To you, maybe, and to those he loved,' Susa spoke very quietly. 'But to many he was a bully and a tyrant. I'm sorry, Tamar, but it's true. And from what you say, Yuri is like him – only much, much worse. You don't want to be like that.'

'Shota tried to tell me the same thing once. He said swords weren't everything, but I didn't believe him.' Tamar smiled suddenly. 'It might be easier if I had your face.'

But Susa did not smile back. 'You're wrong.' She was angry. 'My face hasn't helped me, Tamar. Our mother's face didn't help her. Men don't fight for beauty, if that's what you think. They fight for what they want to protect, for what they believe is good and pure.'

The sound of horses echoed below them. Many horses. The king was returning. Tamar waited for the dull thump of dread to steal over her limbs and immobilise her, but nothing happened. She felt calm, composed. She walked to the window and looked out. Away above the rooftops, as day folded into night, she saw the quiet glint of the evening star.

Deep in her belly, something tapped and quivered. Yuri's child was quickening inside her.

Chapter Thirty-six

Yuri – with the strut of a man who knows his heir is growing in his wife's belly – and a rumbustious gang of favourites swaggered across the courtyard and piled into the great hall, bellowing for strong wine and pig-meat, their chests puffed and cocksure, their voices still hoarse from battle. Most were bearded, some were wounded, blood-crusted bandages wrapped about their arms and legs, but the gold in their pockets flashed in their eyes. Victory clung to them. The palace, which had been quiet, was kicked awake by this exultant onslaught.

'Are you sure it is wise to go down there?' Susa asked. 'I have never seen men so wild.'

Tamar shook her head.

'I will not cower up here and wait for the king to come or not come as he desires. I will not listen to the shrieks of their girls. The absurd fights. No. Enough. I will go down there and remind him that he is king only because I am queen.'

Susa followed her to the door.

'Then I shall come with you.'

Tamar was surprised and pleased.

'You're not afraid?' she asked.

'No. Not unless you are. Are you?'

'Yes, Susa. Yes, I am.'

Together, they walked down the corridor to where the door opened from the royal apartments into the back of the hall. Tamar pushed it open and they entered. It was dim; the fires had not been lit long. For a while, none of the men noticed her. Her grey dress, pale face and dark hair might look like nothing but shadows flickering on the high dais.

Tamar remembered how easy it had been for her father to

259

cow many of the same men into mumbling submission. She would never have that simple power he and Yuri shared. The power a boy has over the world around him. The power to pull the wings off a fly, to tie a firebrand to a cat's tail, to tip chicks out of their nest – and to revel in it.

Below her, Yuri was deep in a raucous cabal, shouting some story in his mangled but very effective Kart. A dozen men were laughing up at him, repeating his jokes back to him, trying to outdo each other, laugh the loudest, the longest. They were like a litter of piglets clambering over each other, rooting for their mother's teats.

The older men sitting near the fire saw her first and fell silent. But the pack crammed about the king did not notice – not until Yuri himself sensed a change and looked up. His eyes found her straight away. He rose to his feet and his chair crashed on to its side. Everyone was looking now. Swaying very slightly, the king stretched his arms in front of him in a broad embrace.

'My lady comes to greet her husband. Honour, my lords, big honour. I understand – my lady grieves while I am gone. Grieve not. Good news, lady queen, no Turkoman bastard live in Shirak. I kill many and rest run away. You want to thank me? Come.'

Yuri made a show of beckoning her towards him, ready to enact the reunion of loving husband and grateful wife. Gleb and a couple of others sniggered – and not quietly. Tamar did not move.

Yuri's expression hardened. 'No thanks? No kind word for soldier?'

The hall had resolved into a brittle silence. Every man would be able to taste the danger in the air.

Yuri hawked and spat. 'Go to bed. I come later.'

He turned his back on her. Gleb jumped up to right his chair and Yuri sat down, stuck his legs out in front of him and snarled something in his own language. Silence. Everyone was staring at the queen.

'What problem?' Yuri shouted. 'Talk. Drink. Your king commands.'

One boy launched back into the story he had been telling before Tamar entered, but his voice jumped into empty air, cracked and faded before he'd said a dozen words. Nobody else spoke.

'Yuri, please will you accompany me to my chambers. I would speak with you in private.'

Tamar spoke as quietly as she dared. Yuri did not move.

'My lord?' A little louder. 'Would you do me the honour—'

'I heard. You not hear me? I come later.'

Tamar took a deep breath and raised her voice another notch.

'No, my lord. You come now.'

He lurched to his feet and trod, slow, a little unsteady, up the fourteen steps that let on to the dais. The planks shuddered under each footfall, but that was the only sound in the hall. He came to a standstill so close to Tamar that she could see the flecks of white spittle dried at the corner of his mouth and smell the old meat on his breath.

'Thank you, my lord.'

She turned to go, but he took her arm and held her back.

'What you want to say to me?'

'Better in private, my lord. I would not shame you in front of your men.'

'Shame?'

'Shame, my lord. Do you know what that word means?'

The blood flowed fast to his face, making the vein that ran across his forehead bulge. 'Speak. You cannot shame me.'

'Very well. The next time one of your men dares to touch one of my household, I will punish him – severely.'

'No,' came the flat reply.

'My lord?'

'I said no. You cannot punish my men.'

'I can and I will. Your men are my men. You are my man. Do not mistake me, Yuri. You may be my husband, but I am your queen. And you will obey me.'

Tamar never saw the blow coming. She was staring at his face, the skin puce, his pupils gyrating, then a thunderclap sounded in her left ear and she was off her feet, falling off the dais. Her sister screamed. Men shouted out. She didn't have time to put her hands out to break her fall. She slammed on to her front and tried to move, but couldn't, tried to breathe, but couldn't.

I'm only winded. It's all right.

But then something came to life in the pit of her stomach, twisting, grabbing, tunnelling. She moaned – she couldn't stop herself – and doubled up, trying to pull her knees into her belly, trying to muffle the pain billowing deep inside her. Her eyes were open but she couldn't see. Hands reached under her and horrified faces loomed above. She felt herself being lifted into the air.

'She's bleeding—'

'Quick!'

'The queen, the queen—'

A whirl of faces, the roof spinning overhead, lights stuttering, then her head lolled and blackness swept over her.

'She did it on purpose.'

The words swam into her ears. Who was speaking? Voices in her head? She stared about the shuttered room. Nobody. Then the voice again, clearer this time.

'You can say what you like, but that was no accident. She must have goaded him into it.'

It was her aunt, outside, yelling at somebody. Male voices, muffled, confused, then her sister, piercing and defiant.

'You were not even there! How dare you accuse a woman of such a thing? It is plain you yourself have never had children. For shame. These gentlemen would never countenance such a gross, such a disgusting, such a vile idea. Be gone. She is ill enough as it is without your horrible insinuations.'

Footsteps stamped down the corridor, the door creaked open and Tamar shut her eyes instinctively. She felt a hand on her arm.

'Tamar?'

It was Susa. She opened her eyes.

'So you've met Rusudan?'

Her sister smiled.

'I know her kind. Constantinople was full of them. Listen, two men, Mkhargrdzeli and Gamrekeli, are outside. They are both mortified – as well they might be. A fine husband they chose. They have been begging to be allowed to see you. Do you think you are strong enough?'

Tamar put her hand to the left side of her head and winced. It was swollen and throbbed and she couldn't see out of her eye. Her sister thought she was embarrassed.

'You do not want them to see you like this? I can bandage it. Or I can tell them to come back later.'

Tamar shook her head. 'Maybe it is better if they see.'

'You're right.'

The two men walked in, adrift, unsure how to handle what had happened. Their eyes flitted between her face and where her belly lay beneath the blankets, unable to settle anywhere.

'Gentlemen. You are wondering what has happened to my child, to the heir you all so long for. He is gone. Dead – at my husband's hand.'

They were silent, stricken. Her sickbed intimidated them.

'I cannot fight for myself. I cannot put up my fists, draw my sword and defend my own honour. I have no father, no uncles, no brothers – and now, no son. You say we must defend our lands – our mountains, our rivers, our plains. But what good are scores of dead Seljuks if you cannot protect one woman? I am Kartvelia. You would do well to start by protecting me.'

Sargis spoke first.

'Yuri has fled with his men. Gone, we know not where. The Kipchaks are angry. Sirchak wanted to go after him, but I did not want fighting in the city streets. I fear some others have followed him. Vardan has vanished and that means Con is gone too. They may yet make trouble, but do not fear – we can deal with them if it comes to that.'

He dropped to his knees beside her bed, his head bowed, penitent.

'The devil was in that man, but I did not see it. Forgive me – forgive all of us.'

After a brief hesitation, Gamrekeli eased himself down beside Sargis. 'I must beg you to pardon me too. The fault is ours. We chose ill. I have sent to the bishops and they are already drawing up the contract for your divorce. You are free of him.'

Tamar nodded and shut her eyes to stop the tears of relief rolling down her face. They took that as a dismissal and she heard Susa usher them from the room.

Her sister returned and tucked another pillow under her head, then sat down by her side with a bowl of something that smelt comforting.

'Here,' said Susa, handing her a spoon. 'Eat this. Nino's doctored it with herbs to stop the bleeding and ease the pain.'

Tamar sipped a couple of mouthfuls of the broth. Swallowing hurt. Her whole body hurt. Suddenly she was shaking so hard, she could no longer eat.

'Did you suspect that he might do something like that?'

Tamar said nothing, but Susa carried on as if she had spoken. 'If you did, do not think any more about it, that is all I wanted to say. Life plays strange tricks sometimes.'

Before Tamar could reply there was laughing and scuffling outside. Susa jumped up.

'Sorry, it's Alexeios. I'll ask Nino to take him away.'

'No, no, bring him in. I think it would do me good to see him.'

The door opened and a boy, beaming and tousled, stood on the threshold. He ran over to Susa and held his arms up to be lifted on to her lap, nuzzling his head into her shoulder while she stroked his hair. After a moment he wriggled free and started to explore the room while the two women watched.

'Susa, sister, thank you. I am so glad you're here.'

Their eyes met and they both burst out laughing.

'Really?'

'Yes, really! God knows, I never thought I would say it.'

Tamar looked over at her nephew again.

'We're the last of the Bagrationi now. Were I to die tomorrow your little Alexeios would be king. Although he might have to kill Yuri and one or two others first.'

The boy heard his name and stamped across the room, brandishing the poker for a sword.

'Kill, kill, kill.'

Tamar held up a pillow as a shield.

'You're a brilliant fighter already, my love,' she said.

'Sos show me.'

She must have misheard. Maybe it was a Hellên word she did not know. She looked fast at her sister and caught her expression emptying.

'Who showed you, Alexeios?'

But the boy clammed up and ran behind her bed.

'Sister?'

Susa's cheeks had flushed pink.

'Sister? What did he say?'

'He asked me not to say a word. He had helped us so much that I could only promise to do what he said.'

'But how?'

'He found us – saved us from the mob. He was bound west, but he turned back to bring us home.'

'Where is he now?'

'I know not. I begged him to come to the palace, but he would not.'

Tamar's mind was spinning.

'But he's here. He could be in the city?'

Her head was singing.

'Yes, maybe, he can't have gone far.'

'Quick, call Sirchak, Zakari, my guards, anyone. Find him!'

Chapter Thirty-seven

The guard knocked and Sos heard Tamar's voice pronounce a *yes* from beyond the door. It opened, but before his eyes could find her, Sargis had folded him into an affectionate embrace, muttering, 'Well done, lad, well done,' in his ear and Gamrekeli offered him a solemn, meaningful handshake, repeating, 'Well done, my lord, well done indeed.' Only after he had thanked both of them with all the proper words could he turn, as if artlessly, to the corner of the room where the queen stood, waiting, with Rusudan by her side. The older woman inclined her head, a nod of acknowledgement, nothing more.

The messengers who had overtaken him on the west road had told him Tamar had been taken ill, and he'd expected to find her diminished in some way, but she was undimmed. She looked taller and, if anything, stronger.

'My lady.' He dropped her a slow bow. 'You bade me return.'

He tried to keep his voice formal, but he could feel his happiness tugging at the corners of his mouth. He wished the others were deaf and blind – or at the bottom of the sea – not standing attentively at his side.

'My lord Soslani,' she began, 'I have learned that I owe you a great debt – the greatest. Without your aid, my sister and her sons would have perished in the dungeons of Constantinople.'

He shook his head.

'No man,' a small smile darted across his face, 'even one exiled by royal decree, could have done otherwise. But I begged her not to speak of it. I did not want to embarrass her – or you – before the king.'

'Nor, my lord, did she – not one word passed her lips. She did not break her promise to you, but my nephew is not, thank

266

God, so discreet. But he is almost inconsolable to have forgotten you were such a great secret and longs to see you to beg your forgiveness. I fancy he rather idolises you.'

She paused and her face darkened, a slight crease between her brows.

'But that is not all we have to thank you for. My lord, you saw the Rus's true nature before any of us. You begged me not to wed him. You were right to doubt him then, and you were right later when you drew your sword on him to defend my honour.'

She shifted her gaze to include Sargis, Gamrekeli and her aunt.

'Would that we had all been so astute.'

Sos bit his lip. She was a study in majesty. Sargis made a small, uncomfortable noise in his throat and Gamrekeli nodded sagely.

'But that is in the past,' she continued. 'Tell me, how can we repay you?'

He shook his head and dutifully matched the serious pitch of her voice.

'I seek no repayment, my lady.'

Gamrekeli bestowed a deep nod of approval.

'Quite right,' said Sargis. 'The queen and her sister swore you'd refuse a reward.'

'But the lady Rusudan had a different view.' Tamar turned suddenly. 'Did you not, aunt?'

'And I am sure your aunt will be pleased to admit she has been proved wrong,' Sargis prompted.

Sos smiled to himself. Things had changed at court.

'Indeed,' Rusudan nodded abruptly. 'The lord Soslani continues to make a great impression on us all. Now, if you will excuse me . . .'

She swept out of the room and the atmosphere improved immediately.

'Forgive my aunt's bad manners,' said Tamar. 'She is a little out of sorts. Before you arrived, we had been discussing how to deal with the tavads who had been closest to Yuri. She suggested we confiscate their lands – and execute a few as a warning.'

'But she—' began Sos.

'Exactly. She brought Yuri here in the first place. A fact she conveniently forgot in her rush to acquire other men's gold. She did not like it when I told her I had no desire to take revenge.'

Gamrekeli smiled complacently. 'A woman's mercy is beautiful to behold.'

'Very likely it is, my lord,' Tamar said.

'As Jesus himself once said to the—' continued Gamrekeli, warming to this theme.

'Forgive me, friend,' Sargis intervened, 'but I don't think that's why the lady Tamar is doing this.'

She smiled. 'Quite right, Sargis. Everyone expects some sort of purge, do they not? Men are keeping close to their homes, praying for their lives, waiting to see where the axe will fall. I shall let them fret – for a few more days – and then I shall let it be known that I want their loyalty, not their lives.'

'And you shall have it, believe me,' said Sargis. 'Now, Sos, what are your plans? The queen and I could use you at court.'

'My mother and my sisters must imagine me long since dead, so if you will permit me, I shall first ride north and show them my face. After that, I shall, of course, continue to serve the queen however she wishes.'

His eyes met hers and she smiled.

'Thank you, my lord. Go to your family with my blessing. But—,' she paused and Sos wondered whether a twinge of uncertainty coloured her voice, 'I too have business in your lands. I have not yet visited the graves of Aton and Albina and I owe them my prayers. I believe I shall accompany you.'

That was unexpected.

'I would be honoured, my lady.'

'Forgive me, my lady,' Gamrekeli broke in, 'but are you well enough to travel? It is not long since—'

'I'm fine, sir,' she cut him off. 'Mountain air always did do me good.'

* * *

They'd crossed the pass into Sos's lands at dawn and were now meandering down through the high meadows with the queen's escort fanned out around them. Patches of dew still clung to the grass and their horses' hooves left smudged trails behind them. Delicate lines of snow traced the contours of the mountains above their heads.

Tamar was riding what Sos still considered to be his horse – the one she had stolen from him at the foot of the mountains. Its tread was heavier now and it had filled out, but its yellow coat was unmistakable. Did she remember? How long ago was it? He tried to count. More than five summers, he reckoned, but less than ten. Was she thinking about it too? Her face was veiled against the glare so it was hard to tell.

He glanced at her whenever he could no longer bear not to, sometimes turning his whole head, sometimes only his eyes, looking for clues in the tilt of her chin, the set of her shoulders. Was she a queen riding out with one of her subjects or a woman riding out with a man? Did she realise they were weaving in and out in half figure-of-eights, knees almost touching, before shying away to the edge of the path? A strange timidity had gripped him and he found himself testing words, whole phrases, on his tongue.

Look at that red butterfly. You'll like my mother, I think. I've thought about you every hour since I last saw you. It'll be a fine day later.

Why had she come with him now? It was a mark of great favour, wasn't it? It could only mean one thing, couldn't it? But the tavads and her aunt had forced her to give him up once before. Would they do the same again? Or was she now powerful enough to choose for herself?

He was so preoccupied that when his horse stumbled on a patch of shale he almost fell off. That jerked Tamar out of her silence and she burst into laughter.

'Unseated by your horse! You're not Sos – you're an impostor.'

He tried to look injured, but inside he was elated. For the first time since he had returned, she did not feel impossibly regal.

'Blame this nag, my lady. Now if I had such a fine mount as yours . . .'

His words squirmed in the air between them.

'You admire this animal?' she said and patted its neck.

'Very much. And, you know, now that I look more closely, I see that it is very like one I owned as a boy.'

'What became of it?'

'I mislaid it one summer, not far from here.'

'Mislaid?'

'A thief made off with it.'

'A thief?'

'Yes. A despicable youth. And now I look more closely still, I see that you are very like him.'

Tamar widened her eyes.

'You call me horse-thief? Me, your queen?'

'I would certainly call you horse-thief — were you not my queen.'

'I would have to fight you for such an insult — were I not your queen.'

'You would lose.'

'You think? Is your nag fast, my lord?'

'For me she runs fast, my lady.'

'Catch me before the house, then, and my horse is yours.'

She kicked her horse's belly and darted away. He gave chase. The roll of his horse's hooves beat up into his stomach and threw a smile across his face. She flashed before him under the trees, the light blinking bright and dark as they raced between sun and shade, making him blind and dizzy and reckless.

He was overhauling her. His horse slapped into the ford first, the splash of cold water sharp on his face, and by the other side he'd pulled in front, leaning into his horse's neck as it scrambled up the bank. He stopped outside the house, listening to the clatter of the grasshoppers and the tumult inside him.

'You win,' she said. She pushed her veil aside. 'It's yours.'

He shook his head.

'You let me win. Keep him.'

He saw her big, bold grin break across her face – but then Sirchak was beside them asking whether they'd lost their minds and would they eat now or later. Sos heard Tamar reply, her voice maybe a little uneven, that she was not hungry. She took her cross from around her neck, turned and strode towards the two rough piles of stones that marked the graves of Aton and Albina.

Sos sat on one of the log benches, remembering the day he had buried them. At his feet, dandelions and clumps of clover were pushing up between the stones.

The guard – a small enough number, but more soldiers than had gathered in the mountains in half a lifetime – halted at a courteous distance from Sos's house and he and Tamar covered the final two hundred paces on foot.

His oldest sister, Maka, still unmarried, was stitching the hem of a dress in the shade of the old courtyard tree while Keti, the littlest, still skinny as a stick, was lolling upside down in the crook of a low branch, her braids dangling almost to the ground. At the sound of their footsteps, Maka glanced up, gave a strangled shriek and bowled into his arms, knocking the breath out of him, while Keti plummeted to earth and jumped up and down yelling his name. His mother's voice sounded from inside the house demanding to know why she wasn't allowed to have her afternoon nap in peace, then she appeared at the door, her hands over her mouth, gasping, incoherent, as Maka shouted, 'Sos, Sos, he's alive, he's home.'

Within minutes he was swimming in a sea of relatives, small cousins materialising out of nowhere, tugging his tunic, fighting to hold his hand, while aunts tussled to pinch his cheeks and ruffle his hair. It was so glorious that he forgot to be embarrassed. They really loved him. He had been gone for months, years, but they all still felt he belonged to them.

'Sos, Sos,' his mother was trying to get his attention above the hubbub. 'And who is this lady with you, my son?'

Her eyes were popping and he realised she thought Tamar must be a grand new wife he'd brought up from the plains.

'Mother, this is the queen Tamar. My lady, may I present my mother.'

A fluster of curtsies and introductions followed. Tamar was given a chair in the shade, then jugs of watered wine and bowls of curd and honey were rushed out. Sos had presents for everyone, and everyone was delighted and told him he shouldn't have and then they asked him where he'd been and why he hadn't sent word and didn't he realise how worried they'd been and what dreadful rumours they'd heard? He replied only that he'd been busy abroad on important royal business, which started another round of questions: where? – what had he seen? – had he seen elephants? – mermaids? – the basileus?

He tried to answer everyone at once, glancing every so often at Tamar to make sure she wasn't bored, but she looked content to listen, scratching the ears of an old hunting dog that was nuzzling her feet, undaunted, he hoped, by the long loops of drool that swung from its jaws.

'Who are all the soldiers?' a newly broken voice, pitching and yawing unmistakably, shouted above the noise. Sos looked over the heads clustered about him and saw Niko, his little cousin, little no longer, sprinting into the courtyard, bursting with excitement. 'Vakho's coming. He wants to know what's happening. He's angry, bright red angry. I ran ahead to see. He'll be here any moment.'

He stopped abruptly, stunned.

'Wow, Sos, it's you.'

Sos was about to leap forward and embrace him, but his mother touched a finger to his arm and stayed him.

'I was going to tell you, son,' she murmured, suddenly subdued.

'Tell me what, mother? What's wrong?' he replied. Instead of answering she looked up at him, pleading and apologetic. 'Tell me,' he repeated, kinder, when still she did not speak.

Keti piped up. 'Vakho says he's lord now. Says it's his right cos you've been gone so long. I said he was wrong but he said there was nothing I could do about it because I was only—'

Maka grabbed her by the arm and pulled her back, shushing her. 'Sorry brother, you see there was little we could do. Three women, alone, and you – well, we didn't know where you were.'

'Did he harm you?'

'No, no, nothing so bad. But he said you were dead and gone and he was now lord of your lands and your household. And he made sure we never forgot it.'

Keti wriggled free. 'He's no good. He's not like you. He—'

She fell silent and glowered over his shoulder. Sos looked round and saw Vakhtang walking into the courtyard. His sour expression told him everything he needed to know.

'Cousin,' Sos bowed low, 'I am in your debt. You kept my family safe while I was away and I see my lands have thrived. Thank you.'

He made to kiss both his cheeks – he didn't want to fight, not if he could help it – but Vakhtang stepped to the side, fingering the hilt of his short sword, his mouth working as hard as if he were chewing on gristly mutton.

'Your lands? You would still call them that, would you?'

Sos nodded, measuring the distance between them, his hands loose at his sides.

'Yes, I would. They were my father's and his father's before him and now they are mine. Would you deny it?'

'Yes, damn you, yes I would, yes I do. You vanish. We hear you are lost – drowned, executed, turned mercenary – dead, you understand, dead – the devil alone cares how – dead and gone.' Vakhtang's jaw was so tight at first that he could scarcely spit out the words, but soon the bile spurted faster. 'You were never here. You always wanted to be in the south, chasing women, chasing fame. Your father despised it. I despise it. I've looked after everyone. I am the true master here. You – you are nothing to us, nothing. But now when you feel like it, you strut back here, in your fancy clothes, with a gang of thugs to lord it—'

'Am I a thug too, sir?' Tamar called out.

'Don't interrupt me, woman—'

Vakhtang's words wilted on his lips even as he turned on her. Sos normally loved watching how men who had overlooked Tamar quailed as at an ogress when she fixed her gaze on them. But this time he found himself wishing she would hold still.

'Who—' Vakhtang began, but Tamar did not let him finish.

'Your queen. The men you call thugs are my escort and the man you dare to insult is my friend. Have you manners enough to uncover your head before me?'

Vakhtang tugged his hat off and doubled over into an awkward bow. There was a deep hush in the courtyard as his family watched. Sos winced. He wanted to tell her that Vakhtang wasn't bad, that humiliating him would help nothing, and that even the best of men behave like fools when they are choking on pride and resentment.

'You know what the punishment is for disloyalty to your liege lord?' she asked.

Vakhtang shook his head, all defiance gone.

'Death.'

Sos's mother cried out and flung herself to her nephew's side. Sos tried to intervene.

'Tamar, please, there's no need—'

She waved him away. 'Vakhtang, I could order my men to seize you and string you up from this tree right here. Make an example of you. How would you like that? Would that teach you not to usurp your cousin's place?'

It was too much. His sisters were crying, his mother was wailing and Vakhtang looked as if he was about to faint. Abandoning propriety, Sos grabbed Tamar's arm and dragged her into the house away from the bright sun and the shocked faces.

'What the hell are you doing?' he demanded.

'No, what are you doing?' she flashed back, shaking him off. Her pupils were huge in the gloom.

'What am I—? I am asking you – no – telling you not to play the master here.'

She did not flinch, but he saw every muscle in her face harden. 'I play at nothing. You forget yourself. This is my kingdom. Do not tell me what to do.'

'Your kingdom, Tamar, but my house. I honour your commands in Tbilisi, but here it is different.' He folded his arms across his chest and set his jaw. 'I will not stand by while you threaten to kill my father's sister's son.'

'You're being ridiculous. He needed a scare. I wasn't going to—'

'I know that, but he doesn't. He thought he'd seen his last dawn. You saw his face. It was cruel.'

Her eyes narrowed. 'Cruel? Nonsense. You didn't like it, that's all. Men fear me and that unnerves you.'

'You're wrong. If the lord Mkhargrdzeli himself had done as you did, I would have acted no differently. But he would never have shown me so little respect.'

That struck home. She looked fractionally less sure of herself.

'But Vakhtang insulted me – and you.'

'And I would have made him apologise to both of us. I know how to deal with him – I've been doing it all my life. I didn't need you wading in and making things worse.' He shook his head. 'It has nothing to do with you.'

'Yes it does. It's my fault that you have not been at home – my fault that you were not here and Vakhtang was able to make trouble.' She took a deep breath, reached out and touched his arm. 'I'm sorry I sent you away to Shirvan. Sorry that Yuri forced you into exile.'

He flinched. She sent him away? Not the tavads, not her aunt. He turned his back to hide his sudden anger. Immediately, she was close behind him, a hand on his arm trying to make him face her.

'What is it? Did you not hear what I said? I said I was sorry.'

He knew what it must have cost her to say that. It would

275

have been easy for him to smile and accept her apology. Then they could have gone back outside and there would have been eating and drinking under the courtyard tree just like he'd imagined. *I understand. Of course I forgive you.* But those were not the words that came.

'You who sent me to Shirvan. Not Rusudan.'

His words came out flat and cold. She held his gaze for a moment, then looked away.

'I had to do it. It was for the best.'

'For you, maybe, but not for me. I had become inconvenient, and you did not even have the courage to tell me so yourself.'

'Why must we talk of that now? Things were different then, you know that. I had been but a few months on the throne. Please, let us forget the past. We are here. I want us to be happy.'

'Is that a proposal, my lady? Shall I rush outside and spread the good news? Or is it a proposition?' He sounded bitter, petulant, but he didn't care. 'What am I to you? A diversion. A distraction from the real business of ruling. No, Tamar. My lands are not your plaything. And nor am I.'

She flushed. 'You presume too much.'

'Do I? Then why are you here?'

She didn't answer. He strode towards the door.

'Sos, wait.'

'What?'

'You're right. I came because I wanted . . .'

She didn't finish.

'What?' He refused to help. 'What?'

They stood staring at each other. For a moment he thought she was going to come to him. His legs were fighting to run to her. But neither of them moved. He made his body turn and leave.

Tamar seized a jug and hurled it at the wall. The crash of breaking pottery made her feel better. She kicked over a stool and looked about for something else to smash, then remembered it was Sos's house and he wouldn't like her any better if she wrecked it. She smoothed her dress, her anger cooling, hardening into hurt.

Chapter Thirty-eight

Night had long since fallen when Tamar returned through the city gates. The guards' greeting was subdued, even for the late hour, which immediately put her on edge. Then she saw a messenger boy scramble to his feet and pelt through the alleyways towards the palace. She caught Sirchak's eye. He nodded and ordered the others to draw swords.

She'd told Sirchak to ride hard back to Tbilisi, wanting to forget Sos and his mountains and bury herself in the routine of the palace. But as they swept past each landmark on the road home, the memory of how happy – painfully happy – she'd been during the gentle ride north threatened to overwhelm her.

She'd believed that her love was a simple thing, that she loved him because he was handsome and fearless and could make even the sternest Kipchak laugh. But as they rode south, she realised it was his love for her that counted. Without it, something inside her was lost.

When their horses stumbled to a stop in the palace courtyard, only the sentries should have been awake, but torches burned at the windows and shouts flitted through the dark. The door to the great hall slammed open, revealing the confused shapes of a dozen or more people. She heard footsteps and Shota's voice reaching out to her.

'My lady? Tamar?'

'Yes—'

He was at her side and grasped her hand in the dark.

'Thank God, you're back.'

'Come, calm yourself. I'm here. What is it, Shota?'

She climbed down from her horse.

'My lady, a messenger has arrived. He's from – he says – no, better come and hear him yourself. Quickly, I beg you.'

She handed her horse to a groom and followed Shota into the hall where the tavads were stamping their feet, gesticulating and yelling at one other. Their voices sounded very distant, oddly thin and reedy, as if she were listening to them from the bottom of a dark green pool.

She looked over their heads. There, between two Kipchak guards, stood a Seljuk envoy, amusement and contempt rolling across his face. He caught her eye and bowed low. She started towards him, but the others surrounded her like chickens flapping after a farm-girl with a corn bucket, barring her way.

'My lady, don't—'

'It's as I said—'

'We must—'

Tamar brushed them aside. She was tired, her patience thin.

'Silence, my lords, I beg you.'

They stopped speaking but every eye was screaming at her in agitation. It was exhausting and, she thought, undignified.

'Leave us, gentlemen. Go to your beds. We shall talk tomorrow, if talk is needed. Sirchak, choose six men and have them accompany our Seljuk friend to my chambers. I will follow presently and hear what he has to say. In private.'

The tavads fell back slowly and slipped out of the door. She could hear their voices rising again once they were outside, clambering over each other, but she ignored them and turned her attention to her aunt, Gamrekeli and Sargis who had remained in the middle of the hall.

'I bid you goodnight, too. I will call for you if I need you. Fear not, I have Sirchak and his men by me.'

They did not move.

'Goodnight, my lords, goodnight, aunt.'

Sargis nodded.

'Very well, my lady. He is unarmed, but I beg you be careful nonetheless.'

279

And with that he strode out of the door. Gamrekeli hesitated a moment longer then followed, leaving only Rusudan.

'Aunt? Have I not been sufficiently clear?'

'You need—'

'No. I need nothing from you. Go, now – or shall I ask Sirchak to escort you hence?'

'He would not lay one finger on me.'

'He would. And you know it.'

Tamar did not look round at where the Kipchak stood, but her aunt did, and whatever she saw there made her determination falter. She left without another word.

'Thank you, Sirchak. Now we shall have some peace. Go ahead and make sure all is as it should be.'

As she walked past her sister's rooms, she heard the door creak and saw her pale head appear. Susa said nothing, but squeezed her hand and gave her a quick kiss on the cheek. She mouthed *good luck* and then closed the door again.

Tamar walked briskly into her room. The Seljuk was sitting in a high-backed chair near the window, looking ahead of him. The guards stood with their backs to the walls, upright, not leaning. Each man's right hand rested on the hilt of his sword. Sirchak himself lounged easily behind the Seljuk's shoulder. She smiled. Without her telling him, the Kipchak had arranged it all perfectly.

When the Seljuk saw her, he stood up and bowed, lower than was strictly necessary.

'Your people have been all at sea in your absence, ma'am. They require your guidance.'

His Kart was excellent, but his voice marched across the words in an unpleasant monotone.

'My people, sir, do not concern you. Pray state your name and your message and then we can all go to bed.'

'My name is unimportant,' he said with a brittle smile. 'I am nobody but the mouthpiece of his excellency, the most illustrious sultan, Rukn ad-Din.'

He might have been expecting her to react to his master's

name, but she did not give him the pleasure. She merely nodded.

'It is long since we have heard from our neighbour. He is well, I trust?'

The messenger blinked.

'His health is, as always, excellent—'

'I am so glad. Please assure him that I, too, enjoy excellent health.'

'Forgive me, ma'am, maybe we can dispense with the pleasantries . . .'

'Agreed, sir. I tire of them. Speak your purpose.'

'My master would like to make you an offer.'

'Hear that, Sirchak, we have another suitor.'

The Kipchak ducked his head to hide a smile.

'No, ma'am, not that sort of offer.'

He pulled a letter from a pouch at his belt, unrolled it and started to read.

> '*I, Rukn ad-Din, the most exalted of sultans, like as to the angels of heaven, enthroned by God, I tell you, Tamar, sovereign of Kartvelia—*'

and there the Seljuk drew breath and cleared his throat delicately,

> '*that woman is weak in spirit. I command you to abase yourself before my tent, profess your allegiance to my person and embrace the true faith. Then you will live and your people will be spared. If you defy me, I shall destroy you.*'

Tamar laughed. The sound bounced off the walls and sank into the floor. When she spoke next her voice was cold.

'That is not an offer. That is a declaration of war.'

'The sultan does not offer everyone such mercy. You have a choice. Many, believe me, do not.'

She held out her hand for the message. She looked at it slowly, turning it over, trying to picture the man who had ordered it to be written.

'Why now?' she demanded.

'Madam?'

'Why does Rukn ad-Din choose thus to insult us now?'

'My master did not unburden his mind to his humble servant,' the Seljuk replied.

'Condescend to hazard a guess.'

'That is beyond my powers.'

She contemplated the messenger, who was gazing indifferently at a point above her left shoulder. Everything about him, from the oil in his hair to the polish on his boots, irritated her.

'I am not sure I believe you. Sirchak, take him to the dungeons. Find out what he knows. Then kill him.'

Sirchak beamed and grasped both the man's shoulders, nearly hoisting him off his feet. The messenger's legs buckled and his face turned the colour of bad meat as Sirchak dragged him to the door.

'Or we can talk like civilised people,' she called out. 'Well?'

The man spluttered a few words.

'I can't hear. What did he say, Sirchak?'

'He say I barbarian, lady. Rest I not understand.'

'Carry on then,' she said and turned her back. 'You may bring me his head — but only after I have supped.'

That worked. The messenger wriggled, writhed and whimpered to be allowed to talk. Tamar let him exhaust himself and then nodded.

'Very well. I ask again. Why now?'

Sirchak released him and he backed into the corner by the door, rubbing his shoulders.

'You will regret this. There are courtesies due—'

'Courtesies that your master forfeited when he wrote that letter. It is an abomination — and you know it, sir. For the last time I ask you — why now? I suggest you answer me swift and true.'

The Seljuk's throat bobbed up and down as he swallowed, apparently wondering which he should fear more, Sirchak's hands, clenching and unclenching at his side, or his master's displeasure.

'Your husband—'

She motioned to Sirchak, who sprang back to the messenger's side and twisted his collar hard, stopping his breath.

'I have no husband.'

Sirchak let go and the messenger fell to his knees, his face mottled and misshapen.

'Try again.'

'Yuri Bogoliubsky,' he wheezed the name, 'came to our lands and begged audience with my master. My master received him.'

'And why, sir, would the great, the exalted Rukn ad-Din deign to treat with a vagabond from beyond the mountains?' said Tamar, holding the messenger's eyes so he wouldn't see that she had clasped the back of a chair to stop her hands shaking. 'I hope he ordered him washed and scrubbed before he was admitted?'

'The Rus prince was treated with honour as the crowned king of Kartvelia, the rightful ruler of—'

'I'd choose your words with more care, sir,' Tamar intervened softly. 'There is only one rightful ruler of these lands. You stand before her. Her servants will not long suffer to hear her insulted. Continue.'

The messenger glanced about the room at the ring of Kipchaks, coughed and spoke on.

'My master and the Rus were closeted for many days. He—'

But again Tamar cut him off.

'Enough. I can sense well enough where this tends. I do not need to hear you stumble through it. He told your master that the Kart kingdom was weak and divided. He told him to forget the Franks, forget Constantinople and send his armies east. He told him he had many friends in my lands and swore to serve him as a loyal vassal – if only your master would help plant him on my throne.'

She stopped, suddenly tired of the whole game and dropped into a chair. She looked up at the messenger and smiled.

'Is that about the size of it?'

'Yes, madam. More or less.'

'And what, I wonder, was to become of me? Am I not the crowned queen of these lands?'

'You are to be reunited with your – with the Rus.'

'I see. And what answer does he expect, this master of yours?'

'He expects you to sue for peace. You can do nothing else.'

'He is so sure of victory?'

'With good cause.'

The messenger hesitated a moment and looked about the room.

'There is something I would add, ma'am – in private.'

Tamar shook her head. 'You cannot expect me to be alone with you, the devoted servant of a man I have learned is my sworn enemy. It is impossible. Besides, there is nothing you cannot say before these men. They have earned my trust many times over.'

She enjoyed being able to say that: she knew how much it would please them. In truth, she would not have minded being alone with the Seljuk. There was nothing threatening about him, but she did not want to allow him to dictate the terms of their talk.

'As you wish, my lady. What I have to add is this.' He paused. 'My master places a great deal of trust in me.' He paused again. Obviously he was unsure how to frame what he had to say. Tamar waited in silence. 'Forgive me, but he told me to pay close attention to your person. To discover what kind of woman you were.'

'I had no idea I was under such scrutiny. What is the conclusion to your investigation?'

The Seljuk lifted his chin and spoke with a new solemnity.

'I think you are a great queen, my lady. Truly. I have never seen your like before and I have travelled far on my master's business.'

Tamar could only laugh. 'I never suspected flattery to be the sharpest weapon in a Seljuk's armoury.'

'I do not flatter. I merely observe how you handle your men – and how you handle me. Madam,' he lowered his voice, 'my master is unwed. You understand me? If the Rus pleases you so little, maybe we can find another path to peace.'

'He writes a strange love letter.'

'Great kings cannot woo as ordinary men do.'

'True. And the Rus? What becomes of him?'

'He would be eliminated.'

'A sort of wedding gift?'

'If you will.'

Tamar nodded.

'Sirchak, have this man taken to the guest quarters. Feed him if he's hungry and treat him well. Keep a watch on his door. And you, sir, will have your answer tomorrow. My thanks.'

Sirchak motioned to his men to do her bidding. Before he followed them out of the door she stopped him, a hand on his shoulder.

'Lady?'

'Sirchak, do not speak of what was said here. See that your men do not either.'

'Yes. Understand. You not need second no-good husband.'

The quickest grin and he was gone, leaving Tamar drained and alone. She was too tired to sleep. Her limbs were heavy, but her mind was ablaze. Of course Yuri would make mischief. He had nothing to lose, no home, no family. Of course he would try to return. She'd known it, but had refused to admit it. The idea of him revolted her so much that for a brief moment she considered Rukn ad-Din. She shook her head. Madness. The Seljuks were their enemies and always had been. But he was strong, too strong. He held the great plateau of Anatolia. He commanded God alone knew many men.

A knock ghosted at the door. The latch clicked and Susa squeezed past the guards outside.

'I waited up until they'd gone. Have you eaten anything? Don't tell me you're not hungry. I've sent for some food and drink. You'll never sleep otherwise. Come on, change out of your travelling clothes. Your feet must be screaming in those boots.'

Tamar let Susa chivvy her into comfortable clothes and settle her into the chair with the biggest cushions. Nino appeared with a bowl of sweet spiced porridge and a cup of warmed wine. The sisters sat in silence for a long time.

'Will we never be at peace?' The words burst from Tamar's lips. 'Enemies within. Enemies without. How do I stop this? Where does it end?'

To her surprise, Susa smiled.

'Do you remember how we used to fight?'

'Of course.'

'Can you remember a time when we did not?'

Tamar shook her head.

'Think.'

A memory swam into her head. They were hiding in a cupboard giggling. It was pitch black and they were both holding their breath, trying not to laugh, trying not to give themselves away. But it was musty and their noses tickled and they were shaking hard, gripping tight hold of each other. A shadow blocked out the lines of light between the door-planks.

Girls. Girls!

It was the stupid sow who'd looked after them when Nino caught the red-itching sickness. They hated her. She had square, yellowish teeth and a smudgy moustache and smelt of rotten eggs and old vegetable soup. They tormented her. Tamar was in awe of Susa's sly questions about where her husband was and what was the stain on her upper lip. And for the first time her sister had enjoyed playing at hunters, stalking and ambushing. It was bliss – until Nino returned and they fell back into their old ways.

Tamar allowed herself a small smile too.

'Sister, unless my wits have deserted me, you're comparing the sultan's mighty army to a nursemaid?'

'Laugh at me all you like, Tamar, I was trying to think of something heartening. A common enemy might do the tavads some good, that's all I'm saying.' She paused. 'It did us good, didn't it?'

Chapter Thirty-nine

The noise rising from the city streets had changed overnight. Instead of an amiable jumble of arguments, banalities and the sweetest of early morning sighs, every voice, every conversation was obsessed with one thing alone.

The Seljuks are coming. The Seljuks are coming.

The fearful expected to be dead by the noonday meal. The boastful whetted their swords and trimmed fresh arrows. The hopeful scoffed, swore it would come to nothing – the Seljuks belonged in old men's tales, in children's games, not under a fresh summer sky – and carried on hammering, stitching, haggling. And everyone tried to ignore the shadowy figures on horseback that twitched in the corners of their minds.

Tamar did not need to set foot outside her chamber to sense the mad tension that had her city by the throat. She could feel the palace – all Tbilisi – sputtering like one of the living mud pools by the eastern sea.

She was glad to have Sirchak as her gatekeeper so that she could be alone with her thoughts. He ignored every appeal, every threat, saying the queen was at her prayers and would receive her counsellors at the hour appointed and not a man – nor a woman – earlier, no exceptions.

When the sun was high and she was ready, she strode down to the great hall where her aunt, Gamrekeli, Sargis and every tavad who lived within a day's ride of the city were gathered, waiting. Her aunt's voice stormed into the silence that greeted her arrival.

'You see? You see what your wanton imprudence has brought us to?'

Tamar's temper rose to match her aunt's, but her composure did not falter. 'Peace, aunt—'

'Peace?' Rusudan's voice was pitched high. Only a heavy blow to the head could silence her when she was in full spate. Better, thought Tamar, to let her exhaust herself. 'An ill choice of word, niece. We must bid farewell to peace. It is as I warned, the day I returned. You shirk, you squabble, you defy those who would help you – and all the while your lands grow feeble as a day-old baby. It is no surprise the sultan now hastens to exploit your incompetence. He will put us to fire and sword and cover our lands in corpses.'

The tavads looked stunned as her words rang out in a swooping crescendo. Candour they had come to expect from Rusudan, but such a venomous assault on the queen – that was new.

'Aunt,' said Tamar, her tone measured, 'those words are not worthy of you. So speaks a doom-mongering coward.'

'Wrong. They are the words of one who sees clearly and does not scruple to speak the truth. I am only ashamed I did not act sooner.' She took a step closer and her face wove back and forth in front of Tamar's like a snake about to bite. 'But maybe it is not too late.'

Tamar was mesmerised, but only for a moment. As Rusudan swung from her to address the tavads, she knew exactly what was coming next.

'Tamar is not fit to rule. My brother made a gross mistake, an unforgivable error when he appointed her his heir. It is your duty, my lords, to undo the damage before it is too late. Her reign must end today.'

She had struck.

A whisper of movement, but nobody spoke. Tamar's face was burning, her heart cold, her mind a wheeling emptiness. Words clambered over each other in her throat, but none passed her lips. The tavads were undecided, waiting for her to beg, defend herself, curse Rusudan from the room – what should she do?

At that moment, the main door to the hall slammed open and shut and everyone jumped, startled. All attention had been riveted on the queen. It was Zak, arriving late. The men closest tried to hush him, but he pushed them aside and crossed to Tamar.

'My lady.' He bowed. 'Forgive this interruption. On my father's orders I was doubling the guard around the walls. There was a great disturbance at the western gate. Hey—' he turned and shouted – 'what are you waiting for? Bring them in.'

Tamar found herself looking at two men, their faces covered in blood, their clothes muddied and torn. At first she did not know them.

'They were trying to sneak in on a slaughterman's wagon but the pigs were making such a racket they were discovered. If I had not been passing . . .' Zak shook his head. 'They are lucky to be alive. You know what the feeling is in the city.'

Zak took hold of the men's collars and shoved them towards her. It was only when they had stumbled to the floor at her feet, half kneeling, half lying, that she realised who they were.

'Stand,' she commanded. 'I cannot talk to you huddled down there. Stand – you are men, after all.'

They lurched upright, but kept their eyes down. Vardan's elegant nose was spread across his face – his sneer spoiled for ever. Con's looks were harder to ruin, but although his split lips would mend, the missing row of teeth would never grow back.

'So you have tired of Yuri's company?' she demanded.

They nodded.

'Strange – you seemed so fond of him. Why did you desert him?'

'He . . . he said he needed strong allies.' Vardan stopped to cough up the mixture of blood and phlegm that was choking his windpipe. 'We thought he meant the tavads, but then we realised he wanted to go to the Seljuks. We refused.'

'You refused? Your king's command?'

Vardan shrank from her as the word *king* throbbed in the air.

'Please, my lady, no man can treat with the Seljuks and be our king. Never. Not the Seljuks. God forgive us, we are not traitors.'

'That is exactly what you are,' growled Zak. 'Say the word, my lady, and they are dead.'

An ominous bullying mood had filled the hall, and Tamar was relieved nobody was armed.

'Enough, Zakari,' she murmured. 'Vardan, Constantine, you did right to leave Yuri. But why are you here? You must have known your lives would be forfeit.'

'We wanted to warn you, tell you what he planned—'

'Really? And why should I believe you? Maybe Yuri sent you back here to spy? Look around you. Every man here wants me to order you killed. Why should I disappoint them?'

Con started to stutter something but gave up and collapsed into a desperate silence. Vardan's face crumpled and he fell to his knees.

'My lady,' he pleaded, 'on my life, I will serve you—'

'Must we listen to this snivelling?' Rusudan broke in. 'It is simple. Hang them, Tamar. What are you waiting for?'

Tamar looked down at the two men in front of her. Con was rubbing distractedly at the side of his head: his earlobe was ripped, the wound weeping. Vardan's face was hidden but his shoulders were shaking and she knew he was sobbing.

She remembered her father's fierce pleasure at Orbeli's death. Demna's empty eyes. Dato's blood on her father's kinzhal. She knew what she had to do.

She reached forward and touched first the top of Vardan's head, then Con's chest.

'Go. You are free. Any man who seeks to revenge himself on you shall answer to me. Mend fast. We shall need all men who can bear arms in the days to come.' They hesitated, not quite believing her. 'Go,' she repeated, 'now, before I change my mind.'

They shuffled from the hall, leaving her surrounded by a ring of faces, all shocked, some openly angry.

'See how it is, gentlemen,' her aunt jeered. 'Too gutless to shed blood. How will this girl defeat the sultan?'

Tamar ignored her.

'They strayed, my lords, but they have returned, and it was

right to forgive them. The Seljuks will be the only victors if I start this war by killing my own men. That is my decision.'

She allowed her voice to swell.

'And now, my lords, you too have a decision to make. My aunt – respected and esteemed so much by us all – doubts my ability to lead. She says I must rule no more. Maybe we should pay heed. But who is to rule in my stead? Is there a man here, in this very hall, who should be king? Is there someone we should send for? Or should we turn to my aunt, to the lady Rusudan?'

The name fluttered back and forth like an autumn leaf and skimmed, slowly, to the ground.

'Let me tell you something, my lords. I did not spend my youth dreaming of the day I would be queen. When my father told me I was to be his heir, I refused – did you know that? – yet he insisted and I obeyed, as was my duty. But if my duty now is to surrender my throne, I will do it – and do it with a light heart. Name my successor and my crown is theirs.'

She reached her hands towards them, her palms open. The tavads leant forward, involuntarily.

'I place my kingdom before you. You have but to take it.'

She curled her fingers shut, bowed her head and waited.

'Permit me to speak, my lady.'

Everyone turned to look at Sargis.

'We cannot hold Tbilisi. It is not built to withstand a siege.'

Her heart thumped against her ribs and the quick flush of victory stole up her neck. Her commander-in-chief was with her.

'What then would you advise, my lord?'

She kept her gaze down so neither he nor anyone else in the room would be able to see the elation that was burning in her eyes.

'Summon our soldiers to Vardzia. Post scouts along our south-west borders. With your blessing and God's will, I shall hold them when they cross the Mtkvari.'

'So be it. Gentlemen, you heard the lord Mkhargrdzeli's orders. Send to your lands for any man you trust with a horse and a spear. We shall meet again before long. God's speed.'

There was a sudden burst of talk, animated and excited. Gamrekeli stood, hands clasped, as if in rapturous prayer and said they would see the sultan in hell yet. Some men crowded round Sargis, pledging dozens, hundreds of fighters, trying to extract assurances they would be at the front, at the centre of the line. Others seized Tamar's hand and kissed it fervently before hurrying from the room. It was infectious. They all swept out of the door until only Sirchak and her aunt remained. Tamar caught his eye and he followed the rest.

The two women stood looking at each other. Rusudan's derisive laugh broke the silence.

'Surrender your throne with a light heart? I never heard words so hollow.'

'The tavads did not think so, did they?'

'No, your little charade was most effective. They always were a sentimental lot. I imagine they found it moving to see a young woman offer to relinquish that which men most desire.'

'Power. They saw it for what it was. A burden, a cross to bear.'

'Charmingly put, my dear, but you do not believe that.'

'But they believed it, aunt, and that is what counts. You have played a long game – longer maybe than my lifetime – but it is over now. You have lost. They had the chance to choose – and they chose me. You shall never now rule these lands.'

'Maybe not. But you shall not rule them long, that I do prophesy. You will be a Seljuk slave girl. You—'

'Silence.'

Tamar found a new voice waiting in her belly – a voice so powerful that it stilled her aunt.

'The men of our family are fond of killing their difficult relations, and I find myself longing to emulate them. I shall execute you. Hang you by your neck as you bade me hang Vardan and Con.'

'Do not kill me.' A whisper.

'What? You would counsel clemency? You?'

'Do not kill me.' Louder.

'Would it not be gutless to spare you? Squeamish?'

'Please.'

The giantess had vanished. An old woman stood pleading before her. Tamar sighed and nodded.

'Very well. You will go to the most secluded convent in my realm. You will never set foot beyond its walls so long as you live. If you do, believe me, I shall kill you myself.'

'Oh, but I do believe you, my dear,' said Rusudan, a little of her poise returning. 'None of those fools would think you capable of it, but I know you better than they.' She gave the thinnest of smiles. 'The convent it is, then. Perhaps it will do me good to spend some time with God before the end.'

Chapter Forty

At first Tamar could see very little. The air, damp and chill, smelt of hot wax and snuffed candle flames. Only the sound of her breath broke the silence, but she knew she was not alone. If she could make her ears listen right, she would be able to hear God, as well as feel him. Her stomach shivered as the world beyond suddenly felt very near. Invisible hands hovered a finger's breadth from her bare skin and she did not know whether to fall to her knees or run from the cave screaming.

Then the tunnels above, below, to the left and right, started to fill with men and the rocks came alive, humming with muffled voices. They swelled and approached so close she thought they would begin to make sense, but then they swerved away and disappeared. She knew it was the vanguard of her army arriving, but in the cave, alone, it felt as if all the noise was in her head. She wondered whether this was how madmen felt when the devils came whispering.

Footsteps, real and solid, sounded behind her and a monk entered, carrying a bronze oil lamp in one hand. A glow fell across the floor, sending her shadow out in front of her. Without a word, he held the light aloft and she saw God's Son on the walls above her, his eyes large and black. His saints surrounded him, their beards swooping low to their belts, great crosses on chains about their necks. They loomed tall, curving with the slope of the cave, leaning over her. Their haloes and feet were lost in the shadows.

The monk took a step forward. The colours of the paintings brightened and their power dimmed as she could see the hand of the painter, not of God. Her breath steadied and her legs grew stronger.

'My lady, come and look. My brothers wanted me to show you this.'

He swung his lamp to the right and stretched out his left hand to point.

'There. Do you like it, my lady?'

She saw the man first, turned to the right, a sharp-cut beard above long ceremonial robes. Behind him stood a woman, dressed alike, her hair tied under a headdress, her eyes stern.

'You are pleased?'

'It is my father?'

'Yes, Tamar, and you stand with him. Father and daughter. King and queen. You are pleased?' he repeated.

She didn't know what to say. She looked up at herself. It was strange to be removed from her body and placed on a wall amongst holy men. She had lost control of herself. Other people could take her, shape her and make her appear where she was not. Men and women she had never met would see her face – cool, serene and inscrutable – and imagine they knew her. It was a little like magic.

The monk lowered his arm and she was once more lost in shadow.

'My lady?'

'It is beautiful, Theophilus.'

She laid a hand on his arm and smiled.

'Thank your brothers for me. I do not deserve to be placed in such great company, but it does me good to know they are near. I will hold this memory in my heart and draw strength from it.'

The cave city of Vardzia was not old. It lay on one of the easiest approaches to the Kart lands, a broad thoroughfare through which an army could march, sure of water and grass. Her father had ordered it to be built – a holy place for monks in time of peace, a garrison and a refuge in time of war. It was here that her armies were mustering.

A rough tunnel led from the chapel back to the chamber where she would eat and sleep. It wasn't much. Bare rock walls, one side open to wind and rain, nothing but rough matting underfoot, and if she stretched up on tiptoe it was easy to touch the ceiling. Aton's house in the mountains was lavish in comparison. But, she mused as she settled into a mound of cushions, what a view.

The evening sun sprang into her eyes as she sat – higher than the dome of a cathedral – and looked down into the gorge. The source of the Mtkvari lay nearby on the high plateau to the south-west and it danced young and fast below her, nothing like the stately river that flowed through Tbilisi.

From the opposite bank, where the path ran before it crossed the river, all a traveller could see were dozens of holes dimpled into the cliff, as if a baby had jabbed its fingers into a lump of dough. When she first arrived under an overcast sky the rock had been a dull, brittle grey. Now, as dusk deepened, the walls around her were coloured like the richest honey, the kind that takes an age to pour from a spoon. The sun bulged and finally lost its shape as it sank behind the lands, now drenched in red, that were the sultan's stronghold.

Her mind emptied and she saw herself at the doorway of a stone house, her hair scooped up, flour on her hands. Mountain peaks glowed in the same red dusk and a warm breeze blew up the valley. Sos was walking towards her. She shook her head and banished the vision. That was somebody else's life, not hers.

As the glow around her thickened, she looked at the men camped on the valley floor. Sargis had told her with pride that it was the largest army Kartvelia had ever gathered, a triumph, a testament to her.

'Had your father given the order,' he'd told her, 'not so many would have come, or not so willingly. But they are taking the sultan's threat very personally – as if he'd insulted their own mothers, their own sisters and daughters.'

'But will they be enough?' she asked him.

'They'll have to be,' was his only reply.

Then, as at the end of a feast when the servants lean forward as one to snuff out the candles, the last rays vanished. She sat in the grey twilight, chewing her nails and frowning.

'You'll ruin them.'

Her sister sat down beside her and pulled Tamar's hand away from her mouth. She hadn't heard her come in.

'Too late. They're already ruined – casualty of war.'

Susa smiled. 'That's a feeble joke.'

'Feeble's better than nothing, right?'

'True. You should go to bed, Tamar, get some sleep. You can do no more tonight. Forgive me for saying this, but you look dreadful, truly awful. At least eat something. Your bones are sticking out and your hair's like a magpie's nest.'

Tamar was glad of her sister's company. Even when Susa nagged her, it was soothing. It made her feel normal again, a person like any other. It helped her forget the weight of thousands of pairs of eyes, full of hope, full of fear, that now followed her wherever she went.

'Sit with me then and brush my hair and then I promise I'll eat. If I lie down and shut my eyes all I see are Seljuks, mostly nine feet tall and riding fire-breathing horses.' She groaned. 'It's ridiculous. I know they are but men like us – not the monsters from Nino's stories. But a part of me is still convinced they breakfast off naughty little Kart girls, bones and all.'

Her sister was running a comb through her hair. Its teeth felt good against her scalp. She looked straight ahead into the gathering night.

'Why do I let those ogres rampage about my head when the truth is bad enough? Rukn ad-Din overpowered God only knows how many brothers and cousins to secure his throne. His lands are vast, rich, teeming with men. Mountains of gold pillaged from all the kingdoms of the world. If he wants to, he has but to . . .'

She fell quiet. Susa, who had been teasing at a tangle in her hair, stopped suddenly.

'Is that—?'

'Look, down there.'

They had both spoken at once. It was nearly full dark, but a party of Ossets was visible trudging up one of the pathways leading to the caves.

'I thought you said he wouldn't be able to come,' her sister whispered, not that anyone could hear them.

'I thought he wouldn't,' Tamar replied, more to herself than to Susa. 'I was so sure. I would not have come if I were him.'

But he was there with five score men at least, all young, all horsed. The ice in her stomach melted.

A Kipchak guardsman came out to meet him and a torch lit up his profile. Sos and the guard exchanged a few words, indistinct, although she could catch the lilt and rhythm that she would have recognised anywhere as his. Then he passed on, out of sight, his men following him.

He was there. He had come.

'That's one thing you can stop fretting over. Whatever happened in the mountains, he has forgiven you,' Susa said.

She had forgotten her sister was still there.

'How do you—?' she stopped and laughed. 'You wretch. I see you have not lost your skill at divining everything that happens inside my head.'

'Your kingdom is in grave danger, but you thrive on that. I knew there had to be another reason why you were looking like the husk of my sister, like a pomegranate with all the juice scooped out.'

Tamar snorted. 'That bad?'

'That bad.'

'Do you think the others see it?'

'No, they only see a queen.'

'Do you think I am a fool?'

'No, I think you have chosen well.'

'I have not chosen.'

'Yes, sister, you have.'

Chapter Forty-one

For days Sos and his small party of Osset scouts had only passed shepherds and, rarely, clusters of houses ringed by stacks of dung bricks drying in the sun. The men and women spoke their own tongue and cared nothing for soldiers, so long as they paid a little for the food they took.

These blank, endless uplands oppressed him and although none of his men would admit it, he sensed they felt the same. The sky hung too close and even though it was high summer the matted, brown grass told him it was not long since the snows had left. But the ground underfoot rose and fell no more than a long sea swell.

The wind was building out of the west, carrying a steep bank of rainclouds towards him, a towering column of grey soldiers on a forced march. Sos pulled his hood about him and ducked his head to keep the swift downpour out of his eyes.

Somewhere to their left lay the great Armenian city of Ani, the domes of its churches lost below the endless sweep of the horizon. To the north, also beyond sight, a lean line of mountains barred the way to the sea. But around him – nothing.

This was the great plain that Constantinople had ruled for numberless generations until the Seljuks came and made it their heartland, their stronghold. The sultan's army was camped somewhere ahead, and Sargis had told Sos to find it.

Slowly, the land began to change. The dips deepened into valleys and the mounds stretched and became hills. At first it gladdened his heart, but he soon saw these mountains were nothing like his own. The Kavkaz peaks were so white a man must squint to look straight at them, their slopes an inviting muddle of clouded blue streams and sudden flower meadows. Here there was no shade, not enough water and everything was a dull, smudged brown.

He was miles from home, stiff and weary, and still amazed he had left at all.

At first he hadn't heard the boy yelling his name. He thought it was someone furious about a lost goat, but then the sound pierced his head.

Sos, Sos, Sos, Sos, Sos . . .

It was Niko, pounding his pony up the track, howling his name like a hunting call. The boy rolled to the ground, beaming and not a bit out of breath, although the pony looked as if it had been ridden non-stop all the way up from the village.

'What is it, Niko?'

Niko reached under his tunic and pulled out a crumpled message, the ink on the front blurred.

'Here. From Tbilisi. I met the messenger at the waterfall. He told me it was for you. Of course I said you were up here and I said I'd take it . . .'

'Stop, Niko – a message for me from Tbilisi?'

'Yes—'

Sos ripped the letter out of his hand and broke the seal. It was not what he expected. A formal summons to serve the queen. Against who? Sos read on. *Yuri. Seljuks.* All men were ordered to fight. His mind mutinied and he tossed the letter aside.

Niko had been kicking at some tree stumps, desperate to know what was in the letter, but still too much in awe of his cousin to interrupt his thoughts. He leapt after the letter as it rolled past.

'Leave it,' snapped Sos.

But Niko had already puzzled through the few short lines and was staring up at him, his face shining.

'But it's war, Sos.' He grabbed his arm and clung to it. 'War!

Please, Sos, take me with you. I'll look after your horse, your fire. I'll be no trouble, please, Sos, please . . .'

'You're not going.'

The boy flushed and scowled. 'I'm the same age you were when you first went south. I am.'

'That's got nothing to do with it.'

'Then why can't I go?'

Because I'm not going. Because the queen and I quarrelled. Because I'm too angry to help her.

'Sos,' Niko repeated, 'why can't I go?'

He looked down at Niko's expectant face and gave in. If she needed him, he did not have the power to refuse.

'I'm joking, sunshine. Of course you can go, we're all going. And you'll be my aide-de-camp. That's official.'

Niko was already running for his pony.

'Come on, come on, come on!' he yelled back at Sos. 'Hurry or we might miss everything.'

He glanced over at Niko, who was lolling in his saddle. He was a lot less enthusiastic now and Sos didn't blame him.

As they'd journeyed further, the heat had become unbearable. The river worming through the bottom of the valley was the colour of bile. A few skinny trees straggled near the water, interlopers, their bright green leaves suspiciously garish against the pale earth and yellowing, sun-struck grass. On the slopes higher up, nothing grew. The rocks overhead were whipped into tortured shapes – crippled turrets, crooked sentinels – as if God had poured the land out of a big bowl and it had barely had time to harden.

Sos had swaddled his head until only his eyes were exposed to the dust, but even then the dry air cracked his lips until they bled. His mind started to wander until he could almost taste the green glut of watermelons that would now be rumbling into Tbilisi. He was sluicing the red juice over his tongue, hunting for black seeds between his teeth, when his horse twitched and stiffened under him and he tasted woodsmoke.

301

The way ahead tapered into a narrow defile between two blunted hilltops, their sides littered with boulders. A dozen soldiers were sprawled by the trackside. They had just finished eating – the carcass of a bird was propped up over a small campfire – and they were stretched out, their faces covered, their hands resting comfortably on their stomachs.

Seljuks.

Sos whipped his sword clear of its sheath and spurred to the attack, covering the ground between them before they had time to get to their feet. He heard a splintering crack as his horse's front hooves dealt one man a blow to the head and two swift swipes of his sword dispatched two more. Arrows whistled past his ear as his men started shooting and another man dropped, then another. That left three running for their horses. Two stumbled to their knees, arrows bristling from their backs, but one, weaving and dodging, jumped on his horse and sped away down the track, pursued by two Ossets.

Sos decided to trust them to finish the job and waited, panting. The wounded Seljuks were moaning a little. He considered them for a moment and then cut their throats as quick and clean as he could. His men trotted back up the path with a body slumped over a saddle.

'Alive?' he called.

'Very dead. Just being tidy.'

Sos grinned.

'Right. Good work. I'm going ahead to see whether there's more where they came from. If somebody comes to inspect, re-inforce, anything – kill them. But don't take on more than you can handle. Slip away if there's too many. Understood?'

The men nodded and set about hauling the corpses off the track, while Sos hurried forward on foot. Soon the smell of many people and animals crammed into one place began to blow towards him.

Feeling suddenly vulnerable, he decided to get off the path and scrambled up a rock-fall to his right, keeping low. It was hard going. The ground crumbled beneath his feet and came away easily in his hands. He was more exposed up there, but he would be able to see if anyone was coming.

The hillside curved away from him, opening up into a great bowl. He pulled himself up on to a boulder and stared down. The vale before him was cloaked in a soft, shifting haze of heat and smoke, pierced by the tall poles of flagstaffs. At first his eyes could not accept what they were looking at, but then his heart began to pound. This was it. Assembled at his feet were hundreds, thousands, hundreds of thousands of horses, tents, fires, camels and men.

The Kart army, a proud and mighty wave as it marched to Vardzia, now seemed but a gentle ripple, lapping at the sultan's boots. What was he going to tell Sargis? What was he going to tell Tamar?

Voices.

He slid off the boulder and pressed himself into the hollow at its base. A group of men were coming along the ridge, heading back down to the camp. Pebbles tip-tapped away from their feet. They were drawing level, a little to the right. They must see him. He readied himself to spring and run, but they passed by within a dozen paces of where he lay. Sos's head jerked up out of the dirt, and he saw five broad backs walking away from him. And in the middle, unmistakable, was Yuri, a falcon hooded on his forearm.

Sos thanked God they weren't hunting with dogs, eased his bow out from underneath him and reached for an arrow. He could see the pink stripe of Yuri's neck between his helmet and his coat of mail. If he let fly, Yuri would be gone forever.

The blood in his head and the crunch of their footsteps blended into a dark roar and he told himself to shoot. But as the slope slowly hid them from view, his fingers still gripped the string tight. It would have been a feeble reckoning. Sos lowered his bow and snapped the arrow in two.

The falcon shot up into the sky and wheeled in a vast circle before plunging into a steep dive. Sos grimaced and wished them happy hunting. With an army that size, they could afford to enjoy themselves.

Enjoy themselves. They were enjoying themselves.

He waited until he was sure Yuri and the others were not going to return, then clambered back on to his boulder and stared thoughtfully down at the camp. He'd had an idea.

Chapter Forty-two

When the air thickens before a storm, animals do not pretend all is well. Horses charge in circles, cross-eyed, bucking and kicking. Dogs whine and cringe, their tails tucked safely out of sight. Birds streak low under the clouds, away from danger.

Tamar wished she could imitate them – scream up at the sky or beat her wings and disappear down the valley: anything to exorcise the impatience that cramped her limbs. Instead she strode back and forth along the stone-cut walkway in front of her quarters. Twenty paces to the left, turn, twenty to the right, turn.

Brooding did not help, she knew that, but there was nothing else she could do. She had no armour to grease, no sword to sharpen. Talking was too much effort, especially when she feared her words would come out warped and quavering. As each day passed and no news, good or bad, came up from the west, her mood blackened.

Footsteps flapped towards her and she rearranged her face as Gamrekeli's head appeared.

'Lady Tamar,' he began, gasping and sweating from the climb. She was surprised; normally he made such a point of moving sedately. 'The lord Soslani has returned.' He paused to catch his breath or, maybe, to make what he had to say sound more portentous. 'He has seen their army.'

'What? Where? How far off? Why do not the warning signals sound?'

'They have not begun their march – not yet. The lord Soslani reports them still camped on the borders of the sultan's lands in a place known as the Vale of Basiani. He says – but he can tell you himself. Come, the lord Mkhargrdzeli is gathering the captains for a council.'

She nodded and sped down the path to where Sargis's tent was pitched close to the river: to be closer to the men, he said, but Tamar also suspected the caves made him uneasy.

'Out, out!' Sargis's voice bellowed. A clutch of younger soldiers streamed from the tent and crowded nearby. She sympathised. They were as desperate as she was to hear the news. The whole camp must sense that, at last, something was about to happen.

Gamrekeli made a show of clearing a path for her, but it was not necessary. At the sight of their queen, the men fell back, bowed and quietened. Some were staring at her feet, she realised. She looked down and saw that she was barefoot. She hadn't noticed.

In the middle of the tent, surrounded by Sargis and his captains, was Sos. He was pale, obviously exhausted, but Tamar caught a glint and glitter in his brown eyes. The general came forward to greet her.

'Welcome, my lady.'

And he nodded to Sos to speak.

'My lady,' he bowed, 'the lord Mkhargrdzeli told me not to waste words, so I shall be brief. The sultan's army dwarfs us. It is a behemoth. What I saw was not a camp, but a town – a town of soldiers. The odds are grim. At best, they outnumber us ten to one.'

His words tolled in her head, reverberating until she felt dizzy. This was never going to be a quick scuffle, a border skirmish, but that wasn't an army. That was a curse, a plague – an act of God.

'Are you sure? Could you have been mistaken?' she asked.

'No, my lady.'

'You did not count servants? Non-fighting men?'

Sos shook his head. 'No, my lady, of course not.' He took a step towards her and everyone else faded a shade darker.

'My lady, they are many, that is true, but I swear they are not bent on fighting. What I saw looked more like a herders' carnival than an army ready for battle. Their horses are penned apart. They were feasting and I heard music. Music! The air smelt sweet – they were burning spiced logs. They are camped in an easy valley, close to water, on low ground. There was only one ring of guards, close in, and a few scattered sentries. They are so big they have no fear. They are waiting, idling, until we send to them and plead for leniency.'

His voice grew stronger.

'We could never defeat them in open battle. No, nor hold them long in a siege. But if we attack now, immediately, and take them by surprise with their cattle among them, their swords blunt, their women still in their beds, we have a chance. We must strike, my lady, and we must strike now.'

He finished and Tamar dragged her eyes away from his. All around her men were shaking their heads.

'Did the sun bake your brains on the ride back?' demanded Gamrekeli.

Tamar frowned and put a hand up to still him.

'These are difficult times, my lord, but not so difficult that we should forget our manners. The lord Soslani did well to get so close and I know we all want to show our gratitude.'

Gamrekeli bowed to Sos. 'Forgive me, my lord. I misspoke. I admit you acted with both courage and caution.'

He paused and his tone changed.

'But what you suggest is madness. My lady, do we want to see our army destroyed before we can be certain whether the Seljuks even mean to attack? Maybe the sultan's threats have some simple purpose. Maybe he seeks a concession, in land or gold.' He gestured towards Sos. 'This young man believes they are waiting for us to send an embassy. Well, let us do so. There is nothing to lose. They are not barbarians, not any more. We can treat with them, reason with them. I am not scared of battle, God knows I am not, but nor do I think we should heed – forgive me – excitable young men. Mkhargrdzeli will tell you the same – will you not, friend?'

Tamar turned deliberately to Sargis.

'What do you say, my lord?'

He tugged at his beard and frowned. 'There is no shame in

307

seeking a parley when we find ourselves so outnumbered. No man would blame you, my lady.'

'No shame, you say. No shame, but little honour.'

A light went on in Sargis's eyes. 'My lady?'

'As ever, I value the lord Gamrekeli's opinion. He speaks sense. But—'

'Sargis, tell her—' Gamrekeli broke in.

'But I am loath to do as he suggests. Wait, talk, haggle – and in the end we may have to fight all the same. But by then the fight will be on their terms and not on ours.'

Sargis was looking hard at her. Their eyes met. He took a step towards Tamar and spoke so low that only she could hear. 'My lady, before you give the order to move, you must ask yourself whether you are prepared for the worst. I cannot promise you victory.'

'But to submit would be very like death. Yes, Sargis, I am ready.'

She turned away from him to face the men gathered about her.

'Tomorrow we march on Rukn ad-Din.'

Gamrekeli threw his arms up in the air. 'This is insanity. You're not King Davit!' The words landed like a blow to her stomach.

'No, she is Tamar,' Sos called, suddenly at her side. 'Davit was but a man when he first picked up his sword and decided to fight. Maybe his advisers thought that he should bargain and plead rather than risk his kingdom, but we don't remember them. We only remember that Davit refused to bend his knee to any man – and it is his blood that now runs thick in Tamar's veins.' He paused and turned to her. 'And I would follow my queen until death, wherever she leads.'

She smiled her gratitude and spoke into rapt silence.

'The sultan counts on mercenaries, rounded up with gold, to steal our kingdom from us. But I place my trust neither in riches, nor in arms, but in you, my men. I ride tomorrow – to war. Who follows me?'

Her arms had flown up into the air, like the wings of a bird, a great eagle soaring. All around her men punched the air and roared their approval. Never had she heard cheers so loud. Then the confusion of many voices settled into one word.

'Tamar! Tamar! Tamar!'

The cry was taken up by the men outside. Never had she felt so alive.

Tamar travelled with the army to within one long march of the sultan's camp, and there she promised to remain. She waited in her tent while her captains came one by one to pay their respects and receive her final blessing. That night, they would cover the final miles under cover of darkness and on the morrow they would fight.

'Come in,' she called to the next man.

Sos's head appeared in the doorway.

'You're a captain too now, are you?' she smiled.

'Fresh promoted.'

He thumped his chest proudly and, despite everything, she laughed.

'My congratulations, soldier,' she said, as solemnly as she could. 'Thank you, Sos, for everything,' she added, in an entirely different voice. 'I didn't think you'd come.'

He shook his head. 'They say Yuri rides at the sultan's right hand. That is one reason. You know the others. They are the same as they have always been. I find I do not change. Whatever happens.'

'Neither do I.'

Their hands touched briefly. Nothing more needed to be said.

'I must go, Tamar. Others are waiting to see you.'

He paused at the entrance and turned back to her.

'The men are pleased you have come this far with them, that you haven't taken sanctuary. The captains admire you and the soldiers speak of you with real reverence. It is wonderful to hear, truly. Take courage from that. Men fight better when they know why they are fighting, who they are fighting for.'

'That almost makes it worse. I fear for them, Sos. I dread how tomorrow must end.'

'It might end well. You might win. Defeat the Seljuks.'

'Defeat the Seljuks. You make it sound so easy.'

'And you make everything look easy.'

'What do you mean?'

'What I say. Farewell.'

'Sos,' she called him back.

Her father's kinzhal was in her hand and now she held it out to him.

'Take this. Wear it out of sight.'

He turned it over in his palm.

'It's beautiful. What is it?'

'Luck.' She paused. 'And love. We may never see one other again.'

Chapter Forty-three

The captains had roused the men at sunset for this, their last march. Before they saddled their horses, they ate their fill by firelight. They would take no food with them. If they won, there would be plenty waiting for them. If they lost, dead men did not go hungry.

A column of soldiers, every hoof of every horse muffled with rags, followed Sos up one of the rocky gullies that led on to the ridge above the sultan's camp. His Osset scouts had reported there were five passes where men could cross into the valley, so the Kart army was split into detachments – a raiding party on a huge scale. Sos tried to pretend all that lay ahead was a dozy homestead guarded by a dozen rusty-armed horse thieves. But however hard he tried to bolster his spirits, he could not help feeling like a very small, very feeble mouse sneaking up on a very large, very sharp-toothed cat.

The noise of the soldiers moving up the slope behind him was deafening to his ears, louder than a blacksmith's forge, but he knew they were walking as soft as hundreds of men can. But the horses could not understand the need for silence, and every snicker, every snort made his heart throb uneasily. He pictured thousands upon thousands of Seljuks standing beyond the crest, swords drawn, waiting to cut them down like piglets in a run.

Moonlight spilled down the hillside, turning his companions' faces pale, shimmering grey, leaving their eyes and the hollows of their cheeks a sullen black. The wings of a nightjar returning from its hunt on the heights cracked above his head and Sos shivered. He clenched his teeth and tried to stop his thoughts running away from him. He did not want to die, but he must not fear death. No man could fight well if he hungered to live. If he clung too hard to life, fate would prise his fingers free.

The moon sank out of sight and he grew calmer. It was waning. He did not know whether that was a good omen, or ill.

He raised his hand and the men behind him stopped. The scouts were tucked out of sight in the boulders jumbled at the rim of the bowl, but they came promptly when Sos whispered a watchword in their own tongue. They rose like ghosts from their hiding place and murmured their report. The camp had been loud until late in the night. Now all was silent, peaceful.

Sos edged forwards. As his face topped the rise a stiff, westerly wind buffeted his face. Good. It would have masked their approach. He gazed down. The sultan's standards, turning red and green in the first hint of dawn, streamed towards him. Now all they had to do was wait for the day.

He looked over his shoulder. The sun was still below the eastern horizon, but the patch of grey was stretching, broadening, climbing. They would attack when the bottom curve of the sun lifted clear of the plain. Already the first darts of orange were shooting up into the sky. A thin line of fire burned the land, too bright to bear, then it softened, swelled, rounded and the sun began to climb free. The night was over.

Sos kicked his horse into a fast trot and his men followed. The defile broadened until three, five, ten men could ride abreast and Sos saw the bowl open out before him like a pair of cupped hands. They were coming down in between two fingers, while the Seljuks lay in the soft palms.

He risked a look to the right. Streaming through gaps in the mountainside, like water through a sieve, the rest of the army was hurtling downhill. The line at the far end was ahead, Zak hunched over his horse, straining to be first. Sos urged his horse faster, refusing to be second.

The way was steep, and for a moment Sos feared his horse might refuse, but he coaxed it onwards, downwards, holding a straight line towards the valley floor. The Kart army was locked in an unstoppable stampede. Nesting birds rose screaming into the air before them.

A horn howled, keening shrill and desperate above the din of hooves. Someone had seen the dust cloud billowing above the camp or felt the insistent rumble of horses.

A battle roar welled in his throat and he wrestled his sword free of its sheath, his mouth wrenched open, something inside yelling, yearning to escape. Other cries, deep from men's bellies, surrounded him, an avalanche of sound, overwhelming his own voice.

The enemy took shape at last. Women screaming, boys running, men fumbling weapons, too late to form battle order, time only to decide whether to turn their back and flee or stand firm and be trampled.

Sos fixed his eyes on a squat man gripping a staff, bare-chested and screaming out hatred and fear. Sos swung his sword high and struck. The Seljuk had no chance.

He scythed through the outer defences, nothing in his head but the need to kill, no thought of death, of past or future, of pain or dread. He opened heads, split throats, hacked limbs, slashed backs until blood ran down his arms, and around him every Kart did the same.

Tamar watched from the heights with Sirchak by her side. Although she had promised Sargis to wait at their final camp until he sent word, she had ordered the Kipchak to saddle her horse as soon as the army had disappeared into the night. He hadn't bothered to protest.

The battle was spread out below her. The land towered over the two armies, diminishing them. Everything was strange and distant – the shouts as faint as memory. Streaks of cloud in the sky, stretched by the winds, distracted her. Plumes of orange told her fires were storming through the camp, but she could not feel their heat. She stood, aloof and impassive, when she had expected to feel wild or fearful.

313

'What happens now, Sirchak?'

'Must wait, lady,' Sirchak said. 'War is waiting.'

Around Sos men crashed to earth as if an invisible hand had flicked them from their saddles. Smoke filled the sky so he only saw the arrows when they drove into the ground or found a target. The shafts bit through legs and arms, sewing men to their horses, which ran wild, their dead riders joggling slack-jawed on their backs.

Sos swore. The Seljuks had organised fast. A phalanx of bowmen were clumped on a hillock above the camp, unleashing wave after wave of arrows, not caring whether they killed their own men or their Kart enemies. They had to be stopped.

He spied Zak's pale hair and Sargis's standard and raced to join them. The general was rapping out orders.

'Zak, gather as many men as you can and take the left flank. Sos – there you are – you do the same on the right. Then we can—'

He stopped, in the middle of a word. Sos thought something ahead of them had caught his eye and instinctively followed his gaze to see what he was staring at. Nothing. He looked back: Sargis's head hung down, as if gripped by sudden despair. Then he saw Zak's grey face and the arrow buried in Sargis's throat.

'Father . . .'

Zak was trying to prop him up on his horse, while Sargis waved his hands in front of him as if to tell him not to bother. Sos wheeled to the other side to stop him falling.

'Don't touch the arrow,' Zak shouted, his voice shrill and cracking. 'I can take you back to the camp. We can find—'

'No good,' Sargis whispered. 'No time. You must attack.'

And he reached up and ripped the shaft from his throat. Blood spilled over his hands. His eyes rolled back and up and he slumped into Zak's arms. Sos and Zak stared at each other over his body.

'There's nothing we can do, Zak. We must do as he

commanded. Ride down the archers. Leave his body. Come on, Zak. Ride, Zak, ride.'

The lookout shouted a warning. Tamar's guards notched arrows and pulled back their bowstrings, but then a voice panted the watchword and one of Sos's Osset boys gasped round the bend. His horse was shaking its head violently from side to side, spit flying between its teeth, its eyes bulging, knees trembling. The boy – his face patterned with blood and grime – fell on to the ground and gulped at the water cup someone thrust into his hands.

Tamar rushed to his side and crouched beside him.

'Niko? It is Niko, isn't it? Can you speak?'

The boy heaved to his feet, all his weight on his right leg. He had a filthy gouge down his left shin and she saw an alarming flash of white bone. He tried to talk, but he winced and shuddered, then started again. His words were slurred, as if his lips were numb.

'My lady,' his accent so like Sos's it hurt, 'we killed many in the first charge. They scattered. But then their bowmen rallied above us. We were dying. The lord Mkhargrdzeli fell—'

'Who leads the men now?'

'His son and my lord. Zak and Sos. They led us against the archers. We followed. But then the bowmen vanished and there came many, many Seljuks on horses with Yuri at their head. That's when Sos ordered me to gallop back to the camp. *Tell Tamar to go before it's too late. Tell Sirchak to bear her to safety.* I swear I did not want to leave them. But he ordered me to. He said he'd kill me if I didn't. I rode as hard as I could. I swear I didn't want to leave . . .'

He had started to babble. He was only a boy and he had seen more than he had bargained for. Tamar realised she had stopped breathing. They were losing. She swallowed hard.

'Sirchak – ready your men.'

'Home, lady?'

'No, Sirchak. To battle. Break the Seljuk line.'

'You not safe alone.'

'You cannot idle here waiting on me like nursemaids. Go. Go!' she yelled the last word.

For a moment, Sirchak stood stubborn. But then he nodded and barked an order to his men. It wasn't necessary. They were already racing for their horses, waiting done. Sirchak fell to one knee before her, grasped her hand in his and kissed it.

'Goodbye, lady.'

Tamar watched him vault on to his horse and disappear into the dust bowl below. She was dizzy and weak, close to despair.

I'd give anything . . . anything . . . only don't let us lose. Dear God, please hear me, anything, you hear me, anything.

The Kart soldiers had seen Yuri unleash his battle frenzy before, but always at their side, killing their enemies, not howling mad red blood in their faces. Like a bonfire ripping across a field of stubble, he carved great circles of death through their ranks. All but the bravest fell back before him. And those who dared oppose him, he slew.

It was a dirty, grim battle, every face twisted into the same grimace, hidden behind soot and gore. Most of the men had lost their horses and were slugging each other on foot, heaving, shoving, grunting, all exhilaration gone.

Sos hungered to face Yuri, but the fighting had not yet pushed them close. Then suddenly the men separating them fell away. They were staring at one other, no more than two paces apart. Their swords tangled, their shoulders collided and they were grappling, scrapping. Yuri lost his footing and fell, dragging Sos down with him. They rolled, locked like dogs, swords lost, until they tumbled into a burning tent and the heat sprang them apart.

Yuri leapt back at him, but Sos followed his aim and arched his body to the right. A dagger swept past his cheek. Yuri pounced again. Sos wasn't fast enough and the blade tore the side of his neck as he swerved clear.

Yuri grinned. Sos remembered the last time they had fought and his head fogged. Yuri was driving him backwards. It would

316

end the same way. He didn't know what was behind him. Panic bubbled in his throat. He stumbled. It was happening again. He ducked another stroke, but the next plunged deep into his belly and he was on his back.

This was death. An ecstasy of acceptance flooded his body.

He waited for the blade to bury itself between his ribs and stop his heart, but instead Yuri's knee landed on him, punching the air out of his stomach. A massive pair of hands closed about his throat.

Sos stared up. Blue eyes, red veins, orange beard, yellow teeth, nothing but Yuri. He struggled underneath him and Yuri smiled harder, his eyes bright, his lips parted. Sos shut his eyes. His head screamed. His lungs burned. His hands flailed helplessly at his side. His luck had run out.

Luck. Tamar.

His hand groped for the dagger hidden in his boot. The cold metal touched his palm like a balm, giving him the strength he needed, and he drove the blade into Yuri's back.

For a moment, Yuri did not react and Sos feared he was dreaming, a vision before death. Then a wonderful spark of surprise filled Yuri's eyes. His mouth opened wide in a long, blank moan, his face glazed over and he collapsed forward, twitched, and then lay still.

Sos tried to rip the dagger free, but his muscles wouldn't listen. His arm flopped limp on the ground. He tried to heave Yuri off, but there was no power in his limbs. His ribs would not rise up and take in breath. The stench of Yuri filled his nose, but he couldn't turn his head away. He no longer knew whether his eyes were open or shut. Red and black clouds rolled above him from somewhere beyond sight and a high ringing noise shook his body. He cried out.

Help. Somebody. Tamar.

But the words didn't leave his throat.

The two armies rippled at her feet, a black, heaving mass like a medusa bulging below the surface of the sea. She envied the

317

vultures their wings and sharp eyes and, in her heart, she swooped low over the battlefield and urged her men on.

The sun was falling away to the west. How much longer could they last? Her army was adrift, many miles from friendly lands. If they turned their back, they would be hounded to their death across the plains. She looked down at her boots, cracked and dusty, at her grey-brown cloak. Would the Seljuks know who she was? Would she tell them? Or would she let herself disappear into the slave pens while Yuri sprawled on her throne? No, she must not be swallowed up by the battle. For her people's sake, she must be ready to act like a queen. She did not have the right to die in battle like a king.

When the sun goes behind the mountain, I will leave.

It dropped, fast and heavy. The light left the valley. She turned for her horse. But as she took one last look, she saw that the shape of the battle had changed.

The far side was beginning to crumble, tiny dots breaking away, a few dozen, then a hundred, then more than she could count. The Seljuks running, a forest of soldiers in flight and her own men, victorious, giving chase. It was beautiful. It was impossible. But it was real.

The ground beneath her feet swayed, lurched, and tipped her on to her knees. She tried to hold herself up with her hands but they would not bear her weight. Someone was choking, sobbing, gasping. She saw tears disappearing into the dust and realised it was her, shaking with joy, with relief.

She heard hooves. For a moment, she feared a party of fleeing Seljuks, but then she heard familiar voices roaring her name. She leapt to the side of the path as they nearly rode her down.

'Zak! Here! Zak!'

He careered to a halt and slid off his horse, panting, followed by Sirchak.

'My lady . . . They said you were here. We feared – God must love you to keep you safe this close. You should never—'

'It's all right Zak. I'm safe. Now, take me down there.'

* * *

318

Gamrekeli, bounding like a boy, jogged up to her and spoke in a new voice.

'A great victory, my lady, the greatest in generations. I salute you. I honour you. Your name will live for ever.'

And he bowed deep as she passed.

When she had walked across a battlefield with her father, she had felt invisible. Now every man gazed at her in wonder as if an angel was floating by. They bared their heads. Many bowed or fell to their knees. Some wept and kissed her hand, saying *thank you, thank you, my lady*. All stopped whatever they were doing to shield her from the reality of the blood and looting. She was pale and untainted amid the slaughter.

She had a smile and a word for every man she met, but the murmur of disquiet in her head grew louder and louder. Where was Sos?

She craned her neck. He must be about to gallop out of the dark and romp up to her, eyes white, giddy with all that he had done. Maybe he would kiss her hand and she would look down at the curls winding about his neck. Then he'd look up and she'd see the gold in his eyes.

She was allowing herself one last dream, then she would ask Zak. He would tell her how bravely Sos had died. She would nod and swallow the pain. She would cry later, maybe. Not today. Today she was a queen who had won a great victory, the greatest in generations. She put a hand on Zak's arm.

'Where . . .' She found she could not finish, but Zak understood.

'Yuri and he killed each other, my lady. I saw it. It was a great deed – and it gave us all strength. The Rus was a terrible enemy and with him gone we found our courage. We drove them back. We won. But not Sos. He's – he's gone, my lady. He's somewhere on the battlefield. But there are so many bodies, so many dead. We've looked but—'

He stopped and she saw his face was lost behind tears.

'Forgive me, my lady.'

'No. Cry. He deserves your tears.'

Zak shook his head. 'I never thought he'd fall. Not him, not—'

He was interrupted by three soldiers waving and pointing a hundred paces away.

'What is it?'

One of them was already rushing towards them.

'The Rus, my lord, we've found the Rus.'

Zak ran over and Tamar followed, slowly. It was too dark too see clearly so Zak yelled for a torch, which arrived fast. He thrust it downwards and Yuri's face sprang out of the night. He was sprawled on his front, his face turned towards them, his eyes staring open, his mouth slack. She waited to feel joy at his death, but none came.

She looked about her.

'Maybe Sos fell nearby?'

Together they traced circles around the body, Zak leaning down, peering into dead men's faces, tugging at dead men's shoulders, but none was Sos.

'My lord? What shall we do with the body?'

'Leave it. Let the sun and the insects and the birds deal with him.'

Tamar nodded, looking at the corpse at her feet. Then her mind finally listened to what her eyes had been trying to tell her.

The hilt of her kinzhal glittered close to Yuri's spine. She fell forward and started to wrestle with the Rus's body, heavy with death, and haul him to one side.

'Don't, my lady, please, what are you—' Zak was trying to pull her off.

'No, help me, quickly. Roll him over. Quickly.'

Together they pitched Yuri away to one side. She gazed down at Sos's body, her lashes plaited with sudden tears.

'It's Sos, Zak. It's him.'

Zak put an arm out to steady her, but she had already fallen to the ground at Sos's side. She took his hand in hers. It was cold, lifeless.

She touched his stomach and her hands came away covered with blood. His eyes were closed. He looked horribly young, horribly lost. She leant forward to touch her lips to his, to say goodbye.

His lips were warm.

She felt his breath brush her cheek. Then his eyes flickered open and his mouth twitched into a smile.

Epilogue

So ended the troubled days of Tamar's youth and the prosperous years of her prime began.

She married Sos – or King Davit Soslani, as he became known – and they remained true to one another until his death. They were blessed with two children – a son called Giorgi and a daughter called Rusudan – and together they presided over the greatest years of Georgia's long history, a glorious golden age.

When Tamar died in 1212 she left behind an empire that at its zenith stretched not only across the Caucasus, but south and west into lands later known as Turkey, Armenia, Iran and Azerbaijan. Her nephews, little Alexeios and Davit, founded the empire of Trebizond after Constantinople was sacked by Frankish crusaders. Her armies – led by her husband and Zakari Mkhargrdzeli – were all but invincible.

Yet Tamar's triumphs were not only military. Civil society, the arts, tolerant religion and philosophy, all flourished. Shota – or Shota Rustaveli to give him his full name – found time to finish his poem. *The Knight in the Panther's Skin*, a tale of love and adventure dedicated to Tamar, is Georgia's undisputed masterpiece.

Sadly, her best qualities were not repeated in the generations that followed. During her son's reign, the Mongols devastated the Georgian kingdom. The Persians followed the Mongols. The Russians followed the Persians. Her great empire is now no more than a proud memory.

But not everything has been lost. Her portrait at Vardzia, Davit's grave at Gelati, the cathedrals of Tbilisi endure, and Tamar herself, like the Mtkvari river or the Caucasus peaks, still lives on. It is hard to travel more than a few miles without

passing a bridge, a stream, something named in her honour. She
will never fade.

Let us leave the last words to Shota.

> *Their tale is ended like a dream of the night.*
> *They are passed away, gone beyond the world.*
> *Behold the treachery of time.*
> *To him who thinks it long, even for him, it is but a moment.*

Historical Note

Now is the moment to own up to any liberties and short cuts I took when telling Tamar's story.

Much of what you have read is true, as far as we can know it. Orbeli's rebellion against Giorgi, the tavads switching sides, the king's surprise decision to appoint Tamar his heir, Qutlu Arslan's rebellion and arrest, Rusudan's power in the early years of Tamar's reign, Yuri's vile character, the insulting message from the Seljuk sultan, the muster at Vardzia, the battle of Basiani, won, so the annals tell us, because their camp was disordered – that all happened.

But – and here I must apologise to both historians and Georgians – some of the facts have been massaged to make for a more enjoyable story. I do not know where Tamar was during Orbeli's rebellion, still less whether Sos saved her in the mountains. Andronikos did visit Georgia and his son married a Georgian princess, but there is no agreement as to whether that princess was Tamar's sister. Qutlu was arrested, dramatically, but we can only hope it was by Sos and Zak. Similarly, we have no idea how Tamar's nephews escaped after Andronikos's downfall, but again Sos made a good candidate. Yuri did try to recapture the throne after he was banished and a vast Seljuk army did threaten Georgia, but I have conflated the two events. Finally, and this is the only serious chronology switch, Tamar and Sos married before the battle of Basiani. History, in this instance, was trumped by story-telling.